NORTHERN

SPIRIT

NORTHERN SPIRIT

LINDSEY J CARDEN

KELDAS
CHRONICLES

Copyright© Lindsey J.Carden 2011

Cover illustrations, design and logo by Paul Middleditch©
e.mail paul@middleditch.com

All rights reserved. No part of this book may be reproduced, stored in, or introduced into an information retrieval system, or transmitted(in any form or by any means, electronic, mechanical, photocopying, recording or otherwise) without the prior written consent of the publisher.

Published by Keldas Chronicles 2011
www.keldaschronicles.yolasite.com

This book is a work of fiction. Names, characters, businesses, places and events either are a product of the author's imagination or are used fictitiously. Any resemblance to actual persons, living or dead, events, or locales is entirely coincidental.

Printed and bound by CPI Group (UK) Ltd, Croydon, CRO 4YY

ISBN 978-0-9569442-0-7

A catalogue record for this book is available from the British Library

Acknowledgements

I would like to thank the following people for their
invaluable help and advice with this book:
Chris, Donna, Liz, Jill, Lorna, Mozzy, Paul and Teddy.

Alastair

Life isn't always a sylvan stream
Where anglers watch and cast and dream
But if by chance you catch his eye
A salmon leaps and takes the fly
And from dark water hope can burst
And love that embraces those that thirst

CONTENTS

1. PROMISE:1973
2. WITH SILVER
3. AN ELEMENTARY MAN
4. DARK SIDE OF THE MOUNTAIN
5. THE GLASS SNOWSCENE
6. THE TOWER
7. SLOW FEVER
8. UP HIGH – IN DEEP
9. NARCISSUS
10. ON HIGH AND VERY WHITE STONES
11. FLIGHT OF THE WILD GEESE
12. ROCK SOLID TRUTH
13. VALLEY OF DEEP SHADOW
14. THE BRASS BED
15. LIBERATOR
16. THE GRANITE CITY
17. KICK START
18. A VISITOR
19. KELD HEAD – THE RETURN
20. MAN OF CLAY
21. CAPTIVE AUDIANCE
22. WITH GOLD

1

PROMISE: 1973

The blue flash hurt David's eyes; he couldn't believe the audacity of the press to come to the funeral. As if they hadn't got enough photographs, and that would be another one in all the papers tomorrow, showing him tired with his dark hair bedraggled, looking older than the twenty-three years he actually was. His mother would be clinging to his arm, leaning on him heavily, yet strong and defiant as usual. And what an irony that every photograph they ever printed of his father, he was always looking handsome. It was usually a copy of the one that was hanging over the kitchen fireplace, taken several years ago. David couldn't comprehend how his mother could leave it there when it meant nothing but shame. But there would be no more photographs of George Keldas. Anyone would think it was David that was the offender, and yet it was he who was to suffer for his father's impropriety. And today it was the funeral and it should be all over, except for the humiliation, and David would have to live with that.

Stopping as he reached the summit of the hill, David could see Keld Head clearly, as the farm with its outbuildings and tower dominated the landscape, and then surrounding it a cluster of cottages and houses. Keld Head was one of those houses that you looked at twice. Not because it was particularly pretty, or imposing, it was because it looked wrong. The old Pele tower that had stood there for generations somehow didn't fit with the rest of the buildings. Wordsworth had said that houses like

PROMISE:1973

this had grown, rather than been erected, by an instinct of their own out of the native rock. And though this place was natural, its genetic make-up was defective.

You also looked at Keld Head in awe, like it was a living thing; it must have been because it had influence over the people that dwelt there. And today, Keld Head was languishing in grief as it was burying one of its sons and it revelled in the morbidity: the drama of the funeral cortege, the gloom of a November day, the weeping of a grieving widow, yes, it feasted on everything, loving the feel of the sorrow swathed around its stonework

David stood motionless, in pure silence; he could hear nothing other than the sound of raindrops falling on leaves. He stared at the farmhouse but didn't want to go inside. He knew it would be full of relatives and guests who'd come to pay their last respects, so the seclusion of the country lane suited him and he would keep this grief to himself.

David ignored the rain as it blinded his blue eyes and curled his hair like it always did when it was wet. He kept his hands in his pockets and his shoulders bent low, feeling the damp seep through the fabric of his suit and into his shoes, yet he still walked carelessly through the puddles. If you knew David well, you might have thought he was drunk and, although he had had several beers, it was grief that made him stagger and nothing else. David didn't particularly need to look where he was going because he'd walked this lane all his life, sometimes alone, sometimes with his friends, but often with his father. This was a path that could lead him away to seclusion, or back to the farmhouse where if he wanted the company he knew his brother and sisters would be waiting.

Today his mother had been generous with her invites. Aunts and uncles had travelled long distances and David knew they would want to see him, but he couldn't face them. From leaving school he'd worked solely with his father, alone with the cattle and sheep and conversation wasn't one of his strong points. He was only capable of using his thoughts; his mind

PROMISE: 1973

absorbed in the deep feelings he had, as he reflected on the strange events of the last few weeks of his life.

David was pulling a black tie loose from around his neck when he heard the crack of a gunshot. A rush of adrenalin flushed through him and he dropped to the floor, curling his body up tightly with his hands over his head. 'Man alive . . . Please don't shoot . . . !' and all the tears he'd suppressed that day, ripped out of him, and he started to cry like he hadn't done since he was a little boy. David knew he was acting irrationally, because he'd seen the gamekeeper's Landrover on the lane and he would only be shooting rabbits.

As he wept, he could think of nothing but grief, with the pain his mother must be carrying and the sense of responsibility he had for his younger brother and sisters. He thought that the burden would be too big for him. Yet, the weight had fallen firmly on his broad shoulders. David remembered the words of the clergyman who seemed to look only at him. He'd talked about the responsibility of the young to look after the grieving. That those with their vital energy should assist the helpless, but David had only been half-listening and felt uncomfortable with the eye contact and turned away.

And now as he lay there on the wet earth, he promised himself that he would never leave his mother as his father had often done and vowed to stay at Keld Head, even if this meant he would never marry and have children. Why should he inflict his unhappiness on anyone else? He would try to take care of his brother and sisters and not treat them harshly as his father had. Maybe he could give them the love and support they all needed and compensate in some way for the way his father had behaved.

Tom Keldas sat fidgeting on the sofa. It was difficult for the eleven year-old to keep still. He was listening as his grandparents lecture his mother on how she should conduct herself. How she should treat the children and how she should try to sell the farm and buy a new bungalow in Windermere.

PROMISE: 1973

Tom hoped his mother wasn't listening, like she didn't listen to him sometimes when he had important things to tell her. He would hate living in Windermere and have to make new friends. But Tom wasn't given to patience and interrupted them. 'Mum. . . . Where's Davey?'

His mother didn't give his bad manners a second thought and was just happy that her second eldest son had interrupted. 'He'll be getting the dairy ready I hope.' She too was troubled that David hadn't come home and she hadn't seen him since the service had ended. 'Why don't you go and see if he needs something to eat.' She doubted David had eaten anything all day.

As the boy left the house, a black dog followed. Tom didn't put a coat on but just ran carelessly through the rain. His father would have called him a pratt if he were here and, if his mother was out of earshot, something worse. At least that was one thing that would change.

He approached the dairy, but was disappointed to find the place deserted. Usually he would hear the milking machines or the music from David's transistor radio and, glancing into the yard, he saw the cattle were paddling about in slurry, standing waiting. He stood for a moment in the rain, unsure of what to do. It was twilight and his eyes were slowly coming accustomed to the semi-darkness. He grabbed the dog's collar to reassure himself.

They were both startled when they heard a noise coming from the lane. Tom shuddered as it sounded like someone was crying. The dog's tail twitched and she raised her hackles and set off to find the source of the noise, but Tom couldn't hold on to her and he momentarily froze, but then was compelled to follow.

David was still lying on the wet footpath and, exhausted, lay there in a daze. He was stirred by the wet tongue and warm breath of the dog licking his face. 'Shove off Moss. . . . Go away.' David raised himself up a little, as Moss kept on washing his face and licking his damp hair. As he tried to stand to his feet, he saw Tom standing at a distance, his young face pale and troubled and unsure of whether to approach or not.

'It's all right Tom. It's only me.' David spoke softly.

'Good grief! I thought you were a Rusky - a spy or summat.'

There was a truth in his brother's words, which David knew he would never understand and he wanted to say: *If you see any strangers about the place, tell me,* but he resisted and to cover his fear, said: 'There are no spies up here, Tom. You watch too much telly.'

But Tom didn't believe him and knew differently, because he had seen them.

David struggled to stand and started to brush the wet and the grit off his trousers and jacket, he couldn't stop himself from checking if there was any blood. He'd once heard that if you've been shot, it was the blood you saw first before you felt any pain, but of course there was none.

'If that's your best suit, Mum'll kill you.' Tom wanted to touch his brother and help him but daren't. 'What are you doing on the floor anyway?'

David didn't reply, but threw his wet arms around the boy and led him back to the farm, pleased it was almost dark and his grief had been hidden.

In reflection, David was glad that he'd wasted the time at the pub in Grasmere, standing at the bar and staring into his beer glass, submerged in his own self-pity. He hoped most of the visitors would have left the farm by now but, as he guessed, he was already late for milking.

'Will you do me a favour then 007, saying you're so interested in the underworld. Sneak into my bedroom and bring me my work things. See that Mum doesn't hear you mind.'

David quietly slid open the door of the dairy and put on the lights, as once again his sore eyes winced in the brightness as the fluorescent lights flashed on. He rubbed his hair dry with an old hand towel and struggled to remove his wet jacket and shirt that was sticking to his body. As he roused himself, he shivered as the damp and the cold finally reached his brain.

He rubbed himself with the towel and muttered, 'Come on Tom . . . hurry up. . . . Don't mess about.'

Tom crept into David's bedroom and looked around for his brother's work clothes and found them folded on his bedside chair. On the floor lay the cushions of makeshift bed that his mother had made up for him. He would have to share David's room for another few nights until his grandparents and Great Aunt Betty went home. But Tom didn't mind, it made him feel grown up to stay with David and have his little sister out of the way in his mother's room. Tom loved his brother's bedroom and, as David suspected, he lingered. He browsed around, looking at the bookcase. Then he fiddled with some of David's possessions. There were framed diplomas and certificates from agricultural college. Tom read the inscriptions on some brightly coloured rosettes pinned on the wall that David had won as a boy from showing the cattle and sheep. He picked up a model tractor and spun the wheels, round and round, in his hand. David would have made it, sat upstairs alone in his room, looking to get away from an angry father who barracked him constantly, saying he wasn't doing his job right, saying that he was stupid, even insinuating that David's quiet nature showed ignorance and weakness.

Tom hoped one day he would be able to go to agricultural college and get diplomas of his own. Maybe go to young farmers' meetings like David did and dance with pretty girls.

When he was satisfied with his tour of David's bedroom, Tom edged down the stairs carrying the bundle of clothes. He stole into the kitchen and, juggling with the clothes in one hand, stuffed a piece of cake in his mouth, and then gathered some things from the leftovers of the buffet for David. He chose a few sandwiches, a sausage roll and a piece of chocolate cake, wrapped them in a serviette and, unceremoniously, shoved them into the pile of work clothes.

Tom dawdled across to the dairy and the familiar humming sound of the milking machine engine that he'd listened for half-an-hour ago was now in full flow.

PROMISE: 1973

David was standing inside, shivering, with a large towel across his shoulders. He grabbed the warm pullover from the boy's arms and, as he pulled it over his head, ruffled up his tattered hair.

Tom stood and watched, looking closely at David's adult body, hoping he would grow to be as strong; he'd already noticed a few premature changes to his own and was apprehensive.

David wasn't particularly a tall man, but what he lacked in height he gained in stature. He had a good posture and usually walked proudly and, for a man, gracefully, carrying his head tall and his back straight. His chest was still bronzed from spending long days in the fields that summer, hauling hay and straw bales to help his sick father. His young body reflected well his strength.

Tom was glad his brother was strong because he had feared his father; he'd made Keld Head a dangerous place to live. David had protected Tom several times from a beating, as George grew impatient with the young lad. David had taken some of the endless criticism from him and, more than once, a good hiding. They hadn't told their mother, guessing she too was under strain from looking after a sick and unreasonable man. Yet, despite all his misgivings, David loved his father.

Tom couldn't understand why his father treated them as he had; he knew he could be awkward at times, but David, as far as he was concerned was faultless. So consequently, Tom hated his father and loved David all the more for his courage.

'Can I help you with the milkin' tonight, Davey?'

'I tell you what. How about getting the next lot of cattle out of the yard for me, eh? And then go and get me a coffee to go with these dry sandwiches.'

This time Tom quickly responded, and his willingness and kindness brought a warm smile to David's hardened face. A glaze of moisture covered his deep blue eyes and softened his countenance.

* * *

PROMISE: 1973

Kathy Keldas was listening to her parents and her aunt discussing the latest story-line in Coronation Street and knew it was time to leave, glad at last she was no longer the focus of their conversation. She went into the kitchen with the pretence of making a fresh pot of tea, but in reality wanted to use the vantage point of the kitchen window to check that David and Tom were working.

Looking out into the darkness, she was pleased to see the lights of the dairy shining across the yard. She knew that David was upset today and more so than the other children. He hadn't spoken much the whole of the day and she was disappointed he hadn't mingled with the other mourners. In some ways she could understand his feelings, but hoped he may have shown the common decency of circulating more than he had. Although David was a quiet man, he was well liked and usually polite.

Kathy stood reflecting, holding her hand to her chin. She was still dressed in her mourning suit: a black crepe outfit with a flash of red on the collar; a silent and defiant gesture. It also had a fetching scooped neckline, which flattered her slim body, which was purposely chosen for the members of the press. It also highlighted her blonde hair, which was pinned on top of her head. Kathy was only forty-two and just like David had begun to look and feel much older.

Knowing that David was working hard reassured her. He had supported her and helped her again in a time of crisis. She felt a pang of anxiety hit her as she thought how brave he was, and hoped he wouldn't be harmed by the last few hard years of his young life. A time when most would be looking for selfish pleasures, David was bound day and night to the farm. He had done this without complaint and with complete acceptance. But Kathy realised David was mortal; she had felt the strain and she guessed he had too.

She had found herself surrounded by tragedy and had wondered sometimes if it was real, or if her body had just switched from reality to fantasy; like she was playing the role in a drama that would soon end and the curtain pulled back so she could go back to the world of normality again. She would have to try and talk to David though, but not yet; not just after the funeral. She must know his feelings and reassure him. What would his ideas about the future be? Kathy even wrestled with the thought that one day he may want to leave. He was a mature lad and popular and she couldn't expect him to stay single forever.

David had already met several girlfriends and Kathy knew some he was fond of, but he rarely brought any of them to Keld Head. He would be afraid of them meeting his father, of being taunted in front of them and, worse still, George embarrassing them with drunken slurs and innuendoes. But as soon as any young woman heard of George Keldas's reputation, it was usually the last David saw of them.

Kathy was naive and hoped that things would be different now and David could begin to lead a more normal life, but there was something inside her that wanted to hold on to him.

Yes, she would have to talk to David, but not today.

The following morning a fresh westerly wind was rattling a loose pane of glass in Kathy's bedroom window. She huddled up closer to a large pillow placed lengthways in her bed where her husband once lay; someone had told her it would keep her warm, and it did.

She'd heard from across the hallway David's alarm clock and hoped he'd heard it too. She sat up a little, not daring to sleep, but the loud click of the bathroom light switching on answered her.

Kathy wanted her life to take on some stability and hoping the weather would stay dry, she decided to do some washing, after that, maybe clean the house; it would be good therapy to have something menial to do, as if every little task would heal her. Then once her visitors were fed, she would turn her attention to her younger children, which she knew had been neglected of late.

Kathy also knew there was gossip in the village about her husband, which may have penetrated the schoolyard. She wanted to put a stop to it for the sake of her youngest children and the family name. A decision to call at the school and have a discreet word with Dorothy Hargreaves, the head teacher, would be her first mistake that day.

Kathy knew her youngest daughter Sarah was, for a child, quite thick-skinned. She appeared to cope better than Tom. She was only seven years old, was a slightly built girl and much like her mother, had golden blonde hair, and despite tragedy in her family had remained a happy girl, perhaps too young to realise the enormity of their problems. She had witnessed the anger of her father but had rarely been the brunt of it.

George Keldas had idolised Sarah. She was his little angel. He would cuddle her and protect her, always siding with her if there was an argument between the two younger children, even if she was teasing David and being a nuisance she was never to be in the wrong. George would buy her gifts and purposely leave the boys with nothing. It was only she and her elder sister Linzi who ever received any sort of love from George Keldas. Yes, for Sarah life had been wonderful, but Kathy now feared her world would change as she grew to miss her doting father.

For Tom, she feared differently. She didn't think he missed George at all.

Tom was much like David in that he was sensitive, although more talkative than David ever was. He too had the fair hair of his mother but he was a well-built boy, reared since birth from the breast to the milk of the land. He was a healthy and fine boy and he had his father's handsome face, and Kathy could see as his young personality began to develop, he would become a tall and attractive young man. But Tom was also perceptive. One evening, when he'd come home from school he'd asked: 'Mum, what does the word adultery mean?' Kathy shrugged it off and said, 'Why?'

'Oh, just that the kids at school were on about it. And I've heard Dad say it. It's a bad word isn't it?' Kathy knew what he was referring to. She'd had a row with George in front of the children and in a drunken rage he'd accused her of adultery, again. David had tried to defend her but George started on him. 'What do you know about life, Davey? You don't know what it means to love a woman. Just because you've been to college and got your head full of nonsense, you think you know it all, besides, keep your nose out of my business lad.' The anger was clear in David's eyes, and Kathy suspected if George hadn't have looked so ill, David may have retaliated.

George's cutting words had sliced through her. And although him being drunk at the time gave some excuse, it was the things that he said when he was sober that hurt her more.

Kathy walked boldly through the village thinking all eyes were upon her where, in fact, most didn't even know her and, of those who did, they only had respect for her. She was desperate to keep a sense of dignity and preserve the family name. They had to remain in Keld Head. There was no running away.

'Come in Mrs Keldas.' The head teacher gestured for Kathy to sit down. 'I didn't expect to see you here so soon.'

But Kathy remained standing as she nervously interrupted her: 'We must get back to normal as soon as possible Mrs Hargreaves. I don't want my children to be affected any more than they need to be over our situation.'

Dorothy Hargreaves was temporarily stunned by the younger woman's courage and insisted that she sat down and, this time, Kathy complied.

'I want to talk to you about my children's future. You see I don't want them to be treated any differently.' Kathy sat proud and upright in the chair, but she was shivering with nerves. 'I want you to treat them just the same as you did before. David and I intend to carry on and run the farm together. We won't be leaving Keld Head. I know there have been rumours.'

'I haven't heard that you were thinking of leaving.'

'No, but maybe you've heard other things. And I just wanted you to stop any gossip that may be going around the school about my family.'

The head teacher's heart was changed from sympathy to defence, as she felt her integrity and the good name of her school challenged.

Kathy continued with her objections, before Mrs Hargreaves could again defend herself. 'Of course you must realise . . . I'm not in a position to stop gossip that may infiltrate this school from the village, painful though it may be. But I will have a quiet word with my teachers and the other members of staff about your children. And we'll do our best to see they get all the help they need.'

Kathy was humbled by the older woman's common sense and thanked her. Her voice then softened. 'I come from a respectable and hard-working background. My husband's family has farmed in this area for generations, and it's sickening to think how disloyal some of my neighbours are.' Kathy was trying hard not to feel aggrieved again. 'Oh, yes, the village folk are nice enough to my face, but I know they're talking behind my back. And true, George did cause some serious problems for us, but that won't stop us from being a normal, happy family.'

Dorothy Hargreaves raised her eyebrows; she took off her glasses and threw them on her desk. In her mind she was thinking that it was Kathy Keldas that was making all the fuss about her situation and not the village folk, or her members of staff; they only pitied her.

She thought it peculiar that when people in desperation attempt to cover over some wrong, they actually bring it more to the foreground, and this was exactly what Kathy had done. This was a well-respected young woman. Yes, she had suffered for years, and now it appeared that her problems would subside, she wished that Kathy would just let things be.

Then Kathy noticed the older woman peer across and look at her pullover. She glanced down and saw a small coffee stain on the cream coloured fabric. Her face flushed; she should have taken more care. What would this woman think? Then a deeper thought crept inside her, like the headmistress had noticed a stain on her soul. Like she'd seen one sin lead into another: lies, deception, and violence, as interwoven threads in a coarse fabric. Yes, she was reaping what she'd sowed, as this woman probed further and deeper into her heart. Kathy felt she must have seen all her sins, and a great shame fell over her, like her secrets, (because she had several), had been exposed.

Kathy waited for her to say something and outwardly condemn her, but the teacher didn't need to because, by the expression on Kathy's face, she'd condemned herself.

2

WITH SILVER

'What made him do it then, Davey?' the postman said as he leant out of the window of his red van.

David narrowed is eyes as he looked at the man and wanted to swear, but before he could, both men turned their heads to the sound of some laughter coming from the farmhouse.

'It's okay to go in for morning coffee, then, is it?'

'Looks like it.' David's voice was raw.

'You'll miss him, son.'

'Yeh. ... Like a hole in the head!'

And David jumped in the tractor and drove slowly through the paddock. He could just see across to the garden, his shirts and the children's clothes pegged on the washing line and blowing in the breeze. It was as if nothing had ever happened. He wondered how his mother could carry on like this when he still felt confused. He wanted to talk to her but she seemed to be distant and unconcerned. David felt she was trying to minimise things and make things appear normal, when he knew they weren't. Maybe she was ill herself or in some kind of shock. He was certain she and his father were never completely happy together, so how could he expect her to miss him now? Did she miss him at all? Perhaps that was the problem. Was she behaving like some kind of "merry widow" or a divorced woman, liberated from years of an unhappy relationship? Yet David was certain his father did love his mother and it was only those crazy ideas in his head that made him unreasonable and jealous, that the accusations his father made were born out of desperation, to rationalise the cold feelings Kathy had towards him, and blaming everyone other than himself for the breakdown of their marriage.

David hadn't just thought of this, he was too lazy in mind to have deduced this for himself. They were ideas of his sister and friends that had been collected over several years of trying to explain the unhappy situation at Keld Head. And despite her age, David knew his mother was still a beautiful woman and his father should have been as proud of her as he was. And no matter what his father said, David was certain she was completely loyal to them all.

He'd also noticed the same beauty developing in his sister, Linzi, as she turned eighteen. But Linzi, like David, had the dark hair and tanned skin of their father.

David found himself comparing his own features as he stared into the rearview mirror of the tractor cab, yet could see no beauty in himself. He'd heard people say how much he was like his father, but his mother always objected and David guessed she knew how much this upset him. She would defend him and say he was milder and that there was no similarity at all. Others thought David probably wasn't as handsome as his father.

As he sat and stared, looking at the colour of his eyes and the shape of his mouth and every curve of a premature wrinkle, he became mesmerized at his own reflection. He felt his heartbeat quicken and a flush of blood ran to his head. Wanting to avoid the sensation, he roused himself and forcefully pushed the mirror to one side.

Then droplets of rain fell heavily and suddenly on the windscreen and cocooned him in a bubble-like prison. It had been a wet autumn and the rain had hardly stopped since September. The rivers were swollen and the ghyll was flooded, constantly spluttering water, mud and gravel onto the farm track. David pushed the tractor clumsily into gear and drove back towards Keld Head, with the wheels splashing water from the puddles across the yard. His mood had taken control of him, and much like his father, David wanted to run away, but he didn't know where to, or who from. It would be foolish to walk the fells today as the rain would persist and get the better of him. Yet he had an overwhelming urge to leave, as he had become afraid of his own image, and David thought he would never look in a mirror again. And as much as he'd despised his father's actions, his feelings where vindicating the thoughts he had, that he was becoming much like him.

He parked untidily in the gate way, jumped down from the tractor cab and was about to put on his waterproof jacket, when he noticed one of the dairy cows standing alone in the corner of the fold yard, swishing her tail from side to side, fidgeting, paddling her feet and in some discomfort.

He crept in beside her and rubbed his hand gently down her spine, and easing himself behind her, saw what he suspected. A long stream of pink slime, was falling from her rear-end and staining the animals black and white coat. The cow was about to give birth.

'It's okay, Silver.' David spoke softly and, recognizing his calm voice, Silver turned to him and nuzzled his jacket.

David had worried about this animal for months, as they'd struggled to get her in calf, and no calf meant no milk. He'd argued with his father to be patient and give her one last chance; George had said she should be sold for slaughter. But David's patience was about to bear fruit and Silver was going to give the results. And as he gently rubbed her thick coat, David recalled what his late Uncle Fred always said: "kindness - kindness - kindness." And the memory of him and his compassion softened David's mood and, through his own kindness and persistence, Silver was about to repay him and save him from a reckless action, providing him with a thread of hope.

He separated her from the other cattle and put her into a loosebox, then scattered around some fresh straw bedding, gave her a wad of hay and a bucket of clean, cold water. He looked at the animal and smiled for a few moments as he leant back on the wall. Sighing, he rubbed the skin taught on his face with his hands, as he knew she had prevented him from running and the danger had passed.

As the day drew on Silver continued in labour, but couldn't produce a result. David checked her as often as he could and tried to give her the privacy she deserved, hoping he wouldn't have to send for the vet. And today he found it difficult to decide whether he was being overly cautious or careless in his choice. It wasn't the first time he had to make this decision, as his father would often disappear at inappropriate times and then return, only to accuse him of interfering.

So David decided to give Silver a deadline: If she hadn't calved by tea-time he would have to call the vet. But tea-time came and went and there was still no calf.

When Tom came home from school he helped with the watch, constantly wandering from the loosebox to the dairy to tell David of any progress. But Silver was beginning to look tired. And David could see as she lay on the dry straw bed, that one of the calf's front legs was the only visible sign of birth. He took a bucket of warm soapy water, lathered his hands and arms and started to examine her. He could feel inside the cow's warm body, the neck and head of the calf. But the calf's other front leg was, unusually, bent backwards and David hadn't the confidence to rectify the matter himself. If his father was here, he knew he could have easily solved the problem, but there was no more he could do, and to save Silver anymore discomfort, reluctantly, went to call the vet. He couldn't risk losing either of them.

When the vet's Mercedes pulled into the yard, David was waiting in the kitchen and he felt uneasy. He should have been pleased that Barry Fitzgerald had come quickly, but David was unsure of how to greet him, because he was sickened and ashamed of some of the things his father had done, and he hadn't spoken to Barry Fitzgerald since. David had also ignored Barry at the funeral as he'd done the rest of the mourners.

David had once read in the paper about a young man whose father had killed two children, and how the fear of turning out the same, had haunted him; David had felt pity for the young man and thought he too was branded for life and tattooed with an unrepeatable word; a description of his father that people had struggled to say, because they couldn't think of a word evil enough, as no word yet existed.

But David should have trusted Barry Fitzgerald. He was a warm, kind, man and well respected and, at the age of forty-nine, had matured into a competent vet. He was also a local man, born from a long line of men in the medical profession. His father was a doctor, but Barry preferred to look after sick animals and lead an outdoor life. He was one of the few men that George Keldas had tolerated, and David guessed Barry would be as concerned with his family's welfare today, as much as the cattle.

David could discern through the lamplight Barry's dark and greying head; his familiar face radiated feeling and his eyebrows frowned against the sharpness of the electric light in the yard. As David watched from his vantage point at the kitchen window he felt reluctant to move. If not for the sake of Silver, he would have made some excuse and sent his mother.

The passenger door opened on the estate car and David saw a young woman clamber out. He was now even more reluctant to leave and hesitated. He continued to watch them unpack the car and dress in some green overalls, when Tom came from the loosebox to meet them. David knew he was being irrational in allowing the moods of his father to enter into him again, and could no longer resist. Inwardly moaning, he pulled on his boots and left the house.

Barry Fitzgerald came forward to meet him and shook his hand and, in a sympathetic gesture, warmly pressed his other hand on top of David's.

Feeling reassured by this kindness David found the confidence to turn to the girl, but Barry spoke up first. 'Davey, this is Hannah Robson. She's from County Durham.' Barry put his arm across David's shoulder. 'She's training with us for six months; I hope you didn't mind me bringing her?'

David was stunned as he looked into the eyes of the young woman, and was instantly attracted to her and couldn't speak.

She held out her hand to his but driven by a desire to keep his promise, David ignored her gesture and pulled his hand back. He muttered a brief "hello" and headed for the loosebox. As he walked away, he knew he'd been bad mannered and justified his actions by wondering what possible use she could be. He thought she was far too small to be a vet; boyish in appearance, yet she had striking brown eyes and short strands of auburn hair that curled around the nape of her neck. David's actions wouldn't have hurt him so much if Hannah weren't so beautiful.

They followed David to the loosebox and Barry saw straight away what the problem was. Silver was standing in a corner grunting and pushing; she was becoming drowsy and swaying from side to side. The black nose and one hoof of the calf were protruding from the cow's rear end.

'Should have called me sooner, Davey. Looks like we've got a leg back. It'll take a bit of maneuvering to get this one out.'

David held his head low, disappointed and embarrassed with his judgment, which did nothing to change the mood he was sinking deeper into. He was pleased when Barry sent Hannah back to the car for some ropes.

As Barry started to examine the cow, David struggled to hold on to her halter and she fell crashing to the floor and started to thrash about.

Barry then lay on the floor and pushed his arm deep inside the cow's body and tried to untangle the legs of the calf, but had to fight with the forces of nature; the more he pushed the calf back to reach the other leg, the more Silver tried to push the calf out. 'Dang it, Hannah. Where are you? Come on, hurry up. Where's the rope?'

As Hannah rushed back, her face and neck were flushed with embarrassment and, with trembling hands she tried to tie one of the soft calving ropes to the calf's leg.

David felt sympathy towards the girl and was sorry his mistake had caused her to be reproved. He bent low and reached out with his hand to help, but Barry shouted, 'Watch what you're doing, Davey. Keep hold of the cow's head!'

Barry grimaced and writhed on the floor, his whole arm now lost inside the cow's body. 'Ahhh . . . gotcha!' and he gently eased out the calf's other leg and snatched the other rope from Hannah and tied it to the calf. 'Right . . . come on, Hannah, you can pull.' But with one big push from Silver, the calf easily slipped out with a flood of mucus and water.

Silver immediately staggered to her feet and swung around to wash her newborn calf, nudging it with soft grunting noises, as the calf thrust its head about looking for the teat of its mother.

To see his mistake corrected David felt humbled, and bent over the calf to examine it and said, 'It's a heifer.' He then muttered a half-hearted invitation to Barry, 'Do you want to come in for a drink.' And he gestured to Tom who was peering over the loosebox door. 'Go and ask Mum to put the kettle on Tom, to make Barry and . . . and . . . this young lady a cup of tea.'

And unseen by anyone, Hannah Robson bit her lip for the third time that evening.

'That's okay, Davey,' Barry interrupted. 'We won't stay. We've another call to make in Langdale and we don't want to be late home. Please give my regards to your mother, though.'

David brought a bucket of warm soapy water and a towel from the dairy to wash their hands and arms in and as the two vets started to remove their overalls, David watched Hannah as she struggled to pull her damp overalls off from over the top of her jeans. As he caught her eye, she showed great contempt for his indiscretion, and the indifference in her eyes humiliated him and he quickly looked away. To hide his embarrassment, David started to wash the calving equipment and then threw down some fresh straw to bed the cow and calf down for the evening. He purposely turned away as Barry left.

Realising David's remorse, Barry returned momentarily and put his arm on his shoulder. 'Don't fret, Davey. We've had a good result tonight and none of them will be any the worse for it. Ring me if you're ever worried, wont you. I know it's going to be hard for you all. I just . . .' but David interrupted, and pulled away before Barry could say anything else that would embarrass him further in front of this girl. 'We'll all be fine,' his voice was uncharacteristically cold. 'Don't worry about us.'

David watched the headlights of the Mercedes disappear out of sight, and the only brightness outside came from the kitchen windows as a shaft of light fell on the cold and damp farmyard floor. He left the lights on in the loosebox and walked outside into the evening's air. He noticed that the yard gate was left undone and felt compelled to close it.

When David came in the house he ignored his mother and didn't seem to hear her as she asked after Barry Fitzgerald. Kathy was disappointed in him, but before she was able to repeat her question, David had disappeared upstairs.

Kathy was used to difficult teenagers, as Linzi was still only eighteen and during her weekend breaks home from college was capable of causing friction. But these moods of David's were alien to her. His lack of restraint and bad manners worried her. She'd rarely ever needed to be heavy handed on him, George had always seen to that, perhaps unnecessarily at times. Kathy had learned to cope with a difficult husband, and wondered how she could possibly cope with a difficult son. She had suffered years under her husband's repression, with his barrage of unreasonable questions and accusations and was longing for freedom. Kathy had always found David to be her saviour, yet, despite that, she was reluctant to deal with his distress.

She wondered if he was going through some kind of crisis and, with all that had happened to him it would be no surprise. But this anger and this aggression, why couldn't he just relax and make the most of the freedom they all had? Kathy was about to follow him upstairs and try to talk when she heard the shower running and knew the moment had passed by again. She looked at his wasted meal on the table, covered it with a tin plate and put it back in the Aga.

Barry and Hannah drove on through the darkness to their next call, hoping their long day would soon be at an end. Hannah was tired and rested her head back on the car seat and shut her eyes. Barry was quietly thinking of David Keldas when Hannah suddenly spoke. 'I hope we don't go to that farm too often! He's an ignorant lad isn't he?'

Barry paused before he spoke, to best phrase what he had to say. 'Don't judge him harshly, Hannah. I admit he was rude to you, but it was uncharacteristic of David. He's usually a likable, placid sort of lad. I'll spare you all the gory details, but he's just been through a nightmare. Well, his whole family has.' Barry sighed. 'You don't want to know what happened up at Keld Head, and I won't gossip about this family, I rather like them. But David's father, George Keldas that is, was a difficult man and I could never weigh him up. He's given them all hell these last couple of years, for various reasons. But let's put it this way, he'll never harm anyone, ever again.'

'Oh no . . . I'm sorry. I didn't realise. I suppose I'll have to get used to these farming types won't I. I'm really more interested in treating small animals; maybe dealing with the general public - Dachshunds and Westies and all.' Hannah rested her head back again on the car seat and stared out into the darkness.

Barry gave a wry smile. 'I wish you wouldn't be so idealistic, Hannah. I suppose you'll want to work in Cheltenham and have all your clients as middleclass housewives with blue-rinses in their hair!'

'Okay . . . Okay, I get the message,' she scowled. 'I'll try and act with a bit more understanding in future. Perhaps I can use this as a learning curve.' Hannah knew she'd upset Barry, but felt there was no excuse for David's behaviour. If she couldn't get on with the locals, she thought, at least she could enjoy the beautiful countryside for a few months.

There was a long silence before Barry started up again. 'It's funny but we did something today at Keld Head that we haven't done for years. Something that you would never have noticed. We parked in the farmyard.'

Hannah now intrigued, looked at Barry.

'If you thought David was rude, you would have hated to meet George Keldas - an awkward devil! Most people around here preferred to deal with David. George always insisted that we parked in the lane, and the gates were to be kept closed. The only people allowed to park in the yard were his family. It was like a fortress there sometimes. George didn't like anyone snooping around, you see, and he never trusted a soul - suspicious to the point of being obsessive – guilty conscience I think. It made life difficult at times, carrying stuff backwards and forwards from the car. You had to remember to close the gate behind you each time. So it was strange today to see those gates open. It sounds silly to us I know, but we have to respect their wishes, as weird as they may be – future custom you know. So don't despise David. He's really a grand lad. He's just had a lot on his plate.'

Hannah shrunk low in her seat and hoped Barry would leave the matter alone. 'What's wrong with the sheep up in Langdale?' she said.

Tom and Sarah were sat in the lounge watching television. Tom had told Kathy, in detail, how Barry Fitzgerald had managed to deliver Silver's calf with the help of Hannah Robson, who he described as a boy-girl. He was glad at last to be able to watch what he wanted on the television as his grandparents had taken Great Aunt Betty out for a meal, as a treat for their last night together, before they took her home to her cottage near Hawkshead; they were to return to Lancaster.

Kathy, still wearing her printed apron from washing the dishes, flopped down on the sofa and drifted off into a much needed sleep. She was stirred as she felt the cushions on the sofa sag with someone's weight. She opened her eyes and it was David, now washed and changed. His dark hair was still wet and curling in its familiar way. He smelt clean and manly, his face and body covered in aftershave lotion, and he was obviously going out. As he bent over and struggled to put on a pair brown suede boots, Kathy watched him for a while wondering where he was going but glad that, momentarily, he'd decided to sit down.

'Davey . . . Please don't go out before you have your tea.'

'I'm not hungry.' He spoke softly and deliberately.

'Will the calf be alright now?'

'Yes. I've left the light on. You could maybe check her for me later, if you will? I'll look in on her when I get back. If you're worried, I'm only at the pub.' He stuffed some money into the pockets of his jeans, pulled his sweater over his head and was gone.

Kathy slapped her hands together. 'Right you two,' she jumped up. 'Sarah. . . . Let's get you in the bath. And don't disappear, Tom, because you're next!'

It was a cool evening, the rain had stopped and David enjoyed his walk down the hill. The village was quiet. He felt at last a sense of freedom, but wondered how often he would be able to do this in the future. David did like a drink, but he hadn't always had the chance of late. He had stayed in, compelled to try and keep the peace between his mother and his father, and he didn't always feel like the company. He was often not just tired with working, but from spending hours wandering the hills looking for his father, afraid he may come to some harm. And now as he walked out to the pub, he hadn't considered that his mother might have wanted to spend some time alone with him. David was also still sulking over his mistake with Silver, and his lack of courtesy with Hannah Robson, and was deep in thought.

Passing one of the cottages on the hill, David saw a man lighting up a cigarette in the doorway. He stopped, glanced quickly and turned away. He knew it was foolish, but he thought how much the man looked like his father. And as he walked on, he guessed the man was behind him, just a few paces away, and it took every ounce of self-restraint not to run. David remembered how he'd teased Tom about seeing spies in the woodland, yet he was reacting just the same. He desperately wanted to be lighthearted again, but couldn't be.

As David entered the pub, the warmth from the log fire immediately soothed him. He went across to order a drink and was resting his elbows in the bar, when someone's hand fell heavily on his shoulders.

'*Where have you been, my lovely?*' a voice was singing softly in his ears.

David lunged forward and almost spilt his drink. 'For pity's sake, Tony . . . !'

'Arhh . . . How did you know it was me . . . ? You've spoiled all my fun.' Tony Milton grinned at David. 'So you've finally come out of hiding, have you?'

'Well, I reckon I need all the friends I can get right now. I'm surprised you want to be seen with me - bad company and all.'

'Don't talk stupid. I'll take that risk.' Tony gestured. 'We're all over here.'

As David turned and looked across the crowded room he saw a handful of his friends over in the corner: Tony's sister, Joanne, and Darren Watson an old college friend; he must have walked straight passed them.

'Come on over and lighten up, mate?'

'I want to . . . believe you me. I need a bit of fun in my life, but I don't know if now's the right time?' David shook his head.

'Then at least try.' Tony led him across and, almost childlike, David complied.

Tony and Joanne Milton were David's neighbours. They looked like they were twins, in that they both had long red hair, but they weren't. They had been David's schoolmates, playmates, and collaborators and had lived in the bungalow down the hill from Keld Head as long as David cared to remember. They were close childhood friends and had seen David through most of the highs and lows of his life, understanding well the problems the Keldas family had been through, but somehow, much like David, had tried to learn to live with them. As friends and neighbours they'd become intimate with the domestic difficulties of each other's family. Their own mother had left them some years ago, leaving their father to bring them up single-handed. This caused no embarrassment, but served to bond them all; keeping confidences, being discreet as not to promote village talk, respecting each other's lives with a kind of trust and dignity that they deserved.

Tony understood the changeable moods of David's father. And from being quite small he had learned when it was a good time to stay and when it was a good time to leave. He remembered as a child, playing on the floor of the farmhouse kitchen, when George Keldas came in and tipped a box full of grass cuttings all over the kitchen table. He was incensed because Kathy had only made a salad for lunch; he'd shouted that they would all have to eat like animals to get some belly-fill. Tony Milton had calmly taken hold of Joanne's little hand and led her away home, picking up their toys as they left.

Tonight, David found he was able to relax with his friends, but as the evening drew on, it was clear that he was still, understandably, grieving. He drank too much and he talked too much; considerably so, for David. And he was beginning to be the worse for it; laughing at things he shouldn't and apologising when he needn't.

As closing time approached, one by one, the group of friends left, leaving only David, Tony and Joanne Milton to walk back up the hill to Keld Head together.

'Come on, Dave. It's an early start for you tomorrow?'

'I'm not bothered about that now,' David slurred. 'Alan Marsh is milking tomorrow.'

'Oh, he's getting his foot back in the door again is he?'

'What choice do I have? I can't work every day for the rest of my life can I? Besides, it was Mum's idea.'

'Aye. It would be.'

'Haven't you got a calf to check on, Davey?' Joanne said. 'You haven't forgotten have you?'

David had forgotten.

The three of them talked in the cold night air, and warm breath escaped as a fine mist from their mouths as they joked and chatted all the way back to the farm. They reached Keld Head with strained voices, breathless with the incline. Tony was a pace behind.

'I could have walked home with my eyes shut following your trail of aftershave,' Tony gasped. 'Or are you trying to cover up something else? What on earth is it?'

David ignored his question, but Joanne knew exactly what it was; she loved the smell of Brut.

Tony then fumbled in his pockets. 'Man . . . ! I've left my keys on the table.' He wheeled around and started to jog back to the village.

Joanne went across to the old Pele tower to shelter inside its sturdy walls as they'd often done as children, when David took her arm and restrained her. 'Don't go in there, Jo, please. '

'I'm sorry Davey . . . I'm so sorry. I didn't realise.'

'No . . . no, you wouldn't.' He took her hand and led her across to a wall, lifting her petite body high onto the slates. They huddled together in the cold, sheltering under the side of the farmhouse; Joanne was shivering.

Why David didn't invite her into the house, she'd no idea, but she knew him well enough not to let that trouble her. He must have his reasons, and the answer, as she thought, soon became clear. David was slow to appreciate how cold she was, but eventually pulled himself across and gave her his jacket; throwing it over her shoulders. As they sat closely together he put his arm around her and pulled her closer to him. Her long red hair blew with the breeze and touched his face. And as he tried to tame it, he looked at the beauty and innocence in Joanne's young face and his senses sharpened. He now felt more at ease with himself than he'd done all day; more carefree, or care-less, as he was soon to find out.

Joanne Milton was five years younger than David and Tony. She'd only just turned eighteen and David hadn't been slow in realising she'd grown into a beautiful young woman, and he'd been the protector of her many times. She was a delicate girl and sensitive by nature. He was always telling her to toughen up a bit. David felt her fragile nature made her appear like a china doll; she was easy prey and vulnerable. And tonight it was David who unwittingly became captive to Joanne's spell, and he understood how others had felt as they'd tried to win her over.

As he held her hair in his hands, and saw her face, pale and blanched, she became unreal to him. Then he did something he would regret for the rest of his life; he kissed her, not as a friend, but as a lover. David didn't know why he did it. Perhaps it was the feel of her hair; he loved the touch of a woman's hair. Maybe it was because he felt comfortable with her as she never demanded of him. But at the time, he didn't care why he had kissed her; he only knew he just had to do it.

Joanne didn't try to stop him - for a start, she couldn't, but then why should she waken from this dream? One she'd always wanted. Perhaps David wasn't out of her reach and she was no longer just the girl next door. Maybe she was old enough for him to love her, not as a friend, or a kind of brother, but as an equal.

They sat quietly for a while in a long embrace. Each numbed by their feelings. Joanne wondered at the implications. David thought of nothing except how her lips felt on his, how cool and soft they were and tasting of wine; nevertheless, neither wanted to move.

Then the noise of a car fast approaching with its headlights beaming, stirred them. Tony jumped out of the passenger seat, thanked the driver and, realising what he had just witnessed, looked at David hard in the face. He held his gaze and shouted. 'I thought I could trust you, Dave?' and he grabbed Joanne's hand and pulled her off the wall.

As David watched them walk away, Joanne turned back and looked longingly at him.

David didn't move, but continued to sit back against the cold stone wall of the farmhouse. He was amazed that he'd allowed this open display of his feelings to be master over him. His total lack of self-control confused him and felt his very thoughts were to be published in some trashy newspaper for everyone to read along with all the dreadful photographs. He wondered what was wrong with him. Did he not care anymore? Had his bad judgment and upsets of the day just been too much for him? He was trying and failing to be introspective of his life when he suddenly remembered the cow and calf.

Jumping down heavily off the wall and staggering in the process, he unlatched the gate and, in the darkness, went across the yard to the loosebox. His mother must have been over earlier as she had promised and put the light out. David switched it on again and saw the calf nestling close to its mother. The cow was cudding, resting in the clean straw, no worse for her ordeal. 'You have someone to love, Silver?' he crouched low and pulled at her ear.

Satisfied they were well, David looked about him, and noticed his grandparent's car parked in the yard and he guessed by this time they would all be in bed. He put out the light in the loosebox and tried to creep into the farmhouse and locked the back door. He clumsily tiptoed upstairs to his room, didn't undress but just lay on his bed not wanting to disturb Tom, fast asleep, on the floor. Then as much as he tried to sleep, he somehow couldn't.

Tony Milton pushed the back door of his bungalow open with his foot. The door was swollen and catching on the lintel like it did every autumn, and had been neglected. The place was empty as their father was away for the week. Tony was now in a temper but Joanne was elated and went straight to her bedroom, leaving him irate. She squealed softly as she flopped, face down onto her bed. Could she really understand what had just happened between her and David? She could still almost feel his warm arms around her body. She began to envision, over and over again, the pressure of his lips kissing hers, his manly odour and his soft voice. She felt impelled to pray and quietly said, 'Dear God, please let what just happened be real? Please let it happen again? Please don't take him away from me?'

She slowly rose and went across to her bedside cabinet, humming a song she had made up, and took out a small black musical box. She pulled out a diary and a few photographs, neatly wrapped in white tissue paper and browsed through them. She took out her pen and started to write.

At two-thirty in the morning David was still awake and was unsure what to do. First he felt sick; he had clearly drunk too much. Then he was too hot; he should have undressed. Then he was too cold; he should have been under the covers. His head was aching and his mind rushing through the events of the day: his mother, his friend, Barry Fitzgerald, the young student vet he'd been rude to, and then Joanne.

He tried a few mental exercises to slow his thoughts down but failed. He tried to think of one of his friends back at the pub, Darren Watson, who'd just bought a new Mini Cooper and had invited them to come and see it on Saturday. Then his disagreement with Tony would come flooding back, and his kissing Joanne. He had flashbacks of his father, how many times had he heard him walking the floor of his bedroom late at night, the boards creaking under his heavy stature.

By three in the morning David was still awake and beginning to feel distressed. Disturb Tom or not, he would have to get up again and make himself a hot drink. Thank goodness he hadn't to be up for work in the morning. He sat on the side of his bed for several minutes with his head in his hands, his body shivering. Rubbing his tired eyes he wandered down the stairs into the kitchen, his stocking feet paddling quietly across the cold tiled floor. As he waited for the kettle to boil, he thought of Tony once again. He decided in his mind to try to make amends and would go straight around to the bungalow tomorrow and apologise. The relationship with Tony was one he would have to depend on, and he couldn't risk losing a friend, especially with the solitary life he had promised for himself. He didn't know what he would say to Joanne.

As children they had often argued, as children do. Tony had usually gone too far with his fooling around, saying David was slow and clumsy, laughing at his serious nature. David had usually been stable as a child, always the worker, not just at home but also at school, spending most of his time if not with

Tony, then with his father. And Tony's teasing usually demanded David making reprisals, and this he did. He would make fun of Tony because of his red hair. He would call him Tinkerman, knowing Tony hated that. David would insinuate he was born in a caravan on the roadside. He said when he grew up he would become a traveller, selling goldfish and dusters, or collecting scrap metal from door to door. Tony would fly into a rage, with his quick temper getting the better of him. He wouldn't come to the farm for a few days, even weeks sometimes, but without any interference from their parents they would eventually make up and act as if nothing had happened. Then it would be David's turn to care for his friend and use his strong body to fight for him. As a child, Tony had a stammer, it was more apparent if he was nervous, but he had grown out of it now. When they were children, the other kids would tease him about this and, although David didn't understand it at the time, there had been an unspoken rule that, as best friends, they could laugh at each other, but no one else was allowed to.

And now this flirting with Joanne, well that was a different matter. This was something new, and as David was about to learn, would be painful. As the steam from the kettle dampened David's face, he remained deep in thought, wondering about Tony and Joanne, if they were asleep right now. Was Joanne dreaming? Her thoughts far away from David Keldas, the boy next door, the one with the evil and eccentric father.

What he would say tomorrow, he didn't know. He hadn't the soundness of mind at that time to concoct any explanations. But resolve this he would. Put the wrong to right and start all over again.

In a haphazard way, the tea was made. He took the hot mug upstairs, stepped over his brother and, this time, undressed in the darkness. Tom only turned and moaned at his appearance.

David sat back in bed and sipped his tea and never really resolved his dilemma. He woke up to the voice of his mother shouting up the stairs. David looked at the clock; amazed it was 9.30am, an empty mug was still lying on his bed covers. There was no sign of Tom.

'David . . . ! Are you getting up? Aunt Betty's about to leave.'

He rolled in his bed, and the empty mug fell on the floor.

'Oh, my life . . . ! Why won't you let me have some peace,' he muttered.

3

AN ELEMENTARY MAN

Kathy Keldas was sat with her parents and her elderly aunt around the breakfast table, slowly sipping coffee. The suitcases were packed and standing by the door.

There was an air of concern about them all. Brian Walker was concerned for his daughter, Kathy. Stella Walker was concerned for Aunt Betty. Aunt Betty was also concerned for Kathy. And Kathy was concerned for David.

Tom and Sarah had been up and dressed for some time. Tom was helping Alan Marsh with the milking and Sarah was hindering her mother. When David eventually appeared in the kitchen he looked wild. Once again his shaggy black hair was unbrushed and his blue eyes were reddened and puffy and half-closed with tiredness. He was unshaven and barefoot. As he slumped down on the fireside chair his elderly aunt was the first to respond as she carefully rose and, clutching to a walking stick with her arthritic fingers, went and poured him a mug of coffee.

Betty had respect for David and it had been well earned. He hadn't been a silly boy, never one to cause his father shame; it was always the other way around. David had flourished on the love he got from her and his late Uncle Fred. They were really David's great aunt and uncle. (Fred being the brother of David's grandfather, Robert.) They had been frequent visitors to Keld Head and had farmed at Spickle Howe, near Hawkshead, the twin farm to Keld Head. Both farms had been divided on the death of David's great grandfather between the two brothers. Fred was given Spickle Howe and Robert was given Keld Head. And after Robert's death, the farm was automatically passed on to his son, George, David's father.

And Betty was now the only surviving relative of that generation, and had since sold Spickle Howe to retire to her cottage near Hawkshead.

The two families had worked closely together, helping at hay-time and harvest, with sheep shearing and dipping, loaning implements to one another and, sometimes, loaning money.

Today Betty was looking forward to getting back to her cottage. She was in her ninety-second year and now a widow, but was still happy to be part of the family she'd married into more than seventy years ago. She had remained childless and these were the closest and most loved people to her. And, as she left Keld Head, she had secret teardrops in her eyes. At ninety-two, she never knew if she would see any of them again.

Kathy gently hugged Betty, feeling the fragile bones of her spine under her hands. Brian Walker helped her into his car and Tom went to unlatch the yard gate as they waved goodbye.

They drove slowly down the tree-lined track as shadows from the branches dappled on the road in the bright winter's sunshine. The road was still white in places where the early morning's sun hadn't touched the frost.

After a short silence, Stella was the first to speak, giving Betty time to compose her emotions. 'I thought Kathy looked remarkably well, didn't you think so Betty?'

'Yes, she did look well, but looks don't always say what you feel inside, do they?' she spoke softly.

'I think the children will keep her too busy to worry, and I know David will look after her,' Stella continued.

'Yes, but there's a lot of responsibility on that young man's shoulders. He's not a child anymore. He'll want a life of his own someday.'

Then there was silence, as each person remained deep in thought. They passed the lake, which was covered in a thin film of ice. Wildfowl were preening and then diving into the water, enjoying their first spot of sunshine in weeks.

Betty thought of the time when she first came here from Yorkshire and married into the Keldas family. She had come from a large estate near Thirsk and her high breeding still showed. And she was still proud to be part of some local history but, at the time, not realising the anguish she would suffer in years to come. Yes, George Keldas's behaviour had touched them all. And although Betty was no blood relation to any of the Keldas children, she felt so much a part of them. This feeling was constantly reinforced by the love she received from them all. But now she admitted to herself that David wasn't quite as attentive to her as usual.

She had known David's grandfather well, and found him to be a likable man, yet he too had struggled with his own personality; he could be wayward and unreliable at times. And like David's father, he wandered the fells alone, sometimes missing for days at a time. It would be Betty's husband Fred, who like David, would walk in all weathers looking for him. But thankfully, her Fred was more placid and carefree and very different.

Betty was surprised when the young, balanced and attractive Kathy Walker, from a middle-class background in Lancaster, had decided to marry George Keldas; yet she could see the appeal. George was a handsome man and he knew it. He lived on the edge; just the right side of dangerous. He was charismatic and Betty wondered whether to warn Kathy of the family's history. But guessed it was wrong to interfere, yet she thought Kathy would never tame him. She knew how much she herself had loved this way of life that the Keldas family had given her, living and working among these beautiful hills. And there was no way she could deny this young woman that pleasure. The mountains, the lakes, the blue-stone walls, and the Lakeland atmosphere were always a consolation for any troubled soul. Then when David was born not many months after they were married, Betty understood why Kathy had stayed.

Kathy always appeared to cope well, especially during the early years of their turbulent marriage. But George could be so loving and repentant, always looking for forgiveness, which he usually got. Kathy was herself bewitched by his dark features, his strong and elegant stature, and his piercing blue eyes, which gave him the forgiveness he wanted, well, until the next time - and the next time always came.

Slowly, George did begin to manifest his father's character and Betty hoped that in David things would be different, that he would be more like his mother. His quiet nature seemed to answer this for her yet, nevertheless, she still lived with the fears - and would probably die with them - that David would turn out like his father. She hoped the memory of David that she had up to this time would be the one she would take to the grave with her. Always hoping, always praying that this family would at last find some peace and that perhaps David would be the peace maker.

Betty glanced up and saw her cottage under the hill in the distance, and she started to fumble in her handbag for the house keys. She reached across the back seat for her small suitcase, in a hurry to be out.

They pulled into the yard and Brian took the old leather case from her hand. All she had inside it were a few clothes and keepsakes rattling loosely around. He went straight inside to light the fire and Stella made some tea.

'I'm going to worry sick about leaving you.' Stella was anxious.

'Oh, I'm getting used to it now, with Fred being in hospital all those weeks before he died. But I still hate to be alone. Your Kathy would have me back anytime, and I can go to the day-centre in Ambleside, if I have a mind. Freddie would have wanted me to stay at Keld Head, but those bairns get a bit noisy for me at times. Besides, Kathy can do without worrying about me now.' Stella smiled and poured the tea into Betty's best china cups.

Foxglove Cottage was already feeling warm as the flames from the fire jumped up the chimney. Stella stood and looked out of the window into Betty's garden. There was mist creeping across the fellside and sweeping down from the green hills above. Some blue tits were feeding from the nut bag hanging from the bird table. She knew Betty would be far more comfortable here in the peace and quiet of this cottage, as she knew she could be if she were ever left alone. Stella started to fiddle with a red flowering cactus on the window-sill and remove some dead flowers, leaving pink shadows reflecting on the clean white paintwork. Betty always had a plant in this window. In summer, it would be a red geranium.

On the mantelpiece there was a photograph of Fred and beside it one of David. David was perhaps only thirteen at the time. He was smartly dressed in his school uniform, his young face tanned, his warm eyes reflecting his pleasant disposition, but beginning to look like a farmer's son; his hair even then a little unkempt. There were no other photographs displayed.

Brian Walker finished his tea and glancing across at Betty, saw her eyes were closed. He nodded at his wife and they rinsed the few cups and plates and left the cottage. Normally, Betty would have waved at them from the window, but today she only dreamt she had.

David rushed back upstairs, found some warm clothes and was single-minded in his mission. Without having breakfast, he left the farmhouse and called the dog.

Joanne saw David through her bedroom window, her face hidden behind a lace curtain. She panicked as she realised he was headed her way, as she was still dressed in her nightie; her beautiful red hair was unbrushed and tumbling over her shoulders.

David didn't need to knock on the door. He could see Tony through the kitchen window making the breakfast. He pushed the door with his shoulder and walked straight in and stood nervously beside the fire. Tony was the first to speak. 'Hoping to see Joanne again, are you?'

Silenced by shame David was slow to reply. He didn't look at Tony. 'It was nothing. It didn't mean a thing.'

'No. To you, maybe not. But what about her? You know

what she's like. She's easily led.'

'She'll know, won't she?'

'Will she . . . ? You tell me. It's not like you were just snoggin' some bird in the back of the pub car park – she's my sister, for pities sake. And this morning she's a whopping great love-bite on the side of her neck, which, I presume, you gave her. Dad'll kill her if he sees it. What were you thinking?'

'Thinking . . . thinking. . . . I don't do much thinking anymore mate. I'm done with that. All the thinking's been knocked outta me.'

Embarrassed at David's outburst, Tony continued to butter the toast, then scraping and clinking a marmalade jar with his knife, he put the last of the contents over the warm bread. He kept his back to David. But David was disturbed by the silence and sat down and fiddled with a newspaper on the table, pretending to look at the sports' page. 'Look . . . I'm sorry Tony,' there was frustration in his voice as he flicked quickly through the pages. 'I repeat, it was nothing. Please, can we just forget it and start again? I'd had too much to drink that's all.'

Tony's face softened and he came across to David and playfully pushed his head away and David didn't retaliate. 'Here . . . have some toast! But you'll have to apologise to her.'

David accepted the gesture of peace and knew he'd been a fool and said, 'I'm going up to the tarn with the dog. I need some space. Do you want to come?'

Joanne rushed to the bathroom to splash water onto her face and body; she quickly pulled on her jeans and t-shirt and tied her mass of hair up into a tortoiseshell comb. Gazing into the mirror and seeing how pale she looked, she slapped her cheeks. She took a deep breath and calmly walked into the kitchen, but was disappointed to find it empty. She saw Tony's house keys lying on the table, picked them up and hurled them across the room, smashing them onto the fireplace.

Joanne wandered back to her bedroom, fell onto her bed and this time sobbed into her pillow, incensed with her brother. She knew it was him who'd drawn David away. He wouldn't want any relationship to form between the two of them. Nothing that would spoil their precious friendship.

She felt she was old enough to choose for herself who she dated. She didn't even care what her father would say. He didn't understand the Keldas family as she did, and Tony was only being jealous because she knew he had a crush on David's sister, Linzi. And what's more, Joanne knew that Linzi disliked Tony, because she considered him a fool.

Calming down, she went back to the kitchen, her pale skin now red, blotchy, and stained with her tears. She saw on the table two empty breakfast plates scattered with toast crumbs. She put her hand on one of them, dabbed some of the crumbs onto her fingers, put them into her mouth and sucked. Then once again flopped down on the empty chair and wept.

'How often will Alan Marsh cover for you? Hasn't he got enough to do with his own job?'

'Hmm. He said once a week, either Saturday or Sunday. It'll give me a break I suppose. Trouble is, in some ways, I'd sooner do it myself. The place is always in a mess after he's finished and the cows never milk the same. He treats them well, but they don't like change. They just got used to Dad and me.'

They continued with their small talk; David having reached as he'd hoped his objective and Tony was just pleased to have a friend again. 'We could go and see Darren's Mini later. We'd better go before he has it in a ditch!' Tony asked.

But David didn't reply and Tony knew this meant a refusal.

The track to the tarn steepened and the men found it harder to talk and walk at the same time. As they approached the tarn the mist started to draw in on them, the path became firm with the altitude and the cold. A silent breeze swirled around them, cocooning their young bodies in an eerie fog. They weren't afraid; they knew exactly where they were. Then suddenly the mist cleared as quickly as it had arrived and the fell top became visible. The higher ridges swept up before them and beckoned them to continue. But they resisted. They could now see clearly, as the dead bracken lay as a carpet, bronzed and golden in the muted light. The grass, bright green, sustained and watered by the Lakeland rain. They heard a splash and they knew they must be near the tarn. The dog had arrived first. Then the two men were enveloped in a peculiar orange glow as the morning's sunshine tried to break through and push the mist further up to the higher fells once again. As they stood and contemplated, their hair dampened and curled in the mist.

'There's not much to see here today.' Tony was anxious to keep moving as he watched David, almost in a trance, staring at the tarn. But as they were about to leave, the mist cleared completely and revealed a silken sheet of water, rippling gently as the dog swam towards them.

By ten-thirty, they had reached a gully and were running and jumping, sliding on the icy ground like two children, tugging each other's jackets and then stumbling on the hard cold earth. They ran down the steep hill, their legs aching, taking the strain off their tired lungs until they reached the flat green pasture below. Both men were gasping, silenced by the exertion. The deep tones of their heavy breathing and laughing swept off up the valley and carried away.

They stopped to rest, bending over, tired now and resting their hands on their hips. Tony started to tease David, throwing stones at him, splashing water in his face from the beck. When this failed to make a reaction, he resorted to name-calling. David smiled at his friend's childish behaviour, happy that nothing really had changed. And David foolishly thought because he'd restored his friendship with Tony that would be the end of the matter. He never said another word about Joanne.

David's mother was sitting at the kitchen table with Alan Marsh. They were both drinking tea. Alan was leaning back in the chair, straining the buttons on his shirt after finishing breakfast, when Tony and David barged in. Kathy, lazily, slid up from her seat and offered them a cooked breakfast.

Kathy was pleased to see David with Tony. Tony's fun-loving

nature had brought her son into much better spirits than he had been in for days. Yes, this could be a normal Saturday morning. David happy again; the two youngest children playing upstairs; Linzi due back from college, even having the stability of Alan with them gave her a feeling of security. No one to harm them or abuse them anymore. Yes, this will do, she thought. Things can stay like this. She broke the eggs into a frying pan, and the noise of the gentle spitting and cracking gave her a satisfied feeling.

'Come on Alan, get off your jacksie!' Tony said. No one was surprised at the insinuation that Alan was lazy. But Alan spoke up for himself, looking for some commendation. 'The cattle milked a bit better today, Davey.'

'Oh, good. I think they're getting used to you.' David didn't look up, but started to eat the breakfast set in front of him. 'Did Silver come in alright?'

'Aye, she was unsteady on her feet, though. She's well enough now. She's got a grand calf.'

'How's business been this week, Alan? Have all those chemicals you've sold, brought us any closer to doomsday?' Tony asked as he got his breakfast and again his comments were ignored.

'It's slack at the moment. These farmers do plenty of talking and not much spending.'

Tony interrupted with another sarcastic comment implying that David did neither.

Alan laughed loudly and grabbed the arms of the chair like he was master of the house. He had been a regular visitor to Keld Head and, along with the vet, was one of the few men that George Keldas tolerated. He supplied minerals and detergents and like most sales representatives, knew where he was welcome for a warm drink, a hot meal and a good rest. People in small communities stick together, they know each other's backgrounds intimately and respect that. Alan understood that to be good at his job he had to be loyal and not gossip to anyone, but he couldn't always live up to that. He knew all about the problems of this family, having been an eyewitness to many of them. He had respect for David, for the hard work he put in, and admiration for Kathy, knowing her since they were teenagers. Alan was Best Man at their wedding, and seen David born, then the others, one by one, and as one of George Keldas's only true friends, was the obvious one to help when the crisis arose.

'What time is Linzi home?' David asked as he pushed away his empty plate.

Tony's eyes flashed at the question and inwardly moaned and wondered why David hadn't told him this on the walk. But he guessed it wouldn't have even entered his head, and neither would David have been playing games with him; the one that says: *I can't have your sister, so you can't have mine.* Tony only sighed at David's lack of thought.

'I've to meet her in Keswick at twelve.' Kathy replied.

'I'll go if you like. I'm not doing much today.' David answered, showing more enthusiasm in his voice and demeanour than he had done in weeks.

Tony sat devising in his mind a scheme in which he could travel along with David. And with one hand to his chin and his elbow resting on the table, and using only his fork, he began to play with the last sausage on his plate and remaining unusually quiet. Tony wondered if David would invite him along anyway. But no, because he had just told him he was going to see Darren Watson's new Mini Cooper. What does a young man do to get his way? Women, Tony gathered, find it easier to talk about men. But Tony couldn't talk to David, not about Linzi, and certainly not after last night. And David would never have guessed that Tony liked Linzi. The two friends could talk about most things together, but they seldom discussed women. And that would explain why David had soon dismissed in his mind the problem with Joanne.

Tony knew that only Joanne held his secret, but he didn't know if she would keep it; in some ways, he wished she wouldn't. He felt frustrated and couldn't comprehend why he was confident about everything else in his life except for Linzi. He wished he didn't always have to play the fool, but maybe it

AN ELEMENTARY MAN

was she that made him this way. Why couldn't he be more calm and quiet like David? He couldn't do anything about the colour of his hair or his pale complexion to make her like him more.

When they were still at school, other children used to tease him about his red hair. And Tony had reasoned that when you have a so-called defect it was best to laugh about it, so he became a joker. And he believed Linzi hated him for that, so how could he expect her to like him when he really didn't like himself? Tony knew David would never ask him along unless he put the thought there himself. He doubted Linzi would want him there anyway. She would be tired from travelling and in one of her moods perhaps. He decided he'd better wait until later to see her and let David take all the sulking. He could handle it. He was used to it. Maybe, he wouldn't even notice.

In complete resignation, Tony slouched down in his chair, grabbed his knife and ate the last sausage.

And so it was to be: David left Keld Head alone to meet his sister.

David was glad to be away from the farm, as he sped up the familiar Raise to Keswick. He looked across to Helvellyn and could see the summit wrapped gently in a blanket of snow, which hadn't yet caused any lasting effects to the lower fells. He felt pleased with himself now. He had solved his problem with Tony. His mother seemed to be happy. Linzi would be home for the weekend. Yes, things looked much brighter. David put his foot down hard on the accelerator, and the car responded as he enjoyed the feel of the Rover's powerful engine surging on up the open road.

As he approached Keswick, it started to rain.

Linzi Keldas sat upstairs on the bus and was glad to be away. But for her it was the tedium of college life. She was anxious at the thought of seeing her family again, wondering what the atmosphere would be like at home without her father's dominant presence. She looked out through the dirty windows on the bus, as the landscape became familiar. The rain started to fall as she approached Keswick. That was hardly a surprise.

The bus pulled into the station and Linzi saw David sat in the car waiting for her and she was pleased he was alone.

The rain fell heavier as she ran from the bus to the waiting car, clumsily hauling some carrier bags and luggage with her. She jumped into the car and flung her arms around David's neck, wetting his face with hers. They started to drive away, when David hesitated. He saw a young woman watching them from the confines of a bus shelter. The car lunged forward again as he put his foot down on the accelerator and drove on.

'Who was that?' Linzi asked him.

David wanted to stay quiet but she persisted. 'Who is it Davey?'

'Oh . . . she's Barry's new student,' he said at last, his voice husky.

'Shouldn't we pick her up then? She'll be waiting for the 555.' Linzi looked back over her shoulder to get a better look at the girl.

'It's too late now. I'm not going back.' But it wasn't too late at all.

Hannah Robson had been watching David and hoped he hadn't seen her. She leant back behind the bus shelter and peered out. She had watched him rest back in his seat and read the paper, and wondered who he was waiting for. She was surprised to see this dark and attractive young women rush off the bus and be so enamored with him. She felt embarrassed when she realised he had spotted her, and now David's manner had done nothing to change her opinion of him, leaving her standing in the cold and damp. She was pleased he didn't stop.

'Davey, your hair's a mess. You look like a thug,' Linzi teased, half looking at him, and half arranging some carrier bags at her feet.

'Now when do I ever get time to go and get it cut?'
'Then I'll do it for you this weekend.'
'No you won't . . . ! I'll get it cut next week sometime.'
'Well, see you do.'

'You're beginning to sound like Mum,' David said as he tried to concentrate on the volume of traffic.

'Huh. . . . She doesn't say enough to you. She's always quick to find fault and criticise me. She never questions you!'

'Don't you believe it,' David replied knowing well that his mother was always interfering with his life; pushing him into things he didn't particularly want to do.

'Anyway, how is she?'

'Bearing up well I suppose.' David had to shout a little now as the noise of the wiper blades and the speed of the roaring engine muffled their voices. 'In fact, too well, if that's possible. I think she's switched off. It's as if nothing's ever happened. I can't understand her.' David felt himself becoming agitated again at his mother's indifference.

'Maybe it's just self-preservation.'

'Aye, maybe,' David softly replied then said, 'You should have come to the funeral, Linzi.' He had to say it; he hoped Linzi hadn't heard him, but she had.

'Don't start preaching to me, David! You know I couldn't face it.'

'Who am I to preach?' he sighed. 'I had enough preaching from the vicar. His eyes never left mine during the whole of the service. It was like he was only talking to me, and to no one else.' David gripped the steering wheel a little harder.

'Oh, you're just beginning to sound paranoid like Dad. Or maybe it's a guilty conscience!'

'What do you mean? What happened wasn't my fault, Linzi!'

'Calm down . . . I was only teasing.' She now wanted to cry.

'Well, that's not a bit funny, and you know it.'

They didn't speak for some time and, as curtains of rain fell steadily, sweeping across them in drifts, they continued their journey south. The mountaintops became invisible and again shrouded in mist. Linzi leant back, shut her eyes, and attempted to restore her breathing so she didn't burst into tears. She tried to picture where exactly she was on the route, wondering if they passed the Castle Rock yet, or were they anywhere near Thirlmere.

It was David who broke the silence with a gesture of peace. 'Shall we all go out tonight?'

'Who do you mean by all? ' Linzi was reticent.

'Well, us two . . . Darren Watson, Tony and maybe Joanne.'

'Only if Jo's coming. I was hoping to see her this weekend. Is she still working at the nursery?'

David found it hard to talk about Joanne, and now a guilty conscience did begin to creep in, but not the one that Linzi had intended. This one he guessed she knew nothing of, and so he pretended not to hear.

Linzi also stayed quiet. She'd guessed for some time that Joanne loved David, but had kept this idea to herself. She knew David would never understand women's intuition. It was a strange thing but she believed it to be true. She thought that she was certainly more intuitive than David, and that wouldn't be difficult. David appeared to her to go through life with his head in the clouds. He would never assume anything. Maybe she was just more observant than him and she had seen the signs many times. Like she also knew that Tony Milton liked her, but he had never dared to tell her.

David drove up the hill and into the farmyard. Once again, and much to Linzi's surprise, the yard gate was wide open. Tom and Sarah were playing in the old tower and ignoring the rain, ran out to meet her, asking countless questions but never giving her time to reply.

Later that afternoon as he had promised, David tried to ring Tony to arrange the evening out. He was taken aback when Joanne answered the phone. This he hadn't considered. Too slow to even think this might have happened, and not even considering this young woman's feelings, he blindly continued on his course of destruction and invited her and her brother out for a drink.

AN ELEMENTARY MAN

The intuition of a man certainly failed in David's case. The basic instincts were there: the need for love, the hunger, the thirst, satisfaction of a hard day's work and a good night's sleep. David was an elementary man and in many ways lacked very little. He was a man of his time. He went along with the changes in morality that had started to spread from the 60's, neither knowing if they were good or bad. But as for the understanding of women, well, that was not only something he hadn't yet considered, he was to learn it would be completely beyond him; way out of his grasp.

Joanne was elated to hear David's voice. She didn't note that the hesitation in his voice was any different from his usual indecisive manner.

So what does a young woman do at four o'clock in the afternoon when the man she loves has just invited her out? She spends the next three hours day-dreaming. She spends ages in the bath, then in front of the mirror, then rummaging in the wardrobe, and finally trying to get in the right mood. She listens to some of her favourite music. She listens to some of David's favourite music. She pulls out her box of cherished photographs. She looks through all her keepsakes and reads her diary, and writes in it a further inscription. She irritates her family by becoming preoccupied and not eating. The hours in the pub with her friends will be enjoyed, but that isn't the time she's waiting for. Yes, she will look at David, delighted to be in his company. She will watch him laugh. She'll listen as Tony pulls him down, and David not always understanding, or even if he does understand hardly ever retaliating. She will watch him lean back in his chair stretching his legs in front of him. Then she will watch him throw his body forward when he wants to speak, but that would be seldom. He would sit and absorb the insults, and rest his beer glass in his usual manner on his folded arm.

She will understand nothing could be done in gesture by him to show the others how he feels about her. That would have to remain their secret. But poor Joanne wasn't aware of the conversation that had occurred between David and her brother. She had been misled and was an innocent victim; not realising that soon her expectations would be erased.

By eight thirty, the young friends were all installed in the pub. Linzi talked mostly of college in Newcastle and the boredom of her Business Studies and the peculiarities of the Geordie folk with their strange and incomprehensible accent.

David remembered Hannah Robson again and thought how likeable her accent was.

Joanne watched the clock and wished time would hurry. She could hardly bear to wait until closing time. She would walk back up the hill much as they had done the night before and then she would wait for the others to leave, and then sit on the wall once again with David. She would hold him and kiss him. She would encourage him and tell him how much she really loved him.

But Tony had other ideas. He had no delusions of romance for himself, and understood that he must see David and his sister separated. He must preserve his friendship and protect Joanne from becoming prey to David's needs again. And by eleven-thirty, he had succeeded. Joanne lay crying in her bedroom and Linzi and David were sat in the farmhouse kitchen talking with their mother about old times, unaware of the gloom that shrouded the bungalow down the lane.

Joanne Milton rolled off her bed, and grunted back the liquid from the tears she'd shed. She fumbled on top of the wardrobe and pulled down a black and chrome camera. It was her father's old one. She dragged open a drawer in her dressing table, and rummaging through it, untidying underwear, tights, and packets of tampons. She found a small box full of paperclips and clutter, and pulled out a new roll of film.

'Yes . . . yes,' she whispered.

4

THE DARK SIDE OF THE MOUNTAIN

Linzi heard from her bedroom the sound of the milking machine engine stop; it was a noise she'd lived with all her life. It was reassuring for her to know David was up and working. She'd resisted getting up any sooner before he came in for breakfast, because she didn't want to be alone with her mother and risk having a confrontation. David had always been the peacemaker when there had been any trouble between their mother and father; Linzi had depended on him then and she depended on him now.

She had skilfully managed to distance herself from the problems of her family and in some ways this had been a blessing, and being away at college sheltered her. She dearly loved her father because he dearly loved her. But there were many things she didn't know about him and many things she refused to believe.

Linzi knew their father spoilt her and Sarah but she didn't realise the magnitude of it; she just soaked up the adoration. And like Tom, Linzi couldn't understand why her father hated David. How could anyone hate David? And yet, she believed that people with no apparent imperfection could be infuriating at times. She was certain that David was no angel, yet he surely didn't deserve all his father's contempt; she should have taken a share of it.

If only her father had known what she got up to in Newcastle, far away from his restraint. And yet, she guessed his cavalier nature had brushed off on her more than it had David. And that perhaps her father hated David because he was too cautious, too indecisive and, as she had heard him once say, too meek. She therefore assumed that David should hate her. She would certainly despise him and be deeply jealous if things were the other way around. But somehow David wasn't; he was as noble and faithful to her as a brother possibly could be.

She didn't know if David had ever sat and worked things out like she did. But perhaps he never even noticed the lack of love, and that would be as well. Or maybe it was worse; maybe he didn't even care.

David wandered in for his breakfast humming some song he'd probably just heard on the radio. He slid off his wellingtons and pulled loose pieces of hay and straw from his socks and went to the wash basin to scrub his hands, satisfied with a steady morning's work. He enjoyed his breakfast and was sat reading the paper, when Linzi, came downstairs still dressed in her nightie, her black hair falling untidily and unbrushed about her face. She sat down on the sofa next to David, curling her slim legs beneath her, and snuggled closer to him. All was peaceful, all was quiet, and then, carelessly, Kathy changed the feel of the whole day.

'We were disappointed you didn't come to the funeral, Linzi.'

David's hands tightly gripped the newspaper and he felt Linzi's body respond to the criticism and she sat up rigid beside him.

'Oh, Mum . . . ! I told you why I didn't come and I'm not going to go over it all again. Why do you do this to me?'

'I do this because of what people think, lady!' Kathy stood her ground.

'Well, why are you always trying to cover over the truth?' Linzi was over reacting. 'Our family's in a mess and you know it. And so does this whole village for that matter!'

With that, David threw down the paper, put his wellingtons back on and left the house. He whistled for the dog and walked at pace down the hill to the silver-birch plantation. The morning's sky was grey and fog was swirling around the lake as he took an indistinct path through the damp woodland.

David's light heart had become heavy again. It seemed to him that his whole life had become a see-saw of emotions and he was unable to keep the right balance. Things had become like his happiness was elation and his disappointments were tragedies. He remembered how reckless he was the night he kissed Joanne and then, the day after, had disregarded her feelings. When he loved, he loved too much. And when he hated, he hated with such intensity that he sensed a sinister fear grip over him, so strong that he might do someone some harm. David felt like he had a heavy iron weight slung around his neck. Some days he would be impelled to carry it, the weight so great that it pulled down his neck and shoulders. But, try as he might, he didn't seem to be able to get rid of it. Then on other days, it had gone, as if someone were looking after it for him. It was safe and still belonged to him, waiting for his return and ready for him to pick it up again. He wondered when he would collapse under its strain; because he guessed, one day, he would have to.

David walked on and thought he heard the snap of a twig behind him. He called to Moss, but she was well in front, sniffing in some rabbit hole. He looked about him, his deep blue eyes searching the woodland, listening like a man with a thousand senses, and every one of them a burden to him. David guessed he was just being stupid, as there was no one in sight. He wondered if his mother had followed him but, after waiting a few moments, he realised, apart from his dog, he was alone. He leant back onto a nearby tree, slid his body down to a squatting position and held his head in his hands.

Back at the farmhouse, Linzi began to wash and dress. She looked at her face in the mirror as she combed her dark hair, trying hard not to cry. She knew she would have to make some gesture of peace to her mother.

Linzi returned to the kitchen and sidled up to Kathy, putting her arms around her neck and leant on her shoulder. 'I'm sorry Mum. . . . Do you think our Davey will take me to see Aunt

THE DARK SIDE OF THE MOUNTAIN

Betty sometime today?'

'I'm sure he will if you ask him nicely.' Kathy was pleased for once that Linzi had taken the initiative to bring about some peace. 'That's if he comes back in time. He's very upset you know. . . . He's a changed man.'

'We're all upset, Mum. But we've just got to get on with things haven't we?'

David crouched low by the lake and splashed water onto his face. He was unable to move as he took in the tingling feel of the icy cold water on his skin, thinking of nothing else. He was disturbed when he saw a flash of blue light. David glanced behind, and his eyes roved about the woodland but saw no one. He shouted, 'For pities sake . . . ! Leave me alone.'

When he returned to Keld Head, Linzi was at the door waiting.

'Davey . . . ? Will you take me to Hawkshead?' Linzi looked into her brother's eyes and thought he looked upset. She wanted to ask why, but resisted.

The red Rover car sped down the winding lane to Hawkshead. David drove on recklessly, hoping to get this errand over and done. Linzi was just pleased he had brought her. She wished now that she were back in Newcastle and vowed she wouldn't return home until Christmas.

Betty Keldas trembled with happiness at the sight of David and Linzi. Linzi was sitting, drinking tea and listening carefully to her Great Aunt. She was glad she'd come and felt she'd satisfied not only her mother, but also this dear and well loved lady. David was standing by the cottage window and was restless. He'd hardly greeted his Aunt, but was selfishly consumed in his own reverie. He wasn't absorbing any of the beautiful scenery, only experiencing overwhelming anguish.

It was Betty who broke the silence. 'You look tired, Davey. Come and sit down.'

David turned and relented. He came across the room and

kissed the pale, paper-thin skin on her cheek.

'Take no more thought for tomorrow, Davey, for tomorrow will take thought for itself!'

'I know,' David replied, smiling at her now. 'But that's easier to say, than it is to do?'

'Yes, it is. . . . I've had anxiety for what seems to be ninety years or more and I've always left things to the Lord to sort out. I prayed hard for my Freddie and for your grandfather. He was just like your father. Yes, he used to walk the hills alone, your poor grandmother never knowing where he was – worrying herself to death - off for days on end. He couldn't cope with being tied down, you see. He said he needed to get away. When your father was a little lad, my Freddie used to love and take care of him, as your grandfather didn't have the patience with him. Freddie would cuddle him and sit him on his knee. George was a bonny lad and what a handsome man he once made.'

The two young people listened carefully to her. Linzi especially endeared to the love and kindness this old lady showed, and the compassion she spoke of her father. David felt the opposite. This was not what he wanted to hear, as Betty continued. 'We always hoped your father would turn out differently, but it wasn't to be, was it. And it breaks my heart to think how much my Freddie loved him. He loved him too much I think?'

'Oh, please . . . don't Aunty.' Linzi dared to interrupt.

'No, Linzi. Things have to be said. But don't you worry now, Davey. You're much like your mother.'

'God knows, Aunt Betty . . . I wish I was!' David muttered. 'She's like a rock - nothing will move her. It's like nothing's ever happened.'

'It's her way of coping, Davey. Don't take that away from her. She's had to learn good and hard and she's succeeded.'

David didn't speak again; he just listened as Linzi and his aunt discussed life in Newcastle. He couldn't understand how his aunt could be so frank. And he once again became embarrassed at his own weakness. Tony was always telling him

THE DARK SIDE OF THE MOUNTAIN

he was too soft. If his father were here he would say he was being slow and stupid; yet David was a grown man, and these feelings he had were childlike so, being judge and jury, David condemned himself and found himself guilty.

He began to stare at the fire as its flames leapt up the chimney, glowing blue and red and then orange. They became a source of comfort to him as he continued to stare long and hard. He became fully focused on them, as they helped him not betray his feelings.

Throughout the coming week David absorbed himself in his work. There was plenty to do on the farm in winter. The winter's feeding programme meant extra work in itself. A shortage of lush grassland made it harder to fill the cows' bellies and it meant feeding silage, hay and grains. The cattle were kept in the cow-kennels for the winter, with brief trips around the fold-yard. This also meant more work; constantly keeping the cattle clean and the yards swept. The manure would freeze solid on the yard, making it harder to remove. Then the snow came, and the mixture of snow and manure was a poor one. The slush was another obstacle. The thawing snow would pour into the drains; the water level rising so high that it would flood the dairy. David's hands froze, as he spent hours on the tractor, clearing the muck and the soiled straw from the concrete floor.

He was pleased he only had to call the vet out again on a couple of occasions, and only for minor problems. It was a relief on the farm budget and a relief that Barry Fitzgerald came alone. David never asked after Hannah Robson and pushed any thoughts he had of her to one side, preferring to remove an embarrassing day from his memory. He still didn't want to meet any more strangers, but on the few occasions he met Barry Fitzgerald, found his gentle sympathy reassuring and David was genuinely comforted by this kind man.

Life for Kathy also began to settle. She put more wood on the fire and the house felt warmer; the chimneys were alive with wood-smoke, drifting on up the valley and across the lake. And with the children back to normal life at school, it became apparent, without George Keldas's dominant presence that more children called at the farm. When it snowed, they were allowed to play in the garden and make a snowman as George would never have let them; they hadn't to disturb and spoil the snow. It was some notion of his that the snow protected his family from intruders. George told them a story of how David's grandfather, Robert, was once besieged behind Keld Head's strong walls for days, fearing someone's wrath. And it was the checking for footprints in the deep and pure white snow that protected him

Linzi, as she had planned, didn't come home much, just for a few days over Christmas and then quickly back to college to be with her friends. Tony visited the farm regularly in the hope of seeing her and he continued to be a good friend for David. They would walk the fells together on better days and on poor ones, would go to the pub. Tony had noticed a difference in David - he had become quieter, if that were possible. He was also more insular. He was edgy, never still, and Tony knew that he didn't sleep well. He tried to offer him a hundred remedies but was never taken seriously. Tony even wondered if he should have interfered between David and Joanne, thinking that David would have been happier if he had Joanne to love and for someone to love him. He didn't like to see his friend in such low spirits, but felt there was little he could do to help.

Joanne was equally as broody; isolating herself in her bedroom most of the time and, when it was fine, she too was out walking the lower fells, but always alone, and never with the men. Tony knew that she was unhappy and put it down to teenage mood swings.

Joanne had kept her diary up to date, recording every sighting of David and the exact words he spoke to her - which was easy, as they were so few. She also started to write some poetry and it was always melancholy, of what life would be like without him. She listened to her favourite music; usually a love song; keeping her caged in her own black thoughts. Her father worried, thinking she was anaemic. Her skin was pale and she had dark circles about her eyes, and he wanted her to see a doctor. No other girlfriends ever called at the house and Joanne would turn down any invitations; always hoping that David would visit. She would sit up until the early hours of the morning with her bedroom light on, hoping he would see it and secretly call. She could see the farmhouse from her bedroom window, and could see David's bedroom light on well into the night, and wonder what he was doing. Then she would dial his number and replace the receiver when he answered, afraid to speak to him, but happy just to hear his voice. She hoped she might bump into him on the lane, as she knew he often walked out alone. Joanne hoped to meet him so he would hold her and kiss once again. She hoped that those fleeting moments of passion for her were not just casual interest. She knew David well and, although he was popular, he was never one to fool around with girls, so why would he play with her feelings. She just prayed and prayed that one day they could be alone again together. Then he could tell her how much he really cared for her.

Alan Marsh also spent more time at the farm and, as Tony had implied, not just for selling minerals or relief milking. Alan was a bachelor, so had plenty of spare time on his hands to visit who he liked. He'd spent several years looking after his elderly mother and that was the reason many suspected he had never married. Others had different ideas about him. He now lived alone in a large house in Grange-over-Sands, but he would usually be seen in the local pub; his large body propping up the bar, telling some yarn or joking with the regulars.

One morning after David had finished feeding up the cattle, he came into the kitchen and found Alan and his mother kneeling together on the floor of the adjoining lounge, surrounded by receipts and papers, and they were adding and subtracting. David didn't like the idea of Alan knowing the farm business, but he supposed his mother did need some guidance. He was never good with figures himself and neither was his father. Kathy had always been left to balance the books. The farm usually managed to support them, but only just.

Kathy and Alan were so absorbed in their calculations, that they ignored David. Kathy giggled and mocked at Alan's efforts to add up. David pretended not to notice their flirting with each other as he put the kettle on the Aga and started to make some tea. He paddled about the kitchen in his stocking feet, wandering from side to side; no method in this. Where was the tea-caddy, the cups, the biscuits? He started to open and close the doors of the kitchen units at random. As he tried to remove the lid of the tea-caddy he'd finally found, it slipped from his hand and all the contents spilled over the floor. David cursed his own stupidity. But before he could move to clear up the mess, Kathy was there to see what had happened.

'I'm sorry, Mum. I don't know what's the matter with me?'

'You need a good night's sleep, that's what the matter!' Kathy shouted, annoyed at the mess. 'It's time you got yourself to the doctor?' Then she held her hand to her throat, knowing she should have kept quiet.

David looked at her and, momentarily stunned by her outburst, calmly said, 'I'm not going to the doctor's. There's nothing wrong with me. It's perishing out there. . . . My hands are frozen.'

Kathy tenderly clenched her son's hands and was ashamed he was right.

David finished his tea and went to check some cattle that were wintering out on the lower pasture. Kathy returned to Alan deep in thought. 'I think he should see the doctor, Alan. The lad's not well, but I doubt if he'll go?'

'Why don't you go then?' Alan sounded genuinely sympathetic. 'Maybe Doctor Reed can give you some advice. David's probably in shock and you know these youngsters - they don't always know how to express their feelings.'

'He can't go on with this sleeplessness. I can hear him at night, up and down, just like George.'

'It's going to take time, for him to sort things out in his head, but he'll settle down again I'm sure.'

'I know your right. I think I will go and see Michael Reed,' Kathy replied. 'He did say if I was ever worried about anything, I must call.'

'Well there you are then, and while we're doing some doctoring, I've got some advice for you. Don't you think it's about time you got yourself away for a break, a change of scenery or something? It would do you good. Your mother would look after the kids, perhaps just for a weekend or so and David can look after himself for a change.'

'Oh yes, and where would I go? The Bahamas! With these figures looking the way they are, I just couldn't afford it. And anyway, what would I do on holiday on my own sat in some little bed and breakfast place.'

'Well, just think about it that's all?'

The following morning Kathy went to Keswick. She dressed in her best skirt and pullover. She did her hair up properly for the first time in weeks, and put on some make-up and perfume. She felt a sense of freedom. She had managed to leave while David was up the hill mending a stone wall that had tumbled down, and she hoped to get back home before he missed her.

It had been some time since she'd actually left Keld Head, barring necessary trips to the supermarket, the bank and the school. And today it was a cold and fresh January morning; the Lakes were pleasantly quiet for a change. Kathy enjoyed looking around the little shops. She went for a coffee and a buttered scone, and felt contented as she sat reading the morning's newspaper, in no hurry for her appointment. She was enjoying the peace and the freedom as she wandered up to the surgery, happy to see a few friendly faces on the way.

Dr Reed was pleased to see Kathy and thought she looked surprisingly well. Over the years of her turbulent marriage, Kathy had found she had made a good ally with this young and supportive doctor. He had seen her through a troubled pregnancy with Sarah, hoping that she wouldn't have any more children. The young doctor had stood by her on many occasions, giving her the resolve to go on, despite the desperate situation she often found herself in.

As much as this young doctor liked Kathy, he had a great disliking for George Keldas. He found him difficult to handle and, although respecting his position as a good provider, he couldn't comprehend how this attractive and articulate woman could abide to stay with such a man.

Michael Reed respectfully rose from his chair as Kathy entered his office. He took her hand and held it momentarily, then beckoned her to sit down. 'You look well, Kathy, if I may say so. I thought you'd have been to see me sooner than this.'

'Well, Michael, you're the only one who thinks that. Everyone else thinks I'm worn out and only fit for the scrap heap.' Kathy slid graciously into the chair.

'Their words or yours? Perhaps that's what they think you should be like.' The young doctor grinned at her.

'I hope this doesn't sound awful, Michael, but I feel like I've had a great weight lifted off my shoulders - tragic though it's been. I feel I can look forward to some kind of future.'

'I wish more people could feel the same as you, and then my surgery wouldn't be half as full. So whichever way you're coping, keep doing it - it's obviously working.'

The doctor dropped his pen down on his desk, sat back in his chair and folded his arms. 'So what can I do for you today?'

'It's David. . . . ' Kathy hesitated. 'I don't know if you can discuss his health with me, he being an adult. But I'm worried about him – he's acting strange, almost suspiciously, like he's hiding something from me.'

The doctor sat forward in his chair and tried not to appear alarmed, as the familiar subject he'd discussed in the past about George, seemed to be resuming about David.

'He's not sleeping, he's jumpy, bad tempered, and he's shutting himself away most of the time. David interrupted Alan Marsh and me doing some book-keeping yesterday, and I felt his eyes glare at me, just like a jealous husband. Yes, just like George. I was waiting for the accusations to start all over again.' She rubbed her hand across her forehead, relieved she had unloaded this anxiety from her mind.

'Maybe it's you that's over-reacting now?'

'Well, maybe so. I don't know anymore. I was so used to the cold feelings between George and me, but now with David. I don't think I can bear it again.'

'What are you hinting at, *like father - like son?*'

Kathy was alarmed at his inference. 'I know that's what it sounds like, but no . . . I didn't mean that. I'm sorry if it sounded like that. It's just his nerves, I'm sure. If he could only get a good night's sleep, then I know - I just know, he'll be better.'

'I can't prescribe anything for David unless I see him, and I would like to see him. Could you persuade him to come in?'

'He'll never come, and what's more, I daren't tell him I've come here today.'

'Then perhaps I could call at the farm sometime on a routine visit. It's a while since I've been, so maybe he won't be too suspicious. But Kathy,' the doctor hesitated, 'you must understand that David will have some trauma. And he's lived with George's influence – what, twenty years or more? He could be affected - all the children could be.'

'Do you mean they could all turn out as evil as George?' Kathy began to fidget in the chair and, much like her visit to the school weeks earlier, wished she hadn't come.

'I'm sorry, Kathy. I didn't mean to alarm you; I can say this now as things are out of my hands, but I always found George to be awkward. I don't even know if he could help himself.'

Kathy interrupted: '*Awkward,* is an understatement, Michael. There's always been a dark side to this family. George could turn on the charm when he wanted, and then be downright wicked. Sometimes there was a fine line between the two!'

'Well, whatever he did, Kathy, whether he intended it or not, you must understand that David, Linzi, Tom and Sarah could be badly affected by it in one way or another.'

Kathy was disappointed. 'No, Michael. . . . None of my

children have ever shown a hint of George's behaviour.'

The doctor was now bemused. What did she want him to say? She had just accused her eldest son of imitating his father and then, in almost the same breath, denied all knowledge. He was perplexed. 'So how can I help you?'

Kathy realised she'd unwittingly contradicted herself. 'Please, Michael. Please come and see him. Try and talk to him. I couldn't bear anything to happen to David.' And she looked completely helpless.

'I will come to Keld Head, and soon. But I can't make any promises of whether I can help. Some of that will have to come from David.'

Kathy looked at this young man, his sympathetic voice and kindness had helped her once again, and yet the subject of her concern was no longer her husband but her son.

She saw the familiar photographs of his wife and children placed on his desk, and she wondered how happy they were. What kind of home did they have? His dear little children would never have to suffer as hers did. Had life just dealt her a slap of the face, a restraint for her short-lived happiness?

Kathy left the surgery feeling trapped. Her momentary freedom had fled and the plan had backfired. Why didn't she listen to her own mind instead of letting people persuade her to do other things? She was coping, and she was doing well. Then she found herself selfishly cursing David for his sensitivity and his weakness, and blaming him for losing her sense of freedom.

Kathy walked away from the surgery, blindly, looking at no one. She didn't notice the rain touching her face. She wanted to cry as the muscles in her throat started to constrict, and thought she would choke if she didn't release the tension, but the tears would not come. She hadn't cried for George, or anyone else, and she would not cry for David.

She jumped into her parked car and, looking in the mirror, could see her bedraggled hair strewn in tatters about her face. Mascara had smeared about her eyes as she'd rubbed away the unwelcome moisture. She hoped no one had seen her, but she couldn't be certain. Kathy tried to remember leaving the surgery, but her mind was blank. She must have crossed the main road at some stage, and shuddered at the thought of what could have happened. She must try and pull herself together and be calm and keep her visit confidential. She would tell no one of Michael Reed's inference and just hoped that when he did eventually call at the farm, he would be professional enough to hide the motive for his visit.

She brushed her hair, wiped her face dry, powdered her nose, and set off for the short journey home.

When Kathy arrived back, she was surprised to see David in the kitchen and he didn't appear to be unduly worried about her absence. When she saw her son sat contentedly in the kitchen, Kathy felt guilty about her thoughts. She wanted to hug him and tell him everything that had happened, but that would be impossible. She felt, more than ever, that she needed some masculine logic to reassure her. She wanted to feel David's strong arms around her, to console her, but had to be content with his presence. And as he sat quietly in the chair, Kathy started to feel calmer inside as she could see he was having a better day. He told her that the morning's milking had gone well, his voice was soft. As she peered into his face, she saw his eyes looked sleepy and he spoke without any emotion. He wasn't looking at her at all, but appeared to be staring across towards the window. She hoped he could settle. He just had to.

At four o'clock, children's voices sounded as Tom and Sarah passed the kitchen window home from school. There was no time for Kathy to dwell on gloomy thoughts. They mustn't see any unhappiness in her speech and actions. But she found herself observing their behaviour more than usual: Sarah so small, delicate and sensitive. She had missed her father dearly and would often weep with her head buried in Kathy's lap, yet she could change as quickly, if she were offered a treat or a game to play. David had been good to her in trying to make her feel secure, but George had so overwhelmed her with love.

David did help, but then Sarah would get angry with him and scream if he teased her.

Tom was different: he idolised David.

Kathy worried about Tom. He didn't have many friends, but he didn't seem to mind. He spent most of his time with David and would rush straight upstairs as soon as he was home from school to get changed, and help with the milking; something he never did when George was around. It was strange to see how their roles had all changed. They had all stepped up a place in the family unit. Kathy remembered watching David when he was a boy, following George. David would walk down the lane behind him, sometimes having to run to keep up, as George strode on regardless. She would watch David imitate his father's posture. He would walk tall and straight-backed just like him, and with an air of arrogance, like they owned the very county, and not just the few fields that surrounded Keld Head. He would show David how to repair the stone walls, and how to mend the fencing. He taught him all he knew about animal husbandry: which cow to breed off and which to replace. He taught him how to tell when a cow was due to calve and how to deliver it. He showed him which fields were wet, and which were dry. Which meadow to cut for hay and which to leave. Kathy could see David teaching these self-same things to Tom, and he loved it. So consequently, friends to Tom were unnecessary; he had all the companionship he needed and that was with David.

5

THE GLASS SNOWSCENE

Kathy wasn't surprised that evening when Alan called. When she heard a car pull into the yard she knew it would be him. David hadn't gone out, but was sitting alone in his room.

Alan lumbered across the kitchen towards Kathy as she sat at the table mending some of David's work trousers.

'You went to the doctor's then?' Alan said, standing tall above her and blocking out some light.

'Yes, I did and I wish I'd never gone,' Kathy softly replied, mindful of David sitting upstairs.

'And why's that?'

'Oh, I just think I can manage better without any interference from doctors.'

'What about Davey, did you tell him about Davey?'

'Yes, I did, and he's coming to see him, "*discreetly*" he says, and I hope he is discreet.' Kathy continued to carefully thread her needle, holding it up towards the light.

'Michael Reed would only be trying to help you - not interfering.'

Kathy knew full well that she could never tell Alan exactly what Michael Reed had said but understood Alan's concern.

'Sometimes I feel that everyone's trying to steer this family in different directions and yet I'm the one that's holding the reins.'

'Oh, and I suppose I'm included in this am I?'

'I'm sorry. I didn't mean that at all.'

'The trouble is, you keep trying to push things aside and you can't do that.'

THE GLASS SNOWSCENE

'I know - I know I do. Linzi said that once. I can't help it though, things have been bad for so long. I can't - I don't want to fight any more. I don't want to make any more excuses for our family. I want things to just go away so I can get on with my life.'

Alan paused before he spoke. He crouched low and held her by the shoulders and looked her square in the face. 'Sometimes you have to face things - accept things. If you run away, problems only keep following you. If you can face up to things, have a good cry, dry your eyes and start again.'

'What have I got to face up to?' Kathy was frowning. 'I thought all was solved.'

'So where do you want me to start? What about this place? Those figures we looked at yesterday didn't look too good.' Alan stood up again to ease his aching knees.

'Now you're beginning to sound like Mum and Dad. All they want me to do is sell up and buy some bungalow in Windermere. Have you ever thought if I did that what would happen to David? This farm is his life, it's his future not mine. I couldn't sit back smug and see him waste his life struggling to find a job. He'd end up on the dole or something.' Kathy stood up and couldn't help but raise her voice.

Alan pressed his hands gently on her shoulders and sat her down again. 'You say Linzi said this and your mother said that. Well maybe - just maybe – we're all right.'

'Oh I don't know any more what to think. Don't you see, we have the chance to be a normal family. Things will eventually settle down and Davey will get better.'

'I hope you're right.' He took Kathy's hand and gave it a squeeze and tears began to well up in her eyes.

'Have you thought any more about a break, a short holiday or something?' Alan took out a handkerchief, thinking she might cry at last.

'I've thought of nothing, only my kids and my son.'

'Well, I know this might sound pushy, but I wondered if I could take you away for a few days. We could go to Blackpool or some place. I realise you can't go anywhere alone. It would all be above board. Just as friends - nothing more.'

Kathy pulled her hands away, realising the gesture from him was an honest one, but she was also aware that he had called a lot recently, and the funny thing was, she welcomed it. She needed the adult company and his strength and soundness of mind, but this new idea of his was overwhelming and Kathy wasn't ready.

'I don't know if it's a good idea, Alan. Besides, I want to see Davey better. I can't leave him while he's unwell, and although a holiday would be all above board to us, it wouldn't be to other people and I don't want to start any more gossip.'

'Who needs to know? Your mother and Davey, that's all. No one else.'

Kathy got up and went to mend the fire. 'Let's just leave it Alan, please.'

David, up in his bedroom, was aware that Alan was here again. He didn't like the idea of his mother being alone with him, but neither did he have the inclination to join them. He didn't want to talk and he was desperately tired.

David had begun to dread the evenings. He looked at the clock and it was nine-thirty. He was almost afraid to go to bed, lying there and not sleeping. How could he face another day's work, up at six-thirty and then slog through it all when he was so tired? Why couldn't he give in and go to sleep? At one time in his life, he couldn't keep awake. A busy day on the farm with his father and he would easily fall asleep in the chair after tea, and even on his day off he would have difficulty getting out of bed before lunch.

He wondered if he should give Tony a call and go out for a drink; that would certainly pass some time. But to go to the pub meant having to talk, and talking was the last thing he wanted to do. So David decided, although it was late, he would go for a walk and, despite the darkness, there would be no difficulty finding his way. It was a frosty evening and there was a good moon; he would enjoy the fresh air and maybe feel like sleeping when he returned.

THE GLASS SNOWSCENE

David didn't go into the sitting room before he left, he just shouted from the kitchen to say he was going out, making the excuse he was checking the cattle.

It was a beautiful January evening and David's eyes soon became accustomed to the darkness and he started to enjoy his stroll. The faint traffic noise from a few cars on the main road below the village broke the silence, but the peace was welcoming. The night was already feeling milder and the moon had become as covered in filigree lace as clouds pushed in.

David wasn't surprised when he felt a few specks of snow on his face, and as he walked the scene before him quickly changed to a winter landscape. Large snowflakes were falling as confetti all around him. The lane quickly whitened and the darkness turned to hazy light, as David was speckled in snow. And, as he walked, the fresh snow crunched under his feet as it compacted with each step.

As the light improved, he decided to walk up the rocky ghyll. The energy used exhilarated him as he scrambled up the slippery path, and he wondered if this was a good idea after all, as instead of feeling tired he was beginning to feel wide awake. He only hoped that once he returned home, the warmth of farmhouse would soothe him to sleep.

David struggled on up the ghyll, grasping at the rocks with his bare hands, his fingers tingling with the cold. His knees ached as his trousers were dampened with the melting snow. Reaching the fell top, David could see in the distance the lights of Grasmere flickering like tinsel in a little glass snow scene globe, like the ones as a child he would love to shake. He recalled his Great Aunt Betty always had a snow scene in her china cabinet. It was of Dove Cottage, and if he'd been good, he was allowed to play with it. She told him to shake the tinsel and watch it fall and imagine if you were ever troubled by things in life, watching the tinsel settle would show you how life could eventually turn out. He would hold it close to his eyes and allow himself to be mesmerised by the flickering tinsel, and remove himself from the real world around him.

THE GLASS SNOWSCENE

And he wanted to do that now.

David felt a shiver as the cold night cloaked him in eerie splendour. He jogged back down the cart track to the bottom of the fell and returned to the lane, his legs now numb with the rigours of the descent and the cold. As he walked back towards the farmhouse, he noticed his outgoing footprints already being covered with a light film of new snow.

With his head down and his chin on his chest, he suddenly noticed another set of footprints beside his, as if someone had walked with him. He assumed the footprints not to be his, but perhaps some fell-walkers out enjoying an evening's stroll. But stamping his boot into the snow, sure enough, one set of prints matched his own. He carefully examined the other footprint and it was from a walking boot much like his, but smaller in size and the pace in between each step was shorter. David's natural instinct was to look behind him, and a rush of fear shot through him, just to remind him he was still in this world that he so despised. He waited for a while expecting someone to catch him up and, concealing himself behind a tree, sat down on a broken branch, but no one appeared. He contemplated retracing his own tracks, but was beginning to feel tired and he violently shivered. David had never feared the fells; they had been his lifelong friends. He didn't fear the dark, and the snow made this particular night welcoming. It was only his own thoughts that stupefied him.

He must have crouched there for a good half-hour with still no signs of any one, when he heard the faint chime of the clock on the village church strike eleven and, feeling colder than ever, David stood, his knees clicking as they straightened, and headed back to the house.

When he opened the back door, Alan had gone; Kathy was sitting alone in the parlour waiting. She smiled as David came across and stood in front of the fire to warm his hands, blocking all the heat. Then he softly questioned her. 'Have you been out, Mum?'

'No love, why?'

'Oh, nothing really. When did Alan go?'

THE GLASS SNOWSCENE

'He left only minutes ago. I'm surprised you didn't see his car leave. Are the animals all okay?'

David mumbled a reply and encouraged Kathy to go to bed.

Once she'd left, he settled down on the sofa and stared into the fire, feeling the warm glow as he'd anticipated, and soon began to relax. And sitting quietly, musing over his mystery, without realising it, David missed the moment that he fell asleep.

He was still there at six-thirty the next morning when Kathy came back downstairs.

Keld Head was in full splendour that morning as the turrets on the tower held a good covering of snow. Azure blue sky framed the hillside beyond. Fronds of dead bracken and moss peeped through the blanket, with hints of bronze and green.

After milking, David decided to finish the dry-stone wall he'd been repairing. It was too beautiful a day to stay indoors. He felt refreshed from the best night's sleep he'd had in weeks, despite being on the sofa.

He went back up the lane where he'd walked the night before, but couldn't find any trace of the footprints he'd seen, only little paw prints from a rabbit ahead of him. He wondered if he'd dreamt going for a walk last night. Did he climb the ghyll or not? In the clear light of day, things appeared to be more logical.

He set his tools down and cleared some snow away with his hands from where he'd been working, re-set his line and started to sort through the stones to repair the wall.

David enjoyed his work and became so absorbed in it, that his thoughts were fully focused on the repairs.

The young doctor could see David at the head of the lane and, anticipating a pleasant stroll, locked his medicine bag in the car as to look less formal.

As he approached, David was startled so much that he almost fell backwards on the rocks.

'I'm sorry, David. I thought you must have heard me.'

David laid his hands on his chest to try and steady his rapid beating heart. 'Oh, man. . . . Hello Michael . . . I must have been miles away then. You could have dropped out of the sky for all I knew. What are you doing up here on a day like this?'

'Exactly the same as you, I suspect. To take in some fresh air and get away from that germ ridden surgery.'

'Have you been to see my mum?' David asked, too slow in thought to understand the real reason for the doctor's visit.

'My next port of call.' Michael didn't lie.

'Well, she's about somewhere, I think.'

And as David was speaking, Michael Reed began to observe his behaviour. The first thing he noticed was that David was edgy, and this was uncharacteristic of a lad who, only a few months ago was steady and unruffled despite the family problems he had. Nevertheless, David did look well. His face was fresh and ruddy, stimulated by the winter's chill. The eyes, though, looked tired and heavy and perhaps a little reddened, but his general appearance was the thing that alarmed the doctor the most. David's hair had grown long, and this didn't suit him, and it made him look wild. Even his clothes appeared more ruffled and dirtier than was usual, and Michael Reed could understand why Kathy was worried about her son.

'How's your mother doing?' The young doctor questioned him.

'Everyone says she's doing fine, but I'm not so sure.' David replied, nervously fidgeting with the trowel in his hand.

'And what does everyone say about you?'

'I would imagine they're saying I'm acting crazy!' He looked at Michael with eyes that pleaded for a reply.

'And is that true?'

David leant back on the wall and, with a wry smile, said, 'They say a man with no conscience doesn't know when he's doing wrong. He thinks all the others are self-righteous fools.'

'And is that what you think, Davey?'

'Huh . . . my thoughts tell me I'm probably as evil as my father.'

Michael Reed put his hand to his chin and replied. 'Then you do have a conscience, David. And by your own theory, you mustn't really be as bad as you think.'

David laughed, 'I suppose you must be right,' but inwardly, David didn't agree; he couldn't possibly tell the doctor, he believed everything that had happened to his family was his fault, and he'd proved it by being reckless with Joanne.

'So if you're not evil, David, what are you?'

'I'm a tired man, that can't sleep, who worries about his mother and thinks people are following him all the time.'

Michael Reed, through a process of elimination, knew that there was no reason for guilt in David Keldas, and his comments were those of an over-tired and wearied man. But he did wonder why David alluded to someone following him. That thought niggled him.

Michael liked David. He sincerely hoped that nothing would be wrong with him. He didn't want to think David was deluded, and neither did he want to think he was speaking the truth, and yet George Keldas had often said the same. But no, the truth must be that David was a level-headed young man, who was suffering some considerable strain from having to look after a farm and a small family at a young age.

Yes, that was the diagnosis - the prognosis? -well, that had to be a good one. He would recommend medication on a short-term basis to help him rest. Give some practical advice on how to relax, and hope his family life would settle.

'I could give you something to help you sleep.'

'I don't want to start relying on pills,' David was dogmatic. 'I'll be okay. Don't worry about me.' And he slapped a heavy stone down on top of the wall.

'Well, lay off the booze and the strong coffee then. Take some warm baths before bedtime. Get yourself away from this place now and again, and don't be looking over your shoulder all the time.'

Michael shook David's hand and as he returned to his car, he met Kathy in the yard.

'Have you seen him?'

'Yes, we've had a little chat.'

'And what did you think?'

THE GLASS SNOWSCENE

'Well, David's tired. He wouldn't accept any medication, but I'm sure he'll be all right. Let's just keep an eye on him for a while. He's a healthy lad, so let's settle with that for now shall we? He does need a break though. Would that be possible?'

'It might be, if he would take it. I'd have to get someone in to cover for him, and this time of year no one wants to be in a cold milking parlour at six o'clock in a morning.'

'Would Alan Marsh do it?'

At this suggestion, Kathy flushed. 'I don't know. Let me think about it.'

The doctor drove away slowly and carefully down the snow-covered road. Kathy stood in the yard awhile watching him and thought of the dilemma she had, wondering if Alan would help David instead of her.

David continued with the walling, and thought what a decent man Michael Reed was. He hadn't wondered why he'd called and presumed he'd just come on the off chance to see his mother. David continued to carefully select the right stones to fit the damaged wall, brushing the wet snow off with his bare hands, looking at the shape of the rocks, and fitting them together as pieces in a jig-saw. And as time drew on, hunger pangs burnt in his stomach, so he packed up his tools to go for lunch. As he wandered back, he saw more footprints had compressed the snow on the lane.

Passing the style to the ghyll he looked up the fell and saw a few walkers struggling up, as he thought he'd done last night. He stood watching for a while then, looking down, noticed a set of prints isolated from the rest. He crouched low for a closer inspection and wondered if these were the same he'd seen last night. It was impossible to tell of course, but David felt compelled to brush the prints away with his hands, as if to erase them from his memory. Then, as if someone had switched on the light to his brain, he hurried back to the farm, and couldn't stop himself from shutting the gate behind him. He walked into the warm kitchen without removing his boots, leaving the back door wide open. 'Have you been interfering?

THE GLASS SNOWSCENE

Did *you* ask the doctor to come and see me?'

Kathy looked around to see David's eyes glaring accusingly. She walked closer to him and shut the door. 'Oh, Davey . . . I can't lie to you, love. I did it for the best. I've been worried sick about you.'

'Look, I'm sorry Mum, but I've told you before, don't worry about me, worry about yourself.' David was angered at her admission, but he didn't want to argue with her.

He moved to the back door to remove his damp clothes and Kathy was glad that he'd backed off. 'Look Davey, you need a rest. Will you take a holiday or something? Maybe I can get Alan in to help.'

'I don't particularly want Alan doing any more than need be. The cattle don't milk as well when he comes, and at the moment we need a few good cheques coming in.'

'I just thought if you could go away, perhaps with Tony, before the spring starts – things will be hectic then.'

'Oh yes, and where would I go?' David's mind was easing as he came and slumped down at the kitchen table.

'Well, I thought you could go to Blackpool. . . . You could have a couple of good nights out. The change would do you good.'

David remembered some of the holidays he'd spent with Tony when they were younger and they would get into all kinds of trouble, unbeknown to their parents, so he paused and made another excuse. 'I don't think Tony could get any more time off work.'

'Just go for a long weekend then. You ask Tony and I'll ask Alan.'

David didn't look at his mother; he just got up to wash his hands.

When Alan called in that evening, Kathy explained her new plan. Alan was obviously disappointed, and thinking his idea had been snubbed, sat quietly for some time sulking, before Kathy broke the silence.

'Alan, it's not rest I need, but peace. If I can see Davey well again my whole mind will be at ease, and then I know I'll feel much better.'

Alan wasn't a parent, and found it hard to understand her reasoning, yet gave his consent to do the extra work if David would agree. Kathy now had to make certain that David would invite Tony, and she knew he wouldn't mention it if she didn't, and hoped she could see Tony first herself.

Her wish was granted when he called that evening to see if David wanted to go for a drink.

'Would you two fancy a few days in Blackpool . . . ? My treat.'

David looked astonished.

'I'll book you into a nice B and B.'

Tony looked David in the eyes, excited that he could restore their flagging friendship, and didn't wait for a reply but said, 'Then book it . . . . Thank you.'

That evening in the pub, Tony talked constantly of places they could go and what they could do in Blackpool. But David wasn't as enthusiastic, and sat peering into his drink. 'What can we do on a cold January weekend? It'll be miserable.'

'We'll go to a football match for a start. Man U are there soon for a cup-tie. Then we'll go to the Tower for a few drinks, and maybe they'll have a Disco on later, and then on to a night-club. Pick up a couple of birds.'

'If it makes you happy then I'll go, but believe you me I don't want to. Drinks and football, yes! But definitely no women!'

Later that night David went out to check the cattle before he went to bed, and he saw a small figure standing by the tower. He saw immediately it was Joanne.

'What are you doing out this time of night?' He walked slowly towards her.

'I've come to see you.'

David was hemmed in a corner. He didn't want to be alone with her in the dark, and the only means of light would be inside the tower.

THE GLASS SNOWSCENE

Reaching into the gloomy corners of the old building, he fumbled for the light-switch, and felt as if a cold hand was touching his warm heart. As he struggled to find the light, he trembled, expecting someone would put their hand on his. But the light came on and he was safe and, as he stood inside, he could see Joanne clearly and was disturbed at her appearance. She looked thin and drawn and had obviously been crying. He felt embarrassed at the situation he'd got himself into. He knew he had to look after her, but he couldn't touch her, not any more.

'You've been crying, Jo. What's the matter?'

'What's the matter? Are you men stupid or something?'

'I'm sorry; I don't know what you mean. Has something happened at home?'

'Tony tells me that you two are going to Blackpool. How can you leave me, Davey?'

This statement struck David hard in the face and he stuttered. 'What do you mean?'

'What about us? You and me?' she said.

'Look, I didn't realise . . . ' and before he could say anymore, she wrapped her arms around him and sobbed bitterly against his chest.

David was at a loss, he didn't want to hold her again, but he couldn't bring himself to leave her. As Joanne clung to him, her hands pulling on his jacket, he could only touch her shoulders with his fingertips, afraid any response would be misconstrued. He knew he'd acted recklessly and cursed his lack of judgement. 'Come on, Jo. I'll take you home. I'm sorry, this is all my fault.'

David reluctantly put his arms across her shoulder and walked her down the hill to the bungalow, steadying her from slipping on the frozen snow.

Joanne buried her head in his chest and, as they walked together in the darkness, David knew after all, now, would be a very good time to get away. He mustn't let Joanne feel any longer that she had some claim on him, but he couldn't bring himself to tell her.

THE GLASS SNOWSCENE

'Joanne, listen,' David softly pleaded. 'We're only going away for the weekend, like we used to. When we get back we'll all go out together again, the three of us, like old times.'

'I don't want old times, Davey, I want new times!' She pushed him away and left him at the garden gate. Then as she stepped into the lamplight by the porch, she turned and said, 'I pray for us every night, Davey,' and went indoors.

David kicked the gatepost, muttered some indiscernible words, and recalled his father saying: "*What do you know about women, Davey?*" And in this, David thought his father was right, as he realised he knew nothing.

6

THE TOWER

They were just two faces in the crowd; a sea of tangerine and red. Bodies were swaying backwards and forwards as they waved scarves and banners, and all the more so as the tension in the game mounted.

To be in a football crowd after spending your life isolated on a farm was difficult, claustrophobic even, but also exciting. Tony, more vocal than David, joined in enthusiastically with the chanting; the noise at times was unbearable.

They had stood on the Kop before and they knew what to expect; Tony had said the atmosphere would be better. The man standing next to David had been drinking and as David caught the smell of his stinking breath, it nauseated him.

They started by leaning on the blue rails for support but each time the crowd surged forward it crushed them against the metal bars. As the crowd receded, they dodged underneath the rails, but with no support at all, found themselves being jostled around even more. Tony was amused, like it was a game, as several times he became separated from David. The drunken man next to David had what appeared to be his son with him. The boy must have only been about eight or nine and looked vulnerable in the huge crowd, but the man was unconcerned. David wanted to help the boy, and pulled him back several times to his father.

On the train journey down to Blackpool, David had felt carefree and like a child himself, and was happy that he'd come away.

When Tom knew they were going to a football match, he begged David to take him with them, and almost succeeded. But Kathy had intervened at the last minute, so David left Tom at the door, still pleading, and he promised to take him to another game soon.

As United scored an equalising goal, the two friends were separated again. David was pushed forward and he felt the young boy squash into his stomach and he tried to protect him by shoving the man in front away.

Suddenly, a loud crack sounded from behind as some supporters let off a firework. David's instinct was to fling himself over the boy to shield him; his body tense and electric with muscle spasms and fear. Someone had done this for him in the past and, although he didn't know it yet, David would have to do it again in the future.

For a few moments David held the boy tight to his body, then he felt a hand heavy on his arm and, as he turned around, the boy's father punched David in the face.

With the fierceness of the blow, he struggled to keep his footing and he started to fall. Blood trickled down his cheek and saturated his t-shirt and David knew that if he did fall, the crowd would be on top of him. His instant reaction was one of survival, as he grabbed the arms and legs of those about him to stay on his feet. He didn't know what had happened to the boy but felt stupid as he struggled for breath. Then he started to choke as his clothes tightened around him, and the collar of his t-shirt cut into his neck. He felt himself being dragged backwards and once again struggled to keep his footing; he thought he would die here in this noisy, dreadful place, with chanting noises that would remain in him; like some monotonous dream.

Then suddenly it became dark and a cold draught immersed his body and David was alive; still choking, as he finally fell to the ground with someone struggling beneath him.

'Get off me, you idiot!'

David was cradled in Tony's arms as the two of them sprawled on the steps in the corridor. Tony was laughing as he wriggled free and pushed David out of the way. 'It's me you fool. I had to drag you out or you'd have started a riot! What in God's earth were you doing? Why did he hit you?'

'I don't know. I only tried to protect the boy. There was a crack and I thought it was a gunshot!' David sat up and held his hand to his face and, momentarily, closed his eyes.

'It was a firework, that's all!' Tony pushed a handkerchief on David's lips and dragged him up on to his feet. 'I think we'd better get you out of here.'

As they left the stadium, silence met them. The singing and chanting, restricted by the height of the roof became a faint muffle and the peace was now comforting.

David's mouth throbbed as the strength of the pain intensified and he felt the warm blood drip from the wound and onto his face. Holding his hand in the sleeve of his jacket and pressing on to the wound, he fumbled in his pocket for another handkerchief. Tony guided David by the arm, but they were stopped as a St John's Ambulance volunteer asked after his injury and, as the man removed the second handkerchief from David's mouth, it exposed a jagged wound.

The middle-aged landlady saw David's battered face and surgical sutures and gave them some warning looks. She expected to have trouble with these two lads tonight.   'Doors are locked at midnight, boys. . . . No noise and definitely no visitors in the bedrooms!'

David threw his holdall on the bed, went straight to the bathroom and looked in the mirror. He ripped off his blood stained t-shirt, filled the washbasin with hot water and started to scrub his t-shirt clean. As he scrubbed and looked at the pink coloured water in the basin, a wave of dizziness came over him and he had to hold onto the sink, thinking he might faint. He'd done this all before.

'As soon as you're ready we'll go and get some fish and chips.' Tony shouted.

'I'm going to lie down, my head's killing me.' David muttered, still mesmerised by the pink water.

'A quick shower and you'll feel better.'

David knew he wouldn't.

THE TOWER

'Oh man . . . I just want a kip.'

'We'll have a few beers and then go to a night club.'

David slumped on the bed.

Tony unzipped his holdall and tipped the contents on his bed.

'You go if you like . . . . I'll join you later.' David said, laying his aching head on a pillow.

'You're not sleeping now, Dave.' Tony persisted.

And he didn't.

Dressed in purple corduroy flares, an orange tie-dye t-shirt, and green velvet jacket, Tony Milton bought his friend a drink. His long ginger hair was now shining and clean and curling down to his shoulders; David was more casually dressed in a red check shirt and jeans.

'Thank goodness it's dark in here, you look a pratt.' David said.

'We'll see who looks stupid before the night's out. You'll never pull any women dressed like Desperate Dan, and look at the competition!' Over in the corner by the bar was a group of youths, local lads, of only eighteen or nineteen and all dressed alike in black baggies and white shirts.

David had already seen them and guessed they were eyeing them up for trouble, and knew his blood stained face would attract more problems. He'd already decided to keep his head down tonight.

The flashing lights and the loud music didn't do much to help David's headache as the whole of the discotheque floor appeared to throb, despite only a few girls dancing around a group of handbags that were carelessly thrown down on the polished floor. And with the ultra-violet lights, any white on their clothes was illuminated and turned to a translucent purple.

David usually enjoyed music but tonight he was indifferent as Mowtown and Northern Soul played constantly. The music was to Tony's liking but perhaps too loud. He would sit for hours at home in his bedroom composing melodies and

THE TOWER

writing songs, something more bluesy or jazzy than this, and then jamming into the night with his acoustic guitar; the melodies eerily resounding up the valley, and more so if the air was still. When David could hear it up at the farm he always knew Tony's father was away.

Hopes of becoming a songwriter were as dreams to Tony, but David was always quick to shatter them. He did have to admit some of the songs were good, but said he didn't live in the real world and that he shouldn't waste his time thinking of getting anything published, but he knew Tony could do better for himself than working in that little record shop in Keswick.

Tony eyed some of the girls dancing together. They too where all dressed alike: dark coloured mini-dresses, platform shoes, and they all had the same short, feathery hairstyles. But he was particularly attracted to a small blonde-haired girl in a red dress.

'If she's not with the mods in the corner, I'll buy her a drink later. Do you fancy her mate?' Tony quizzed.

David had already noticed the thin girl dancing, but said, 'I told you. . . . No women tonight!'

When the girls came to sit down just behind them, Tony picked up his drink and went across to talk. But David became increasingly anxious about the group of youths. Although it didn't seem that the girls were with them, David got the feeling that if they didn't leave, there would be trouble. They were local lads and these were probably local girls, and David knew the rules: *Even if we don't want them, you can't have them. Keep your hands off them, and if you dare tread on our patch, we'll have to fight you for it.* Lads like these were only here for one thing and although David didn't want to spoil Tony's evening, he knew that if they didn't go now, they would both end up being beaten.

Tony pulled David across to the bar. 'The thin girl's got a weird taste in men and fancies a bit of rough, Dave. You're in luck!'

But as they stood amongst the crowd, jostling to get drinks, two of the mods pushed purposely in front of them. 'Hey...

pretty boy... you want another kiss on that busted lip of yours? Come an 'av it?' Their voices grated as one of the youths curled his fist into a knot and held it up to David's face, as another youth made kissing sounds.

David lowered his head, backed away and ignored them. He'd reacted before and had a few hidings in the past in Blackpool, Carlisle and up at the University, and didn't want any more. He discreetly tried to pull Tony away and pleaded in a low voice: 'Let's get out.... Now! I've had enough. My head's killing me. If we stay any longer, we'll be back at the hospital.'

'Are you mad? I'm not going now. The little blonde thinks I'm a rock-star!'

David was exasperated. 'If you don't want to leave, that's fine, but I'm off.'

'Look. . . . Let's bring the girls with us . . . we can go somewhere quieter. They're local, maybe they'll take us back to their place.'

'No! Either we go together, or I go alone.'

'Oh, man. . . . Will you stop this misery! I'm fed up to here with your moods.' Tony gestured and walked away.

It was only 11 o'clock when David left the night-club and walked back through the town, alone. It was a dry night and he hoped the clear air would relieve his headache. He was happy to leave, but worried about his friend, yet Tony would have to take care of himself. These disagreements between the two of them were not new, both knowing that their friendship revolved around the highs and lows of each other's lives.

He zipped up his jacket and pulled his collar up around his face and, as he walked the little streets of Blackpool, he realised he wasn't sure where he was going. The rows of boarding houses and hotels all looked alike. He fumbled through his pocket and pulled out his booking slip and the address, and only hoped Tony could remember where they were staying when he finally made his way back.

He decided to would walk back along the promenade and guessed it would be quieter, passing just a few drunks staggering about the pavements and some courting couples making their way home. A late-night tram rattled along the sea front, narrowly missing him. He bought a bag of chips and ate them from newspaper as he walked and laughed to himself at Tony's dilemma, wondering what he would do with the two girls.

He was sorry Tony had lost patience with him and guessed that with his moods recently, it was just how everyone else was feeling. Maybe this was why his mother had been so keen that he should get away, because she was tired of seeing him moping around in his own self-pity.

Safely back at the boarding house, David put the television on, slowly undressed and fell into bed, but was soon bored by the programmes. He then tried to sleep but, as usual, found he couldn't settle as he was now worrying about Tony.

He considered going back to look for him, but knew they would both be locked out. Sleeping and then wakening, he listened for a while, and in the middle of one of these naps he was disturbed by a noise against the window. David put the light on and, screwing his eyes together, looked at his watch. It was 2:30, am.

David stumbled towards the window and through the lamplight below saw Tony standing there alone. His long hair was blowing about his face, his shirt was half-undone and in disarray, but he was apparently unharmed.

'Let me in. It's perishing out here.' Tony said, half-whispering and half-shouting.

David crept downstairs, wearing nothing but his t-shirt and paisley pyjama bottoms, and quietly tried to unlock the front door. But Tony started to laugh as soon as he got indoors as he saw David's dishevelled hair and his battered face.

'Shh . . . you idiot!' David whispered and followed Tony back to their room.

'Oh, man. . . . You missed out tonight, Dave. . . . The blonde was called Janet.' He ripped off his shirt. 'She only lives just around the corner.' He unzipped his trousers and struggled to speak as he pulled them over his feet. 'But the thin girl turned out to be the nicest.' Then he went to the bathroom and splashed his face with cold water. 'The mods never bothered me after you left,' he shouted back, then gargled as he cleaned his teeth. 'It was you that looked threatening.' He returned to the bedroom, stretched and patted his stomach. 'No body's afraid of a skinny dude like me!'

David slumped back in bed and tried to distance himself. 'Look mate. . . . I don't want to hear anymore, I just want to get some sleep!'

'You just want to be miserable. I'm brassed off with you. I suppose you want to pack up and go home tomorrow.' Tony threw a wet towel down on the floor with his clothes.

'I don't want to go home!' David snapped. 'I never want to go back if I can help it.' And he threw his head back on his pillows, recalling how uneasy he felt when he was hemmed into the old tower, and his last conversation with Joanne.

Tony stopped what he was doing and realised that this wasn't just another argument between them. It was hard to control his thinking; he'd had far too much to drink, but could see his friend was unhappy.

He'd thought David would have enjoyed being with the two girls. He always used to.

Tony came and sat on the bed beside him. 'What do you mean, *"You NEVER want to go home"*. I thought you loved that farm?'

David pushed himself up in the bed, crossed his arms behind his head and sighed.

'I hate the place. . . . I despise it! Everywhere I go I see my dad's face. It's like he's hiding in every field, every wall, every building. Like he's tormenting me.' He was starting to raise his voice and Tony gestured with his hand to try to calm him.

'I'm sorry mate. I didn't know you felt that way.' And, instinctively, put his hand on David's arm.

'I'm bound to that place now,' speaking more calmly. 'Don't you see, I can never leave, get married and stuff like that. Well, not until Tom grows up, or my mother marries Alan or something stupid.'

THE TOWER

'It's a good job you've got me then, isn't it?'

Then the sympathy of his friend released something woven inside David; something sharpened like barbed wire, and it was being ripped out. He dropped his head down into Tony's chest and he sobbed.

Tony had never seen David cry like this before - well, not since they were children, and he felt at a loss to know what to do.

As David's weeping intensified, Tony held him in his arms like a child and just sat quietly for a while, but David's breathing became erratic as he let go of his feelings. He guessed this all had to come out, and it did. Months of anguish, fear and sorrow; relief mingled with shame.

'Shush, SHHH, now. Don't cry so loud! You'll waken the whole house. You're freakin' me out now mate,' Tony whispered and pulled away to get David a glass of water.

'I'm sorry . . . I'm sorry.' And David composed himself.

'Look, don't be sorry mate. . . . I'm the one that's sorry.'

They sat quietly together for some time, before Tony realised that David had fallen asleep on his arm. He gently pulled away from him again, got into his own bed and put out the light, but for him, the thought of imminent sleep had fled.

It was David who woke up first and saw that it was 8:50 am. Just ten minutes to get dressed and ready for breakfast.

As he rose from his bed his head pounded even more than last night, and he felt a sharp pain in his lip. Tripping over Tony's green velvet jacket, which was still lying crumpled on the floor, he went to pull back the curtains.

'Come on, Superstar. It's time to get up. You've got five minutes. Get your strides on.' And David threw the corduroy flares at Tony's face.

Tony cursed as he slowly turned over in his bed and, squinting against the light, took a good look at his friend and with words barely legible, said, 'Good grief man. You can't go down for breakfast looking like that.'

David went across to look in the mirror and saw why his face

THE TOWER

was hurting so much. His right eye was half closed and his cheek badly swollen. His face was now bruised purple and yellow. He touched his cheek gingerly and winced. 'Well, I'm not missing my breakfast ... I'm paying for it!'

Tony, still moaning, slid from the bed and dragging his trousers on, hopped and stumbled about the small bedroom.

The other guests were just leaving when they eventually arrived into the dining room and they got some condescending looks. They took their places at the table, just in time for the landlady to slap down in front of them their breakfast plates. 'You're only just in time, lads. There's your breakfasts and your bill!'

David picked up the half-folded piece of paper. 'Bill . . . ? What do you mean the bill? We're here till Monday.'

'You might be in Blackpool until Monday, lads, but you're sleeping under the pier tonight. So enjoy your breakfast, you'll need it.'

'Don't worry, Dave. I know where Janet lives.' And Tony poured tomato sauce all over his plate of bacon, sausage and eggs.

As they packed their bags, David insisted that as soon as they found new lodgings, he would be the one to choose what they did that day. But a walk along the Golden Mile confirmed what he'd already suspected; there wasn't much to do in Blackpool on a cold January weekend. The thought of his bed at home, the comfort of the sofa in front of the fire; yes, Keld Head, with all its misgivings, was the place he wanted.

Most of the arcades were closed, except for a few bingo halls, and David didn't want to waste his money in there. Then Tony wanted to have his fortune told, but once again David dragged him away. 'We'll go up the Tower! We've never been up the Tower.'

'As long as you don't try and jump off.' And Tony froze, immediately realising his comment was unkind and unfeeling and wanted to take it back. But a wry smile came on David's face. 'Well, if I jump, you must promise to wear that green

THE TOWER

velvet jacket and those purple kecks at my funeral!'

The metal lift trundled its way slowly to the top, climbing five hundred or so feet in the process. The climb silenced them for a while as they both leant anxiously on the sides of the lift for support.

At first they found the view overwhelming as they wandered around the platform in silence, trying to acclimatise and adjust to the height. They leant on the rails and looked over through the grill. They could see the whole of Blackpool and beyond; the little trams going up and down the promenade; the colourful rides on the Pleasure Beach; The Big Wheel and The Big Dipper.

'Look. I can see Janet's house from here!' Tony pointed.

'Yes, and I can see yours,' David was looking north towards the Cumbrian fells on the horizon.

Today the fells looked welcoming. Their soft green slopes were a gentle contrast to the harsh red brick and grey concrete buildings of Blackpool below. Even the distant snow-capped mountains looked calming, like soft meringue covering a cake.

The resplendence of his home county tempted David; it wasn't Lakeland's fault his family had problems. At least he would have his troubles in one of the most beautiful places in the country, and that would be some consolation. His head felt clearer from unburdening his mind to Tony; saying things he thought he'd never say. And David remembered his promise to look after his family, and knew he could keep it.

'Look, Dave . . .' Tony pointed. 'I can see Alan Marsh in the paddock. And is that your mother holding his hand?'

On the train home on Monday lunchtime, David felt well. He'd slept better on the last night, and the fresh seaside air and a good meal had restored him. Shopping in the town, they'd managed to buy some gifts: little white chalk images of Blackpool Tower for Tom and Sarah, a bottle of perfume for his mother, a glass snow scene globe with Blackpool Tower in it for Joanne, and a small bottle of whisky for Alan.

THE TOWER

David shut his eyes as the train rattled on, and he thought about the boy at the football match and guessed he would be at school today. He reflected on how protective he'd been towards the boy, and was glad. At least he'd found some love in himself, unlike the harsh and selfish manner of his father. David was even grateful to the boy's father for the smack in the face, as it had awakened his senses. He opened his eyes and smiled; Tony was asleep, resting his head on his shoulder.

The brotherly love Tony had shown, had confirmed their friendship for one another. David knew he wouldn't always be there for him as Tony would, someday, have to move on. They hadn't bonded any closer; that was impossible. But he did understand his friend a bit better and knew he should try and give him something back.

They walked into the farmhouse kitchen and at the sight of her son's injured face, Kathy dropped the basket of washing she was carrying onto the floor.

'Don't worry Mrs Keldas. We've only had a fight, been thrown out of our hotel and spent a night under the pier.'

Alan, spoke up. 'You've had a good time then?'

David went over to his mother and hugged her, nearly taking all the breath from her. 'We've had a brilliant time,' he softly replied.

'My goodness! What on earth's happened?' Kathy brushed David's cheek with her hand and made him flinch.

'We were at the wrong end of the stadium. . . . They thought we were Man U supporters. . . . David dragged me out, before I started a riot!' Tony was enthusiastic with his fabricated story.

David lowered his head and removing himself from the lie, went upstairs to unpack, pulling from his bag the presents he'd bought, and putting the chalk images to one side, ready for the children when they came home from school. He took out the glass snow scene and shook it to watch the snowflakes fall and settle down on the tiny beach. He held the glass close to his eyes and let himself be mesmerised by the tinsel as it danced and sparkled, taking him back to another world of magic. And the memories brought back a sweet taste to his mouth – fish and chips that tasted of sand and sea. He gave a wry smile and put the snow scene on his bookcase; he wouldn't give it to Joanne; that would be a mistake.

7

SLOW FEVER

Tony Milton walked down the hill to the bungalow, with his overnight bag hanging loosely over his shoulder. As he walked he scuffed his soft brown boots carelessly in the gravel road; carefree, happy and singing out loud. He didn't care who heard him, in fact, he hoped somebody would. He was a true extrovert and loved the sound of his own voice, especially when it echoed around the Lakeland valleys.

He threw his bag down on the kitchen floor and went straight to the tap for a cold drink. But, in a matter of seconds, Joanne was there beside him, looking tired and sullen as she coldly muttered, 'You sound happy.'

'Oh I am!' Tony leant back on the kitchen sink to drink his water. 'Why aren't you at work, Jo?'

'What's it to you?'

'It won't make any difference to my life whether you go to work or not but it could make a lot of difference to yours!'

'I couldn't care less,' she said.

Tony picked up his bag to go to his room. He'd had a good weekend and he was happy and he didn't want his sister to destroy these feelings, but Joanne shouted back at him. 'What did you do then?'

'Oh . . . this and that.'

'Come on. . . . Don't irritate me. What did you do?'

'You mean what did David do?'

The friction between brother and sister had begun well before Tony ever left for Blackpool. They had argued more recently and especially the few days earlier. Joanne blamed him for taking David away, and she knew he would try his best to see that David met up with some other girl and, in this case, she wasn't wrong.

Tony didn't really want to hurt Joanne, but he was no psychologist, he was a straightforward guy. But all these questions and him having to play the mediator, was just getting out of hand.

Tony was pleased with himself in the way he'd handled David's distress. He knew only too well what a strain David had been under, but perhaps hadn't realised how much it had affected him. When David had displayed such heartfelt emotion, it had touched him deeply and he'd found it hard to hold back the tears himself, and had to wipe his own cheek dry while he was comforting David. He guessed that things would soon be sorted in David's family life, and hoped they could all get back to as they were before; they just had to.

But Joanne couldn't leave it as she glared at him. 'If you won't tell me what you did, then I'll go and ask Davey.'

'Now don't you go bothering him.' Tony pointed his finger at her. 'Just leave it!'

'Davey will tell me everything. I'm going to see him now.' And with that she started to leave, but he got to the door first and pushed it hard shut, almost trapping her hand.

'Leave him be, Jo.'

David had tried not to think about the farm while he was away, but with renewed zeal, he wandered across to the dairy to look at the milk receipts. He'd purposely waited until Alan left, as he didn't want him to feel he was checking up on him; he knew what that felt like. So when David saw the shiny, blue and silver bulk tanker arriving in the yard to collect the day's milk, he thought it a good time to go and check.

'The milk's down a bit again, Davey,' the driver said.

'I thought as much. What was Saturday morning's reading?' David looked anxiously at the slips of paper, flicking them in his hand.

'That was down a bit as well.'

David remembered that the cattle hadn't milked so well the

SLOW FEVER

Friday night before he left for Blackpool and he knew he couldn't blame Alan for that. He looked in the milking parlour and found it as untidy as he expected. The glass milk jars were grubby and the floor didn't look like it had been swilled down properly. David decided to leave it for now and have a good tidy up session before the evening's milking. He wandered into the foldyard where the cattle seemed clean and content, munching on hay, but over in the corner he saw Silver standing alone.

Silver should have been at her peak by now, but David thought on Friday she hadn't given as much milk as usual, and that would explain the drop in the bulk quantity. He would have to watch her. He didn't want to make another error of judgement, but later that evening, David noticed a drop in Silver's milk yield again. She was also jumpy and irritable and tried to kick him as he handled her. Her coat was dull and she ate very little.

He couldn't see any swelling in her udder that would show she had mastitis, and there were no other apparent reasons for her sickness, although he did have an idea what might be wrong, he needed some advice to be sure, so David decided to call the vet straight away.

Over the phone, Barry Fitzgerald reassured David and said he would come in the morning if there were still no improvement and at next morning's milking, Silver was just the same. David tried not to let this worry him. He knew with animals, life was unpredictable; in fact, through all the last few months of trauma, the cattle were the last things he'd worried about.

David felt refreshed today. He'd slept well and found it hard to rouse himself when the alarm went off. He rang Barry early enough to catch him before he went on his rounds and arranged a visit. Kathy was happy to see David talking confidently on the telephone, at ease, and once again taking an interest in his work.

He put Silver in the isolation box ready for Barry and did some jobs around the buildings to be on hand when he eventually called. There was no hiding behind closed curtains today.

When Barry arrived, it was about 11 o'clock and the first thing he noticed was that the yard gate was closed again and he had to send Hannah out to open it.

David saw the young woman struggling with the latch and felt compelled to help. But it wasn't until he was close, that he recognised Hannah. He saw the large brown eyes and long lashes and was struck by her appearance; no longer did she look boyish and her auburn hair had grown as it curled attractively around her neck.

As Hannah struggled to open the latch on the gate, David put his hand playfully across hers to help. 'Here, let me do that for you.' And with the broad smile on his face, Hannah noticed for the first time the countenance of an attractive man, and was momentarily taken aback. Then, not wanting her heart to tell her she'd misjudged him, she searched David's features, looking at his clean white teeth and noticed one of his teeth was crooked and slightly prominent. Next she saw the surgical sutures on his lip and she pulled away from him.

Hannah hadn't wanted to come to this place again. When Barry's receptionist had told them to call at the Keldas farm, she'd tried dismiss herself by claiming the office needed tidying up. And, when they'd arrived at Keld Head, the structure and architecture of the place chilled her. She'd only ever seen the farm by night or at a distance from the main road but in daylight, every piece of stone appeared to jump out at her, and she realised it wasn't just David that she felt uneasy with.

Barry too had noticed David's injury and didn't like to ask what had happened, but he also saw his manner was more like the one of old, as David enthusiastically shook Barry's hand and even offered his hand again to Hannah. And this time she reluctantly accepted it.

Reassured by David's mood, Barry broached the subject of his battered face, and David tried to give the same explanation Tony had given his mother. 'Football match . . . . The Kop...

Need I say any more?'

'Hmm . . . supporting the wrong team, eh?' Barry raised one eyebrow. 'So what about this beast then?'

'Yes, I think she may have Slow Fever.'

'And what are the symptoms?'

'Drop in milk yield - lethargy - eating very little,' and then looking straight at Hannah he continued, 'and irritable.'

Hannah rolled her eyes at David's flippant remark and was incensed. Barry wanted to laugh at his guile, and knew this would irritate Hannah even more, but not wanting to give another lesson in communication skills, immediately brought the subject back to the cattle.

'Right then. . . . let's take a look at her.'

David put a halter on Silver and tied her securely to the loosebox.

Barry took the cow's temperature, looked into its eyes, and checked her rear-end and udder. 'Get hold of her head and smell her breath, Hannah?' Barry asked. But she didn't know if he was joking.

'Come on, what does it smell like?' He laughed at her as he repeated his request.

Hannah reluctantly grabbed hold of the animal's head. 'Well, very sweet and sickly.'

'Yes, that could be the *Peardrop's* smell! Let me try.' Barry leant forward and stuck his face close to the cow's mouth. 'Yes, Davey, I think your diagnosis is right. She's got Acetonaemia, more commonly known as Slow Fever. The sweet smell on her breath is an accumulation of ketones in the blood-stream. This is acetone you can smell. You've probably not been giving her enough roughage and too many concentrates, and she's having difficulty digesting everything properly.' He let go of Silver's head and wiped mucus off his hands onto his trousers. 'Do you know what to do, Davey?'

Barry Fitzgerald enjoyed quizzing the young people. He knew that David had a good knowledge of the animals, not just from his time at agricultural college, but he was taught well by his father. Yes, George Keldas, despite being a bad husband was a good farmer. He'd always kept the place tidy and looked after his livestock well and David was now doing the same.

Barry noticed Hannah was listening carefully to his short lecture. She was a good student, conscientious, and enjoyed her work. She was probably one of the most promising students he'd had in a long while. When she'd first arrived from Durham, much like David, Barry thought her too small to ever be a good vet but soon realised that, although she was small in stature, she was strong willed. But he knew precious little else about her, apart from that she had lost her mother to cancer and that she rarely spoke of her father. Hannah did travel back home regularly to County Durham, but seemed to want to keep her private life to herself, and Barry was diplomatic enough not to intrude.

Nevertheless, she had come with good recommendations and Barry had begun to like her in the few weeks she'd been with him, knowing when she finally left he would miss her, and have to get used to a new student all over again.

Barry could have a joke with Hannah and he loved to tease her. She always fell for his tricks and managed to wind herself up, as she'd just done with David. But Hannah could never leave things and would usually try to get her own back.

Yet Hannah's main weakness continued to be her communication skills. She had continued to show a dislike for some of the Lakeland farmers. Barry knew they could be an awkward breed, but Hannah's obvious disinterest was something she would have to work on. And he told her several times that she may not get enough work just treating small animals; she would need the custom of farmers like these for her bread and butter.

This problem wasn't entirely her fault, and Barry knew that. On the last visit to the Keldas farm, David had been rude to her, but he'd hoped with David's change in spirit, Hannah might have felt a bit better about him. That was until David worsened the matter by flirting with her and making his impudent comment.

SLOW FEVER

When David invited them in for coffee, Barry decided to accept, thinking this might help her. But Hannah was vexed. *Why go in for coffee here? We never go in for coffee*, she thought, and hoped that David wouldn't join them.

As for David, he was pleased his diagnosis had been right, and when Barry questioned him on what treatment to give, he was also correct. 'Molasses and plenty of roughage?' David said.

'Yes, and give her a bit of exercise as well. Cut down on the concentrates and build her feed up gradually.' Barry suggested. 'And if you get time, walk her around the yard, and if there's no improvement in a few days give me another call.'

David took them to the farmhouse kitchen and politely introduced Hannah to his mother and then left.

As Hannah shook Kathy's hand she couldn't believe the contrast, that this beautiful blonde-haired woman could possibly be David's mother. Kathy just wasn't what she'd expected. The farmhouse was also a surprise as it was immaculate.

Kathy was keenly interested in Hannah when she discovered she was from Durham. And a conversation quickly started about Linzi, who was at the university there.

Barry was pleased to see Kathy looking well and was happy to shake her hand. He hadn't just known the Keldas family through the veterinary work, but his wife, Eleanor, had been a close childhood friend of Kathy's. And they'd spent much of their teenage years together, going out as couples.

Hannah sat quietly taking in the atmosphere of the farmhouse while Barry chatted to Kathy. She noticed the furniture was mostly of antique pine and the soft furnishings were of blue and white gingham. The heat coming from the Aga was welcoming; a little black cat was curled up on the clip rug on the floor in front of it. This was a clean house and the smell of home baking and the pleasant manner of Kathy Keldas softened Keld Head's brash exterior.

On the wall hanging above the fireplace Hannah noticed a large portrait photograph of a man, about thirty or forty years old, who was holding a silver trophy. She was struck by how handsome he was; dark hair, piercing eyes, a strong jawbone and an attractive, sculptured mouth. She was saddened when she realised this was probably Kathy's husband and David's father.

She then had a feeling of foreboding and had to look away. But soon became tempted by her own imagination and had to look at him again. She was feeling bewildered, when a little girl ran in, delicate and fairylike, and unconcerned, thrust a colouring book on Hannah's lap.

'Sarah. Don't pester Hannah; she's come in for a rest.'

'I don't mind,' Hannah replied, glad of the intrusion. 'Let me look at your book.'

The little girl promptly ran back to her room to bring her crayons.

'Oh, Sarah, you're supposed to be ill.'

'Well, I was sick last night Mummy, but I feel better now.'

Hannah took some of Sarah's crayons and started to help her draw and momentarily forgot where she was. The kitchen door was opened and David returned, he too was ready for a break; he was hungry and it was getting close to lunchtime. He was amused to see Sarah sitting at the table with Hannah, but his amusement became embarrassment as Sarah dragged him across the room to see her colouring.

'Now, Sarah. Hannah and Barry will have to leave soon; they've got lots more sick animals to see to.' Kathy intervened.

Barry didn't like to leave just as David returned but they'd already stayed longer than he anticipated. He looked at David and said, 'If you like, Davey, I'll take those stitches out for you.'

'You're not going to manhandle me like you do my cattle!'

'Then we'll let Hannah do it.' Barry knew this would annoy her. 'She does a good job in the surgery - stitching up and the like.'

Just as Barry assumed, Hannah was annoyed at his suggestion - almost repulsed, and she looked at him sternly, hoping once more they could leave.

'When are you coming again?' Sarah said, tugging at Hannah's pullover to give her one of the drawings; it was of a weird looking pony.

Hannah pushed it into her pocket, knowing she couldn't answer the girl's question, but hoping that it wouldn't be too soon.

When they finally drove away it was Barry who was quiet this time. He was pleased to see them all well, and wasn't worried at all about Silver. But he was thinking of Kathy, wondering how she managed living there alone, looking after this young family. He assumed David hadn't given a lot of emotional help recently, perhaps he'd even added to her worries.

Hannah was the one to break the silence. 'What a lovely farmhouse. I was quite surprised.'

'What did you expect? Wuthering Height's! A little, fat farmer's wife with a pinny on and chickens walking on the kitchen table?'

'All right. I get the message. Don't be sarcastic.'

They were both silent for a while. Hannah recalled the image of the man in the photograph; it was hard for her to forget. She tried to put it at the back of her memory but, again, it wouldn't go away. She felt so sad.

Barry was thinking of David and was bewildered. He was like two different people at the moment. He knew David could be shy sometimes and that shy people can often appear aloof, but this condescending attitude with Hannah was unlike him. David didn't know her well enough to speak in the way he did. He'd gone from the sublime to the ridiculous!

David sat at the dinner table, where Hannah had sat only moments ago. It had struck him how comfortable she seemed with Sarah and his mother. Hannah looked so different and he was all the more attracted to her femininity and felt embarrassed once again of how he'd treated her. But her dislike of him was more apparent today; her eyes had made it clear, and David wasn't used to this. It was only his father, and him alone, that had hated him;

He thought of how he'd treated Joanne, teasing her with a kiss like it was some kind of sport and was appalled at his own chauvinism. David was sure he didn't used to be like this. Yet, he knew that was just the way his father treated his mother at times. The young men in Blackpool were protective of their women and David knew it was foolish to think the way they did: *Even if I don't want them, you can't have them*! Why should he spoil everyone else's aspirations just because of his own? Like a child that's been naughty and told it can't play with its building blocks anymore, so it knocks them down and says: *If I can't play with them, no one else can!* And David was just the same: he wanted it all.

Kathy watched him for some time sitting quietly daydreaming, and putting his lunch in front of him said, 'Penny for them?'

'You'll need more than a penny for these, they're priceless.' David mused as he started to eat his meal. 'I don't really understand what I'm thinking; it's all a bit beyond me.'

'What's beyond you?'

'Oh, just stuff,' and he wouldn't commit himself.

'Does your face hurt today, love?'

'No, it's okay. I think it probably feels better than it looks.'

'I think YOU feel better than you look, don't you?'

'I suppose I do. Do I look a mess?'

'Well, sort of.'

'You mean my hair, don't you?'

'Err, well, amongst other things.'

David looked at his mother standing in front of him, her arms folded. Her blonde hair tied neatly up on her head, with just a few stray curls hanging loosely down. Her pale blue eyes weren't cold like his, but soft and warm. She looked beautiful today. He felt proud she was his mother and realised she wanted to be equally proud of him.

David got up to look at himself in the mirror and said, 'I never get time to get my hair cut anymore.'

'Then let me trim it for you after dinner?'

SLOW FEVER

Sarah immediately ran across to the kitchen drawer to get the scissors. 'Yes, Mummy. Let's cut Davey's hair!'

'Only a trim, mind. . . .' he reluctantly agreed. 'I'll maybe go to the barber's on Friday when I get my stitches taken out.'

'And maybe you won't!' she said.

After they'd finished lunch, Kathy put a towel over David's shoulders and started to cut. She didn't really know what she was doing but trimmed large chunks off David's hair. She hid some in her apron pocket, not for a keepsake, but afraid he would complain if he saw how much she'd really cut.

As soon as she was finished, David went upstairs to the bathroom to wash his hair and see the results. He combed the curls back off his face to reveal his strong forehead. His dark eyebrows were visible and lay in a peculiar curve that looked neither angry nor happy.

David had had this expression from childhood and it could get him into trouble with his schoolteachers because, unlike his family who knew him well, they never knew if he was scowling or smirking. And as he looked in the mirror, his long black sideboards became more prominent, so he took a razor and trimmed them, just long enough to finish below his ear.

He felt happier with his new appearance and although his hair still wasn't short, Kathy had succeeded in making him look presentable.

When he came back downstairs to the kitchen and Tony was there and was sitting in the makeshift barber's chair. His ginger locks also falling to the floor and mingling with some of David's hair.

'I want to look like him, Barber.' Tony pointed at David watching them from the doorway.

Kathy looked up and saw David standing there. Her heart swelled with pride. With most of his long curls now gone, his striking features were more apparent. His whole countenance had changed since his visit to Blackpool. His face was less drawn and almost plump in appearance; his deep blue eyes were clearer and shone with some vibrancy; they looked stunning. Even despite his swollen cheek and surgical sutures, he looked more becoming. 'You want to look like me, eh.' And David wandered across to Tony sitting in the chair and clenching his hand into a fist, made a playful attempt to punch him.

Sarah shrieked. 'Hit him, Davey. . . . Hit him.'

'Sarah. . . .We'll have none of that! And David, you should know better.' But no one was listening, so she backed away, delighted at the horseplay in the kitchen once again. Memories of their childhood antics came flooding back to her: two little boys playing on the kitchen floor with their toys.

Kathy's love for David grew at this point to a dimension she hadn't known before, and it would soon become almost obsessive. She'd always indulged David more than her other children, and all the more so as George showed his intolerance of him, and maybe this would cause an anxiety that she couldn't possibly anticipate.

When the scene in the kitchen began to settle once again, Kathy asked after Joanne.

'She's a bit miserable at the moment,' Tony said as he winced with every snip of the scissors.

'She didn't reckon much to Dave - er - I mean us, going off to Blackpool without her.'

Kathy found this reasoning of Tony's strange and thought Joanne wouldn't usually have expected to go on a trip with the two lads. She also wondered why Tony had chosen his words carefully. 'Yes, Tom didn't think much to it either, did he, Davey?' She looked across to David to see his reaction, but he was one step ahead of her and leaving the house.

Silver struggled when David tried to put the halter on and attempted to lead her out to the yard. Tony was soon to follow and was now leaning on the wall watching them. 'What are you trying to do?'

'Barry said she's got Slow Fever and some exercise will help to get her system going.'

Silver pulled her head down, determined she wasn't going

anywhere, but David had other intentions and, with one huge tug, managed to get her as far as the yard.

Tony stood watching David for some time, amazed at his patience, then choosing his moment said, 'Jo's on the warpath, Dave.'

David, still struggling with Silver and only half listening to Tony, breathlessly replied. 'Warpath? What do you mean? Oh, don't be stupid, animal!' He growled at Silver, pulling her again. But Tony continued, 'She thinks she loves you!'

David heard clearly what Tony said but was silent for some time, then quietly replied. 'I thought as much, and don't say I told you so. But what can I do?'

'Did you ever apologise?'

David stood motionless and couldn't look Tony in the eye. And, as he softly spoke, it was like he was speaking to Silver, as his mouth was close to her ear. 'I couldn't do it. I'm sorry.'

Tony breathed in deeply, his chest expanding, and then mercifully said, 'Just keep your distance for a while then, and all being well, with your face as hideous as it is with those stitches in, she might go off you. She's threatening to come and see you. Oh, and by the way, she hasn't been to work since we left for Blackpool.'

He left David struggling with Silver in the yard, unsure himself if his sister would ever "*go off*" David, as he'd put it.

Later that afternoon, David started to tidy up in the milking parlour. He managed to get the glass milking jars shiny and clean again. He scrubbed the stainless steel bulk tank, and the little milking parlour with its grey painted walls was starting to look better as he worked away in the familiar surroundings that he'd so hated the night he bared his soul to Tony. He became absorbed in his work, doing it like second nature. As the dairy herd slowly wandered in for milking, he started the milk pump engine, put on his transistor radio and started milking.

David heard some noise faintly in the background, as if someone were in the dairy. He presumed it was his mother coming to get some milk. He listened for a while and then, silence. Then he heard the noise again but this time was startled. *Dr. Reed told me to stop looking behind me,* he thought. Yes, he was just being irrational. But when he heard the sliding door slowly opening, his body froze, and a burst of adrenaline shot through him, as he looked anxiously at the door.

'Don't worry, Davey. It's only me.'

David bit his lip. He was relieved in one way to see Joanne standing there, but not in another.

She came down the steps into a small recess and stood close to him as he resumed his work, not wanting any eye contact, and hoping she hadn't noticed he was afraid.

'They're all talking in the village Post Office about you, and saying that you've been beaten up. Oh, look at your face!'

David closed his eyes momentarily, not wanting to hear any more comments about his face and, as she came close to him, he could smell her perfume, pungent and tantalising.

She raised her hand in an attempt to touch his wound and, sensing her movement, he walked away to check one of the cows. But Joanne followed him closely and then pushed something into his hand.

David held up the little package to the light and relented. 'I'm okay, Joanne. I haven't been beaten up. What's this?'

'It's a present. I've missed you and you've been hurt.'

David wasn't surprised she'd missed him, but wished she hadn't. And now this gift. He began to feel guilty about not giving her the snow scene globe, but Joanne's overwhelming affection was too heavy for him. He would have walked away from her if he hadn't been working. He desperately wanted her to leave, but couldn't tell her. He knew Tony was right with his assumptions and yet once again felt powerless to do anything about it. He thought if he could just keep his head, things would settle down. He tried not to look at Joanne as he thanked her, and put the package down on the step, and promised he would open it later.

Joanne stayed for some time, trying to draw out of him what they had done in Blackpool, but David remained non-committal. He tried to play things down, stressing only that he'd enjoyed the football match and the film they'd seen, and he hoped his silence would make him a poor lover. But Joanne was happy just to watch him working, and it wasn't until Kathy called in for some milk, that she decided to leave.

'What did Joanne want?' Kathy said as she cautiously balanced a large enamel milk jug in one hand and held onto the door with the other.

'Oh, she heard I'd been beaten up,' David laughed. 'Can you believe it? They're already talking about me in the village.'

Kathy could believe it all too well. 'Jo doesn't look in very good form these days. I wonder if we should persuade her to see the doctor.' And, as she glanced down, she saw the small gift on the step and noticed David blush.

Kathy's interest in Joanne was not unusual. She'd kept a gentle eye on both the Milton children since their mother left. Keith Milton, their father, was a hard working man and had succeeded in providing well for them materially, but perhaps the emotional support was minimal. And when David made no further comment, his disinterest disturbed Kathy. She felt that he could have shown a bit of compassion for Joanne and she sensed there was friction between the young people.

Later that evening, David settled in his bedroom and lay on his bed, wanting some peace from Tom and Sarah, who'd already begun to irritate him again.

He was just dozing and then daydreaming, when he suddenly remembered Joanne's small package. He lazily slid off his bed, took the package from the bedside table, and carefully removed the paper. He found a small box of mint chocolates, and then, concealed in a Get Well card, were two photographs. One was of his father, which he'd never seen before. And the other was of him, taken by the lake. He couldn't recall recently being by the lake with Joanne.

8

UP HIGH – IN DEEP

'This wretched winter!' Kathy mumbled as she stood over a calf, trying hard to make it suck her fingers. Then she tried dipping its head into the bucket of warm milk, but it didn't want to cooperate, and consequently tipped the contents of the bucket over her trousers and down into her wellingtons. 'Blast . . .!' she said, as her warm breath drifted like smoke into the frozen air of the calf pen. 'You poor thing. You didn't ask to be born in February did you, baby?'

The calf feebly suckled her fingers once again and warmed Kathy's hands with its soft mouth, but still refused to lower its head. She would have to stop soon, as she was quickly running out of patience and only hoped the calf would drink later when it was hungrier.

Next she started to scrub the milk buckets clean in an old galvanised bath in the dairy, warming her cold hands in the hot water. Even the farm cats wandered inside and rubbed themselves around her legs, with the hope of some warmth and a chance of a few drops of leftover milk.

During the depth of the winter, Kathy had begun to feel restless; the feelings of euphoria and freedom had gone and she found no comfort at the life before her. Much like David, she had felt bound to Keld Head, and began to feel contempt

UP HIGH – IN DEEP

for the farm that had been her home and livelihood for some twenty-three years or more. It was like Keld Head was fighting back.

The winter had made the place hostile. Drains were clogged up with ice and the bath water wouldn't run away as the downspouts became blocked. Falling snow would freeze and then melt in the farmyard in regular cycles for days on end. Each morning frost coated the inside of bedroom windows with unique mosaic patterns. Even the rain would be welcome now; if nothing more than just a change from this hard winter.

'Right . . . ! That's it . . . !' Kathy groaned; brooding about this cold would do her no good, so she decided to do something constructive and visit Aunt Betty. She hadn't seen her for some time, only talked to her over the phone and Kathy had guessed that if she was feeling depressed with this winter, Betty would be feeling just the same. She didn't know if she had the ability to cheer anyone at the moment, but felt she at least wanted to try.

Foxglove Cottage looked as welcoming as ever and as Kathy approached from the lane, she could see smoke rising steadily from the chimneypot. Walking through the front door, she was comforted by the sight of her late Uncle Fred's hat and coat still hanging on the hall stand.

Betty was thrilled to see Kathy and she was ushered into the warm room. 'Come on, love, sit down and let me get you a cup of tea.'

'No, you sit down,' Kathy insisted. 'Let me do it.'

Kathy settled the old lady down and took charge of the kitchen, hunting for the best cups and saucers which she knew Betty would want to use for visitors. But the china cups hanging on the dresser were grubby and tea-stained and the worktops and kitchen sink were marked and dirty. This wasn't like Betty.

Kathy felt the pangs of a guilty conscience and had to bite her lip as she realised that this old lady must have been struggling for a long time without anyone ever realising it.

UP HIGH – IN DEEP

David and Linzi hadn't mentioned the state of the cottage when they'd last visited, but they probably hadn't even noticed.

'How are you feeling then, Betty?' Kathy began.

'My arthritis is bad at the moment - but I can't complain.'

She never complained and that was the problem. If she had, maybe more would have been done for her. Kathy noticed that Betty had been slow getting to the door and was walking with two sticks instead of one. 'Mrs Challenor's still helping you, isn't she?'

'I don't know what I'd do without her. But she's no spring chicken; she's seventy-five you know. And this will be my first winter without Freddie. He was fit for a man of his age - he would get all the wood in and the like.'

Kathy reflected how honourably poor Fred had looked after Betty. He'd been a healthy man for his age and his death was untimely. 'You must miss him loads.'

'Yes, it's no good without your husband, is it?'

Kathy didn't know how to reply, for she knew that despite her feelings today, she'd been much happier without George, so she turned the conversation back to Uncle Fred.

'I miss Freddie too. I miss him coming around the farm and I know David thinks about him a lot.' Kathy spoke with a hint of sadness.

'Yes, he will love. . . . He will.'

'I notice you've kept some of his things.'

'It gives me comfort to see them around. Makes me feel a bit safer, you know.'

Kathy smiled to think how safe Betty could have felt having a ninety-year-old man around the house. Fred was well, but he wasn't that strong, yet despite the frailties of old age, this man had looked after his wife very well.

'You look a bit tired today?' Betty said, sympathetic toward Kathy and she carefully rose to put some more coal on the fire.

'Oh, I'm just a bit fed up of this winter. It's been a long and a sad one.'

Kathy sipped her tea and started to think of David working

out in the cold and she hoped he'd come in for a warm up. He'd been struggling with the tractor all morning; it too was refusing to work.

'When did you last get a break?' Betty asked.

There was a lapse in the conversation as Betty gasped and fell back into her chair again and Kathy waited until she was comfortable. 'Oh, I can't remember, Aunty. But, do you know, I feel like running away myself sometimes. George had the right idea I think, wandering off from time to time.' Kathy sat back in the armchair with her hands cupping her tea. 'At first, things were such a relief to me, if you can understand that. I think I went into a state of euphoria. Does that sound awful? Then I spent weeks worrying about David, but when he came home from Blackpool he'd changed, so I relaxed again. David seems to have resigned himself to his role now. I thought I had, but I'm feeling unsettled again. I don't know why. Oh, I'm sorry. I shouldn't burden you with all this. I came to cheer you up.'

Betty leant across and put her cold hand on Kathy's warm one. 'It cheers me just to see you and hear my David's doing well.' Then Betty put her cup very slowly and deliberately back on its saucer and, by the customary pause that came, Kathy knew she was about to get some advice. And so Betty started: 'You've had a rough time of it my love, and so has Davey.'

Kathy wanted to say, *and so have you.*

There was a long pause again. 'You're both still young, and Davey . . . well, he can make a new life for himself if he wants to.'

Kathy didn't say anything to Betty but she didn't like to think of David doing anything that would take him away from her as well.

Betty continued, 'You've got the two youngsters still left at home,' as if she was reading Kathy's mind, 'they'll keep you busy for years and who knows, Linzi may come back someday to help.'

Kathy didn't think too much about the idea of Linzi coming home to help either.

'Why don't you try to get away for a break. Maybe go to your mother's for a while?'

'I have been offered the chance to go on holiday,' but before Kathy could continue Betty interrupted. 'Then take it, and I'll treat you to a new outfit to go away in. How does that sound?'

Betty hadn't even considered who the offer might have been from and there was no way that Kathy would enlighten her. Then, before she could resist, Betty pulled herself out of the chair, unlocked a walnut display cabinet and took a wad of notes from the inside of an old teapot. She rolled the money up and squeezed it into Kathy's hand. 'There. . . . You've got to go on holiday now haven't you?'

Kathy didn't know what to say, but was moved to give the old lady a hug. 'I'll have a good time on you then, Aunty!'

The money was safely bundled into Kathy's handbag, knowing it couldn't be returned; to do so would hurt her aunt deeply. Kathy also knew if Betty had any inclination it was a man who'd invited her, she would strongly disapprove. Kathy didn't want to be deceptive, but felt that there was no way out of this, unless she chose another partner and that would hurt Alan once again.

Poor Alan, he had been so good to them. He'd given them all the physical help that was needed, and in that he'd been tremendous. He didn't need to give up some of his weekends to help David. He certainly didn't do it for the money. The paltry wages they gave him were only a token. The emotional help was there too. Kathy knew that with just one phone call he would be around; Alan was as sound and as steady as they come, and he asked very little of her in return.

Alan Marsh was a man of basic needs. He liked his pint of beer, his food and his golf. He had an impressive company car and had inherited his mother's house in Grange-Over-Sands. He'd once been labelled the most eligible bachelor in Cumbria. But after caring for his sick mother for years on end, time had passed by for Alan, and now with too much weight from too many beers, Alan's handsome features had ballooned. Nevertheless, he was still one of the kindest men that Kathy knew.

She found herself comparing Alan with George. Yes, George had been fun as a young man and willing to take a risk. His carefree attitude and lust for life had excited her.

She'd first met him at a Farmers' Ball in Carlisle and was besotted by his good looks. She remembered how tall and slim he was, his skin like David's, bronzed by the weather. He too had dark hair and blue eyes, which didn't lose any vitality even during middle age. George had been hard working and hard playing and did everything to the limit - sometimes to excess.

Kathy recalled when they were younger, on a night out with Barry Fitzgerald and Eleanor, George had carelessly turned their car over into a ditch, and as they all crawled out of the battered vehicle, he could do nothing but laugh; never mind that they could have all been killed. This thought then brought back another one that had been lodging in Kathy's mind of George, and how he'd laughed when he heard that Uncle Fred had died.

Choosing the right day to tell David about her planned trip was awkward. Kathy had already called Alan and there was no turning back. Alan couldn't believe her change of heart and decided in a matter of minutes over the telephone what they could do and where they could go.

Kathy's mother was also agreeable and said she would have the two youngest children, providing they could be brought to Lancaster. She wanted to see her daughter happy again, and had secretly hoped that she might "take up with Alan in the future," as she'd told Kathy's father many times. But she'd thought that this was far too soon to start a new relationship; but Kathy had always been impulsive. She'd been so when she had married George and she'd surprised and worried them all with her choice.

Kathy planned to tell David at morning coffee about her trip. Providing that the milking had gone well, he would be alert and in good spirits by that time of day.

She waited for a fine morning; waited until Silver was better, and then for the tractor to be mended, and finally the right morning came. The only drawback was that Tom was off school. He had a heavy cold with a high temperature and she would have to keep him upstairs out of their way.

The kettle was boiling and she mended the fire; even taking the trouble to put up her hair for she knew David liked it like that, and she waited.

Peering through the small kitchen window into the yard, she nervously fiddled with a strand of hair, knowing he would soon return. David seemed to be in good form that morning, at breakfast time he'd teased Tom about his cold and said he was soft for not going to school, and then sat up in the bedroom with him, reading some of his comic books.

As Kathy waited, she wondered why David was late, and then she heard footsteps in the yard and the farm gate click shut. She ran upstairs to get a better view from the arched window on the landing to see who'd just left, and saw Joanne walking away, down the lane, back home.

Kathy felt irritated that while she'd nervously waited, David had been held up by Joanne. She knew Joanne had spent a lot of time with him recently, especially at milking time, but wondered why she never came into the house any more.

She heard David come into the kitchen and by the time she got down the stairs he was already at the washbasin with his back to her and scrubbing his hands. As he twisted around, he had a harsh look on his face, and without saying a word, he turned his back again and continued washing.

'Okay, love?' Kathy tenderly enquired.

'Aye.' David was blunt, and carried on washing.

'All gone well?' Again, she asked gently.

David yielded a little. 'I'm sorry. How's Tom?'

'Oh, he'll be all right in a day or two. . . . Come and sit down and get your coffee.' Kathy put her hands on his warm shoulders to try and motion him to the kitchen table and poured the coffee.

UP HIGH – IN DEEP

He didn't notice her breath in deeply as she said: 'I'm going away for a few days. . . . Aunt Betty's treat.'

'That's nice.' Yet his voice was cold.

'Will you be alright on your own?'

'Course I will. But what about the kids?'

Kathy sidled beside him and touched his arm. 'Grandma can have them.'

No reply.

She continued, her hands now shaking. 'I'm going with Alan, Davey.'

'What?'

'Don't ask me to say it again. It was hard enough the first time!' She moved away swiftly.

But David sat quietly trying to absorb what he'd just heard: *she wants to go away with Alan Marsh*! He didn't touch his coffee, but pushed himself back from the table, his wooden chair screeching on the hard floor and he headed for the door.

Speaking to him like he was a child, Kathy shouted, 'Where are you going, David?'

He stopped, looked at her and frowned. 'I just don't understand you.' His eyes glared and his eyebrows almost joined above the bridge of his nose as he scowled, and the scar on his lip made him appear sinister. 'Are you determined to make a laughing stock of this family?' he gasped, bending down and pulling his boots back on.

'How dare you speak to me like that . . . I need a break and Alan's offered. You had a holiday and it did you good. Although heaven knows why you're back to these moods again. And I didn't question what you were up to in Blackpool!'

David saw her trembling and held his head low.

'You're only thinking of yourself.' She angered him once again.

'Yes, and who are you thinking of? Not Dad, not the kids, not me!'

'Look, David. . . . Nobody else needs to know.'

'Oh, and that makes it all right does it?'

UP HIGH – IN DEEP

From this moment, the love she'd had for him turned into hate - instant hate. How quickly her feelings had changed with his reproof. She stood and glared at him. His head was held high again and his face flushed with colour, bearing a self-righteous expression. She desperately wanted his approval but with or without it, she would still go, if nothing more than to prove she wouldn't be ordered around by anyone ever again.

'Don't be a hypocrite, David. It's okay for you to be fooling around with Joanne Milton when we're all so busy.'

'You don't know what you're talking about, Mother. You know nothing!' and David grabbed his jacket and, without saying another word, left her standing and slammed the back door behind him.

Kathy, thinking she was alone, stood for some time staring at the closed door. Then she heard a noise and she turned and spotted Tom just leaving, quietly closing the hallway door to return upstairs.

Keld Head revelled in being an unhappy place again during that third week in February. David hardly said a word to his mother. Kathy was still anxious for his approval but knew it would never come. She started to prepare for her holiday with Alan and ruthlessly enjoyed a trip to Carlisle to choose a new outfit with Aunt Betty's money.

David continued to be engrossed in his work, much like a man that had joined the Foreign Legion to forget an unpleasant experience. He had the mentality that thought: *If I just work and work, my problems will go away.* He didn't have any other ideas, so he just worked and became numb to all around him. Not caring, not loving, not even hating, just indifferent to everything. The winter had probably got to him as well, and yet with the imminent approach of the spring, he'd no thoughts of better days and warm sunshine. This was despite the fact that the snowdrops and aconites were in full bloom, as carpets of them rolled through the trees. The daffodils would soon be out and their buds were already fattening ready to burst open at the first sign of warmth.

UP HIGH – IN DEEP

* * *

Kathy left with Alan one Wednesday morning after leaving the children in Lancaster with her parents. They were excited to be having a few days off school.

When Alan met Kathy outside her mother's house, he was full of anticipation and his spirits were heightened as she walked out clutching a small overnight bag. She was wearing a red wool suit with a tightly fitted skirt and a thin black polo-necked sweater. Her blonde hair was immaculately tied back and neatly held in a black comb. Her slight figure was still appealing.

Alan felt like a man about to elope, but knew he must keep his promise and honour her reputation and not spoil their friendship. But there was a thought deep inside him, a hope that she might change her mind and that this could be the start of a closer relationship. And, as he sat beside her on the train, he wanted people to believe she was his wife, for he noticed she was still wearing her wedding ring.

As for Kathy, at that moment, she didn't care what anybody thought, she was happy just to be with Alan and experience the safety of his company, and she guessed how he would be feeling. She knew she looked good today. Putting on her make-up and dressing that morning, she had taken more than the usual care; in fact more than she'd done for years. There was no farewell kiss or loving embrace from David, and Kathy felt like the teenager that was leaving home and he was the aggrieved parent. But, as she sat on the train, Kathy did feel some guilt; not because of her trip with Alan, but because she was leaving David alone.

She'd left several frozen dinners in the freezer for him and if David didn't eat them, well, that was his own problem. Kathy didn't even know if he was listening when she tried to tell him what to eat, and when.

David was incensed with his mother and couldn't believe she was going through with this foolishness. She had almost taunted him with her appearance, knowing this angered him more. He hadn't watched her leave, but stood in the damp and cold, as the emptiness of the cobbled farm yard and its tower and outbuildings enclosed him.

That same day Kathy found herself in Paris; she thought it would be Blackpool or St.Annes. She couldn't believe Alan had brought her here. He'd secretly conspired with Kathy's mother and Tom, and between them they'd managed to find her passport. She was glad she'd packed some decent clothing and taken care over her appearance, and when an olive-skinned French man sitting on the train, winked at her, she flushed with colour. He reminded her of George.

They stayed in a quaint Parisian hotel. The bedrooms lavishly decorated with blue flock wallpaper and a bathroom fully tiled and with antique fittings. Alan kept his promise and slept in the room across the landing, but each morning he brought her a tray of coffee and croissants, and sat on the side of her bed as they shared breakfast together. They walked by the River Seine and visited the Arc De Triomphe and Sacre Coeur; had a glass of Champagne on a boat on the river and ate in wonderful restaurants. They bought gifts for the children from street-side markets, and, finally, he took her to the top of the Eiffel Tower.

Kathy looked out across the Parisian skyline just as David had done in Blackpool only weeks earlier, but their aspects were different: David had changed his mind and wanted to go home, but Kathy didn't.

'Are you all right?' Alan noticed the shine had gone from her face and he put his arm around her.

'I'm sorry, Alan. This is a bit much for me. I'm obviously not very good with heights, but I want to take it all in.'

'You are very quiet. I guess you must be missing the children.'

'Would it sound awful if I said I wasn't!' She couldn't tell him that each flashback she had was always of David; thinking of what he would be doing and how he would be feeling. She knew the little ones were safe with her mother. But David was alone and unpredictable.

'You don't want to go home then?'

'Home . . . 'she paused. 'I don't feel at this moment that I ever want to go home again.'

Alan found her vulnerability seductive and desperately wanted to kiss her, and his arm tightened a little on her shoulder. 'I love you Kathy. . . .'

She looked around at him and softly spoke. 'I know you do, Alan.' She stood closer to him, feeling his warm breath in her hair, her arm pressed against his body, and she shivered with the cold. 'Please don't say any more. Can we go down now? I feel uneasy.'

They walked silently back to their hotel, both thinking of what had just been said. The admission of his feelings were of no surprise and, inwardly, Kathy had welcomed them. Just like David, she craved for the attention and admiration, and was desperate to be loved. And like David, she knew she wasn't in a position to return it yet.

'Have you enjoyed it then?' Alan broke the silence.

She took his arm again and squeezed it. 'It's been wonderful. Absolutely wonderful! I'm sure this break's already done me good. You were right . . . I think I did need to get away from the farm.'

'Try not to think of the farm, Kathy. Not just yet.'

'I know . . . Davey will be doing a good job,' she said with a hint of sadness in her heart.

As he left her at the hotel room, she gave him a kiss on the cheek. Alan waited expectantly, but Kathy was more cautious. 'Good night Alan. And thank you,' and he knew she had made a wise decision.

He'd already let his guard down in declaring his love for her and for the cautious bachelor he was, that was an embarrassment. But he was happy she understood how he really felt and he wanted to be ready when the right time came.

Alan found this parting harder than expected and didn't go straight back to his room, but went for a walk through the night. He hoped the darkness and the anonymity would hide his disappointment. He'd told Kathy something he knew was true and what he had often thought; something he'd never told another woman. He found comfort in the neon lights and the street bars, illuminating green, red, and blue streaks, as they reflected on the damp roads and pavements, as he walked the busy streets of Paris, alone.

9

THE NARCISSUS

The kitchen table which was normally strewn with children's toys and piles of ironing, was bare. There was no aroma of coffee, no teatime smells of roasting meat or cooked vegetables. The fire wasn't lit and the Aga had been neglected and gone out.

David hurried indoors when he heard the telephone ringing. He snatched at the receiver but there was silence. 'Hello . . . hello. . . .' still no reply, then the line went dead. He mused for a while: that was the third time that day. If his mother had some message for him and couldn't get through, well, tough, he thought.

David stood in the stone cold farmhouse in silence, he opened the fire door on the Aga and slammed it shut again, cursing himself for letting it go out. He put a match to the dry sticks in the parlour fireplace and threw on more sticks and coal to restore matters. He put the electric kettle on and then, peering into the fridge, found a packet of small pork pies. David chose one of the pies for his tea and opened a tin of baked beans. Glancing at the clock he could see it was time for the early evening news.

The yard gate clicked and then the sound of someone singing; *Tony?*

He knocked then popped his head around the kitchen door. 'Where is everyone?'

That question was ignored.

'Do you want some tea?' David spoke, with his back turned on his friend.

'What a miserable specimen!' Tony replied, as he picked up

one of the small pies and put most of it into his mouth and tried to eat and speak at the same time. 'I'm sorry. . . . Was that your tea?' spitting pastry crumbs over himself and David.

'That was tomorrow's and the day after's!'

'So then . . . I'll ask you again. . . . Where is everybody?'

David emptied the tin of baked beans into a small pan and stirred them with a wooden spoon. 'My mother has cleared off with Alan Marsh for a day or two, and the kids are at my gran's.'

'You poor little mite! Is that why you're looking so dejected? Your mummy has left you has she?'

David ignored the banter by putting out two mugs; he carelessly threw in the coffee and then filled them with hot water. 'According to my instructions . . . it should be fish and chips tonight but I can't be bothered to go to Keswick.'

'Oh, wonderful. And where might your mother be dining?'

'Probably some hotel in St. Annes that, Alan, and a hundred other reps stay at. They'll be talking about how much a gallon of sheep dip costs, over a romantic dinner. Anyhow, wherever she is, and whatever she's eating, I couldn't care less.'

'You selfish beggar! I bet she didn't think that when you were drinking and fighting down in Blackpool. Besides, you don't really mean that. You're only feeling sorry for yourself.' Tony pulled a chair up to the kitchen table and watched David spooning the hot beans over the cold pie.

'Anyway. . . .' Tony continued, 'never mind them. Do you fancy coming out for a drink? It'll be warmer in the pub than in this god-forsaken place.'

And a glimmer of a smile appeared on David's face as he started to eat his meagre meal – Someone cared for him at last.

The men had a welcome drink, a game of pool and a plate of sandwiches, and as they struggled back home up the hill the evening turned windy; their voices were muted.

David left Tony at the bungalow and walked briskly back to the farmhouse. He was as content as he'd been in weeks and, this time, as he opened the kitchen door, the warmth

THE NARCISSUS

embraced him and he guessed the Aga had finally stayed lit. Yet, despite its heat, there was still a coldness and an eerie silence and an unwelcome feel to the house and he realised, that in all his twenty-three years, he'd never stayed in the house alone at night.

He went into the parlour and touched the radiators with his hand, and they were warm. The fire was smouldering in the hearth, belching out puffs of smoke from a draught coming down the chimney. He felt tired and still a little hungry so, making a jam sandwich and a cup of coffee, took himself straight upstairs to his bedroom.

Quickly undressing, he put on his pyjamas and got straight into bed. And sitting up in bed, David sipped his tea and ate his supper. The alarm was set for six-thirty and he put out his bedside lamp. He was ready for drifting off to sleep when he heard the latch on the backdoor downstairs click. It must be the wind.

He sat up further in his bed and listened – he thought someone had come into the house, and hoped it was Tony fooling around. Not daring to move, he rested back in bed, mesmerised in the darkness. He listened for many minutes, his heart beating like a car engine. Then, as he peered into the darkness, his bedroom door slid open and he saw the form of a woman moving in closer toward him. He sat bolt upright in bed.

'Don't be afraid, Davey. . . . It's only me.'

'Good grief, Jo! How did you get in?' David, still disabled by fear, didn't move.

'I haven't lived next door to you for eighteen years without knowing where you keep your spare key,' she whispered.

'Well, what on earth's the matter?' Still shaken, he rubbed his eyes and reached out for the bedside lamp.

Joanne came across the room and firmly took his arm, preventing him from any further movement. But David found the energy to stir and threw back the covers and stood up quickly but he clumsily knocked the lamp and it fell crashing to the floor and broke in pieces.

THE NARCISSUS

'I'm sorry . . . I'm so sorry, Davey.' She knelt down to pick up the fragments, then sat down on the edge of his bed.

David could just see her appearance through the darkness. Apart from a white t-shirt, she was completely dressed in black. She wore a leather jacket and a short skirt and was shivering with the cold. Her long red hair was falling loosely about her face and shoulders.

'Tony told me you were all alone, so I've come to keep you company.'

David was confused as to her motives and groaned, 'I'm - I'm all right. Please, please, you're shivering - you're cold. What's the problem, Jo?'

'Nothing. . . . Not now. . . . Not now that I'm with you. I saw your light on and I thought I'd come and talk to you, that's all.'

David brushed passed her, pleased that tonight he was wearing his pyjamas. He reached for the light-switch by the door. Both of them squinted.

'Don't spoil things, Davey. I wanted it to be just you and me. Don't you want to talk to me?'

'Joanne!' David was exasperated. 'I love talking to you, but not now - not in the middle of the night! I have to be up early in the morning. Come downstairs and I'll make you a cup of tea, and then you MUST go home.'

He put a pullover on over the top of his pyjamas, as she stayed motionless on his bed. David headed for the door. 'Please. . . . Come downstairs,' his voice was cold. He simply had to get out of the bedroom, but she resisted. 'Joanne. . . . Please . . . I can't have you here while my mother's away.'

'I thought you would want me!' And with that, she started to cry but David didn't notice that the tears were false.

'Oh, no. Please . . . please don't cry.' He went back to the bed and, taking her hand, pulled her up towards him and led her from the room. 'You must have some tea and then go home,' he repeated. 'If Tony finds out you've been here, he'll kill me.'

'Tony . . . Tony . . . I don't care about Tony. I only care about you.'

'And I care about you, Jo, but this isn't the way to do things. It just won't do!'

'Well, you're treating me like a child now. Can't you see I'm not a child anymore?' Her eyes flashed.

David looked at her, knowing well that she looked anything but a child. She was a beautiful young woman, but this was madness, her being here. He also knew that, for once, he must do the right thing and take her out of his room; even force her if that were necessary. And, as he gently pulled her hand, she obliged and followed him and he managed to get her downstairs and into the kitchen.

The tea was made with resignation, as David clumsily clattered the kettle, the cups, the milk jug, and then sat, reluctantly, at the table. 'Does Tony know you're here?'

'No. I left him sleeping in front of the telly.' Joanne weaved around him, curling her body smoothly and seductively close to his.

'But he'll hear you coming in again.'

'Then I'll stay longer. And he'll be in bed and won't miss me at all, will he?'

'Then I think it's time to go, Joanne.'

'If you kiss me like you did before, I'll leave.' She stood close to him and rested her arm on his shoulder.

It was foolish and irrational and yet he complied, anything, to get rid of her.

He gently kissed her on the forehead and held her shoulders slightly as he did so. 'Now you must go, Joanne and I'll see you tomorrow.' But she started to kiss him full on the lips and with passion. Desperate now, David backed away and went to the door. 'No... no... no.... Don't please....'

With her face shrouded in disappointment she finally gave in, and David was relieved to see her through the door, and walked as far as the yard gate with her. He gave her a torch and promised to watch until she was safe in the bungalow. He knew she was hanging around for another kiss so he backed away.

As he stood shivering in the yard, he pulled the sleeves on

his pullover down over his hands and folded his arms. He then jogged back indoors and, without any hesitation, put the safety chain on the door.

Unnerved by Joanne's intrusion, David wandered around the kitchen, not daring to go back upstairs to bed. He thought of sleeping on the sofa and leaving the kitchen light on. Then inwardly cursing himself for his stupidity in kissing her again, he decided his punishment should be to have the uncomfortable night downstairs.

As he contemplated getting pillows and blankets from the airing cupboard, he wandered across to the laundry-room door and, as he passed the Aga, he saw the mirror hanging beside it glistening in the light, and David suddenly stopped. His blue eyes now wide open and sharp, saw something that made him shudder. Scrawled across the mirror was some graffiti. And, as he allowed himself to read it, it said: *Come outside to play.*

It was an innocuous statement if he could believe it was written by little Sarah or even Tom, and he desperately searched his mind, trying to recall seeing it a day or so back before they left for his grandmother's house. He touched the cold glass and the writing smeared pink on his finger and he realised it was lipstick.

David backed away and crashed into the dining table, catching his foot on one of the chairs. He spun around and stumbled, then kneeling on the floor, crawled to the kitchen sink, and dragged himself up and turned on the hot tap, full flow. He grabbed a cloth, dowsing it in washing-up liquid, and with water and soap dripping down his arm; not caring that it was soaking his pullover, he scrubbed the mirror clean.

Joanne managed to get back into the bungalow without disturbing Tony. He was still asleep, with the television on, as some politicians argued about the rights and wrongs of Britain joining the Common Market.

She put away her jacket, went to the bedroom and fumbled through the dressing table drawer to find her diary. Humming to herself, she lay on the bed and began to read:

MARCH 10th.Tuesday

Helped Davey with the milking again tonight. He told me of his plan to move to Scotland. He told me how much he loved me and that as soon as his mother could cope, we will elope together. Then there will be just him and me.

Then she began to write:

MARCH 11th. Wednesday.

Helped Davey with the milking again. He told me how miserable he was living at home and said he couldn't wait until we leave and get married. He begged me to stay the night as his mother is away for a few days.

MARCH 12th. Thursday.

I came home at 6:30 this morning. David is now at work. He didn't want to get up and leave me for milking but I persuaded him to go. That was my very first night at Keld Head alone with him. His mother is home tomorrow so we must be careful of when we see each other again. I do love him so much.

Kathy, still dressed in her red suit, stood at the desk looking at the mail. She sighed as she opened each envelope. 'I can't believe how many bills can come in just three days!' She placed several invoices back in the correct envelopes and putting them in a wire basket, shoved them back on the desk.

David was relieved to have his mother home and admitted to himself that she looked well, in fact, she looked radiant; but he couldn't forgive her. He found it hard to believe that Alan had taken her to Paris, and as he looked carefully at her appearance and demeanour, he tried to see any marks of unfaithfulness in her, not just against his father, but mostly against himself.

He recalled how his mother would act when she'd made up with his father after they'd had some massive argument, and there would be open displays of kissing and whispering between them. She always had an air about her that should have pleased David, but it never did, it always sickened him, and today she seemed the same. And then he recalled the suggestions and accusations of his deluded father, who didn't trust anyone, and David realised he was thinking just the same.

Kathy had hugged David on her return and sensed his resistance. Then hoping she wasn't to get another scolding she tried to pacify him. 'Are the animals all okay, love? Did milking go well?'

'Well enough.' David was sitting at the table trying to mend his broken bedside lamp; there were bits of wires everywhere.

'Have you been out at all?'

'Just to the pub. Tony called in for me.' Still a rebuff.

'What happened to the lamp?'

'I just knocked it, okay.'

'Did anyone else call?'

'No, not really.' David tried to concentrate on his repairs.

Kathy wondered who constituted a "*not really,*" but decided it would be better not to ask. She was glad to see he was safe, and wondered why she'd worried about him so much; he was driving her crazy. She opened the fridge door and noticed from the contents that he'd eaten very little. She hoped at least that he'd had some fish and chips.

'Oh, by the way,' David stood from his chair, frustrated that the lamp still didn't work. 'Mrs Hargreaves phoned . . .' he paused as once again he looked intently at his mother for any clues of deception in her eyes. 'She wants to speak to you about Tom.'

'Oh no . . . ! What's the matter now?'

'She just said it was important that's all. Oh . . . and Linzi called to say she'll be home at weekend and wants picking up from the bus.'

'Did you tell her where I was?'

'No, Mother, I didn't. . . . You tell her!'

The following morning Kathy started to dress in her familiar clothes: blue denim jeans and a baggy pullover, then she had second thoughts. And not wanting to lose the wonderful feelings of peace by being anxious over Tom, decided to go to the school and get it over with. She had to call into the village post office and a detour wouldn't be out of her way. She decided to wear something that, the sensible, Mrs Hargreaves would approve of. Her new red suit would certainly raise some eyebrows in the village and provoke some unwelcome comments. So Kathy wisely chose something less seductive.

It was a fine day and the long walk to the school would give her the opportunity to compose her thoughts. She couldn't help but wonder why she'd been summoned, and only hoped it was nothing to do with the children being taken out of school again. She wanted to be as discreet as she could and give the Head Teacher no further reason to view her disapprovingly.

The village was crowded as she walked over the bridge; she stepped off the pavement into the road, past the church, and stopped for a while to watch a robin hopping around the headstones in the churchyard. The bakery was open and the aroma of freshly baked bread filled the cool spring air.

Looking up to the fells, she could see the mountains looming over her, and the light and the clear day made them appear like they were made of brilliant glass. The summits were shrouded in a carpet of bright green, lush turf, and bronzed with dormant bracken, looking resplendent as moisture glistened on the wet rocks.

As a precaution, Kathy decided to do her errands before going to the school, recalling how on her previous visit she'd had to make a hurried return home.

The Head Teacher was in her usual dominant spirit. The strength of her character appeared to ooze from her very presence and, without uttering one word, Kathy felt intimidated. She took a deep breath and sat down on the chair before her; glad she'd considered her appearance.

Dorothy Hargreaves got straight to the point. 'We seem to have a problem with Tom, I'm afraid, Mrs Keldas. One of our

THE NARCISSUS

parents has complained that he's been bullying their child.'

Kathy was astounded. 'I can't believe it! Not Tom.'

'I'm afraid so.'

'May I ask who the child is?'

'The parent wishes him to remain anonymous and, under the circumstances, I think it best if it stays that way.' Mrs Hargreaves was resolute. But Kathy was provoked and wanted to say: *'The circumstances . . . the circumstances. . . . What circumstances are these?'*

There was silence as both women eyed each other and contemplated. Kathy was the first to speak. 'If this is true . . . because it's not like him. What do you want me to do about it?'

In her thoughts, Mrs Hargreaves disagreed, as she believed it was typical of Tom Keldas.

'I've noticed a big change in his behaviour recently. He's become inattentive and his schoolwork has suffered. Children who bully often do it because they feel inadequate in some way, perhaps even jealous of the other child.'

Kathy didn't want to admit it, but she knew she'd given Tom and Sarah very little attention recently and she'd channelled every waking thought into David and her own selfish pursuits.

Kathy didn't need to rush home as she'd expected. Yes, she was disturbed and perplexed, but her renewed vitality gave her a clear aspect of this new situation. She tried to recall David as an eleven-year-old, but couldn't think of any time he'd been accused of bullying, though he had been in a few fights at school. She smiled to think of his recent one in Blackpool and how he had the scars to prove it. She would usually blame Tony Milton's sharp tongue for most of the trouble David found himself in, but she knew David wasn't perfect and neither was Tom.

Yes, Tom was a strong and tall boy for his age, but to think he might use this as a means to provoke others vexed her. He was certainly used to the rough and tumbles of life; George had treated him badly. And David tried to give him some of the time that George had neglected, but this often resulted in play fighting. David had ended up being the victim of Tom's playfulness with a bloodied nose and a broken tooth. So, consequently, she decided that David would be the best one to speak to Tom purely on a man-to-man basis.

As soon as she was home, Kathy got straight to it and asked David to help.

'I wouldn't know what to say to him. Why me?' David shut his eyes. He was trying to relax before the evening's milking.

'Because you can relate to him more than I can. He'll listen to you.'

David wanted to say, *Why? Because nobody else listens to me!*

'Take him for a walk or something. You two haven't been up the fells for a while. Perhaps you could take him to that football match you promised. Anything, but please . . . please help me with this, David.'

'Okay . . . okay. . . . I'll do something with him this weekend while Alan's milking, but don't expect too much. I'm no social worker. But he'll natter me to death. You know he can't stop talking; he drives me crazy sometimes.'

Kathy had to hide a smile as she realised she'd got her way with him and felt, this time, she'd won the battle. She knew she had pushed him and forced the issue, and it showed in David's countenance. He looked grave. He looked thinner in his face, and was developing a scowl, which drew his dark eyebrows ever closer together as he sat pensively, resigning himself to his obligation.

Linzi Keldas opened the fridge door to view its contents: a lemon, a packet of lard, some Stork margarine and two eggs.

'Thank goodness for eggs.'

The dismal contents of the fridge only served to enforce her decision to go home. She had missed lectures for nearly two weeks because of a heavy cold, which had left her feeling drained and in poor spirits. She'd no money and felt miserable and, although the thought of home was small comfort to her,

THE NARCISSUS

it still had a glimmer of appeal when she considered the lowly straits she'd found herself in.

Wearing only pyjamas and a blue bathrobe and slippers, she wandered through to the kitchen. It was lunchtime and she was famished and her head was thumping with too much sleep. In just one hour she had to be in Newcastle to catch the express coach to Keswick.

'What a mess!' she said, as she attempted to wipe some grime from the cooker, her cloth soon becoming smeared with sticky grease. She then whisked the eggs and poured them into a clean pan, to make scrambled eggs.

'This place stinks!' she grumbled, as she looked about the dingy flat. The kitchen sink was clogged with dirty pots and pans; the waste bin was over-flowing with empty cans and bottles; her fellow flatmates were all as guilty as she for the mess. She shuffled across the sitting room and pulled back a pair of heavy curtains to reveal clouds of dust and spiders' webs floating across the room exposed by the early spring sunshine. The gas fire was only just managing to put out some heat.

Linzi wanted to cry at the pathetic state she found herself in. 'Does nobody ever do anything around here?' Her two flatmates, both in college, had left the remains of their breakfast on the coffee table: half-eaten bowls of Rice Crispies floating in milk, several cups of cold coffee and side plates strewn about the sitting room which had been left for days, maybe even weeks. She was about to start and clear them away, but thought better of it, and went back to the kitchen to butter some toast.

Linzi managed to make an effort with her appearance as she bathed and washed her hair, putting on jeans and layers of t-shirts and pullovers. She found an overnight bag and stuffed it as full as she could with dirty washing to take home, put on her navy Parka and wrapped a red scarf about her neck that almost obscured her face.

She just caught the bus in time, and could relax for a couple of hours as they progressed across England. She made herself as comfortable as possible on the back seat and was mesmerised by gazing aimlessly out of the window as they left the busy streets of Newcastle behind.

As the coach stopped at one of the suburbs, Linzi noticed a young woman boarding. She watched for some time as the girl paid her fare then wandered towards the back of the coach and sat just in front of her.

Where have I seen you before? Linzi was perplexed as she peered out from over the top of her scarf. Then she realised this was the girl David ignored at the bus station a few months earlier and the memory of that intrigued her.

As the girl settled down in front of Linzi, she carelessly dropped the contents of her purse on the floor, and the coins rolled about under the seats. Linzi felt compelled to help. 'I think we have a mutual acquaintance.' Linzi said, stretching to pick up some of the money and giving it to the girl.

Hannah Robson looked up and said 'I'm sorry. . . . Do I know you?'

'No, I don't suppose you do. I'm Linzi Keldas.'

Hannah's large brown eyes flashed wide open and thoughts of David came straight to her mind. *This girl must be his wife*! Hannah thought, as she recognised Linzi behind the layers of clothing. She couldn't explain why, but felt disappointed as she realised this was the girl she'd seen David embracing at the bus station. 'Oh! Do you mean David?' Hannah was cautious.

'Yes. I believe you know him?'

Hannah, immediately wanting to play down much knowledge of him replied, 'Oh, only in that I work with Barry Fitzgerald.'

'Yes I know.' Linzi was disappointed in Hannah's complacency.

Hannah sat half-turned in her seat and was surprised that Linzi had recognised her from what must have only have been a fleeting glance at the bus-station a few months earlier.

'Are you going back to Windermere today?' Linzi asked.

Hannah turned again and guessing Linzi wanted to talk, was

glad of some light conversation that would help pass the long trip back to Cumbria. 'Yes. I've had the week off. Barry wants me back for any emergencies over the weekend.'

'Are you going home too?'

Linzi sighed as she replied, 'Yes, but reluctantly I'm afraid. To tell you the truth I've had the flu and I'm broke and I need to borrow some money off Davey. That's if he'll cough up!'

Hannah mused and thought it a strange request to have to borrow money off your own husband - still, they were a strange family.

As Hannah looked puzzled, Linzi tried to explain. 'I'm a student you see, and I can't manage on my grant.'

'Doesn't David help you out?'

'Phoo! Why should he?'

'I'm sorry. I didn't mean to pry.'

'That's okay. It's just that my brother's probably loaded and he doesn't like opening his wallet, especially to me.'

'Oh, your brother. . . . He's your brother.' Hannah was surprised to find she was relieved. 'I'm sorry. How stupid of me.'

'Who did you think I was?' Linzi laughed. 'Oh my goodness. Surely you didn't think I was his wife! I wouldn't be good enough for Mr Perfect. I'm afraid Davey's got a severe case of narcissism. Whoever marries him would have to be better than him, and he thinks no one like that exists.'

Hannah was uncomfortable in the way the conversation was turning. 'So what are you studying?'

'Oh . . . Business Studies; book keeping and stuff like that. Well, I'm supposed to be, but I've just had two weeks off sick and, to be honest, I don't know if I'll go back after the Easter break.' Linzi surprised herself at how open she'd been to this stranger, but Hannah's smile and her warm brown eyes had drawn out her very thoughts and compelled her to speak.

'How much longer do you have to do? I'm sorry; I don't even remember your name.' Linzi continued.

'Hannah . . . Hannah Robson. I've just less than two years until I sit my finals. How about you?'

THE NARCISSUS

'I'm in my second year, but I very much doubt I'll finish.' Linzi winged.

'You can't give up now! You're nearly there. If you flunk out now, the last eighteen months will have been wasted.'

Hannah sounded enthusiastic and Linzi wondered how she could be; being a student herself, she must understand how difficult it was. But Hannah was free. She wasn't stuck in college, day in and day out. At least Hannah could do some practical work and travel about.

'Oh, it's just so very, very boring. Please don't tell Barry, will you? He knows my mum and if this gets back to her, she'll worry sick and natter on at me. Have you met my mother?'

'Yes. She's a lovely woman,' Hannah smiled 'I've met your little sister too.'

Linzi warmed to Hannah and guessed for the first time in years, that she'd made a new friend. 'Does your family live in Newcastle?' Linzi had recognised her accent.

'No, we live in a small village just outside Durham. Just Dad and me, that is.'

'Do you have any brothers and sisters?'

'No, only me. My mum died of cancer two years ago.'

'I'm sorry,' Linzi paused and sounded sympathetic. 'You know about my Dad, do you?'

'Well . . . sort of. I'm sorry too.'

'I think my mum's just beginning to pick up the pieces now. I'm not sure about Davey though.'

Hannah thought it strange that this surly young man should be referred to as "Davey". Barry had called him that once or twice and, somehow, the name of affection didn't lend itself to his person.

'Men are peculiar things,' Hannah continued. 'My father never talks about my mother, and I think if he did he would feel better.'

'I get the impression Davey wants to talk about Dad, but my mother, as fragile as she looks, is a tough cookie. She sometimes doesn't seem to care.'

'I'm sure she does. Your mother seems a lovely person. It'll just be her way of coping.'

Linzi knew this was just what everyone else was saying and continued. 'Are you going straight to Barry's?'

'Yes, I live in the flat above the surgery.'

'We'll give you a lift, then. Either Davey or my mum will meet me today. We can't leave you standing at the bus stop, can we. We must make up for our Davey's ignorance last time.'

Hannah didn't want to be a nuisance. The practice was a long drive from Keld Head, and yet she was intrigued to see how Linzi interacted with David; maybe it would reveal something about him and that thought tempted her. 'Well, only if they have time.'

'Would you like to come out for a drink with us on Saturday night?' Linzi next asked.

'Who would be there?'

'Me . . . Davey. . . . His friend Tony Milton. His sister Joanne. Then there's Darren Watson from Langdale. I have my eyes on him; he's a dish. . . . Just those few. That's all.'

'Oh, I don't know. You're kind, but they might not want me there. I'd feel like I was intruding.'

'Rubbish! You'll bring some culture to our group.'

With the spontaneity of their conversation the girls were soon looking at the Cumbrian fells, and as they fast approached Keswick, Blencathra and Skiddaw were there to welcome them, looming above them in the last of the early evening light. Mist on the summits and a sprinkling of snow in the gullies were just visible to the eye.

'Do you like the Lakes, Hannah?'

'Yes, I love it here. I've settled here better than anywhere else. But, I must admit, I don't like these farmers. They're a cantankerous lot'

'Oh, you'll get used to them. It's probably because you're a woman and they don't think you're up to the job. I hope Davey was kind to you?'

Hannah couldn't tell Linzi what she really thought of David.

But as they jumped from the coach, Hannah found herself disappointed to see Linzi's mother sitting in the Rover waiting.

Kathy had decided that she'd given David enough to think about with her problem with Tom and daren't ask any more favours of him.

'Mum. I think you know Hannah? Can we give her a lift to Windermere? We can't leave her standing at the station, can we?' Linzi looked at Hannah for any hint of a reaction but there was none.

Kathy wound down the window, popped her head out and saw in the semi-darkness, Barry's pretty assistant. 'Jump in, Hannah. Of course we'll take you home.'

During the drive to Windermere, Hannah asked after Silver and her calf. Kathy described in detail how David had spent hours, under sufferance, walking around the fold-yard trying to give the animal some exercise, and was happy to say she was now doing well.

'I'm sorry about the state of the car.' Kathy apologised, as she noticed Hannah remove a half-empty packet of crisps she'd just sat on, and pulled away several lengths of baler string and pieces of straw.

Sitting in the back of the Rover, Hannah felt comfortable with Kathy. Then she noticed a man's brown woollen pullover that had been thrown carelessly on the backseat beside her. She couldn't help but pick it up, gently fold it, and rest it on the seat beside her.

10

ON HIGH AND VERY WHITE STONES

'She's from County Durham.' Linzi cuddled Sarah then struggled to release herself as the child hung on firmly around her neck.

David had just come in from a hectic milking session. Several cows had developed mastitis and he wanted them all safely treated, so Alan wouldn't have any problems with them in the morning. He went to the wash-basin and, quietly unconcerned, washed his hands.

'Yes. I liked her as soon as I saw her,' Kathy said. 'Sarah hasn't stopped talking about her since. How much longer is she here for?'

'Only until July, I think. Depending on whether Barry needs her over the summer.'

David continued to scrub his fingernails with his back to his family, only half-listening. *Who on earth is she talking about?* he thought, not really caring. *Barry needs her over the summer; Sarah knows her.*

'Anyway, I asked her to come out with us tomorrow night. Is that all right with you, Davey?' Linzi looked longingly at her brother.

'Mind what?'

'HANNAH ROBSON . . . COMING WITH US . . . FOR A DRINK . . . TOMORROW NIGHT!'

Still confused and embarrassed, David wondered how Linzi knew Hannah Robson. 'I don't know who you mean.' David lied as he turned to her, drying his hands on an old towel, knowing he couldn't give a better reply.

ON HIGH AND VERY WHITE STONES

* * *

Hannah unpacked her holdall and carefully folded the clothes away. Her small flat above the practice still felt warm, despite being empty for the week. Barry's wife, Eleanor, had put the central heating on and had stocked the fridge and larder with fresh milk and bread. Hannah knew Barry and Eleanor spoilt her and they treated her like their own.

If Linzi could have seen Hannah's flat it would have depressed her all the more. Not that Hannah always had it easy. She'd lived in some dreadful places at the university, and some diabolical cottages and caravans supplied by some not-so-generous veterinary practices. She too had struggled and, like Linzi, had often felt like giving up, especially when her mother was ill. And once her mother died, she felt a pull so strong to return home to support her grieving father; Hannah would have given everything up, there and then, if not for the dying wish of her mother to continue. But this little flat of Barry Fitzgerald's was sparse yet warm and Hannah kept it clean. It was painted white throughout, with a handful of Lakeland scenes hung on the wall. She'd just a few essentials: a television, a bed, a sofa and even some luxuries, like the central heating and a shower, and the use of the telephone in the hallway.

The practice itself lay high on a hill, amongst woodland, on the outskirts of Windermere. The grand house that had belonged to Barry's father had once been lavishly decorated and furnished to a high standard, but Eleanor's disinterest had let things get untidy. The money was there, but she had neither the desire nor the will to do anything with it. Barry was always too busy to offer any help and too satisfied to want to. Yet, when things were purchased, they were done to excess.

Tonight, Hannah contemplated the invitation that Linzi had made. She was half-wanting to accept, and then half-hoping she would be called out on an emergency. She thought she would like to see Linzi again and help her if she could. Hannah was glad that she'd stuck with it and knew Linzi would regret the decision if she dropped out now. But the thought of an evening with David brought out a bit of devilment in Hannah. It may be her chance to get even with him, thinking how much she could hurt his narcissistic ego. But Hannah doubted that he would want her there and felt certain no phone call would come to make a definite date.

Hannah hadn't felt particularly lonely in Windermere. When she had a day off, and that was seldom, she would drive off to the lower fells and take Barry's Lakeland Terrier with her. Windermere and Bowness were always alive with visitors, winter and summer. Hannah loved looking around the little shops and boutiques, occasionally treating herself to some quality walking gear and enjoying breaking them in.

Searching through the kitchen cupboards to find something quick and easy to make for her tea, Hannah finally settled down in front of the television with a plate of tinned spaghetti on toast, when she felt a hint of uncertainty creep over her.

'Come on, Davey.... Get up!' Tom was jumping up and down on David's bed.

David pulled the covers over his face to screen him from the light and from the claws of the black dog that was standing with all fours on top of him.

'Go away, Tom. It's too early!' David's voice was muffled under the covers.

'Mum says we should get an early start!'

'Clear off NOW . . . ! And take the dog with you, for pity's sake. Come back in an hour and maybe bring me a cup of tea.'

David did manage to get back off to sleep and was so comfortable, that he felt reluctant to get up, let alone spend a day walking. Still, he'd promised and didn't want to let his brother down. He hadn't any idea where they would walk or what he was going to say to Tom. He'd tried not to think about it and had succeeded to some extent; except for the occasional niggle in the back of his mind. But an hour later he was sitting up in bed, drinking the tea that Tom had brought him. He still felt uncomfortable and had some disquieting thoughts that he couldn't clearly recall. As he searched his mind, he realised that they were more than just the problem with Tom.

The weather forecaster had promised it would be a dry day, and David finally struggled out of bed, peering through his bedroom window to check that was true. He glanced across to Easdale in the distance and, although it looked cold, the clouds were high in the sky and the fells were clear.

The smell of frying bacon and eggs creeping up to his bedroom was the incentive he needed to get ready. He had a quick shower and, with sheer laziness, decided not to shave. He threw on layers of t-shirts, a warm pullover, and had to rummage through a bundle of clothes in the bottom of his wardrobe for a pair of walking trousers. He couldn't find any clean socks so crept, barefoot, downstairs, not wanting to touch the cold tiled floor with his feet.

Kathy had quickly laid the table, knowing a cooked breakfast would please David. Tom and Sarah had already started and had left the remains of their breakfast spattered everywhere. 'You messy tyke!' David said, rubbing Tom's head as he passed, sorry now that he'd shouted at him.

'Porridge, Davey? - it'll make your hair curl.'

'Oooh! Yes please. If that's no trouble.'

'I've tried to persuade Tom to have some, but he doesn't want curly hair, do you Tom?'

That was certainly true. Tom didn't want curly hair. His hair was fair and straight, no natural curls like David's and he preferred to be like his mother. He didn't like it when people said David resembled his father. *Poor David. I'm glad I'm like my mum,* Tom thought.

'Davey . . . ! Can I come with you?' Sarah was now leaning over his lap, as he tried to eat.

He picked her up, sat her down properly and held her in his arms. 'Now why would I want to take a little princess like you out in the cold, where it'll be blowing a gale?'

'Because I want to see the waterfalls. Mummy says they're beautiful at the moment.'

'On another day, I'll take you. Besides, Mum's taking you to

ON HIGH AND VERY WHITE STONES

Kendal with Linzi. That'll more fun than being with boys.'

Kathy interrupted, 'Yes, and we'll buy you a new book.'

Sarah had a dilemma: see the waterfalls or get a new book. She sat skewing her mouth to one side, then the other. Then, making a quick decision, pushed herself off David's lap and went to her mother. 'Which book shall I get, Mummy?'

Tom was sitting across from her at the table, listening, and hoping that David wouldn't give in; he didn't want a girl with him today. It was just to be him and Davey. If Sarah came she would moan because it would be too cold. Then Davey would have to carry her on his shoulders. Then they would have to walk slower or keep stopping. He didn't think mountains were for girls.

'Come here, Tom. Let's get you kitted out.' Kathy said.

Tom reluctantly complied, hands in pockets, as Kathy began to smother him in scarves and a woolly hat and shoving a spare pullover in his rucksack.

'For goodness sake, Mum . . . ! He won't be able to move if you put any more clothes on him.'

Tom's face flushed, embarrassed as Kathy continued to fuss and he pulled away from her.

'I don't want him getting hypothermia.'

'He's a fit lad. Anyway, walking will keep him warm.' David argued as he slid his empty porridge bowl into the dish water.

But Kathy took no notice and followed Tom. 'I wish you'd wear a different jacket. . . . Your school one's thicker. And mind you wrap up too, our Davey. It's not just kids that get hypothermia you know.'

They walked over the new bridge, across Easdale Beck, and David was as silent as usual. Tom was telling him about the few days he'd just spent in Lancaster with his grandparents; his conversation was non-stop as David suspected. Then Tom picked up a stone and threw it in the beck. The dog was quick to jump in.

'Tom . . . ! We've only been gone half an hour and we've already got a wet dog.' David guessed she'd be in the water at some time before the day was out, but didn't expect it as early as this. 'Come out Moss . . . you stupid dog!' The dog leapt from the stream and shook herself, spraying their legs with the dirty water. Tom laughed, but David wished he was still in bed.

The walk ahead took them gradually up to the falls. From the village below, the froth on the water looked like someone had broken a giant bottle of milk and it was dripping down the rocks. David stopped to look at the water as it noisily tumbled down the hillside. He held the dog firmly by the collar, and glanced down to the village; the cottages and houses were already dwarfed by distance and across the valley he could just discern the tower at Keld Head looming ominously as a formidable landmark.

The day continued grey and cold, but dry. They had little company in the way of other walkers, but David could just see on the path below them someone walking alone.

After a short break they steadily climbed until the terrain levelled. And as they walked into Easdale, they could see the fells high above them streaked with snow, as they swept down to the tarn. David was still quiet; just managing to say a "yes" or a "no" to Tom's barrage of questions, purely because he was unsure of what else to say. He knew he was meant to be helping, but just didn't know how. He wished he could come straight out with it and ask Tom why he'd been bullying, but he couldn't bring himself to do it.

He wasn't even sure if he had the right to do speak to the boy and thought this problem shouldn't be left to him. He couldn't remember bullying anyone at school. Although he'd been caught fighting in the playground once or twice, he believed his own conduct was as white as white. He'd usually only been protecting someone else, but invariably was the one to be caught, and David wondered if that injustice had coloured Dorothy Hargreaves's view of Tom. And, if that were the case, he could recognise a sense of responsibility.

David was irritated to have been given this problem on such a pleasant day. He knew what it felt like to be disciplined, when all you wanted was to be loved. David had spent many hours alone with his father in the hills, but it was rarely a happy experience. It was usually on an errand of mercy looking for him, because he'd wandered off in one of his selfish moods or maybe crazed with guilt after some argument with his mother. Then, if David did find him, they'd spend an unhappy hour walking home, with his father saying he should have left him up there to rot.

The tarn lay just before them; the water still and black as treacle. It was a good place to stop and eat so they bundled their rucksacks down on the shingle, as a flock of wild geese flew up swiftly and noisily from the water, flapping their wings and making a great commotion.

David poured coffee from his flask, and as he sipped he watched Tom gather up some stones and skim them across the water, counting each time they bounced. David looked at the space before him and it settled him. He saw the rocks bordering the lake, splendid in shape and form, black, grey and green. The expanse of the hills and sky stretched out ahead of him; miles of freedom if he so desired. He considered the choices he had today and wondered why he was allowing himself to become embittered, rather than elated with his life. Everything here was real, solid and tranquil, nothing was deluded or the imaginations of a tired mind. He downed his drink, took in a deep breath of air and felt exhilarated for the first time in weeks; the liberty was welcome, and he would have fun today, so picking up a stone, he joined Tom at the edge of the lake.

The game was entertaining and Tom responded to the challenge. But glancing at his watch David realised they must get on. They'd plenty of walking and talking to do and, although he knew his route well, the daylight hours in March were short.

The next objective was to scramble up the side of Belle's Knott, which was a large slab of rock, covered in moss and a damp black slime. Then there was one last pull to the summit of the fell, and then an exposed walk on a good path to

ON HIGH AND VERY WHITE STONES

Sergeant Man and High White Stones.

They spoke in broken tones, as they breathlessly climbed. Tom screamed with boyish laughter as he purposely slithered on the wet rocks. The dog was way ahead of them now. She stuck to the path and waited on each corner. And, each time they approached her, she teased them and ran away again, wanting to keep them at a distance.

David stopped to catch his breath and looked down to the valley way below them. Keld Head was almost obscured in mist. He could still see a great distance behind them, just one person sitting at the tarn at the same spot where they'd rested.

Easdale was a popular route, especially at this time of year when the weather was improving. The sight of other walkers usually comforted David, not because he wanted the company, and not because he was afraid of the hills but, in case of an accident, help was within sight.

He found himself peering into the distance at the solitary figure sitting by the tarn and thought it looked like a woman. David became overly concerned at their presence and, as he continued to amble up the fell, he looked back over his shoulder several times in case they were following him. He continued to watch and climb until, after a struggle, they reached the summit and the stranger was out of sight.

Tom was far ahead of him now, using his energy to keep up with the dog. He shouted back to David, 'Come on. . . . Hurry up, Davey. What are you looking at?'

David quickened his pace and with one last effort finally managed to catch up to the boy. They climbed over the top of the fell and the wind was strong as it hissed passed their ears. They had to shout to be heard. 'This is better than school.' Tom screamed.

At this first mention of school David seized an opportunity. 'You'll only have a few months at Junior's left now.' David shouted back.

'I don't want to go to Keswick in September.' Tom came closer to hear him, nudging into David's body as he carelessly wandered the grassy path.

'I'd make the most of the village school while you can, then.'

'They say they push your head down the toilet on the first day. Did they do that to you?'

'No. . . . They couldn't catch me. Don't you worry about that. It's all stupid talk. You're a big lad. They'll leave you alone.'

'Well, if they don't, they'll soon know about it!'

They pressed on over the grassy fell, keeping to the path and climbing towards the next summit. 'You want to keep out of trouble. . . . Take it from me.' David said more softly.

'Oh yeah!' Tom ran around David and, tripping carelessly on the cobbled path, started to taunt him. 'Is that how you got your busted lip down in Blackpool then?'

David felt a sharp jab at the accusations. 'Anyway. . . . You don't know what happened in Blackpool. . . . I was just in the wrong place at the wrong time.'

'Didn't you hit him back then?'

'No. I didn't. I just got out of the way.'

'I'd have let 'im 'av it!'

David laughed, but he really wanted to stop this aggressive talk and, he realised, that without even trying, he was opening up what was in the boy's heart.

'They call me Killer Keldy at school!' Tom said.

'What . . . !' Stopping, David grabbed hold of the boy's shoulders and looked him square in the face. 'What do they call you?'

'KILLER KELDY . . . !' Tom had a twinkle of mischief in his eyes as he shouted.

'But that's horrible.'

'I don't care what they call me. I can handle it!'

David thought, *Aye, but you don't want to live up to it, though.* And there was no more to be said as he'd discovered, with no surprises, the overwhelming cause of the bullying and knew that his brother wasn't to blame. His father was a bully and he'd left them both with a bitter legacy.

David also knew that he couldn't blame himself for the boy's behaviour, yet that was no consolation. The way Tom was talking, it would take more than a pep talk from him to sort him out. He certainly didn't know what the answer was, but the school and its problems diminished, as his brother's future became David's overriding worry. He would have to leave it to his mother; there was nothing more he could do.

David looked anxiously for the fell top and was pleased to see the summit-cairn just peeping out of the mist. At that moment, he felt it the most inhospitable place on earth. The wind was so strong they could no longer hear each other shout, let alone speak. David took a woolly hat from his pocket and pulled it down on his head and over his ears. He checked Tom to see if his clothing was fully buttoned. He lifted the hood on the boy's jacket and pulled it up and over his head, and tied it, unceremoniously, under his chin, as his young cheeks flushed with the cold.

They didn't loiter, as David led them quickly across the grassy slopes on to the jutting white rocks of High White Stones and then back to the head of Far Easdale and the path homeward. With each step of descent, they quickly escaped from the cold wind.

Tom, still charged with energy, began to run as he could see the way before him, and Moss followed closely, glad to be out of the cold.

'Don't go too far in front!' David yelled. But the wind carried his voice away in a different direction, and Tom didn't hear anything of what he'd just said.

The mist began to clear as they descended into the valley below and the whole of their walk home was stretched out before them. David checked his watch and was happy they'd made good progress and decided that as soon as he could catch up with Tom, they'd stop to shelter and have another hot drink and some more to eat.

David had been thinking what it must be like to be a parent and have the responsibility of a young life, but with the promise he'd made he doubted he would ever be a father. He didn't want the accountability anyway, and neither did he want to inflict on anyone else this inheritance he had. He considered their future and wondered if Tom, in time, would have to carry this same load that he had to bear. Not that his own father had taken his commitment seriously, and David understood that it was only due to his mother's influence that he'd had any kind of family life at all. The only way his father had given him some consideration was that he'd shown him how to run the farm. But these skills had been passed on with such a bitter tongue and, sadly, David had struggled to live up to his standards. Neither did David do any fell walking for pleasure with his father. Most of the happiest times on the fells had been with Uncle Fred. They'd usually been on the same duty of looking for his father, and the old man's remarkable vitality and good company provided a welcome release from the anxiety of the search. Yet, David loved spending that precious time with Fred. But the beauty of the hills had often eluded him because of the grim circumstances he'd found himself in; walking in the cold and wet, when he would rather be in front of the fire. It wasn't until he started to walk alone for some peace that he learned to love the sanctity of the hills. He had favourite routes; ones that didn't hold any bad memories for him and these were the ones he regularly took.

David was daydreaming when his boot struck a rock it jolted him back to reality. He realised that Tom and Moss were only a few feet away from him.

'Davey . . . ! I'm starving. . . . What have we got left to eat?' Tom tugged at the fastener on the rucksack.

'Let's get some shelter first. Look, sit by these rocks.'

David sat across from Tom on a spare pullover, leaning his back against a rock. Comforted by the shelter, he crossed his legs and stretched them out in front of him and he noticed Tom doing exactly the same.

'I've been thinking of going to Old Trafford in a couple of weeks' time. Would you like to come?'

Tom stretched his spine to make himself appear taller. 'You mean it?'

'Yeh, I mean it.'

'What, just you and me, like?'

'If that's what you want.'

'Who's playing?' Tom asked.
'Does it matter?'
'No . . . no. . . . Oh man, yeh.'

They ate their sandwiches and David poured some more coffee. The dog sat in front of them, hoping for something to eat. Her brown eyes drooped, and her mouth drooled, hoping they would feel sorry for her.

'Quickly eat up or we'll get cold. We've done well today. We should be home before it gets dark.'

At the mention of home, the worrying thought that David couldn't recall that morning as he lay in bed hurried back to his mind. *Hannah Robson was coming out with them that very night!* Mixed feelings swam through his brain as he quietly sat eating his sandwiches. *Linzi would have to entertain her. She was her friend, not his.* He even considered staying at home. He would be tired after this walk. But then, as he recalled Hannah's Durham accent and imagined Tony trying to imitate her and tease her, it brought a wry smile to his face and he abruptly said: 'Right. . . . That's it, Tom. Let's get on home.'

11

FLIGHT OF THE WILD GEESE

He walked on the soft grass and his footsteps made no sound. The strands of grass blew frantically in the wind and looked like the waves of the sea, and then they were flattened to the earth by the force of the wind. David stumbled over the rocks but couldn't find the path. He shouted but no one heard, as no sound came from his mouth. The rocks ahead jutted from the ground like the white and savage teeth on a dead jawbone. The people following him were all silent. When he called out to them, they ignored him. He began to run down the hill to safety, but there was none, only grass and rocks – endless, grass and rocks.

'David . . . David. . . . Are you decent?' The voice from the door was female, and when David woke up he saw the form of a woman standing in front of him.

'Joanne . . . ! What do you want?'

'It's not Joanne you fool. It's me.'

David sat up in bed and saw Linzi.

'I'm sorry, Davey. Did I waken you?' She wasn't sorry at all.

David peered through half opened eyes. 'I must have been dreaming. I was well away then.'

'I'll say you were!'

Linzi walked over to his bookcase and started to fiddle with a few of David's things, sorting through his record collection, some of which were strewn about on the shelf and she put them back in their respective wrappers. Then picking up his snow scene globe of Blackpool Tower, Linzi shook it and watched the tinsel flakes falling to the beach, and wondered why he'd thought she was Joanne.

David sat on the side of his bed and rubbed his fingers

through his tangled hair, pushing it back off his face. He was still dressed in his walking clothes. 'Stop messing around, Linzi! What do you want?' and he shook his head to waken himself.

'Can you lend me twenty pounds? I'll pay you back as soon as I can.'

'Twenty quid . . . ! What on earth do you want it for? You still owe me ten from when you were over at Christmas!'

'Oh . . . ! Don't ask stupid questions. . . . It's just for this and that.'

'Twenty pounds is more than "this and that."'

'I've just got behind with things, that's all.'

'So you'd rather owe me than anyone else, eh?'

'Oh, don't be so mean! I've no one else to help me have I? I daren't ask Mum, and I just can't manage on my grant. Anyway, I'm starting a new waitressing job when I get back, so I'll soon catch up again.'

She came across and flopped on the bed beside him.

'Look Linzi, I don't know if it's a good idea to keep lending you money, and I'm not exactly flush myself.'

'Oh, come off it. . . . You can't be broke. . . . You never spend anything!'

'Now don't start getting at me or you'll not get a penny. I'll lend you ten quid, and that's all I can spare, but you'll have to pay me back as soon as you can, or there'll be no more.'

David reluctantly got up from his bed and rummaged through his trouser pockets to find his wallet. He turned away from her and carefully pulled out two five-pound notes and threw them down on the bed beside her. Linzi snatched at them and flung her arms around him, then started to mock kiss him on his neck and on his cheek.

'Okay . . . okay . . . go away now. I'm tired!' And with that, he fell back on the bed.

'Don't forget we're going out tonight, Davey?'

'I haven't forgotten.'

Linzi started to leave, and then looked back at him and said, 'Oh. . . . Will you pick Hannah up then?' and she left without waiting for a reply.

When Linzi returned downstairs she found her mother alone in the kitchen, busy at the sink, preparing the vegetables for tea. Shutting the stairway door behind her, Linzi moved up closer to Kathy and checked over her shoulder that they were alone. 'Is there something going on between David and Joanne?'

Kathy stopped what she was doing, putting the peeled carrots down into the dirty water. 'And what makes you think that?'

Linzi's interest was fuelled by the look of concern on her mother's face. 'Oh, something he's just said . . . something really strange.'

'What thing?'

'There is something isn't there?'

Kathy lifted a warm towel from the Aga to dry her hands and looked towards the stairs. 'I think David and Joanne must be seeing each other. But neither of them seem to be happy about it. I hope to God I'm wrong, though.'

'Oh Mum!' Linzi raised her voice, 'What can be so wrong with David dating Joanne?'

'I'm sorry, love. I don't want to sound prejudiced, but not the Milton girl, she's turning out to be kind of - odd!'

'Well, I'm sorry, but you are being prejudiced.' Linzi was whispering again. 'Joanne's a lovely girl and, anyway, David's not been acting what you might call, rationally, himself has he? Who's going to want him? Who's going to want to marry into this family?'

'Why do you have to be so blunt, Linzi? I just want things to be better for David that's all.' Kathy picked up a kitchen knife and started to peel the vegetables again.

'Better than what? Better than you and Dad you mean?'

'Let's leave it now, please, and don't you dare say a word to him.'

David continued to laze on his bed and closed his eyes, still feeling tired despite his nap; his dream hadn't helped. He guessed his body had relaxed itself too much after the walk. Sleep wasn't necessary, yet his eyes kept closing. He didn't really want to get up, yet he felt grubby. He knew he must wash and change, but was reluctant to do so. Glancing down, David saw the muddied trousers he was still wearing, his woollen walking socks hanging loosely on his feet; he hadn't even brushed his hair. He knew he was procrastinating, so with a surge of energy, jumped up off the bed to rouse himself and went to run a hot bath.

He didn't spend much time in deciding what he should wear; he never did, and with only a bath towel wrapped around his waist and his hair still wet, he reached for his blue, checked lumberjack shirt from the wardrobe. But something made him hesitate, and instead he took out a cream-coloured cotton shirt with dark brown buttons. He carefully examined it to check it was clean then slipped it on his bare chest. He then rooted through his chest-of-drawers and took out a pair of dark, pressed, cord trousers.

When he finally walked into the kitchen with clean dry hair, and more smartly dressed than was usual for him, Kathy cast a worried glance towards Linzi. David took the shoe polish from the sink cupboard and vigorously polished his best brown boots; that was even more worrying.

Linzi had arranged with Hannah that someone would pick her up at 7:30 pm. But she didn't say who that someone would be.

Hannah, like David, felt she just wanted a quiet evening in as she'd had a hectic day in the surgery. As she prepared for the evening, she had bathed and was undecided in what to wear. She was always more comfortable in jeans and pullovers and, not really knowing Linzi that well, didn't know how to dress. Linzi had given her no clues in her appearance at their first meeting on the bus and Hannah recalled Linzi had been unwell and had just dressed for warmth.

Hannah decided on a black, crushed velvet mini-dress, with a modest neckline. And, as a token for the cold weather, wore a pair of black, knee-high boots and a grey, fun-fur coat.

When she heard a car swiftly pull into the gravel driveway, she peered through the window down into the yard. She could see through the street light that it was the red-coloured Rover of the Keldas family. She strained herself further, to see who the driver was, but the interior of the car was in darkness.

Hannah hoped it would be Kathy and she wasn't certain whether Linzi could drive or not. So, feeling hesitant, she grabbed her shoulder bag, ran down the stairs and outside into the cool, windy night and jumped in the waiting car.

Through the momentary illumination of the interior light, Hannah saw her driver was David. But as they sat in darkness together, she had no indication of his appearance.

She briefly thanked him for calling, and he appeared to ignore her, but he hadn't; he'd just nodded politely and his gesture was unseen. All the bravado was gone and David was nervous.

Hannah felt awkward and the muscles in her throat tightened. She hoped she wouldn't have to talk much, at least not until she'd settled. But as David drove speedily through Windermere and then on to Ambleside, Hannah realised she needn't be concerned as it was obvious David wasn't going to speak to her at all.

Hannah was angry, yet she should have expected this rudeness from him. But the silence became uncomfortable and, as David recklessly negotiated each bend, Hannah was glad he was driving quickly as their journey would end the sooner.

In the darkness and the silence, Hannah's other senses were acute. She heard him clear his throat as if he was going to speak, he but didn't. She could smell a manly odour coming from him. Not a bad one, or an unclean one, but perhaps David's after-shave. Glancing at his arm, she saw he was wearing a suede jacket and she could smell the soft, mellow, scent of leather.

Hannah was surprised when out of the silence, David finally spoke. 'Have you had a good day, Hannah?' His voice was husky.

'Oh . . . yes. . . . Very busy.' She stumbled over her words.

'Have you been chasing cattle around?' A little clearer now.

'Oh, not today. . . . Just a few emergencies at the surgery. We had to operate on a spaniel that'd been knocked down and a few small animals to treat.' She coughed to clear her throat.

That was the end of the conversation. That had been enough for David. He couldn't think of anything else to say and he wished he'd brought Sarah with him. But then again, it excited him to be alone with her.

He couldn't make out Hannah's appearance through the darkness and didn't want to look at her. But he could smell the soft, womanly scent of perfume. He could also see her knees close to his hand looking tanned with the stockings she wore. He held on firmly to the gear lever with each change of speed, as he drove the twisty road through Rydal and on to Grasmere and Keld Head. He tried not to let go as he didn't want to move his hand any further away from her.

It was unusual for David to be the first in the pub. He was usually held up checking over the cattle or messing around with some unfinished work, or even just lacking motivation. But tonight he was the first. He'd put his head down as he walked down the lane, thrust his hands in his pockets and walked well ahead of the two girls. Linzi clung on to Hannah's arm, as they huddled together, walking through the cold night to the village pub.

David had easily managed to keep several paces in front of them. This suited Linzi, as the last words her mother said to her was: "*Watch over him like a hawk tonight!*"

David bought the first round of drinks and Linzi was quick to embarrass him and said he'd only bought them now because it was cheaper, before everyone else arrived. But David didn't find it particularly cheap, buying his sister a brandy and Babycham and Hannah a Bacardi and Coke.

The two girls removed their coats and flung them on the chair backs, and sat together in the corner. David stood at the bar, and for the first time Hannah saw him in a clear light. She noticed straight away how clean and well-groomed he looked, despite his dark hair curling over his collar. The wound above his lip was still discernible and left a scar that would stay with him for the rest of his life. He appeared taller than she remembered; perhaps it was just the cut of his trousers or maybe just his good posture.

Hannah felt comfortable from her vantage point, nestled safely in the corner. She and Linzi had picked up their conversation immediately from where they'd left off.

David brought the drinks across to the girls and went straight back to the bar. He rested his boot on the brass footplate, leant on the bar and chatted to the landlord.

Hannah, still suspicious of David, eyed him cautiously, wanting to learn more of his character. She was helped when another couple joined him, a young man with pale skin, freckles and long, red, curly hair. The girl with him was small and also pale, but she had the most beautiful red hair. It was brushed back off her face and tumbled over her shoulders and back.

'That's Joanne Milton. She's one of my friends. And that's her brother, Tony.' Linzi whispered in Hannah's ear. 'She's lovely, but he's a complete idiot and, not surprisingly, is our Davey's best friend!'

Hannah wondered why the girl didn't come across to speak to Linzi; she hadn't even acknowledged her.

Linzi continued to talk non-stop about life at college, but Hannah was distracted, half- listening to her and half- trying to hear what the young people at the bar were saying.

She watched the girl with the beautiful hair, standing close to David, but making no contact with him. She was listening to the two men talking, one much louder and more excitedly than the other.

David turned and stood with his back to the bar. He glanced across and saw Hannah looking at him. She was embarrassed when they made eye contact and she looked away. And several times throughout the evening, Hannah felt he was also watching her, but each time she looked at him, he purposely smiled and kept the eye contact.

Hannah also saw Tony Milton watching Linzi and guessed he liked her. Linzi did look attractive, more so than the poorly girl she'd met two days earlier on the coach. Linzi's dark hair was neatly cut into a bob and, for the first time, Hannah noticed the shape of her eyebrows. Linzi had beautiful, blue, deep-set eyes, much like David's.

As the girls emptied their glasses, Tony ambled across, grabbed a stool and sat at the table with them. 'Another drink, ladies?' he asked. 'So you're the girl trying to kill off Dave's cattle are you?' He looked directly at Hannah.

Hannah rose to the bait and with her view of Tony being coloured by Linzi's comments, took an instant disliking to him. She just smirked back.

Tony went to buy the next round of drinks, and David and Joanne came to sit down. For the rest of the evening they remained altogether. Tony still did most of the talking and, as usual, Linzi became irritated with him. He continued to tease Hannah as David suspected he would. At first David found it amusing but, gradually, he could see Hannah was agitated and that troubled him.

Hannah continued to eye David as she sat across from him. She watched Joanne looking at him, and her intuition told her that this girl was in love with David, but there appeared to be no reciprocation on his part. Joanne had hardly spoken a word all evening and Hannah thought she was either shy, or strange.

Then the more Tony drank, the more he fooled around, aiming most of his jokes either David's or Hannah's way and repeating words she said in her Durham accent. David sat with his legs stretched out in front of him, resting his beer glass on his folded arm and only half- smiling at his friend's jesting. Then, as usual, Tony went too far and he didn't have the self-control to stop. 'You're too small to be a vet, Hannah.'

'I get on very well, thank you.'

'I suppose it helps with the lambing does it? Getting your arm stuck in a sheep's backside and all!'

At this, David sat up and thrust his empty beer glass down

on the table. 'Leave it out mate . . . !'

'What's the matter, Dave? You don't normally stick up for women. She must mean something to you?'

David looked across at Hannah. She had her head bent low and was fumbling nervously through her handbag for something or other of no consequence. He also noticed a blotchy rash, from embarrassment, on her neck. He was incensed with Tony. Yet David should be used to it by now, but somehow this time it hurt, especially as he realised Tony was right. David didn't want the feelings he had for Hannah to end just now, so he ordered everyone a fresh round of drinks and was glad to escape to the bar, before he did or said something he might regret.

Joanne had been watching and listening. She too had felt a little sorry for Hannah. But with Tony's suggestion that David had feelings for the girl, she quickly changed her view. She'd also noticed David looking at Hannah, and consequently felt hatred grow inside her so intense that she felt could actually do her some harm.

She began to study Hannah's appearance and inwardly criticise her. Her stature? Too small. Her voice? Too common. Her eyes? Too big. Her taste in clothes? Too modern. The realisation of David's new-found dress sense also took on a greater meaning.

If anyone had been watching Joanne (and sadly, no one hardly was) they would have noticed a change in the colour of her skin. If you could monitor her heartbeat, you would find that it was beating at a rapid pace. Her teeth were grinding together, and her jawbone was aching with the intensity.

Almost unnoticed by all, Joanne rose, took her jacket and left the bar. It was only when the drink that David had just bought, remained untouched, that anyone realised she'd gone. And, ironically, the one to notice was Hannah.

'Your sister appears to have gone!' She looked at Tony.

But the others all knew of Joanne's turbulent nature and weren't moved or surprised by this. And Linzi, with a mercenary spirit, immediately started to loot the untouched drink. 'Well, there's no need to waste it!' she said.

David felt compelled to take charge of the conversation and steer it into a more sensible direction. But soon a heated debate developed as to who would make the best Prime Minister: a man or a woman. Then they argued about music, employment and politics, the state of the Cold War, and David had to change the subject again.

'I took Tom up to High White Stones today.'

Hannah was interested as David continued to talk passionately about the hills.

'The little monster messed about on the rocks. . . . He's no idea how dangerous that place can be.'

Hannah, intrigued by the change she'd seen in him hoped she could find out more about the walk. But Linzi didn't want to let her brother turn, what should be a happy evening, into a grim lecture on the dangers of fell walking and she interrupted. 'For goodness sake, Davey. Stop preaching!'

David knew exactly what Linzi was trying to do and, as he glanced again at Hannah, he guessed she would be watching him and waiting for a reaction, so he winked at her.

Her face relaxed at his gesture. 'No, please. I would like to know more, David.'

As the evening passed and the bell for last orders rang, David felt smug with his behaviour toward Hannah. He'd whitened his character and that was enough. He walked home ahead of the girls, with Tony in tow. They headed for the Milton bungalow for coffee and supper, assuming that Joanne would already be home.

They bustled into the bungalow and the girls threw their coats down on the kitchen table and headed for the sofa by the fire. David slung some sticks and coal in the grate; his last act of chivalry.

Hannah thought the untidy condition of this house was a stark contrast to the neat appearance of the farmhouse at Keld Head.

Tony shouted for Joanne at her bedroom door and, getting no reply, gently pushed it open, but all was in darkness. He held onto the open door and peering into the darkened room, momentarily wondered, but he knew worrying about Joanne was futile.

The cups of black coffee and cheese sandwiches wouldn't be enough to help any of the men become sober enough to drive Hannah home. It was too late in the night to expect Kathy to drive, so Linzi decided they would share the cost of a taxi. Tony was becoming irritable as he'd started to get a head cold and was searching the house for remedies. David had fallen asleep in the armchair and, unbeknown to Hannah, had done so out of contentment. No more talk was needed. He wouldn't take this any further. He remembered his promise and was satisfied with her approval.

The cab arrived and Hannah picked up her coat to leave. David was now in another world. She was dismayed at his lack of concern and reasoned that those fleeting moments of kindness and playful glances, where just momentary lapses in his normal chauvinistic manner.

Hannah left the bungalow and Linzi walked back up the lane to the farm alone, leaving David sleeping in the chair and Tony still hunting around for some aspirin.

Tony fumbled around in the bathroom and kitchen cupboards, desperately searching for a cure. Then he noticed an envelope on the kitchen table, where the girls' coats had been only minutes earlier. It was addressed to David.

He picked it up and examined it and, seeing that the handwriting was Joanne's, threw it back on the table and went to put the television on. It wasn't until he heard the clock strike midnight that he worried about his sister again. He went back to the envelope, rubbed his aching head and pondered, and then went across to David. 'Wake up, Dave. Wake up . . . !' Tony shook him by the shoulders.

David opened his eyes and, momentarily, didn't know where he was.

'Open this. . . . I think it's from Jo!' Tony thrust the letter right in front of David's face.

'Jo. . . . What do you mean? Where is she?' David sat up in the chair and rubbed his forehead. His eyebrows almost meeting as he scowled.

'Just open the letter, David!' Tony insisted.

And still not certain whether he was dreaming, David tore open the envelope and read:

Davey, I've gone to the tarn. I can't bear to be without you. I love you.
Joanne.

He then re- read the letter out loud to get the sense of it. But Tony snatched it from his hand to read it for himself. 'Stupid woman. . . . You stupid woman!' And went back to Joanne's room and this time put on the light, in a faint hope that she might be there. 'This is all your fault!' He shouted back.

David struggled to stand and he held up his palms in defence. 'Look. . . . Let's keep calm. It's okay. She'll be all right. We'll get some torches and go and find her. She won't have gone far.' Yet David felt anything but calm. He was trembling and he'd been woken up far too quickly. 'I'll put some warm clothes on and get the dog.'

Tony was almost distraught. 'Which tarn does she mean? There are hundreds of the blasted things!'

'Did she hear me say I'd been to Easdale with Tom?'

'No. . . . She'd gone by then.'

'And surely she wouldn't go up there at night! She must mean Kelbarrow Tarn, she goes up there a lot on her own and she knows we go there with the dog.'

'That settles it then. You go to Kelbarrow and I'll go to Easdale. I'll get my walking boots and tell Mum if we're not back by - let's say two-am - to call Mountain Rescue.'

David jogged up the hill to the farmhouse, not noticing the cold and not thinking the situation through properly. He collected some food and drink, gathered up the flashlights and called the dog, and told his mother not to worry. But Kathy wasn't as confident. Every time David went to look for George, either day or night, she always feared for him. 'I knew that girl would bring trouble. I just knew it!'

FLIGHT OF THE WILD GEESE

* * *

When David finally left Tony to search in the opposite direction, he did so with a sense of foreboding. He knew Tony was a good walker, but his headache and sore throat were probable signs of an imminent cold, or even flu. The last thing David wanted himself was to return to the fells, especially at night. He'd done this all before, and the memories were bad ones.

David really just wanted to go to bed. He'd had a pleasant evening; he'd enjoyed the girls' company and had been in good spirits. But now, as he walked, his dog his only companion, he knew this problem was all his own doing. Tony was right to blame him. He'd led Joanne along, when he should have stopped it. He'd hoped it was just a crush she had on him and that it would soon pass. He admitted to himself that he liked the attention, and he hadn't wanted to upset her by rejecting her; yet, his actions and his silence had probably hurt her more than he'd imagined.

He walked on into the wind; the path took him up high to the valley beyond. The night was, thankfully, a clear one. He wanted to save some of the life in his flashlight and once his eyes became accustomed to the darkness, used it only momentarily. Moss followed close at David's heels and her presence comforted him. He put his hand in his pocket and felt the crumpled envelope from Joanne's note, and the feel of it and the task ahead brought reality home to him.

As he walked, he worried if he'd made the right decision and maybe they should have stuck together. It would have been safer. He should have insisted Tony took the dog with him. Then he tried to shout Joanne's name but, again, his voice was lost to the wind. He was glad it was dry and hoped she'd at least put some warm clothes on. He'd worried, as Tony had, that his conduct had driven her to this crazy scheme.

He shouted: 'Joanne . . . ! Joanne . . . !' David was breathless as he reached the steep incline to the ghyll. He guessed he was near the falls as he could hear the rushing of the water forcing its way to the valley below. In the darkness he stumbled and almost fell on some hidden rocks, banging his knees. He walked quickly, almost running at times as the gradients eased again, walking much faster than he'd done that morning with Tom.

'Man, I wish I was in bed!' he cursed, and wondered what he'd do if Joanne wasn't at the tarn. Then he reassured himself, that Tony would probably be at Kelbarrow by now and maybe he'd already found her.

Tony tried to run up the hill, but couldn't. He felt unfit and unhealthy. His torch just managed to light up the path in front of him.

Coming out from the woodland onto the open fell, the wind hit him with such ferocity it almost pushed him over. He desperately wanted to go back, but couldn't. He felt angry with David, which perhaps gave him the adrenaline he needed to keep his body moving.

He couldn't believe David's behaviour. He was always putting him down for fooling around and yet David's constant need for approval and to be loved was far more destructive. Tony also felt angry with his sister. She was just acting crazy, thinking she wouldn't have done this if their father hadn't gone away so much. Nevertheless, he too worried about her sanity - to have walked out on a night like this, and expect David to run after her was mindless. He thought about David on the other side of the valley; how cold it was here on this fell side, and he knew it would be worse in Easdale.

In the hazy distance the lights from the village below comforted him; Tony doubted that David would see anything. He knew he would reach Kelbarrow before his friend reached Easdale and, although David was fitter, it was a much longer walk. A faint noise of the clock chiming from the church below rang out eerily as the wind carried the noise up the hills to him. He shouted, 'Joanne . . . ! Joanne . . . ! It's Tony!' but he didn't get any reply. A few specks of rain touched his face and it urged him to quicken his pace.

FLIGHT OF THE WILD GEESE

* * *

David felt the terrain ease under his feet and could just discern a path leading to the left, and knew he was over the worst of the climb. He guessed he had left Sour Milk Ghyll behind and hoped he was still on the right track. He shouted again but heard nothing. Maybe Tony could hear him as he climbed across the valley, his voice blowing westward.

David's body was hot with the exertion, and he felt his chest and back soaked in sweat under his heavy coat, yet his ears were aching with the cold. He stopped to put on a woollen hat. The dog was still at his side; she too was anxious of the dark and of the cold wind ruffling up her thick coat.

He pondered at how different the day had turned out, from the enjoyment of walking with his brother that morning, then flirting with lovely Hannah that evening, and now the chore of searching for Joanne when he should be in bed. But, as he turned into Easdale for the second time that day, he felt a flash of panic and sensed he was walking into a wall or some kind of trap. This was the place that Wordsworth called (and for good reason) The Black Quarter.

David knew the fells here and he knew the people; the farmers and their men; the mountain enthusiasts; the wild men and the gentlemen. He never feared the spirits of dead poets who once walked these paths, or the vagabonds, rogues and statesmen. Grasmere had housed a few characters and David was generally not afraid of any of them, but he knew for a certainty, that many had been afraid of his father and were fast becoming wary of him.

He stopped for a moment, unable to move, and put his back to the wind. He felt a slight spray of water hit his face, but he had to continue regardless.

He bent his head into the rain and trudged on.

Tony had just passed the forestry marker and guessed he was approximately halfway. Just a steep climb to the summit, then perhaps he would be out of the wind and the rain and safely in the small basin that held Kelbarrow Tarn. He could then search the tarn and shelter behind some rocks. His thoughts of turning back diminished as he realised he was near his objective; climbing higher and further away from safety, his head pounding again and his breathing, fast and erratic. Apart from the wind, his beating heart was the only other sound he could hear.

His flashlight grew dim as the batteries weakened, and he cursed David again for not replacing them sooner. The tresses of his long red hair became tangled and wet as they clung to his head and face. He tried to push his hair aside and wished he'd worn a hat. He pulled up the hood on his army surplus Parka and tied it under his chin, but the wind found every gap.

Safely reaching the flat plateau to the tarn, Tony started to hunt for the space in the wall, struggling and stumbling over the rocks as he did so. He found a gap and crept through to the other side, then fell to the ground behind the slate to shelter for a moment.

He sat there on the sodden turf, no longer caring whether he was wet or dry. The damp from the ground soaked his thighs and his buttocks through the thin cloth of his trousers and coat. The torch was lying on the wet grass beside him, its weak beam now fading upwards into the night sky and, in the faint glow, he noticed the droplets that he'd thought were of rain contained flakes of snow. Tony just wanted to stay there and sleep but knew he must make one more attempt to shout and search around the tarn before he could go home. He wasn't sure if he had the kind of unselfish love needed to put his sister's life before his own as the tiredness he felt overwhelmed him, making his choice harder.

'Dear God, help me?' he begged, as he struggled to his feet again. And he walked on in the direction he believed to be eastward, as the wind swirled around him in all directions. It was pushing him along, hitting the back of his head and jacket, then blowing him aimlessly sideways, then head on into the fell. Then, almost running, his feet splashed in water and he realised he was at the edge of the tarn. Standing on the shingle, he struggled to keep his balance to stop himself from falling. 'Joanne . . . ! Joanne . . . !' he repeated. Then he shone the weak beam of the torch across the watery surface, but he saw nothing, only the small waves of the tarn, whipped up by the wind and splashing against some rocks.

Then he started to run around the tarn and, with his objective now reached, it spurred him on to continue; running and stumbling, but he found nothing, only himself, like a madman, circling the dark expanse of water.

David's fear intensified as he walked further into Easdale. Who was behind him? Who was in front of him? Was the stranger he'd seen that morning still there, sitting on the rocks, waiting for him? He thought he heard a reply, but it was just the wind teasing him. He switched on his flashlight again and tried to face full north, hoping the tarn would stand out before him, but all he could see was a white haze, as snow began to fall, thickly and rapidly. It was like the tinsel in his glass snow scene globe, safely placed on his bookcase at home.

'Thank God, I'm nearly there,' he mumbled, when a sudden flapping noise terrified him. He'd reached Easdale Tarn and the same wild geese that he had seen that morning were startled into flight. And from the safety of the rocks, David could only watch as the grey and white on their wings flashed up and skimmed across the water, off into the darkness, leaving behind them an eerie silence.

He lowered his hands, and like a blind man began to feel for the rocks, then momentarily sat down to get his bearings. Moss stayed close beside him, her wet body pressed against his legs and dampening his trousers. 'Come on Moss . . . find Joanne? Go . . . ! Go . . . !' The dog panted excitedly as David started to run behind her, trying not to stumble on the uneven ground, and flashing his torch across the surface of the water. 'Joanne . . . ! Joanne . . . ! It's David . . . ! It's David . . . !'

On and on he ran, around the tarn; shouting and waiting, stopping and listening, but hearing nothing. David feared that he was too late; Joanne must have been gone hours. She could even be dead by now, if she'd misjudged the weather. 'Joanne!

Joanne, please. Hello . . . ! Hello . . . ! Hello . . . !' David shouted in despair, almost in tears; the snow was hitting him so hard in the face that his skin was tingling and reddening with the cold.

He thought if she were out in this, she wouldn't last long. If Joanne wasn't at the tarn then she must be sheltering, but where he didn't know. He knew no one could go much further unless they had a torch. Maybe she was too afraid and had turned back? Belle's Knott and Easdale Crag surrounded him like a barricade. David knew there was no more he could do, except to hope that Tony was right, and that she'd gone to Kelbarrow Tarn after all. Of course! That would have been her best option. They did go there a lot. She could manage that walk easily. Yes, that's where she would be. Tony will find her, and Joanne will be safe.

Reluctant to leave the tarn, he shouted once more and flashed his torch to the nearby crags and stopped and listened. He looked at his watch under the light and could see it was 1:00 am, and knew he must hurry back before his mother called the rescue team. He could just do it if he ran; hoping all the time that on his return, Joanne would be back at the farmhouse. 'Be careful now. . . . Don't fall,' he said to himself knowing he could easily break his ankle or wrist. Then he began to run, lifting his feet high above the rocks like a fell runner would. The wind was now behind him and he slipped on the wet snow, running and jumping, his flashlight on all the time, pointing its beam to the path below, watching for hidden rocks. Down and down steeply and on past the falls. His lungs were aching with the cold and his heart was pumping hard.

He found a soft level piece of grass just by the ghyll, and for a few minutes rested to shelter out of the wind.

Tony continued to run around the tarn. Three-times he ran. First one way, then the other, shouting her name in despair. 'It's no use,' speaking to himself for reassurance. 'No use at all. She's not here. She must be across at Easdale with David. She must be. I'll kill her when I see her. Joanne . . . Joanne . . . I'm going home . . . I've had enough. I'm frozen . . . I'm done for!' And the beam of the torchlight became so weak that it was near useless, so he hurled it across the water and it splashed into the tarn. He then walked on blindly into the blizzard, stretching his arms out in front of him and feeling for the perimeter wall again. Then stumbling on and over some rocks, his body hit a solid object. Feeling it firmly with his hands to find the base, he realised he was at the wall. Slate and rock tumbled with him as he slithered to the ground for safety and, instinctively, Tony drew his legs underneath him as he huddled into a ball, wrapping his arms around himself. Coughing, and in total desolation, he remained on the ground.

David couldn't settle. He knew it wasn't safe to stop for long. So, with a momentary rest for his racing heart, he lifted himself again and was about to leave when he thought he heard a faint cry, one so soft and weak that it was almost a whimper. The dog's ears pricked at the sound and she ran off, and David followed her around the rocks, towards the ghyll. There it was again: 'Help me . . . ! Help me . . . !'

'Joanne . . . Joanne . . . it's David. . . . Where are you?'

'Help me, Davey. . . . Help me, please!'

The feelings of relief were sheer ecstasy, almost in a frenzy now as David could see in his torchlight, huddled under the rocks and beside the ghyll, the small outline of a woman.

He ran to her, his hands grasping on to the wet rocks as he steadied himself, jumping down, still slipping and stumbling and calling her name.

Joanne couldn't move. She daren't move. She hoped the man struggling toward her *was* David, and the sight of the black dog told her it was. She sobbed tears of relief and happiness and knew what a fool she'd been in doing this to him. But he had come. He'd searched for her in this awful weather.

He crouched down by her side and the wet snow soaked his

aching knees; his whole body was trembling. Joanne used the last drop of energy she had to cling to him, clutching at his body and hysterically calling his name. 'Davey . . . ! Davey! I love you . . . ! I love you.' But he ignored her.

He stripped off his jacket and wrapped it around her, then took out of his rucksack a thick pullover for himself. 'It's alright Jo. . . . You're safe now. You're safe.'

David took out some biscuits and gave her a drink of coffee from the flask. His hands were shaking as he poured. 'We'll soon have you home,' he whispered and came up close to her face. 'Don't cry now. We must go quickly or we'll both be done for.'

He pulled her to her feet, but she clutched at his arm, resisting him. 'Davey. . . . Say you love me, or I won't come back!' Snowflakes were sticking to her face.

David couldn't believe her defiance as he tried to pull her again. 'Please come now! Tony's up at Kelbarrow Tarn looking for you. We've all been worried sick.'

'Then tell me you love me. . . . Tell me! You must love me, Davey. . . . Please, please say you love me . . . !' She began crying hysterically again. 'You must tell me. You must marry me! I love you so much.'

'I do love you,' David lied. 'But I can't marry you. You don't know what you're saying.' He looked hard through the darkness into her face, and shook her by the shoulders, but she persisted.

'Then, if you love me, you must marry me. Tell me you'll marry me! Please tell me. I'll not leave until you tell me.' She struggled to stand up and pushed him away, and the snow whipped around their young faces.

David grabbed her to pull her to the path and tore the sleeve on his coat, pulling it away from her shoulders as she resisted him again. He was cold, he was wet, he could hardly see, he could hardly hear. 'Joanne, stop bitchin' around. . . . Don't be stupid . . . I'll never marry anyone. No one . . . ! Ever . . . ! How can I?'

'But I love you, Davey. No one loves you like I do. So, say it

Davey . . . Say it, please! I beg you.'

'I can't say I'll marry you. I'll never say it to anyone. I'll end up as reckless as my dad. Can't you see it! Who wants a fool for a husband . . . ? Tell me, who?' David pleaded. 'Don't you see it's useless? It's my inheritance. Not the farm - not Keld Head, but just evil - evil stuff. The dice is loaded against me, Jo.'

He pulled her again so hard, holding her by the wrists. He knew he was hurting her, but he didn't care; they couldn't stay any longer. So almost dragging her, they left the confines of the rocks and went together, stumbling and falling, down the steep path below, on to safety, back to the village and back to the warmth.

Joanne never said another word, she just cried. Some were tears of anguish, some of pain at the feel of his strong hands, grasping hard against her wrists and arms. Down they struggled, neither speaking, David with a sense of total bewilderment. He'd felt that with one more plea from her, he would have weakened. He was so close to giving up his promise for her, and it was only brute strength that saved him from a careless declaration. But now he was too tired to think anymore. His only objective was to get her to safety, back to the village and not let her go. What happened after that he couldn't think or say.

The lights of Grasmere peeped through the white haze. The new bridge and the easy path lay in front of them. Checking his watch he realised he was late. It was 2:20 am and his mother would be worried senseless and would have already called the Mountain Rescue. If only he could shout and tell her they were safe. Just the walk across the village and then up the long and tedious lane to Keld Head, and they would be home. Joanne was still struggling, but with less defiance. But David couldn't release his grip; he daren't.

Grasmere was in silence as the snow falling steadily, sticking to the pavements and trees. No one to see them or hear them, no one to worry. David held on to her like a man with evil intent and, hoping all the time they wouldn't be spotted, he walked as quickly as he could, still clutching the girl in his arms.

He could see the lights in the distance up at Keld Head. He wanted to fall to the ground and sleep.

Kathy must have heard the click of the yard gate and, as she rushed to the outside door to meet them, she saw the pitiful sight of her son with the distraught girl in his arms. 'Oh, Davey. . . . Thank God you're safe!' She rushed to him and pulled him indoors. Linzi held on to Joanne, as she fell into her arms and rubbed her wrists, relieved to be free from David's clutches.

'Did you call the Mountain Rescue?' David gasped.

'I had to love. . . . We were worried. I did as you said. Don't worry Davey, at least you're both safe. Get your wet things off. We'll look after Jo and I'll ring them and apologise. Maybe they won't have set off yet.'

David struggled to walk up the stairs, pulling his wet pullover and shirt off him at the same time, not thinking. But as he was about to fall on his bed he suddenly remembered Tony and, half-naked, almost fell back down the stairs to the kitchen. 'Where's Tony?'

'He's not here, love. . . . He must be at home.'

'He can't be at home. We arranged to meet here.'

David grabbed another coat and ran from the farm down the lane and bursting into the bungalow saw it was in darkness. 'I can't do this . . . I can't do this . . . !' He was standing desolate in the doorway, when he saw the blue flashing lights of a rescue Landrover coming up the hill.

The driver spotted David, and as he frantically waved his arms he fell exhausted onto the gate. 'Please help. It's my friend. He's at Kelbarrow Tarn!' he struggled to speak.

David felt the warm arms of his mother rest on his shoulders and she walked him slowly back up the hill, and then up the stairs into his room. 'Come on, Davey. Come home, son.'

'Where is he, Mum...? He should be here!'

'They'll find him...don't worry...he'll be fine.'

* * *

Joanne was still sobbing as Linzi took her to her bedroom. She helped her into some dry clothes and as Joanne undressed and rubbed her sodden hair, Linzi noticed the appalling bruising on her arms that she knew her brother had done. *What's this all about?* she wondered and shuddered.

12

ROCK SOLID TRUTH

Kathy tiptoed up the stairs, not wanting to waken the young children. She was holding a hot mug of tea in her hand as she crept into David's bedroom. He was sitting on the side of his bed with his head in his hands, bare-chested, and had a large bath towel draped over him. She sat down beside him and put her arm across his shoulders.

David leant his head on her chest; he couldn't speak or close his eyes. Crying wouldn't help; he'd gone beyond that. He was burdened with guilt and felt that if anyone should be lost, it should be him. One friend had almost died because of his foolishness and now he thought he was destined to lose another. He was so weak, he could barely move. No one needed to stop him from any more search and rescue; he just couldn't do it, despite the fact that he had let his friend down, and badly.

'You're safe now, son. Don't worry about Tony, they'll soon find him. He won't be far away.' Kathy whispered; her face close to his ear.

David still couldn't speak - not that he wanted to. But now at least he was able to close his eyes, if only to help shut out her words; he couldn't believe what she was saying was true and he wanted to blame himself. He should be the one punished, not Tony.

'Try and drink this tea. You must take in some fluids or you'll get dehydrated.'

There was still no reply as he sat motionless.

'I've rung 999. I think you should see a doctor.'

Still no reply.

Kathy tried to lift his head, but he couldn't look at her. She put the beaker under his lips, but he pushed it away. 'Don't Mum, I can't. Not until Tony's found.'

'I know you won't sleep until he's safe. But please take this drink, for my sake.'

David took the mug of sweetened tea in his trembling hands and sipped. And speaking in low tones with a voice that could melt the snow, he said: 'I've done wrong by Joanne you know, and I've done wrong by Tony.'

Kathy didn't reply and waited for more, but it didn't come. 'What do you mean, done wrong by Joanne.'

'Don't you see. . . . It's all my fault. . . . If I hadn't . . .' then he paused. 'Oh, this is all just stupid.'

Kathy sat bolt upright. 'Hadn't done what, David?' She pulled his head up to face her. 'What have you done? Have you been sleeping with her?' She tried and succeeded to keep calm.

David couldn't answer. He could see his mother looked confused, but for some time he couldn't reply.

'I'll have to marry her now . . . !' And in one bitter breath, David gave up his promise.

All types of crazy thoughts and ideas rushed through Kathy's mind. She couldn't understand what was happening. Linzi had assured her that nothing was going on between David and Joanne but her intuition told her better. And she now assumed Joanne must be having his baby. She wanted to scream at him for being irresponsible, but he looked so pitiful. She started to gently shake him. 'David . . . David. . . . What have you done? Have you got Joanne pregnant?'

David looked at her and scowled, and thought how absurd her question was, not realising how ridiculous his answer would sound. 'Pregnant! Why no, I only kissed the girl!'

Kathy pulled away and pushed herself off the bed and stood over him. 'You're just talking crazy you know that. . . . You don't have to marry Joanne! You've got everything out of proportion, David. You're over-reacting. You're beginning to sound just like your father.'

'Oh, that's what this is all about is it? I know you've all been watching me for weeks. Talking about me behind my back. . . . Don't think I haven't noticed!'

'No . . . no . . . David. You're wrong. That's not what we're thinking. I just can't believe you feel you have to marry a girl because you kissed her. It doesn't make sense, unless you're lying to me. So tell me the truth?'

'I know you don't understand. But this is the truth.' David rubbed his tired eyes. 'I will have to marry her . . . I led her on and it's all my fault. She could have died up there tonight because of me, and between us we may have killed Tony. The only thing I can do is to try and put things right again.' David raised his voice in defiance and gasped with sudden panic.

'You will NOT marry her, David . . . ! And that's that. I won't hear any more of this nonsense.' She had to insist.

In the morning when David woke up he wondered where he was. He was sitting in a plastic chair and leaning slumped over a bed. He could hear women laughing and some were whispering. Doors were banging and the noise was echoing around him. He could smell an odour that was neither pleasant nor terrible.

He tried to move, but his body was stiff; his back ached as he raised himself up from the chair. Wearing only a t-shirt and boxer shorts, he stood up and flinched as his bare feet touched the cold of the tiled floor.

Looking back at the bed, he saw Tony, lying pale and still. His red hair was sprawled across the pillows, and endless tubes and contraptions were hanging from him. Then Tony opened his eyes.

'You're a sight for sore eyes, Dave.'

Glimmers of memory melted the permafrost in David's brain and he said, 'Man, you had us worried.'

'Where are we?' Tony scowled with the brightness of the light.

'In Lancaster, and you're alive and that's all that matters. I'll get the nurse.' And David stood up and walked stiffly down the corridor.

ROCK SOLID TRUTH

Tony drifted in and out of sleep. He was certain he'd just seen David, but he was alone again and lying in a plain white room which was brightly lit. He had a burning pain in his stomach, and he couldn't tell if it was hunger or sickness. He also had a thirst so strong that it impelled him to look for water. He tried to feel around for a glass or a bottle, but was prevented by the tubes and pipes and a sharp needle thrust into the top of his hand taped up with Elastoplast.

Then a woman appeared; she was wearing a blue dress and had some kind of white cap or hair-band on her head. She was the most beautiful woman he had ever seen. Tony thought she could be an angel. She was tall and had soft, rose-coloured skin, and warm blue eyes. Her cool hands touched his arm and comforted him; his body tingled with the gesture.

He saw David again, but this time he was standing behind the woman, and looking over her shoulder. Tony felt comforted by the sight of his friend, and yet somehow he felt angry and he couldn't explain why. He wanted to shout at David, but didn't know what for. But this beautiful woman was interested in him, and she was ignoring David.

The nurse allowed David to stay with Tony. He gave him drops of water to sip, and held small portions of food for him. David didn't know how much memory Tony had of last night's events, and he hadn't mentioned Joanne's whereabouts in any of his waking moments so, as soon as they were alone, David wanted to let him know she was safe.

'Do you know why we're here?' David leant across and whispered.

'I know you've messed about with my sister and she's probably dead on some mountain.'

The words tore at David's conscience, because that's exactly how it could have been. 'No . . . Joanne's safe, mate. She's in another ward.'

'Did I find her?'

'No. . . . You had a good try though. . . . I found her. She was at the ghyll and in better fettle than you!'

'What have you done to her, Dave?' Tony didn't understand

and he sounded almost childlike in his question.

David paused. He didn't know what to say. 'You get some rest now. I'll go and telephone your dad and tell him you're awake.'

Tony couldn't remember anything about his rescue, just glimmers of being manhandled. Then the next thing he knew he was looking at a beautiful blue-eyed girl. The answers to his questions wearied him so he shut his eyes again; his chest felt heavy and it was a labour for him to breath. He wanted to dream again of the blue-eyed girl.

David rang Tony's father, who was still in Scotland. Keith Milton was relieved to hear his son was conscious and reassured by the sound of David's voice, prepared to make the long journey back to Cumbria. He partly blamed himself for Tony's waywardness and knew that Tony and David had been in a few skirmishes in their life, but for Joanne to have become involved, troubled him. Keith also knew she'd been unhappy recently and he would have to make amends. He decided to take her back to Aberdeen with him, to stay with his sister to convalesce.

David had also rung his mother. He told her of Tony's progress and Kathy was glad to hear him speak rationally again. She regretted shouting at him last night, but hoped some of what she'd said made sense. She hoped it was just ramblings from a mild dose of hypothermia that had made David say what he had.

'Is there anything I can do to help?' Hannah hung on to the receiver as she listened to Linzi's sorry tale, and was bewildered like everyone else.

'Could you drive us to the hospital? Mum's up to her eyes in it and our Davey's to be discharged.'

'Yes, of course I can, gladly. I can probably borrow Barry's spare car.'

Linzi hung up and looked at her mother. 'Hannah can help, Mum.'

'Good. Now, you keep Davey well away from Joanne, today.'

Linzi grabbed her Parka. 'You're over-reacting again. But don't worry.' She zipped up her coat.

'You don't know our Davey at the moment, love. He's unpredictable.' And Kathy knew she couldn't reveal to her daughter the truth.

David was at Tony's bedside when Hannah came into the room. She found him just as she had left him – sleeping, with his dignity completely gone. He was unshaven, looked unkempt in every way, and was bare-legged and weary. He was grossly surprised and embarrassed when he woke up and saw her standing before him; he had expected his mother.

If only he'd known Hannah's thoughts, David wouldn't have felt as uncomfortable. She had only tremendous respect for him, because of his brave rescue of Joanne and the vigil he had kept at his friend's bedside.

Hannah didn't know what to say at first, but she realised that the foolishness between them must end here. 'I've brought you some clean clothes,' and she gently rested a small carrier bag down on the bed.

David saw Hannah's uncomfortable posture and rose from his seat. 'Please . . . please sit here. I'll go and get another chair. Thank you for coming.' He took the bag and quickly left the room.

Not wanting to disturb Tony, Hannah tried not to move, but sat quietly looking at the drips, bottles and tubes surrounding him. She was familiar with this equipment, as she'd seen it all before in the surgery, and it revealed the serious nature of his condition. It was hard for her to imagine that this was the same young man that had teased her throughout the previous evening, as he was so still, but thankfully alive.

David returned, fully dressed, but still unshaven. His hair was brushed and he appeared to have more vitality and composure.

Hannah stood up.

'No . . . no. . . . Please stay there!' David gestured with his hands. 'Thank you for coming. I've been discharged, but I really want to stay with Tony. I won't be coming back with you,' and he shook his head.

'But your mum insisted!'

'Yes . . . she would insist, she always does, but I don't always listen!' He raised his eyebrows and Hannah guessed there was a hidden meaning behind his reply which she couldn't possibly understand.

Hannah had a dilemma, but the door burst open. It was Linzi.

David looked determined at his sister. 'I'm not coming back, Linzi,' he repeated.

'Don't be so pig-headed David. . . . You're coming home, and now. Mum can't keep coming backwards and forwards for you. Besides, Tony's dad will be here soon and Jo needs to get home to pack.'

'Pack, what do you mean, pack?'

'She's got to go to her Aunty Marian's in Aberdeen.'

David looked at Hannah and yielded.

Joanne was impatient and restless; she was fully dressed and sitting with some elderly ladies in the day room; angry and perplexed at her father's suggestion of taking her back to Scotland.

'Come on, Jo. . . . It's time to go,' Linzi beckoned.

David and Hannah were waiting in the corridor but at the sight of them together, Joanne retreated to the day room and whispered to Linzi, 'The staff nurse wants to speak to David.'

'Speak to David. Why?' Linzi just wanted to get him home, and was tired and frustrated at this unnecessary intrusion to her short break at home. She hadn't intended staying so long at the hospital as it was. But as they were whispering, the nurse arrived. She beckoned Linzi and David into a small office and closed the door. 'We're just concerned about the bruising on Joanne's wrists and arms. She said she'd done it to herself. Could that be true?'

David was slow to register what the nurse had just said,

when Linzi interceded: 'Yes!' She gasped. 'She probably did do it. . . . She's done it before. . . . She tries to hurt herself. . . . You see, she hates herself.'

David couldn't believe what his sister was saying, and quickly came to his senses as he realised Linzi was covering for him. But how could he have saved Joanne if he hadn't dragged her off the fells.

The nurse had a look of suspicion and David sensed she knew Linzi was lying. He held his head aloft hoping to hide the guilt. But his face flushed and the palms of his hands were clammy and, as he nervously rubbed his hands together, he saw the nurse peer at them and David guessed that his secret had been discovered.

As Hannah drove back to Keld Head, Linzi and Joanne sat huddled together on the back seat of Barry's spare car. David was sitting in the passenger seat next to Hannah, and as she carefully drove the unfamiliar car back through Windermere and Rydal, David found her caution endearing. How happy he had felt almost twenty-four hours ago when he was in the driving seat.

David shut his eyes; the daylight was a welcome change for him. The bright blue sky and sunshine were the result of last night's stormy weather. The snow was thawing and dripping off the roofs and gutters. He felt the warmth of the sun touch his face, the dappling of the branches of the trees shading him from time to time. Green fields, streaked with thawing snow looked like white threads in a silk garment. David knew there was no more he could do for Tony, and worried that he could be implicated with Joanne's injuries, was relieved to be leaving. He desperately needed to rest himself and try to re-think his future under more favourable conditions.

Linzi had been astute in her planning and, as her mother had insisted, never left David alone with Joanne. She took her straight to the bungalow to wait for Joanne's aunt.

When Kathy saw David, she protectively clasped him close to her. Hannah looked on and touched by their reunion felt like an intruder and left, unnoticed.

Hannah was unsettled for the rest of the day. She'd only a scant understanding of what had happened that night, suspecting Linzi hadn't told her the full truth. Why Joanne was alone on the fells at all, Linzi could only guess at, and then fabricate the rest.

The thought of Tony Milton lying in the hospital, desperately ill, while she was safe and well at home, made her feel guilty of how she'd judged him. He really had just been teasing her and Hannah guessed she'd taken things too seriously. She had a vivid picture in her mind of David sleeping at Tony's bedside, and then waking, with the forlorn look on his face. Her feelings towards her new friends had grown, even her view of David had dramatically changed from one of disgust to one of respect, and she found she couldn't stop thinking about him.

Hannah flicked on the television and tried to relax, but couldn't; she must be positive about things. She'd been nagging Barry for weeks about the state of his office, with papers scattered everywhere and bottles of medicine on the shelves that were out of date. Files were in the wrong order and the whole place generally wanted a clean-up. Barry had said if she ever got the chance, she had his permission to tidy things; Eleanor would never have the desire to do it. This surprised Hannah as this was Eleanor's livelihood, yet she showed no regard for it whatsoever.

It was no secret that Eleanor hated the animals. In fact, she detested the rural way of life. She'd rather be shopping in the city, meeting old school friends, commuting on the train to Carlisle or Preston; anything to get away from the Lakes.

Hannah grabbed a large black bin-liner, some dusters and polish. She'd promised Barry not to throw away anything of consequence, but she knew she could certainly find a bag full of rubbish. She started with the medicines, checking each date, and putting to the back of the shelves the newer stock in order to circulate it properly. She tidied the various bottles and packets, neatly arranging them in the storeroom. Her bag was soon crammed with out-of-date packets, no longer safe to use.

This is going to take me forever! Hannah regretted starting the job at such a late hour. She searched through the shelves and cupboards, looking for items to be discarded; for two hours, her mind was fully occupied by the job. She began to tire and decided to spend only half-an-hour more. She was discreet enough not to interfere with the drawers and baskets of statements and private documents, but just straightened a few papers and threw out some old circulars and the like. As she glanced through the box-files high on the shelves, there was one that she hadn't seen before; it was labeled, "Press Releases". Assuming these to be useful documents on new drugs and procedures, Hannah took the file down to look. Inside she found some magazine cuttings of radical ideas that had worked in healing sick animals. There were several advertisements and coupons that Barry had saved, recommending new drugs and surgical equipment. She became engrossed in the contents of the file and sat down in a large black leather swivel chair.

Hidden in amongst the other cuttings were press releases from the various local papers. There were photographs and articles written about Barry and other vets in the area; some were stories about farmers whom she vaguely recognised. She found some press photographs taken at the local agricultural shows of Barry putting rosettes on cattle and sheep and handing out prizes and trophies. She also found some old cuttings of young boys, proudly holding prize-winning calves, along with Barry in his much younger days. His hair was still dark with no sign of the ageing grey colour he had now. She smiled at his handsome face and his youthful appearance.

Hannah read the text under one of the cuttings, and was surprised to see that the boy in the photograph with him was David. It must have been taken when he was perhaps only fourteen or fifteen. Hannah found herself transfixed by the young, dark-haired lad, holding proudly the halter and rosette on the prize-winning Friesian heifer. But she was disturbed when she heard Barry coming into the surgery.

'Hannah. . . . Is that you?'

'I'm in here,' she shouted as she swivelled around in the large chair.

'What are you up to?'

'Come and see.'

'You're taking over then, are you?'

'I thought I better had, before they strike you off for selling out-of-date drugs! Look at this lot.' She rustled the large plastic bag beside her. 'It's disgusting. . . . You're so wasteful!'

Barry looked into the bin-liner and was surprised to see the amount of bottles and packets she'd collected and, picking out some of them out, read the date stamp to check she was right. As Barry continued to rummage through the bag, Hannah carried on looking at the press cuttings, gathering up the small pieces of newspaper and carefully reading them.

She found some cuttings that appeared to be new, not yet yellowed by age, and began to read as the headings caught her interest: Dated October 1973.

HAWKSHEAD MAN SHOT IN FAMILY FEUD.

The police were called out today to a serious incident at Keld Head Farm, near Grasmere. Retired farmer, Frederick Thomas Keldas of Hawkshead, was shot in the chest. 90-year-old Mr Keldas was rushed to hospital where his condition is critical. The police have arrested a man in connection with the shooting.

Dated October 1973

FARMER ARRESTED ON ATTEMPTED MURDER CHARGE

George Samuel Keldas of Keld Head Farm, near Grasmere, was today charged with the attempted murder of Frederick Thomas Keldas and the attempted murder of David Robert Keldas, at an incident yesterday at Keld Head. George Keldas has been remanded in custody without bail.

Dated November 1973
INJURED FARMER DIES

Frederick Keldas, 90-year-old, retired farmer from Hawkshead, died today in hospital three weeks after being shot in the chest. It appears Mr Keldas was protecting his great-nephew, David, when the incident occurred. The police praised Mr Keldas for his bravery, despite losing his life; he no doubt saved the life of his young nephew. Fred Keldas leaves a widow, Betty.

'Barry. . . . Is this about David's family?' her voice, shaky. 'Who are these people?'

'Ah . . .' Barry paused.

'I'm sorry, I shouldn't have been prying.'

'No . . . no. . . . It's okay. You're not prying. These things aren't private.'

Hannah placed the cuttings back in the file, and was about to close the lid when Barry took them from her hand. 'You really don't know who these people are, do you?'

'I'm - I'm not sure. Keld Head is the Keldas Farm, I know that much, but who was the man that was shot?'

'Linzi hasn't told you about her father then?'

'Well, no. . . . Not really. None of them speak of him.'

'Aye, that's right. They wouldn't. I'm not surprised at that really, I suppose.' Barry took an involuntary breath. 'You see David's great-uncle, Fred Keldas, was killed by David's father, George!'

Hannah put her hand to her mouth. 'Oh my goodness!' Gasping now, she tried to stand, realising that her question had stirred up an unwanted explanation.

'Don't leave yet. Hear me out . . . George was trying to shoot David, and the old man, Fred that is, stood in his way. Whether the gun went off by accident or if he intended to shoot, no one knows, only George Keldas.'

'But this is dated November last year, how can that be, we were at the farm then!'

'That's why I tried to tell you to be patient with David. They'd only just buried Fred the day before we called. The lad's had a tremendous shock and that's why he was so sullen.'

'But why would a father want to kill his own son?'

Barry put his arm around her shoulders. 'George Keldas was the most belligerent person I've ever met. . . . He became crazed - jealous too, amongst other things. He accused David and his mother of all sorts of rubbish. He thought David was trying to drive him out and take over the farm, which of course was all nonsense.'

'So when did David's father die?' Hannah picked up the cuttings again and started to read, trying to find the answer.

'George Keldas die!' Barry replied. 'No, he's not dead - though some would want it - he's in prison!'

Hannah quickly returned the cuttings to the file, not wanting to touch them. 'This is bizarre! I've misunderstood everything you said. I'm sorry, Barry, I don't think I can handle this.'

'Well, I don't suppose you can, but then you don't have to live with it do you? David, Kathy, Linzi, and those dear little children do. They have to cope with it every day of their lives. Don't back off from them please, everyone else does. They're not to blame. They should be admired for battling on.'

'What will happen now?'

'There'll be a trial, as soon as the lawyers have finished arguing. Then probably, if justice is done, David's father will stay in prison for a very long time. The experts are trying to decide if he really knew what he was doing, but for now, the Keldas family are all safe and trying to get on with their lives.'

'Poor David. . . . Poor Linzi. And now they've had all this worry over Joanne Milton and Tony!' She thought of David again, and how he was that morning, sitting in the hospital, defeated. 'Oh, Barry. I wish I'd have known sooner. I don't know if I've said anything horrible to them or not! They must have presumed I knew everything.'

'Hey . . . hey. . . . You wouldn't say anything awful to anyone. If you'd have upset them in any way they wouldn't have wanted you to be their friend, now would they?'

Hannah's mind raced back to the conversations she'd had with them all, trying to recall David's actions; Linzi's unhappy life at college; Kathy Keldas, so attractive and balanced, how could that be when she's had so much unhappiness?

'So you see you really didn't know David well enough to judge him as you did.' But Hannah interrupted him. 'Oh, please don't, Barry. I feel bad enough about it as it is. He was like two different people. I didn't know what to think of him. First, he was rude to me, and then he was cheeky to the point of being obnoxious. Then the next time I met him he was charming, almost as if he was trying to win back my favour. He was flirting with me, but then there was nothing at the end of it! When I saw him today at the hospital, all his arrogance had gone - he was like a little boy. His eyes were almost pleading with me; they looked so dark. His strange eyebrows were frowning at me, yet beckoning me. He had teased me - one minute it's *"keep away from me. You're not good enough for me."* (Linzi had given her this perception of David.) Then he seemed to want me around. I didn't know where I was with him. When I met Linzi and Kathy, they seemed, well - dare I say it - normal - different from David.'

'People react in different ways to stress. Linzi's away most of the time. She hasn't been around to see all the trouble her father caused. George was devoted to her. He wouldn't do her any harm at all. David and Kathy always got the brunt of it. Maybe David has reacted badly, but who knows how it feels to stare death in the face through the barrel of a shotgun!'

'I can't believe this, Barry. How can you hate your own son so much?'

Barry chose his words carefully. 'No one will ever understand how George Keldas's mind worked' He didn't notice Hannah shudder. 'Come on. Let's get you some supper. You've done a good job tonight, don't worry about this anymore.' Barry led her away and, dragging the black bin-liner with him, put out the light and shut the door.

Hannah lay on her bed with her brown eyes wide open. She'd had a good supper with Eleanor and Barry; she only ate because they wanted her to. She felt they were trying to make her feel better, which of course they were. But now, lying in her bed alone, she felt uneasy. If someone had said: 'Do you want to go home?' she would have quickly packed her bags and gone with them. She had never in her life been close to so much tragedy as she had this weekend. To run away and keep her distance was the foremost thought in her mind. How could something as awful as this happen in such a lovely place? Murder was for some run down city, not for these beautiful hills and mountains. She knew she was being naive but this tale of Barry's stole away her dream of Lakeland.

She felt she could never set foot at Keld Head again, it would always hold this grim story; and to see David again would be impossible, she would view him differently. She didn't want to pity him, in fact she now felt angry with him for not telling her. But then why should he?

Then moments of guilt overwhelmed her. She felt if Barry suggested that they visit Keld Head, she would almost certainly go with him. In fact, something impelled her to do so; mainly to console Linzi, but also to apologise to David. She understood what it felt like to lose a parent. When her mother died, the emptiness inside had gnawed at her. She had thought it wrong to laugh, and to ever be happy again would be out of the question. She'd just worked and studied - anything to keep her mind occupied. But after meeting Linzi, and wrongly believing her to be grieving too, Hannah couldn't understand how she just wanted to have fun. She wanted to have new friends and start again. Linzi had unwittingly taught Hannah something. But now, as she thought of Linzi and her loss, she realised it was of a different nature, it was much worse, and there was no pride or pleasant memories of a beloved parent, there was only shame.

Hannah had sheer love and admiration for her dead mother who had courageously fought cancer, but Linzi had, in a sense, lost a father who no one will ever love and respect again; a shame that will stay with the family for generations to come; a family who people would gossip and snigger about behind closed doors; wondering if the children would turn out to be as evil as their father, and their fate not even settled.

She remembered the attractive man in the photograph in the kitchen at Keld Head. She was right to have felt uneasy about him. But for his family to keep his image displayed in the house, where he was no longer loved, only despised, she could not comprehend. It was as if he were hung there as a trophy of grim remembrance: *Do not remove me, in case I harm you too.* But what respect could you have from a family who no longer loved you or cared for you, who daren't remove your memory in case you are found innocent.

13

VALLEY OF DEEP SHADOW

George Keldas leant forward on the desk, his thin hands tightly clenched together in front of him with bony fingers knotted and entwined together; the skin on his face, sallow. His head was bent low and he was staring at the desk. You couldn't see his eyes but if you could you might feel that they were burning the structure of the timber beneath him.

In stark contrast was the beautiful young woman sitting opposite him. She was wearing a silver-grey fur coat, snugly wrapped around her. Her soft black hair was falling to her shoulders; her eyes were full of empathy and love.

They didn't speak, but waited for the noise around them to stop: the banging of the doors, the turning of the keys, and the stamping together of a pair of heavy boots belonging to a guard standing at the back of them. Then there was peace, an echoing silence. No noise except for the breath of the man behind them.

The young woman was the first to speak: 'You look poorly again today. Are you feeling unwell?'

'I feel sick all the time,' George whispered. 'My stomach burns like I've a worm gnawing at it.'

'Will they let you see a doctor?'

'This place is full of doctors, Linzi. . . . But they don't try to heal my stomach, they just try and mend my head.' He looked at her lovingly. There was no trace of the handsome face he once had, his deep blue eyes that used to be clear and bright, were now muddied with brown and yellow veins.

'You must ask to see a proper doctor then, Daddy. . . . You must insist.'

VALLEY OF DEEP SHADOW

'I've no right to insist on anything. They would want me dead! Then they would have no problems to solve, and they could all go home to their wives and babies and love them and forget all about me.'

'Don't talk like that, you only make yourself feel worse. . . . Anyway, I've brought you some money and left it with the guard, then you can get yourself a few things.'

'The only thing I need is some powder to kill this worm in my stomach – pain makes you act crazy, Linzi.'

They remained silent for a while. George twisted sideways in his seat, then stretched his spine upwards to ease the pain and cautiously held his side. 'Have you been stealing from Davey again?'

'I don't steal it, he lends it to me.'

'It may as well be stealing. I bet you never give it back again do you? What a joke.' He leant back on the chair and laughed. 'This is good medicine for me.' George gave a wry smile and then bent forward on the desk close up to his daughter and looked hard into her face. 'Take his money now, Linzi, because he'll soon have none.'

'I'll pay him back as soon as I can, you know I will.'

'Don't bother!' he threw his head back in defiance. 'It's my money anyway. And when your mother divorces me, you can have it all.'

'Stop it. . . . She won't divorce you. . . . She's never said a thing about divorce.'

George interrupted her. 'Aye, and do you know why? Because she'll be out on her ear. . . . I'd fight for every penny and see that she gets blamed for her adultery!'

Linzi tried again to alter the tone of the conversation. She was usually clever at this, but today she was losing heart. 'I've got a job as a waitress; it'll pay my bus fares, so I can see you more.'

'Now what do you want to see a miserable old git like me for?'

'You know I love you . . . I'll never stop coming to see you.'

'Aye well, mind you don't. But don't tell them, this is our

secret remember. Just me and you together. No one to interfere . . . no one to push me around.'

'They don't know I come. . . . They haven't got a clue. . . . They never talk about you. It's as if you don't exist. . . . Sometimes I think Davey wants to talk, but Mum just sweeps over things like it never happened. Besides, Davey's not been well. He looks thinner. I think he's doing a good job of the farm, though.'

'No wonder the lad's sick. . . . It's his own fault. . . . He's probably got a guilty conscience eating away at him. Maybe he's got a worm in his stomach too? He has that stupid look on his face all the time. You never know what he's thinking. He's laughing at me, isn't he? It's as well he doesn't come or I'll finish the job off proper.'

Linzi had had enough. She couldn't bear to hear him speak like this. She still loved her father and no matter what he did or said, she would never abandon him. She would always love him. She believed him to be the victim, not Uncle Fred; he just got in the way. It surely was a dreadful accident. She knew David to be infuriating at times with the arrogance he had, and an air of self-righteousness about him. She could have smacked him herself many times. Sometimes she felt she hated David then, other times, when she saw him playing with Sarah and Tom, she loved him for his patience. He would be devastated if he knew she was visiting their father. It had only once been discussed who should go to visit, but her mother had said it best to leave him be, and so they did, except for Linzi.

'I'll come again next week. Please try and see a doctor about your pains,' and with that, she kissed him goodbye.

George Keldas had seen a doctor; in fact, he had seen several. But he didn't remember; doctors were all the same to him. They gave him pills for his stomach, which he confused with pills for his head. He had a dim memory that someone had told him he had kidney stones, or was it gallstones, or even gravestones. George just didn't know. One day they would have to take him to hospital for an X-ray and then maybe some surgery, but to get him to co-operate was another matter. No one could ever get any sense out of him.

He was much aggrieved that he hadn't finished the job he intended to do; David was still alive and free to take his land and squander his money. George didn't expect old Fred to jump in the way. *Stupid old Freddie! Always poking his nose in where it didn't belong.* And George had reasoned, with a heart full of vengeance, that he'd done Fred a favour. *The man was as good as dead anyway.*

'Any way, if I see that lad again I'll wipe that smirk off his face for good!' These were the last words he spoke to Linzi.

It was raining heavily when Linzi left the prison. She ran across the wet pavement to the waiting bus; she was tired and hungry and had a long and complicated journey back to her lodgings. She wanted to cry; she always felt like this when she left him.

She thought her father seemed worse today, but at least he had talked to her. Some days he never spoke at all and only cursed her for coming. And then on other days he would ramble on and on, totally incoherent. Today he was bitter and there was still no repentance - never any repentance. She could tell he loved her and that meant a great deal, as Linzi knew she was his only ally.

Linzi would never tell anyone what he said to her, admitting his guilt or not. She dreaded the trial but, even if it meant going against her mother and her brother, she would never speak against her own father.

If Linzi could have talked to her mother, she would have found that she wouldn't have stopped her visiting; in fact, Kathy pitied George, as did David. None of them hated him; the only reproach they could give him was to ignore him. David had done this purely out of his mother's wishes, not to antagonise him. He knew his father was sick and it did grate on his conscience that he didn't visit; David hadn't seen him since the day of the shooting. As for Kathy, well she'd tried out of duty to visit but George's speech and behaviour was cruel and cutting and it pushed her away and the peace she felt without him was so wonderful.

Kathy knew that the trial would be the final reckoning, that the lawyers pleading his case would have to wheedle out of her any information that could either release him or incriminate him. It remained to be decided whether he was innocent or guilty; and hopefully to understand what his intentions really were. He surely hadn't meant to kill Fred Keldas, but had he meant to kill David? And David was the only witness left to tell, and what he would say no one knew.

As darkness fell, Linzi slipped into her apartment. Her fellow students were all home from lectures. Loud music was blaring from upstairs and the thud of its beat penetrated the bricks of the house. There was a television playing loudly in another bedroom, where someone was trying to compete with the noise.

Linzi's friends had wondered where she was, and why she hadn't been in lectures. She was well dressed but this gave no clue of her whereabouts. One girl presumed that Linzi had a secret lover somewhere and took frequent days off to meet him. She certainly kept them guessing, and in no way would she ever reveal to them her true destination.

Some of the girls did know of her family history and they'd comforted her and pitied her. One of her friends had been back to Keld Head with her, purely because she wanted to meet Linzi's brother. She had figured that a girl so beautiful must have a good-looking brother also. But she'd been disappointed in David's personality and shocked by George Keldas's attitude, so she'd, consequently, kept away.

Linzi made some tea and went straight to her room. Despite the noise and the company around her, she felt alone. But today she didn't mind; she wanted to think and plan how she could best help her father. She wondered how long she could keep this burden to herself, but her flatmates were not the people to confide in, nor were her family; she couldn't possibly betray the trust her father had in her. She guessed David wouldn't blame her for visiting: she lived nearer the prison than all the others. David couldn't possibly go, and he was already under stress as it was with the work load, the trauma of the shooting, and the trouble he'd been in over Joanne Milton. Linzi then had an idea.

She changed into some comfortable clothes, turned her stereo on to mask the other noise, curled up on her bed and started to write a letter. The only person she felt she could confide in without any prejudice was Hannah Robson.

Linzi had assumed like all the others that Hannah knew about her father, and as she'd never met him, would give her no cause to take sides. Hannah appeared to have no particular connections with her mother or David and she'd shown compassion over the *Joanne Milton* incident. So, taking hours in the writing and using pages and pages of notepaper, Linzi scrawled away and poured out her very heart and begged Hannah to keep silent.

While Linzi was secretly visiting her father, David was visiting Tony, as he'd promised. After finishing work each night, he rushed his tea, washed and changed ready to go to the hospital. He didn't care if he were tired or not.

Tony's health improved steadily at first then, as the doctors suspected, he deteriorated, as his cough turned into double pneumonia and he became weak and poorly. But his life was not in danger, and he slowly responded to treatment.

Tony wasn't in any hurry to leave the hospital. Initially he'd been too ill to resist and being severely weakened, slept long and hard, but in his waking moments, he enjoyed the attention he was given. He learned all the nurses names, and he knew who was on duty and when; especially those he particularly liked. He memorised all their rankings by the shade and colour of their uniform: the lilacs, the stripes, the greens and the dreaded navy blues. He knew those who were soon to take their exams, and those who'd just passed; those who were in charge and those who only thought they were. But it was Kelly who kept most of his attention and she gave hers to him; the young blonde-haired nurse who he'd first set eyes on, when waking in the hospital. Kelly was an attractive girl, but it was pure emotion on his part that turned her into an angel.

Although David had visited regularly, some of the nurses were still suspicious of him. To them he was a sullen young man with stunning eyes and, unbeknown to David, some had nick-named him *Heathcliff*. There was also gossip amongst them about David's role in the battered condition of Tony's sister.

Tony had never spoken to any of the staff about why they were out on the hills that night, in that he was loyal to his sister and David. And at times, when he became weak and tired, when his lungs ached with every breath he made, and his cough felt like it ripped his gullet, he did wonder himself what it had all been about.

Tony's father was satisfied with his son's improvement and returned to Scotland; partly for business reasons, but also in an attempt to keep a watchful eye on Joanne, whose poor mental condition worried him more than his son's physical one. Joanne was settled in at his sister's house in Aberdeen where she would stay until she was well.

The relationship between David and Tony had also suffered. At first, Tony was pleased to see his friend, although too weak and tired to communicate much. But, as time passed and he became stronger and more alert, he showed no desire to encourage David's visits. At first David put this down to Tony's illness but after one particular evening when David interrupted Tony and Kelly enjoying a bit of horseplay, he could see he was no longer required. Tony had obviously been flirting with Kelly as he was just taking his hand from her waist when David came into the room. Kelly was embarrassed when she saw David standing at the door and left, but Tony was annoyed.

David apologised, then tried to talk to Tony and admit his mistake about Joanne but, as usual, his words were not particularly well-chosen and he made a bungled confession, which Tony found unacceptable.

Tony knew Joanne had overreacted but she was still his

sister. David should have listened to him weeks earlier and apologised to Joanne face to face, and told her the truth about his feelings.

Quietly closing the door, David looked around. 'I'm going to ask Joanne to marry me, if she's still in the same mind.'

'What?'

'You heard, Tony. Don't make this any harder than it is.' David wandered across to the window and looked out into the night sky.

'I could understand if you . . .' Tony stopped and waited as there were footsteps passing the door. 'If - if you loved her, but I doubt you do,' he put the television on and fell onto his bed, then looked smugly at David waiting for more.

'I can love her.' David spun around.

It was hard to talk this way about love to his friend and the television served as the distraction it was meant to, as neither man looked the other in the eye.

'I once promised myself I'd never marry and leave Keld Head but I reckon with Jo, I can still at least keep part of that promise.'

The cat food advert now showing wasn't conducive to the emotion of the conversation, but the television was left on to be the mediator.

'You're a fool, Dave. You're playing into her hand.'

'I know, I know . . . but what else can I do?'

David had reasoned that he and Joanne could survive on the kind of affection he had for her, and if in some way he could make amends, then so be it. He couldn't live the rest of his life with the troubled conscience he had. And David did love Joanne, but not in a romantic sense, his love was born out of duty, the type that a man may have for a friend or relative, not the kind of love that should be between a man and woman. David knew that a type of love could exist between them, but as soon as it was fulfilled it would go, until next time. The love that was lacking was the type David couldn't understand, and the kind he'd never known.

The reaction David received wasn't unexpected, but he

hoped Tony would see this as a compensatory gesture and that he was trying to put things right and do his best for Joanne. And Tony's reaction was similar to his mother's: not quite as strongly opposed, but blunt and to the point.

'You must do what you think's right. But remember, Jo's infatuated with you, that's all, and it will pass. She's still young and inexperienced and maybe she'll cool off if you marry her. It's only because you're not giving it back, that she wants it. You love more when love is forbidden.'

And so the relationship between the two men continued to be estranged and David's future intentions were still not certain.

One evening while David was mechanically working and feeding up the cattle, he had the idea to invite Hannah to the hospital with him. Tony had spoken of her several times and said how much he liked her for her spunky attitude. He was nervous of making the phone call to ask her, but felt she would be a pleasant diversion for him. She'd shown compassion and had acted with genuine kindness, in giving up her time to help him home from the hospital.

David's decision was made harder because his feelings for Hannah had also changed, although he hadn't seen her since the day she drove him home from hospital. The thought of her friendship and the possibility of some reckless flirting with her would lighten his mood; he thought he could have some harmless fun and hope she may respond in some way. David certainly hadn't learnt by his mistakes, and his need for constant adoration, as Linzi had rightly implied, now showed at its ugliest. He was being a fool, forgetting the harm he'd caused by his meaningless kiss with Joanne and was now bent on a selfish course to win back some approval.

Driven on by anticipation, David pressed forward with his plan and rang Hannah's number. He chatted politely to Eleanor for several minutes, tapping his fingers nervously on the telephone table. She asked him to wait as she shouted upstairs to the flat for Hannah. Eleanor smiled and raised one eyebrow at Barry, when she told him who it was on the phone.

The gentle conversation with Eleanor relaxed David, but Hannah was a long time coming to the phone and the waiting made him nervous. Consequently, when the invitation was made, it was done in such an abrupt and disjointed manner, and was exactly the opposite of how he wanted it.

'I'm sorry, David, but I'm … er… going to a lecture tonight.'

David was disappointed and thought the excuse she gave was a lame one. He felt slighted and wished he'd never called. So on a cold wet night, he made the long journey to the hospital alone.

Driving carelessly through the darkness and with the windscreen wipers' regular beat the only noise to comfort him, David approached Kendal, pulled in to a lay-by and stopped to think. He wondered if he should turn back, thinking Tony wouldn't want to see him either. He would have to spend the whole of the visiting hour struggling for words, hoping someone else would come to help with the conversation. But Hannah's refusal had irritated him the most. Her rejection of him cut him deeply and, as much as he tried, he couldn't get her out of his mind and he began to feel just as Tony had said: *You love more when love is forbidden.*

David slid down in his seat in the darkness, rested his head back and shut his eyes. He was aware of the volume of traffic passing by, as car headlights penetrated and flickered through his closed eyelids. Gusts of wind blew at the car, rocking it gently from side to side. With the engine switched off, the car soon felt cold, so David folded his arms together and huddled them close to himself.

He didn't believe he'd ever felt so unhappy. Yet he was safe, all the danger he'd been through had passed and he'd survived. The anxiety of living with his father and his constant taunts had been dreadful, and now as he silently contemplated his present situation, he felt this was probably the lowest point of his life.

He had lost everyone: his father hated him; his mother had said he was a fool; Tony had rightly turned his back on him;

and now even Hannah had rejected him. The only person he could think of who would love him right now was hundreds of miles away in Aberdeen, and that was Joanne. He even considered that for one ounce of love he would turn the car northwards and drive on through the night to Scotland. It would be so easy, he was near the motorway, a few more hours and he would be there. Then she would throw her arms around him and squeal with delight at seeing him. She would hug him and kiss him; love him and welcome him and feed his starving ego.

David knew his mother had been watching him for days; so concerned at what he might do. He guessed she would be relieved that Joanne had been taken to Aberdeen, out of his way and, initially, he had felt the same. It had given him time to reflect, but his reflections were not balanced and his wayward idea to meet Hannah had further confused an already unstable mind. He didn't care how devastated his mother would feel, if only she knew how close he was to leaving.

He'd barely spoken to her since the night on the fells and a melancholy silence had returned to Keld Head. The only conversation they'd had was when he told her the reason for Tom's bullying, and he'd done this in such a matter-of-fact way that he had hardly told the true story about the name-calling. The seriousness of the situation had also diminished with the selfish yearnings of his own life.

David was startled by the sudden noise of a vehicle pulling into the lay-by behind him. The headlights shone brightly in his rear-view mirror. Not wanting to be spotted, he started up the engine and sped away, the wheels spinning on the wet gravel, flinging it up into the air as he drove on to his original destination. The danger had passed, the moment in his life that could have changed the future. But David's future was still on course.

He arrived at the hospital and found Tony's bed empty, then David heard laughter coming from the dayroom. Several nurses were with Tony. He was still dressed in his striped pyjamas and standing on a small table, singing loudly and performing a private cabaret; Frank Sinatra.

'... *And so ... I did it my way.*'

David stood and watched but didn't have the spirit to intrude, so he eased down on to a chair by the door. But his presence broke up the party and the nurses quickly dispersed. Completely alone with Tony, David was the first to speak: 'You're obviously feeling better then?'

Tony jumped down off the makeshift stage and went across to a coffee table and picked up some books and flicked through their pages. 'What have you done to my audience?' he asked. 'You're about as popular as a dead rat!' And turning his back on David, still humming the melody, he took the books across to a bookcase.

David continued, 'You've made a few more friends then?'

'Yes, and it's more than you've done, Turnip Head! You've driven them all away!'

'Well, that's the story of my life isn't it?' And he stood up to leave; he couldn't take any more abuse. He'd done his duty and was no longer required. As David stood and turned for the door, Tony said. 'They say I can go home tomorrow.'

David stopped and leant on the partly opened door as Tony continued to speak. 'Could you come and collect me then?'

'Depends what time; I can sort something if you want me to. How will you manage at home alone?'

'I'm not staying at home. . . . I've decided to go to London. I only need to sort a few things out, and I'll catch the overnight sleeper and leave at the weekend.'

'Are you well enough to travel?' David turned to Tony who was now sitting by the window, looking out into the night sky watching an ambulance scream in.

'I'm going stagnant here. . . . I've had plenty of time to think. If I don't go now, I never will.'

'What will your Dad say?'

'Who cares . . . ?' With that, Tony picked up a tangerine from a bowl, tossed it in the air and then started to peel it.

'Where will you stay?'

'Remember my cousin, Pete Milton? He's just come back from South Africa. He has a plush flat in Knightsbridge and a good job in advertising. He said he could put me up until I find somewhere myself. He may have some contacts. I'll try and sell a few of my songs.'

There was an unpleasant pause in the conversation as Tony continued to fiddle with the orange and David stood motionless. 'Look mate . . .' David pleaded. 'If this is because of me, I'm sorry - you know that. But you just can't leave like this, not when you're sick.'

'Don't flatter yourself to think this is about you . . . ! You're a fool, Dave, but then I suppose so am I.' Tony threw a small segment of the tangerine up into the air and tried to catch it with his open mouth. 'Do what you like with my sister. . . . I suppose she'll be better off with you than with anyone else, but if you hurt her anymore . . . ? There's nothing here in the Lakes for me - it's dead. A poxy job in Keswick, selling records to teenies. I'm worth more than that, I know I am.'

And David knew he was, but he didn't think this idea of Tony's was a particularly good one; who was he to say what was good or bad, when he was contemplating the most foolish decision of his life. Perhaps they would both completely mess up their lives. David didn't feel there was any more he could do, so without looking at him said, 'Let me know what time you'll be discharged, and either me or Mum will come and get you.'

'Maybe little Hannah will drive me home, eh?'

'I doubt it . . . !'

Hannah Robson had seen the red-coloured Rover parked in the lay-by and she wasn't certain if it was the Keldas car or not. The thought that someone may be in trouble or broken down crossed her mind. This had niggled at her conscience (unlike David, who weeks earlier had left her standing in the rain at the bus stop). She had driven right round the roundabout, double backed on herself and, recognising the number plate, pulled into the lay-by. She didn't know if the driver had spotted her nor did she know who the driver was. But before she could step out of her car the Rover sped away, flicking gravel and muck onto her windscreen, and she had guessed by the speed that it must have been David.

Hannah wondered whether he'd known it was her, and was unaware that in stopping behind him she had saved David from making a rash decision.

She'd borrowed Eleanor's car to drive to the university to attend the lecture. It hadn't been her intention to go out but, she couldn't think of any other excuse to tell David; she had to go out to justify herself.

It was the letter! If she hadn't received it from Linzi she might have gone with him. However, not only had she been told the full truth about the Keldas family by Barry, but she'd also been given an unwanted secret to keep. It had crossed her mind that David could be as wayward as his father and that would explain his roller-coaster lifestyle and mentality.

She felt, understandably, that she could no longer cope with this, and any further intimacy with David would not only cause her to feel she was betraying Linzi's confidence, but also be dishonest with him. This situation was far too difficult for her to deal with. She must keep out of his way. And, if David had seen her tonight and had fled away from her, then her decision was well founded.

Hannah didn't want to play any more of his games.

14

THE BRASS BED

Tony Milton sat with his back to the window of the overnight bus and tried to stretch his thin legs out in front of him, but this position hurt his neck. He twisted again and sat with his head back, but this position crushed his knees into the seat in front. He twisted to one side but this hurt his back and, as the night hours passed and daylight approached without him getting much sleep, Tony was glad when the coach approached London. He would soon be in Victoria and then a ride on the underground or a brisk walk and he would be safely installed in Knightsbridge.

It hadn't troubled Tony to leave Cumbria in fact, he was glad of it. Yes, the blue rocks and fells were beautiful, and although he'd lived with them all his life he thought the stone and the architecture of the city had more appeal. He wasn't so naive to believe that London's streets were paved in the proverbial gold, but felt this might be the chance to make a career in the music industry. Tony knew his songs were good and working in the city would stand him a better chance of success. It was also time he broke free from the security and restrictions of family and friends. For some that would mean marriage but, for Tony, although being twenty-three years old, he was still immature and could barely look after himself, let alone a wife. He wasn't indecisive, as he believed David was. He hadn't been cosseted all his life by an adoring mother and he wouldn't have wanted that, even if it had been offered. And Tony didn't hate the life at Keld Head as David once did. He recalled David's tearful plea in Blackpool, *never to return to the farm*, and then, as if to justify his actions in leaving his home and his friends, he found himself thinking more of David and despising him

Tony had been planning this move for sometime; much earlier than that dreadful night on the fells searching for his sister. And the many nights in the hospital staring at the ceiling had given him further desire to do something else with his life. He'd spent much of his waking hours composing and writing new chords, humming songs and melodies to himself and others.

He'd wondered as a boy what his future might be, but as a child could never envisage any life without the influence of the Keldas family; his exploits with David; his love for Linzi; the kindness of their mother and the impropriety of their father. And, in some ways, that would be the hardest thing to leave. His bungalow was never really a home; his own father was never there. Tony had long suspected he was having an affair with some woman up north, but had never dared to ask. And neither did he feel any more responsibility toward Joanne. She was always telling him she needed to be treated as an adult and no longer wanted him interfering in her life and her foolish craving for David had led her to this conclusion. And this was the turning point for Tony's decision.

Things were also starting to change for David. Tony was once proud to be his friend as David's strong body had protected him many times and his gentle disposition had steadied him. David's popularity had also drawn the admirers; especially the women. But this was all changing as David was. Tony could see David was becoming irrational in his thinking, sitting alone, brooding. He felt David was taking over from where George Keldas had left off. His handsome features were turning into a face lined and rugged, and torn with anguish.

Tony also thought it best to leave before his own father returned from Scotland. He knew he would object and he didn't want an argument. So, after just leaving a note on the kitchen table and a contact number, he left.

He was surprised that David hadn't called to see him the first evening he was home from hospital. He guessed that it must have been for genuine reasons as it was Kathy that had brought him home. It had been late in the afternoon when he'd been discharged and that would have meant David would be working. Tony knew it was cruel not to see David before he left, and maybe one day he would reconcile himself to him again but, just now, he'd had enough. Tony knew his sudden departure would hurt David, but Tony didn't care; David needed to be treated in the way he'd treated others.

As Tony had left Keld Head at 5:00 pm yesterday evening and he'd walked down the hill, the only noise he heard was coming from the pulsator of the milking machine. Tony thought David would be washing down the dairy and tidying up for the night. He could have so easily called in for just a few minutes, for one last goodbye, but no. It was best this way, he thought; Joanne was safe in Aberdeen, barred from returning and irritated to have to stay with her aunt. And, as far as Tony was aware, she still had no clue of David's intentions for her. This was a decision that he knew David would dither about for a while and Tony didn't want to be around to await the outcome.

The coach pulled into Victoria and Tony clambered down the steps, throwing his hand-baggage in front of him and carrying his guitar in its case over his shoulder. He was glad of the chance to stretch out his aching body.

It was a fine morning and the sun was just beginning to rise. He was happy to be leaving the stinking smell of the diesel filled coach station behind him; the fresh air enticed him, so he decided to walk all the way to Knightsbridge. It was too early in the morning to waken his cousin and the walk would pass some time and revive him.

The cool city air lifted his spirits and he started to hum to himself as he pulled out from his bag an A-Z and searched for the way to his cousin's apartment. He thought of Keld Head and, ironically, the only person up and awake would be David doing the early morning's milking. The only other movement would be from the daffodils wagging their heads in the March breezes. But London was alive with street cleaners, dustmen, postmen and milkmen. The bag people were already leaving the warmth of the coach station and begging for money and a hot drink.

The smell of frying sausages coming from a diner tempted him. He ordered a coffee and a bacon roll while he sat at the table with all his worldly goods splayed on the floor.

When Tony started to walk again, he struggled with his luggage and wished he'd taken the tube. He was weaker than he'd anticipated, as this was only his first full day out of hospital. The cold March air hit the back of his throat and felt like it would cut his lungs to shreds. He started to cough and had to stop to hold his aching side.

As he approached Knightsbridge, the prosperity of the area was clear. He passed some high-class stores and looked longingly through the windows: suits, ties, leather goods, all with designer labels, un-priced and, as Tony guessed, unaffordable, at least to him; his own appearance was now out of place. In the Lake District, he would have blended in well with his green army surplus coat and flared denim jeans. He had a hope, one day, if his dreams came true, he could afford to shop here. Maybe buy a new suit and tie and have his own apartment like his cousin.

He checked the street names with his map, he checked the numbers on the doors; admired the beautiful iron railings and the majestic Georgian exteriors of these tall houses; slowly wandering along the tree-lined avenues as early blossom like confetti, peppered the streets. Tony counted the numbers. The buildings grew larger and grander with steps and terraces leading up to front doors with polished brass fittings on glossy paintwork. This was it. This was Rievaulx House.

Glancing at his wristwatch, he pressed the brass doorbell and waited, hoping by this time his cousin would be up and dressed; it was 7:35am. With no reply, he pushed open the heavy front door and entered a hallway, paved with black and white mosaic tiles and walls of panelled in oak. There was a large hallstand holding a heavy vase filled with fresh and

THE BRASS BED

exotic flowers. A gold framed mirror highlighted Tony's unkempt appearance and caused this ordinary lad from up north to comb his red and curly hair. He pulled back the metal shutters on the lift and pressed the button for the second floor and Flat 6b. The flat was soon in front of him but taped on the door was a white envelope addressed to him.

He ripped it open:

Dear Tony,

I've gone to Edinburgh for the week on business. I'm sorry I wasn't here to welcome you. The key is at 6a. Please make yourself at home. You're in the blue room.

Regards.
Peter Andrew Milton.

He collected the key from the young man at 6a. Tony was easily recognisable as Peter Milton's cousin as they both had the same red hair, except that Tony's was much longer.

Disappointed that Peter was away, Tony entered the flat; the early contacts he'd hoped for would have to wait. He was also disappointed at his recovery; when he'd been discharged from the hospital, he'd felt well, but today after his walk he was weaker, in fact, quite unwell. The pain in his back had returned. He felt feverish and he knew he looked sickly. He was always pale; that never changed, but he didn't usually have this deathly grey look about him and today his eyes were reddened and tired looking.

Tony's bungalow in Cumbria seemed a lifetime away from the wealth here in Knightsbridge and he couldn't help but compare. The untidy and grubby condition of their bungalow, (partly his own doing,) stood in stark contrast.

Overlooking the street below was a spacious lounge. It was decorated with just a few choice items: a large red Chesterfield sofa was strewn with velvet cushions. White muslin drapes decked the windows, with heavy velvet curtains cascading to the floor. A cream coloured shag-pile carpet was covered with a deerskin rug. There was a black and chrome Hi-Fi system in one corner and masks and carvings from Africa on the walls. Tony checked his shoes and he didn't want to step inside the

THE BRASS BED

room, in case he soiled the carpet.

He continued to explore and found the kitchen and a blue painted bedroom, which he assumed was to be his. The blue room was neat and yet sparse, just a single bed, a wicker chair and a small portable television standing on a coffee table. He went for his holdall and threw it on the floor and immediately made the place look lived in. He would stay a month; that was the agreement until he could find a place of his own.

There was only the bathroom to find, and one other room left in the apartment. Out of pure curiosity Tony opened the next door and found a large double bedroom fitted with glass panelled wardrobes. There was a sheepskin rug on the floor, and a few modern prints of Van Gogh and Andy Warhol hung on the wall. But the focal point of this room was a large brass bed standing stately in the middle.

The highly polished brass bed was covered with a pure white counterpane, so neatly made that Tony daren't touch it. He was transfixed and wanted to keep silent as if someone were sleeping there. He stood still for a while as he realised he'd entered the intimate sanctuary of his cousin's life.

He stepped forward towards the bed and rubbed his fingers along its brass structure, feeling the coolness of the metal on his hands. His heart surged as he quickly walked around the bed, and thought of the elegant suits in the high-class stores and hoped, if nothing else, one day he too could have a brass bed.

Closing the door, Tony found the bathroom and washed. He made himself a drink of tea and wanted to surrender to the tiredness that was creeping over him. He was in no hurry to begin his new life; he had the apartment to himself; he had a whole week to himself. He would sleep, change his clothes and then search for a few landmarks to help him find his bearings.

Tony woke up to the buzz of traffic noise below him; it was 1:30pm. He was surprised and annoyed that he'd slept for so long, but never-the-less, had benefited and some colour had returned to his complexion. He soaked his aching body in the deep water of a luxurious bath and started to plot out his plans for the rest of the day.

As the spring sunshine cast into the apartment he took out his A-Z, searched for the whereabouts of The Royal Albert Hall and decided to walk again. The traffic had increased since the morning and the streets were alive. Businessmen, wearing the same styled suits he'd seen, replaced the tradesmen. He found the Royal Albert Hall and saw on the billboard just what he'd expected: a charity concert next week, held for the benefit of the street musicians in London. Buskers had been invited to play, their chance for some recognition, and a chance for Tony to meet some contacts.

He bought a ticket.

David hosed down the dairy, tirelessly removing debris and dung that had accumulated from the morning's milking. The cattle were settled and munching hay in the foldyard. He loved to see them like this, as they rocked from side to side on their feet, with steam rising from their bodies and drifting up into the cool air. The cattle were chewing their cud, contented, oblivious to any danger and satisfied.

The sight of the contented animals had a revitalising effect on David and lifted his spirits. He put away the hosepipe and set the dairy up ready for the evening's milking.

He'd had a quiet morning; he'd walked the fields and checked the grassland, knowing that as soon as spring approached the cattle could go out to graze. A few more calves had been born over the winter without any hitches, and there were still several more cows due to calve. David had decided that he needed to call Barry Fitzgerald out for a few necessary check-ups. One cow had given birth and was sick with an infection. Two others, which David had thought were in calf, were showing no signs whatsoever of a pregnancy, and there was also a cow with mastitis; its udder had become hard and swollen with infected milk, and David had been struggling to treat it himself. He would have all the animals ready in the barn for Barry, whenever he called.

David was hungry and felt more satisfied with his work than he'd been for some time. He started to whistle as he worked, talking gently and fondly to the cattle as he moved them around and playfully patting them. Someone had kindly taken the heavy weight from him today. He knew he'd have to have it back, but hoped he could resist as long as possible.

When David entered the farmhouse kitchen ready for lunch, he was surprised to see Tony's father.

'Davey . . . ?' Kathy was the first to speak. 'Did you know that Tony was going to London?'

Removing his grubby overalls and out of breath with the exertion he replied. 'Er . . . yes. He told me on Tuesday. He didn't say when, though.'

'Then why on earth didn't you say anything?' Kathy said.

'I didn't think I needed to tell you everything that happens in my life.'

Keith Milton quickly interrupted. 'I'm just worried about his health that's all, Davey.'

'Well, I shan't be able to talk him out of it.' David softened and went to wash his hands. 'He doesn't listen to me anymore.'

'It's too late anyway, Davey. He's already gone.'

David stopped what he was doing and looked at Keith Milton and his deep blue eyes widened.

'He packed and left last night. Just left me a note. He says he's staying with my sister's lad in Knightsbridge.'

'Well, that's it then isn't it? That's probably my fault too!'

Kathy heard the despair in his voice. She knew David and Tony had been at odds with one another of late and that perhaps Joanne was the cause. Things were slowly being pieced together, but Kathy felt she hadn't seen the full picture. She'd also heard more gossip in the village. A neighbour had taken pleasure in telling her, and all those present in the Post Office, that she'd seen a man, much like David, dragging a young woman out in the snow at an ungodly hour. If it hadn't been necessary for the woman to get up and "spend a penny" she would have missed it all. The woman said she'd peeped through the window when she heard the girl and had feared for her safety. She hadn't known whether to call for help, but then seeing the blue flashing lights up at Keld Head, "*again*", guessed the situation must be in hand. Kathy had refused to let her anger show and wouldn't be sucked into the woman's fact finding mission, so she calmly asked for her purchases and left the shop, knowing full well, the gossip would continue and soon this whole village would turn against her son as they had done her husband.

'Come on, Davey. . . . Have your tea. This is NOT your fault.'

But that was the problem, David imagined everything was his fault. Somewhere along the lines he blamed himself for his father's attitude, thinking he'd driven him to shoot to kill.

Barry Fitzgerald put his equipment back in the boot of his car. In the cold of the farmyard, he stripped to the waist, carefully removing his soiled green waterproof overalls; his job was now done at Keld Head. He was just mulling over the news that David had given him, surprised to hear that David's friend, Tony Milton, had gone to London. It mattered to him that David was worried.

He hadn't rushed his job today, wanting to pacify David. He'd taken a retained after-birth from the newly calved cow, diagnosed that one of the dairy cows wasn't in calf. Barry could see David was disappointed, as it was too late to try and mate her again and she would have to be sold.

David was also disappointed that Hannah wasn't with Barry as he'd expected. He'd hoped the reason was because she was nursing some poorly creature elsewhere, rather than the fact that she was avoiding him.

The dimly lit loosebox was warm and dry and a strong wind was blowing outside. David wasn't normally affected by the cold but had found of late he had an increasing disliking for it. He had intended to invite Barry into the farmhouse for a drink, but after man-handling three boisterous animals for an hour or more, he'd felt a wave of dizziness come over him, and the straw bale behind him was a convenient seat.

The more he sat, the more comfortable he became and an overwhelming tiredness crept over him. In his mind he felt he was just being bone-idle, but he'd had these dizzy spells for a few days now and today he felt a tightness grip his chest. David felt some of the life drain out of him and thought if he could see himself in a mirror he would look pale. These new feelings didn't worry him because he didn't care anymore.

But David did care about Hannah and he wanted to ask after her, but had resisted, and now as he sat quietly, he recalled the promise he'd made to himself on the day of Uncle Fred's funeral, and realised he was failing himself and his mother if he married Joanne. If Joanne hadn't have been so persistent, and if he hadn't have been so reckless, he could have kept his promise. And now there were thoughts of Hannah constantly coming back to his mind. Her influence on him he hadn't expected at all. He'd had other girlfriends who'd been fun to be with, but none of them got to him as she did. Some girls he'd used and some had used him. Some had given him up because of his belligerent father and some, much like Joanne, still adored him. But he guessed that these feelings for Hannah were different, not just flashing moments of desire. And although he hardly knew her, he had little chance of getting to know her better. Why was it, that the girl he wanted didn't seem to care, but the one he didn't want, cared too much?

He'd also had two letters from Joanne since she left Keld Head, which he couldn't bring himself to reply to. At one time the anxiety of all this would have made him walk away, or even run, but all he could do was sit. There would be no one to go and look for him anyway, as he'd done for his father; his dear Uncle was dead and Tom was too young. So David slapped his hands down on his knees, realising he'd allowed his mind to go deeper into the mire than was good for him.

He was about to stand, when Barry returned and sat close beside him on the straw bale. 'Not too disappointed about the barren cow are you, Davey?'

'Ah no. ... Not too much anyway. Some you win - some you

lose.' There was no eye contact as David stared at the floor.

'You must come over to my place sometime. . . . Now that Tony's gone, you and I can have a drink together. Eleanor doesn't want my company much these days and I guess I need a good drinking partner.'

'And you think I'd be good company?'

'Ah, you young ones. . . . I don't know what's the matter with you all. I've another one like you back at the surgery.'

David knew he was referring to Hannah and his senses sharpened.

'Yeh, she's moping around just like you. Hannah used to cheer me up, but now she's miserable, and I don't think it's Tony Milton she's missing.'

'Is she ill?' David asked. 'I thought she might have come today.'

'No, she's not ill, she's studying. . . . Hannah's got a lot of exams to sit this year, and she has her head stuck in medical books. It's good to take your career seriously but I think she's going a bit overboard. She needs a break.'

Both men fell silent, thinking about the troublesome women in their lives. Barry wanted to tell David about his failing marriage to Eleanor, but didn't want to burden him. David wanted to tell Barry of his confused feelings for Hannah, but guessed he would think he was being improper - she was far above him. And then there was this crazy plan to marry Joanne. David reasoned Barry too would think he was being a fool: adoring one woman and yet intending to marry another.

It was Barry who spoke next. 'Do you have date for your father's trial yet, Davey?'

Shocked at his bluntness, David replied, 'No . . . no. . . . It keeps being put off. They've finally diagnosed Dad's stomach trouble – he's got gallstones or something. And until he's well, they won't send him for trial. He has to have surgery and then more waiting, I guess.'

'I bet you wish you could just get it over and done? I can see you're anxious.'

'To be honest Barry, I daren't think much about it. . . . I keep

THE BRASS BED

trying to push it to the back of my mind.'

Then David looked intently into the older man's kindly face. 'You see . . . it all hinges on me, doesn't it? If I say Dad was trying to shoot me, he could go down for attempted murder and a manslaughter charge for killing Uncle Fred. But if I say it was all an accident, Dad will be given a lighter sentence. And for an accidental death verdict, his conviction would be much shorter, if any! And then we'll have to start all over again, him tormenting Mum and me, for goodness knows how long, or until he does something stupid again, and I'm sure he would.'

David paused to take a breath and then continued as Barry listened. 'And then there's Keld Head . . . ? What will happen to the farm if Dad gets life or something? Mum will have no say in what happens to it - it's not her farm and I doubt he would give it to me. So we're like sitting tenants really. Legally, none of us can sell the place unless Dad allows it, or he signs it over to one of us, and he's not likely to do that either.' David didn't stir, only his head and his eyes moved, firstly looking at Barry and then glancing down at the straw under his feet. 'If Mum divorced Dad, she would be entitled to a lot of money and the farm would have to be sold, but then what will happen to her and Sarah and Tom?'

'And what about you, Davey?'

'I don't care what happens to me. . . . I've no particular love for this place any more, but I wanted to be loyal to my mum, but I don't know if I can. Life's a mess Barry - it really is, and I don't know what to do.'

'You must tell the truth for a start - for your safety and your mother's.'

David raised his voice. 'Will they believe me, though. Maybe they'll say it was all my fault anyway - making up crazy stories about him. Besides, how can I stand there and say that my own father was trying to kill me. But I saw him Barry. . . . He held the gun at me. He said he'd shoot and he did. And besides, I couldn't look him in the eyes. He's stronger than I am. He would look at me with those cold eyes of his and wish me dead! Oh, why does everything depend on me?'

Barry put his arm across David's back and he responded by dropping his head.

'It doesn't all depend on you. . . . They'll question your mother too. . . . She'll tell the truth. . . . She knew what he was trying to do.'

Kathy stood shivering outside by the loosebox door, holding a tray of coffee in her hand. She could hear the soft voices of the two men talking. She wasn't one to eavesdrop, but when she heard David raise his voice and, this time at Barry, Kathy stopped to hear him as he poured out his real feelings.

But David looked up, aware of his mother standing at the door and wondered how much she'd overheard. He jumped up and pushed passed her, knocking her body against the stable door. The coffee mugs fell to the ground, spilling the hot liquid on her clothes.

Barry moved quickly. 'Are you okay, Kathy?'

He heard her moan, wounded, as she could no longer hold in the pain and the heartache, and she fell into his arms and, for the first time publicly, she wept.

15

THE LIBERATOR

George Keldas hadn't seen the outside world for five months, and even today the bars of the prison van obscured some of his view. But, true enough, he was outside.

If he could stretch a little taller he would see more, but the guard beside him sat tight, with his hands held low and handcuffs binding him down.

An ache in George's side gave him the excuse to stretch upwards, but not for long; a sharp stabbing pain in his stomach made his body shrink back down.

He could just see a few cars and people, busy and getting on with their lives, not noticing him or caring. He looked at the fields. He hadn't seen fields like this for months, but the hills here were smaller and the land was flatter.

If he could just catch a bus, he would soon be home. The children would be at school and Kathy would be washing. But who would look after the farm until his pain went away? He had no one he could rely on; he had disowned David and he couldn't trust Kathy. Maybe Linzi would come home and help him and Tom, when he came in from school, then they could feed up together. Maybe just two or three days in this hospital and he would be home. Yes, that would be best - have a good rest, then leave.

'Now, George, don't go to sleep. Make the most of your trip. You'll not be getting many more.' The guard speaking was nudging and shaking the prisoner's trembling body.

'I'll be home before you think,' George muttered in a slow, drug induced drawl.

'In your dreams!' the guard said.

Another guard spoke up in his defence. 'Leave him be, Mike. The man's sick. Don't keep tormenting him.'

'If you ask me, he's not sick at all, are you George? You're a devious beggar. You know exactly what you're doing don't you? You just want a couple of easy days in hospital.'

If George hadn't have been restrained he would have punched the guard in the face, but he was powerless. He was getting used to the taunting now. They were always calling him lazy, and saying things about his wife and his daughter. Some things he believed were true, and some of them weren't. If he was going crazy, the guards didn't help.

As the van swung swiftly around corners and up and over small bridges, George started to feel sick. The palms of his hands felt sticky and fine droplets of moisture clustered on his forehead as the heat rose. He tried to bend his back and bury his head down between his knees, but the guard pulled him up again.

'We'll soon be there, George,' the kindly one spoke. 'Take some deep breaths.'

But it was too late. George was sick.

The guard beside him frantically tried to pull himself away, jarring the prisoner's wrists and shoulder. But it was no use; the guard was already spattered with vomit, covering his trousers, his sleeves and his shoes.

'Stop the van . . . ! Pull it over.'

'Stop . . . stop. . . . ' the other guard shouted and banged his fist on the side of the van. But as they stopped, George was sick again.

David found himself singing today. He hadn't felt as lonely as he thought after Tony's departure, in fact, he'd thought very little of him these past few weeks; peace and normality were healing him. David had decided to give the dairy a spring clean. He'd cleaned and polished the stainless steel bulk talk and was now scrubbing the dairy walls. When they were properly dry and aired, he intended giving them a lick of paint. He had some azure blue swimming pool paint ready to give the walls some waterproofing, and it would give the old grey concrete walls a cleaner and brighter look. The sun was shining through the window, showing up the cobwebs and the dust that had accumulated over the winter. Green wellingtons protected David's feet, but his overalls were wet from the scrubbing. His face was speckled with muddy water.

He was swilling the floor clean with the hosepipe when he thought he heard under the noise of the water pressure the yard gate click open. He tried not to react and continued to spray the cold water onto the walls. But, as he tried to force the water on a grubby piece of concrete, he felt the pressure drop and the water stopped running.

Instinctively, David looked at the end of the hose-pipe and shook it, but nothing happened. Thinking it must have come loose on the tap, or even twisted, he kicked the pipe, but still there was no response. So peering down at the pipe, he walked into the yard to look for a kink or an obstruction, but there was none.

He glanced across to the farmhouse door expecting to see his mother, but he was alone. Then he heard the sound of someone laughing, the noise coming from the stone tower. Feeling anxious, he sidled across to the old building. Just in the recess he could see the back of someone crouching by the door; someone with long red hair.

'Tony . . . is that you? Stop messing around.'

But David was surprised to see it was Joanne.

She ran to him and hugged him, smothering his damp body with hers. 'I'm back, Davey . . . I'm back. Are you pleased to see me?' Then she started to kiss his muddied face. 'I've come home for good, now.'

David still smothered in the girl's warm body was shocked and remained silent. *Why has she come back now?* He thought. *I'm not ready for this yet.*

David pulled her arms from him and gently pushed her away. 'Joanne, please. Be careful, I'm wet through.'

'What's the matter, Davey . . . ? Aren't you pleased to see me?' Her pale green eyes looked saddened at his reproof. 'Why didn't you answer my letters?' Joanne wiped the grime from her jacket and continued. 'Oh it's so good to see you,' and she couldn't resist hugging him again.

Pulling away, David went inside the tower to turn the tap back on, but she came closer to him and held onto his arm as he muttered a few indiscernible words, then more clearly said: 'You've taken me by surprise that's all, Jo. I've been busy. There's a lot of work to do now. Anyway, you know I'm useless at writing.' David wiped his mud-spattered face with his sleeve, as all the time she was watching him and grinning.

'Have you missed me, Davey? Have you?'

'I've been thinking about you a lot, Jo.' And that was no lie. 'Look . . . I do want to talk, but not here, not now.' Confused thoughts rushed through his head. She was always one step in front of him; always quicker with words than he was. He needed time to think. It was apparent that she still felt the same about him and, if he couldn't take away any of the harm he'd already done, he must ask her to marry him. But he couldn't do it just now. He wasn't ready.

As she stood before him, she looked well; rested and less anxious. Her pale skin held a rosy glow, blushing her cheekbones. Her hair was falling loose with soft curls that framed her face, the sort David couldn't resist. He wanted to touch, and he now understood why he'd kissed her that night.

Joanne was wearing a green wool jacket with brass buttons, with a mustard coloured scarf wrapped around her neck. Her skirt was short: red tartan, and she wore black tights. She looked like a child.

David peered into her face, something he'd resisted for so long and, although he knew she was still only eighteen, he thought what a beautiful bride she would make.

He held her arms and looked her square in the face, 'Meet me tonight. . . . Not here. Meet me in Keswick, at the Moot Hall. Catch the seven o'clock bus and I'll bring you home. Now please go, Joanne . . . please.'

She obediently accepted the authority in his voice and complied. Giving him one last embrace, Joanne was about to

THE LIBERATOR

leave when they heard footsteps at the door. They turned around.

'What a pretty sight . . . I'm so sorry to interrupt your intimacy,' the man said.

David had to blink; his mouth dropped open, astonished at the sight of his father, who once again was holding a shotgun and was standing in the doorway, blocking out the light.

This cannot be real. David thought. *It's déjà-vu!*

'What's the matter, lad? Dumb as usual. Surprised to see me eh?'

David pulled Joanne closer to his side; she was shaking and unable to breathe.

'You shouldn't leave things like this lying around the place, Davey.' George waved the gun at them. 'You never know if they might get into the wrong hands,' and he started to laugh.

David tried to speak but the words wouldn't come out. He thought only: P*lease . . . please . . . not now . . . not again.*

'Are you scared, Davey boy?' George raised the shotgun a little higher and David now clearly saw the eyes of the man he most feared. He was looking older and thinner and much changed in five months.

'I expected to find you here, Davey, but I didn't expect her to be with you. . . . The little bitch . . . ! She's after you now is she? She'll never leave you alone, won't that one. . . . She got tired of me and now she wants you, does she? Any way, you can have her. You're welcome to her.'

David didn't understand what his father meant; he'd become unaccustomed to unravelling his cryptic messages and manner of speech.

'So I've come to finish the job, Davey. . . . Do you remember? When old Fred got in the way. No fool like you is going to take over my farm. It's not yours to have . . . I want you out. . . . You're no son of mine! Yes, that's right Davey, you're a bastard!' George started to laugh again and the skin around his eyes wrinkled.

'Be careful what you say to me. . . . ' David found words with a strength and dignity that he didn't think he possessed. 'Yes, I am a fool, you know that, so I might actually believe you!'

'Ah, you're no fool Davey and these are not lies. I promised your mother I'd never tell you. But I've done it now. Keeping that secret just to save her face. Looking into the eyes of another man's son for the last twenty-three years was enough to drive anyone crazy.'

Words were drawling out of George Keldas's mouth that David couldn't grasp, then he noticed him sway, and his body wavered a little. George scowled and lowered the gun as he pressed his hand on his side to ease the pain

David noticed the broom handle beside him and was about to grab it and try to knock the gun from his hand, when George raised the shotgun and, this time, pointed it straight at Joanne.

David pushed her to the wall, covering her body with his and then waited for the bang and pain to hit his back. But it was an age before the gunshot was actually fired; the pressure from the blast so loud that they were compelled to hold their hands to their ears.

Joanne and David fell to the cold wet floor in each other's arms, but they never felt any pain, and David couldn't understand why. Joanne clung to David; the deafening noise from her screams pierced his eardrums. Then there was silence, with only the writhing of Joanne's body beneath him struggling to be free.

She pulled herself from his grasp and ran from the tower. David, on his hands and knees, turned and saw behind him the crumpled body of his father on the floor, lying motionless, with a pool of blood about his head.

Shaking with fear, David felt no pity, only relief that his ordeal was over. Perhaps now there would be an end to the suffering and anxiety. He had to step outside and get away from the hideous sight. He closed his eyes and leant against the wall, his body heaved with the emotion and he was sick; he stumbled against the doorpost to keep his balance.

When he opened his eyes David saw three police marksmen in body armour, their pistols raised and pointing at him.

'You have who you want . . . leave me alone. I must go to my mother.'

And David's slow thoughts started to cogitate over the last words his father had just spoken. Never before had he heard him speak such nonsense. Then the spirit left within him surged, and he set out to find Kathy.

Kathy had seen Joanne come into the yard. She was upstairs washing her hair when she heard the yard gate click open. She had quickly wrapped her wet hair in a towel and rushed for a pullover to put on. She hadn't expected Joanne's return so soon. She'd intended to have the fires lit in the bungalow, make the place look lived in and stock the fridge with food. Kathy also hoped she would have the courage to speak to David again about Joanne, and talk him out of his dreadful decision, but she was afraid it might have meant another row.

Kathy knew she loved David more than she thought was healthy, but she didn't want him to make the same mistakes as she had and enter a loveless marriage. She knew he was old enough to make up his own mind, yet she must talk to him. But she'd failed, and now Joanne was home and was alone with David. She must try to come between them before he said anything that he might regret, even if it meant spending the whole of the day with Joanne, drinking coffee or scrubbing the bungalow out. She must separate them.

Kathy hurried to put her clothes on and dry her hair and was about to leave when she heard a great noise, a bang so loud that it shook the farmhouse. Recognising the noise, terror gripped her, and a mother's courage impelled her to run, as she cried out David's name. She heard the girl scream and saw her run from the tower and Kathy's worst fears were now before her. It had to be David this time!

Standing at the back door, Kathy saw police marksmen everywhere; but why were they here? As she ran across the yard towards the tower she saw David, his face spattered with blood and his body trembling as he leant on the wall to be sick. She ran to help him.

THE LIBERATOR

At the sight of his mother, David raised himself upright and forcefully took her by the arm and led her away. 'Don't go in there . . . ! Come away!' He implored her and pulled her back to the farmhouse.

'David . . . please. . . . What's the matter . . . ? Whatever's happened? Are you hurt?'

David pushed his mother into the house and banged the door hard behind her. He pulled her small body to him and frantically shook her and shouted, 'Who am I? Who am I . . . ?' He was close to tears as he spoke.

'I don't know what you mean, David. I don't understand.' Kathy was terrified and tried to pull herself from his grasp.

'You know exactly what I mean! That - that man, lying on the floor. . . . Yes, your husband. . . . He's DEAD! The police shot him. And he just told me something, and I want to know the truth. Who am I, Mother . . . ? Who am I?'

'You're my son, Davey,' and Kathy tried to calm him, yet she was totally bewildered.

'Aye, and who is my father?'

Kathy now understood the nature of his question, but she still couldn't comprehend how George could be here and how he could be dead.

'Tell me . . . tell me. . . .' He shook her again. 'Answer me. Who am I? Who is my father?'

Kathy started to moan words that were barely legible, 'Oh, dear God, what have I done! I don't know David . . . ! I'm so sorry, I don't know.'

'Don't lie to me. You must know!'

'I don't know who your father is David,' she repeated.

'So if I'm a bastard . . . ' he shouted, 'what does that make you?'

She went to slap his face but he grabbed her arm, holding her tightly in his grip. They gained eye contact and a battle commenced as David held her gaze, and it was Kathy who was compelled to turn away.

'You've seen me suffer all these years, taunted by a man who I believed to be my father . . . my own flesh and blood. You've seen me suffer and cringe at the thought that I might one day end up like him, and you never told me . . . never once reassured me. . . . All to save your own face. I've wasted all that fear, that suffering!' and he pushed her away in contempt.

As Kathy wept uncontrollably, David left her and ran outside, down the lane, knowing he must find Joanne. He banged on the bungalow door and pushed it with his shoulder, but it was locked. He shook the handle fiercely, loosening the fastenings. He ran to the window and looked inside. He once again shouted her name and ran around the bungalow peering into each window, stumbling over the plants and shrubs, as thorns of the rose bushes tore his trousers and scratched his hands and legs. He tried the back door, but still there was no way of entering so, frustrated, he leant exhausted on the front porch.

He then heard her shout from inside. 'Go away David. . . . Leave me alone. I don't want to see you again.'

'Joanne, please. . . . I don't know what this is all about. . . . Are you okay?'

'I hate you David . . . I hate you . . . !'

David fell back on the wall of the bungalow and knew that in a space of a few short minutes, his whole life had changed. He'd been betrayed, assaulted, reproached, all for no cause. He had been the scapegoat and now he would have to leave.

Until today, David had never believed anything that George Keldas said could be true. But if one thing was, then many other things could be too and David then began to feel a kind of pity for the man lying dead. And he wondered if he'd finally been liberated.

He slowly walked back home, looked down at his blood stained clothes and said to a policeman. 'Do you mind if I get changed.'

During the quiet of the evening, David started to pack an overnight bag. He put out a change of clothes and some underwear ready for the morning, neatly folding them, as if for the rest of his life the decisions he made would be of his own volition and carefully thought out. He took some soap and his shaving things: deodorant, a comb, and a small mirror. He methodically looked through his wardrobe and chest of drawers and took out various items of clothing: a warm pullover, two t-shirts, two pairs of jeans. He looked through his bedside cabinet for any of his personal belongings: cheque book, passport, driving license. He took all his money from a small tin and pushed it in his wallet. Then he glanced up at his bookcase and saw the small glass snow scene globe. He reached for it and, without any hint of emotion, placed it carefully into his bulging holdall.

David left Keld Head early the next morning in the same way that Tony Milton had left a few weeks before, silently and without notice. He had no reason to see his mother or to speak to her again. All the anger had gone. And as he quietly walked down the lane, he was pleased he'd been able to leave without being spotted.

Kathy was sitting in the parlour with Alan Marsh, who'd been drafted in again and was now consoling her. They were huddled together on the sofa and David had no inclination to disturb their intimate conversation. They were so engrossed in each other that it was the last piece of justification David needed to go. Alan had as much right to be at Keld Head as he did.

He walked to the bus stop and leant on the wall, the early morning sunshine was touching his face. He glanced across to the hills and saw the juniper bushes and gorse bushes climbing up the fell side. He could just see the froth on the waterfalls. And so in the quiet cool air, he waited and meditated. He didn't know when he would return, he would have to one day, but whether he would stay would be another matter. There was just one person he had to speak to, so he could fit together the last pieces of this jigsaw and complete its grim picture.

David took the stairway to the top of Rievaulx House, he was breathless as he climbed, and he realised he hadn't had enough to eat; the meal on the train had been a meagre one. He'd slept most of the journey and yet wished he hadn't. He'd dreamt of nothing else but guns and hills. He desperately hoped that he could find Tony and if he had one ounce of friendship left for him, David could seek some refuge and the answer to some of his questions.

Tony's cousin was surprised to see David standing at his door. He easily recognised him from his youth, as the sturdy young man with dark hair and dazzling eyes. As a child, Peter had spent some of his school holidays at Keld Head, staying at the Milton's bungalow and, as children, playing together on the Keldas farm. But David stood before him now as a man.

Peter Milton welcomed David and fed him. They sat and enjoyed some light chatter, without David revealing his grim news. Peter told David that Tony had only stayed with him a few days, and that he hadn't seen him since. He said he'd taken a flat in Wandsworth and had promised Tony he would help him if needed; he was always welcome to return.

David left for the underground and unlike Tony found the bustling streets of London overwhelming. As he stood, looking at the tall houses lining the street, an overweight woman with a baby in a pushchair reluctantly pointed the way. She must have been only about seventeen. Her baby was dirty and scruffy looking, and she herself was poorly dressed and scantily clad, her fat, bare legs looked blotchy and cold.

Most of the houses in the street had their bay windows boarded up, the grand exteriors, were reduced to crumbling masonry. People were sitting on walls and steps. Men were smoking and swearing and idly talking; no work to go to; no fault of their own. The women were gossiping, oblivious to their children playing on the street corners and in the roads. David wondered if he'd taken a wrong turning. He checked the address from the note that Peter Milton had given him and continued to follow the numbers on the houses, some no longer discernible.

He found a young black youth sitting on some steps, who eyed David cautiously when he asked for the house number.

THE LIBERATOR

The youth looked David up and down.

'I'm looking for Tony Milton,' David quietly spoke. 'Does he live here?'

There was a long silence so David continued, 'He has long red hair.'

'Yeh, yeh . . . top floor. . . . You mean Tinkerman?'

David smiled at the name, remembering how much Tony used to hate it as a boy. And as David was about to walk away, the youth pulled out of his pocket a harmonica and blew through it. The screeching noise was meant to intimidate and it grated on David's tired nerves.

He reluctantly thanked the boy and pushed past him to stride through the doorway.

'I haven't seen him for two days though,' the boy shouted back.

David covered his mouth with his hand from a disgusting stench in the hallway. He climbed the murky stairway, his feet crunching on broken glass and litter. Sitting on the first landing was an elderly man playing a banjo, who ignored David as he squeezed passed him. There was a stench of stale alcohol and urine. David climbed the next flight of stairs and there was only one more door on the landing. David knocked and getting no reply, pushed it open.

When Tony awoke from his sleep, he didn't raise his head but just opened his eyes and saw the strong body and clean skin of David Keldas standing over him. Tony raised his arm and beckoned him. His dream had come true.

'It is you, isn't it, Dave?'

'Yes . . . I'm maybe not as pretty as your little nurse, but I'm here.'

'No, maybe not, but I'm glad to see you.'

David went across to his friend who was lying on an old mattress on the floor, covered with a dirty blanket. Neither spoke for some time. David knelt beside him and touched Tony's pale forehead and wiped some moisture away with a clean handkerchief. Tony started to cough uncontrollably and he turned on his side for relief and grasped his hand onto a stone cold radiator behind him as he coughed. 'Is this a brass bed, Dave?'

'Aye, it's brass all right mate. . . . Oh man, I'll get a doctor.' David whispered and shook his head.

'No . . . no. . . . They're not welcome here. Besides, they wouldn't come anyway.'

'But look at you, you're still sick. . . . You need help. When did you last eat? I'll get you some food.'

'I haven't felt hungry . . . I had two telephone numbers in my pocket, one's yours and one's Kelly's, that little nurse from Lancaster, and I haven't had the strength to ring either of you. Don't bring a doctor here, Dave, please . . . call Kelly and she'll tell you what to do.'

'After I get you out of here I will.'

'No man . . . just leave me . . . I'll be okay.'

David left Tony and promised to return quickly, knowing he was making a bad decision. He found the nearest chemist for some remedies, bought some brandy and food and took them back. It was well into the evening before he eventually managed to contact Kelly and she was as concerned as David was, and reluctantly gave him some instructions.

That evening the two men slept side by side on the same old mattress. David didn't ask Tony how he'd got into such a state, squatting in this old house, and neither could he tell his friend his motive in coming in the first place; he would have to wait.

David decided that as soon as he could move Tony, he would try and get him to Peter's flat or back to Cumbria. Straight away he started the process of nursing him. He bought a small gas burner and a pan to boil water and food in. He regularly gave him liquids as Kelly suggested, holding his head in his hands as he helped him to eat and drink. He gave him warm soup and fresh bread and yet, through all the hours of intimate care, Tony never once asked David why he'd come. He only knew as one day drifted into another, that David had probably saved his life.

Tony was nursed for three weeks with the help of Banjo the

old man and Twist the black youth. They were Tony's friends. They were buskers and they'd all met at the Royal Albert Hall. Banjo had invited them to share his flat, and Tony had willingly joined him without realising it was only a squat. They played on the cold London streets together trying to earn some money; that was until the pneumonia returned. They had earned some money from their takings, but Banjo had stolen most of it and squandered it on alcohol and gambling and had become incapable of looking after himself. He was now remorseful and depressed at the way he had let Tony down. He'd begged David to let him help, but David took charge and felt he was more of a liability.

The boy, Twist, had been more helpful, and one evening returned with a pocketful of drugs and penicillin. David guessed they were probably from a dubious source, but gratefully accepted the medicine and refused the rest.

The two men barely separated except for David's trips to the supermarket for food. And David soon found himself feeding the whole household, as the others realised he had money. He couldn't see the boy and the old man go hungry while he and Tony were satisfied.

The four of them sat and played cards late into the night. Laughing at the old man, telling stories of living rough, busking when he was well and sleeping in hostels when he was poorly. The boy was talented and would sing and play Tony's guitar to entertain them, but then disappear for hours at a time on some nameless errand.

Twist and Banjo soon began to trust David, just as they had trusted Tony. David felt at ease, being accepted for who he really was. He was no longer a victim and much like all of them, felt free, and had no concerns for the future. Each day was enough to satisfy them. They could eat, sleep and occasionally laugh. David didn't think about his family or the farm at all. His main concern was to see Tony get better. But he knew he couldn't stay. He didn't want to live like this, amongst the muck and the squalor, the cold nights and the long days. No fresh water, no baths, and the filthy toilets.

THE LIBERATOR

Through all of this Tony didn't seem to notice David's lack of anxiety. He never once questioned him as to how long he would stay, until one day when the two men were alone. Twist hadn't been seen for two days and Banjo was sober enough to do some busking. David had been shopping in the morning and had left Tony sleeping and had decided today he would take him out for a walk and buy him a good hot meal.

They didn't walk far before Tony had to stop as dizziness and weakness overcame him. They didn't intend going far; despite the day being dry, it was cold. Neither could they go anywhere respectable to eat because of their appearance as both were unshaven and only David was relatively clean.

They sat opposite one another in a diner looking out through greasy, steamy, windows into the street, when Tony took David by surprise.

'Why did you come, Dave?'

David didn't look at him, but continued to stare out of the window. He didn't know where to start, and then wiping some of the condensation away with his hand, said, 'Because the man who I thought was my father, is dead!'

Tony scowled and was unsure of how to reply.

But David repeated, 'George Keldas is dead . . . and I've discovered that he isn't my father.'

'Oh boy . . . I don't know what to say.'

'I know, it's incredible isn't it. But don't be sorry for me,' David smiled. 'You see I'm free now, but God knows who my father is. Mum reckons she doesn't know, but she's no slut. She must know. But all that matters for now is, I'm not George Keldas's son and I'll not end up as mindless as him and I'm free.'

'What happened? How did he die? How did you find out he wasn't your dad?'

'The police said he'd escaped on the way to hospital and had stolen a car. They bungled things up and George got to Keld Head first. He came back to the farm intending to shoot me, but a police marksman shot him in the nick of time.' His words had an impact on both men and David stopped and cleared his throat. 'Joanne was with me. I probably saved her life, but I've something to ask that you that you might find unbelievable.' David spoke clearly and deliberately now. 'I've never believed anything in my life what he said could be true and yet, I wonder, after all these years, if some of it was. . . . ' and he fiddled with the cutlery on the table. 'Did you ever see him with Joanne?'

'I don't understand. . . . What are you implying?'

'I mean, could they have had some kind of affair?'

Tony wondered at David's sanity. This strange calmness he had; leaving home for weeks on end with no word about his mother, his family, or the farm or anything. And now he wonders if the man, who he says is not his father, has had an affair with Joanne. 'Dave . . . you are seriously losing it mate!'

'No . . . for the first time in months - no years, I feel as sane as the next man. Believe me, Tony, this is true. Ring home . . . call my mother, anything, but please, this is important. I was going to marry Jo, you know that. I hurt her so much. She could have died because of me, and she nearly killed you! Then she came home a few weeks ago and she looked beautiful. She was well and happy and, although I knew I was still being a fool if I married her, if anyone could understand me and live with me, I guessed she could. I knew I could love her in some kind of way. I was going to ask her to marry me that very night. I thought what a lovely bride she'd make, and that she would love me and make me happy again, and at least I could put something right. . . . Then . . . Dad arrived and he caught us together. He was jealous, I could see that. It shocked him. Then he told me I was a bastard and if that wasn't enough, he implied he'd had some kind of a relationship with Jo. And the next thing he was lying dead on the floor. And Jo, well she ran away. Poor girl, she must have been terrified. I know I was. I tried to talk to her, but she wouldn't let me into the house. She said she hated me, yes, hated me . . . can you believe that? So now I have to find some answers. My mother admitted I wasn't George's son and now I need you to tell me about Jo. . . . If there's anything you know about her and him? Don't keep anything back from me.'

They were interrupted as the waitress brought in their meal, but Tony just looked at his plate and said. 'I'm not hungry,' and shoved it away. David gently pushed it back and beckoned him to eat.

'I don't know what you want me to say. I'll have to think about this.'

'Don't hide anything. If you think you know something, tell me. I don't want any more lies!'

'I know one thing. You'd be a fool to marry Jo. . . . But that's only my opinion. I must think about the rest.'

Despite the gravity of the situation, David ate his meal, but Tony chased his food around the plate. 'There is something, Dave . . . something I never would have guessed meant anything if you hadn't have brought the subject up . . . I'm maybe wrong and I hope I am, but when she was fifteen, she did have a kind of crush on your Dad. He was a good-looking bloke before he was ill. She was never afraid of him, not like us. She got excited when he was around. If there was some kind of a scene at your place, she loved it. I could never understand why she wasn't frightened of him. He scared the living-daylights out of me. Then once - no twice I think, I'd come home from work early and your Dad and Jo were alone together in the house. I could tell they'd been foolin' around because Jo was blushing and he was laughing. Yet nothing really was going on, but I did wonder why he was there. I guessed he was looking for you or your mum. My dad was away at the time and I thought it was odd to find them together, but George was like that wasn't he?'

David didn't know whether to feel repulsed or relieved at Tony's suggestion. 'Can you help me find out the truth and sort this mess out? Then I can decide what to do about Jo.'

'I'll help you, mate.' Tony was still serious. 'I'll help you all I can. You've probably saved my life and I think I owe it to you. Besides, Jo's my sister, and I need to know what she's been up to. I'll come back to Keld Head with you, but I won't stay.'

'I don't expect you to, because neither will I.'

THE LIBERATOR

Tony started to eat his meal with more enthusiasm. 'Aren't you going to lecture me, at how I managed to get into the state I'm in?'

'Well, I don't reckon much to your lodgings but, to be honest, at least you're free. I guess things just haven't worked out as you expected, have they?' And, at last, David smiled.

The drunken washroom attendant wasn't too happy to be letting them in. It was only because one of the young men looked like Jesus, and he spoke with a soft, quiet voice and walked with such stature. He reckoned that the other young man with red hair was some kind of disciple.

They said they were just two lads from up north, who'd come to London to rough it for a few days. But the washroom attendant knew differently. He'd prayed that one day he might have a visitation; that someone would come and rescue him and help him repent of his sins.

The one with red hair said that the dark young man had been his salvation and, that if he let them in for a good wash, he too could be so blessed.

The attendant watched them strip to the waist and wash their long and scraggly hair, then return to their dirty clothes. And his belief in a saviour came true, when the red haired young man started to sing, *Amazing Grace*, to him and the dark haired one gave him a handful of loose coins, and thanked him for his kindness and blessed him as they left.

David and Tony took a walk through a park and laughed at the joke they'd just played on the attendant. It was like old times, like their trip to Blackpool; at last, they had something to laugh at. They fed some dry crusts of bread to the ducks and talked about some of the skirmishes they'd had through their troubled lives, hoping things would change. But Tony had a deep feeling in his gut that one day, sooner or later, Joanne would hurt David. And David had a hope in his mind that one day he would be free of this crazy life of his.

They travelled back to Cumbria late in the day. They had an

emotional farewell with Banjo and Twist, and Tony promised to return as soon as he could. As they left, the old man gave Tony a small package containing twenty-pounds. Banjo had earned it busking, and in some way had wanted to compensate for the drinking binge that had nearly taken Tony's life.

They arrived back at Keld Head on a cold, wet and misty night. David tried to prepare himself mentally for a confrontation with Joanne and was disappointed that the bungalow was empty; they guessed she'd gone to Aberdeen again to her aunt's. At least it gave him more time to think. The other disappointment was that it meant David would have to make another long journey with his sick friend.

David only glanced up the lane to the farm, and could see that every light in the farmhouse appeared to be on. He had no desire to call and Tony didn't question David's decision to stay at the bungalow. He called Kelly to tell her he was home and safe, and she agreed to come and bring them some groceries. She was suspicious of Tony's secrecy and wondered why they didn't want to leave the bungalow. She didn't trust David Keldas at all, and wished Tony wasn't involved with him.

David lit the fire and had a bath in deep, hot water. They were both stretched out in front of the fire relaxing when someone banged on the door. Tony went expecting to see Kelly but he returned to the sitting room with Alan Marsh.

David didn't make any gesture of welcome and remained seated, half asleep, and this angered Alan. He thought David had a smug manner about himself, and Alan was appalled at his appearance.

'So you're back then.' Alan was flustered and his large body trembled as he spoke. 'What the deuce do you think you're playing at? Leaving your mother like that without a word!'

David had never seen him look as angry and authoritative.

Tony backed away and watched over Alan's shoulder. He wondered how David would reply. How much did Alan know?

David didn't rise from his chair as he spoke. 'I'm sorry, but I had to leave.'

'Had to leave . . . ! Going swannin' off to goodness knows where. What about your responsibility?'

David stood up and attempted to leave the room, not wanting to be involved in another argument.

'Aye, that's it Davey . . . run away like you always do . . . ! Do you think you're the only one who's had to suffer through all this? Your father dead and your mother at her wits end, worrying herself senseless over you!'

David looked at him coldly in the eyes. 'What responsibility is this, Alan? Ask my mother what responsibility I have, eh?' Ask her . . . ! What's the matter, are you finding it hard doing all the work yourself? Not quite what you expected is it?'

Tony winced at his cutting words, but David persisted. 'Besides . . . I thought you wouldn't mind spending a bit more time with her.'

Alan grabbed David by the arm, but Tony intervened and came between the two men.

'Don't be stupid, Alan. Leave him be.'

'Aye, I'll leave him be all right. Don't expect any more pity from me.'

'I never asked for pity!' David spat and stood his ground, and Alan was compelled to move away. But, as he headed for the door, he turned and said, 'Your father was buried last Thursday, and you hadn't even the guts to come to his funeral. I can't understand you David. . . . It's true what they say: *The father eats the sour grapes, but it's the son's teeth that gets set on edge.*' And with that, Alan left.

David was shocked; he became pale and his heart pounded. In all his anxiety over Tony, his search for clues about Joanne, he'd never once considered that he might have missed the funeral. His days in London had blended and time hadn't mattered. Nothing had mattered anymore, except his own self-interest and to see his friend recover.

Tony didn't know how to console him, and could see the shock on David's face, as reality hit him.

'We'll leave for Aberdeen tomorrow. I can't stay here any longer.'

'Do you think he knows the truth, Dave?'

'I'm not sure. . . . It's up to my mother what she tells him. It's not my problem. I don't need to say anything to him to justify my actions. If he thinks bad of me, then so be it.'

When David settled down on the sofa for the night, he knew he wouldn't be comfortable but at least he would be warm and dry. He'd been asleep sometime, when he was wakened. Tony had put the light on and was clattering about in the bungalow. The noise continued and David was about to get up and see what he was doing, when Tony appeared and threw a small book down on David's stomach.

'Here . . . read this. It'll give you nightmares!'

David, still dazed from his sleep, picked up a diary.

'I hope this is all rubbish for your sake, Dave.'

David held the book and looked astonished. 'What are you doing? You can't read someone's diary.'

'Well, if you don't read it you'll never find out the truth will you,' Tony insisted. 'Read it, Dave . . . just read it. Is any of this true?'

David sat up on the sofa, rubbed his eyes and read through the pages of the private book that had been hidden in Joanne's bedroom.

'She must have left in a hurry, to leave this. I knew it existed, but I didn't know where it was. I couldn't sleep until I'd found it.'

David began to read descriptions about himself; details of the clothes he wore, the ones she said she'd liked. Him having his hair trimmed, and then going to Blackpool and being in a fight. The things he'd said to her, about him kissing her that first night. How he walked the fells with Tony and their other exploits, his drinking sessions with Tony and Darren Watson. These were the rational things. But then there were other things; things about her staying the night with him at the farmhouse. How they were to be married and run away together. How he had said he loved her. Then there were things she said they'd done together, vividly described, things that David was appalled to read.

'This is all rubbish, Tony . . . ! This can't be me she's talking about - it must be someone else. We've never done these things. I've never said these things!'

'Well it sounds like you, don't it!'

'That's true, but . . .' David was desperate to clear his name. 'Tony, you have to believe me. Most of the things in here are just incredible. The product of a vivid imagination, or just wishful thinking.'

Tony flopped down on the sofa beside him. 'Don't worry, Dave . . . I believe you, but there's more. Look at this.' In his hand was a small photograph album.

The two men sat together long into the night flicking through its pages. There were pictures of the late George Keldas, ones they'd never seen before, taken some time ago. David was in some, but as a teenager. Then on the back were inscriptions, dates and times. There were also photographs of David sitting by the lake, walking alone, and working in the fields.

'If she didn't have some kind of a thing going with him - what's this all about then?'

'If she's lied about me. . . . How can we know if she'll tell the truth about him? All this other stuff could be lies too.' David shook his head.

They sat engrossed, letting the fire go out, and agreed to leave for Aberdeen at first light.

16

THE GRANITE CITY

Hannah was like any other young woman, nipping in and out of the stores with handfuls of carrier bags, browsing through the sale rails, trying on shoes and matching them up with a handbag, testing make-up, spraying on perfume that she never intended to buy.

In the afternoon sunshine, she walked through the little grey town of Kendal and back to the multi-story car park. As she continued to browse, looking up across towards Windermere, the fells jumped out at her today in three-dimensional aspects, like she could reach out and touch them. The bronzed bracken would soon be fully rejuvenated as the lush green fronds were already bursting out. The blue rocks glistened with water and whitewashed farmhouses nestled lazily under the crags.

Hannah would certainly miss Lakeland. Just a few more weeks then back to the city and to who-knows-where. The only sadness was the solitude as she'd made no lasting friends, and Hannah felt that such a beautiful place should be shared. She had no one to tell when she'd seen a red squirrel or a deer with its fawn, she could tell Barry but he'd seen it all before. Hannah didn't know how she would remember Lakeland - for the loneliness or the beauty, or the tragedy that had touched so close to her.

Then there was her love and pleasure of working with Barry; that had been the greatest education she could have hoped for. To work with such a dedicated man, with his willing and self-sacrificing nature.

She was sorry to leave as spring was turning into summer, when Cumbria would take on another aspect. The rain would continue to fill the rivers, streams and lakes, ready for the summer visitors and give the Lancashire public their drinking water.

And now a cloud hung over the practice since the second shooting incident at Keld Head. When they'd heard a man had been shot, all of them assumed, with anguish, that it was David. But then there was relief to know he was safe, and yet to hear that George Keldas, Barry's old friend was dead was still a dreadful shock. Barry had remained depressed ever since.

They'd all attended the grim funeral, standing around an open grave in the pouring rain, the only brightness coming from one wreath of spring flowers laid on the coffin from a long-suffering wife and children.

Hannah had gone to support Barry and to see Linzi. She didn't particularly want to talk to David or see him in any distress. But David's absence was strikingly apparent and questions were whispered by the partisan crowd, who'd only come to see the final chapter in the Keldas saga end.

But it was Linzi who Hannah had watched sobbing, inconsolable around her father's grave, with Kathy Keldas standing beside her, small and fragile, yet strong and determined as ever.

When Hannah returned to the surgery she was surprised to see Barry's Mercedes parked in the yard, it was unusual for him to be home on her day off.

With an armful of carrier bags, she struggled to open the front door. As she passed the office, she saw Barry sitting at his desk. Hannah peeped around the door and he glanced across. She could see his face was red and his eyes looked tired and sore, his dark eyebrows frowned. It was obvious he'd been crying.

Hannah was embarrassed and, uncertain of what to do, backed away.

'Don't go, Hannah . . . I'm sorry, please come in.'

She hesitated, and put the shopping bags down on the floor.

'You may as well hear my news. You'd have heard it sooner

or later,' he paused as he choked a little on his speech. 'It's Eleanor. . . . She's left me. . . . She's gone.'

Hannah didn't know how to respond, her instinct was to hug him, but this man was her employer, a man whom she'd loved for his skills and his kindness. She wondered how anybody could ever leave such a lovely person.

'Where is she? Where has she gone?' Hannah went over to him and eased herself gently on top of the desk beside him.

'There's someone else. . . . I've known about him for a while, at least she's been honest with me. She did try, but she said she couldn't take anymore of our life. It's all my fault Hannah - not hers. Don't blame her will you. I've never been much of a husband, chasing cattle and sheep around, and putting my job before her.' But before Barry could continue Hannah spoke up. 'Please don't Barry. . . . Don't tell me. . . . This is your private life.'

'I'm sorry, but if I don't tell someone, I'll go crazy!'

'What can be done then?' Hannah reluctantly continued.

'Nothing - absolutely nothing. What could have been done has been tried and has failed. She won't come back now and we'll be divorced.'

Hannah was silent, her mind racing as to what else to say; if there was any comfort she could bring. Now the end to her stay in Lakeland had taken an even unhappier turn. She fidgeted, rubbed her face, flicked her hair from her eyes and, with her hands deep in the pocket of her sheepskin jacket, sat with her shoulders hunched in defeat.

She noticed papers scattered about his desk and Barry started to shuffle them around. She saw some press cuttings about the death of George Keldas. She also saw a photograph, much like the one she'd seen and was mesmerised by, on the parlour wall at Keld Head. But this time was brave enough to peer at it as she picked it up. She looked deeply into the dark piercing eyes of the man she'd become to fear. 'He was a handsome man, wasn't he?'

'Yes. . . . Yes, I suppose he was. When he was younger, he could have taken his pick of the girls around here. It wasn't a surprise when he married Kathy - she was beautiful.'

'I bet you weren't too bad yourself.' Hannah looked compassionately at his dark and greying hair, his warm face, and remembered the earlier photographs she'd seen of him.

'Aye . . . but you can't turn back the clock.' He looked at the young woman sat beside him, her brown eyes tinged with sadness, her auburn hair falling on her face. Her little body was so compact and tidy that he envied her youth.

She picked up the cuttings and carefully placed them in his file and Barry put it back up on the shelf.

'Will this mean I have to leave earlier?' she said.

He was taken aback by her question and his dark blue eyes glared. 'Leave earlier. I'm sorry, Hannah; I don't know what you mean.'

'Well, people will talk, won't they? If they know Eleanor's gone, and we're here alone - living under the same roof so to speak.'

'Then let them talk. Goodness knows it's going to be hard enough after you go as it is. Besides, I could do with you to stay and sort things out until I can get some more help. I'm sorry, does that sound presumptuous. I guess I'm expecting a lot of you.'

She smiled at him, 'I'd love to stay . . . I don't mind what people say. Who cares? *Fame at last*!'

Hannah looked down at his diary. 'Shouldn't you be in Langdale by now?'

'Oh, it's just a bunch of sheep. I think they can wait a bit longer - they're not going anywhere.'

She jumped off the desk to leave. 'What are you going to do then?'

'Mope around a bit, I suppose. . . . Feel sorry for myself.'

'I was going to get changed and go for a walk. It's a lovely day. Do you fancy coming with me? The air will do you good.'

'Me. . . . Walk! Hannah, I haven't walked much further than the length of a field these last few years.'

'Then it will do you good then, won't it. You can take me to Grasmere and show me Dora's field. I want to see it before all the daffodils finish. It's not too far to walk is it?'

'No, but it's going to rain.'

'No it's not.'

Like two thieves, David and Tony left Keld Head early that morning. David had glanced up the lane and wanted to laugh when he thought of Alan milking the cattle and the mess he'd be in. He was glad of his freedom and despite the early hour, it felt good to gratify his own needs for a change. He knew he couldn't continue like this, once he'd talked to Joanne, surely then he would know what to do with his future. He would have to work somewhere; he would have to live somewhere. He was fast running out of money and had spent more on Tony's recovery than he'd intended, and now the train fares up to Aberdeen would be costly.

As they sat on the train David felt apprehensive. He became tired, and as he looked across at Tony, he saw he was asleep. David was glad he was sleeping, as Tony had spent the first hour on the journey coughing and no doubt irritating the other passengers.

David didn't particularly want to sleep; he doubted if he could anyway. Neither could he risk missing any of their connections, so the long waking hours on the train gave him time to plan his strategy with Joanne. He wanted to be alert and, most of all, to be calm. He mustn't alarm her. He guessed if she were feeling as bad as he was at being close to death, then she would be in a poor mental state. He didn't know if he would be welcome and he hoped that Tony's aunt would be there. David began to have doubts if he was doing the right thing. His tiredness was damaging his thinking and nothing appeared in perspective. If only he'd known the truth before - if only she had told the truth.

He looked at Tony sprawled out on the opposite seat and wished they'd taken more care over their appearance. They were both clean-shaven but were accustomed to wearing nothing other than faded jeans and t-shirts. Tony had changed his clothes and offered some clean ones to David, but David's sturdy body, despite losing weight living rough in London, couldn't fit into them. So, although his skin was clean, his clothes remained soiled and dirty and his hair, unkempt.

Hannah had to pull Barry up the steep hill to Rydal Hall by the hand. She laughed as he gasped his way to the top. Barry was relieved to be at the summit and leant on the wall and rested, but Hannah bustled him on and led him through a small wooden gate onto a lane.

She looked across to Rydal Water below as its small waves tossed about on this blustery afternoon. 'It's strange to think that Dorothy and William Wordsworth walked on these paths and we're doing the same. They saw the same rivers, the same mountains and the same views as us. I wonder how happy they were, Barry.'

'They were probably just like us, getting sick and old; trying to earn a decent living.'

'Oh, come on, gloomy. . . . Sit down a bit.'

They sat on a stone slab to take in the view.

'I've never been here before, it's beautiful. Are these Wordsworth's daffodils?' Hannah was looking at the drifts of yellow and gold flowers rising up through the parkland.

'Well, I think the daffodils that inspired Wordsworth were actually at Ullswater. This field was just named after his daughter.'

'It's incredible to think that people come from all over the world to see this.'

'Yes, it certainly brings the crowds to Grasmere.'

'Wouldn't it be funny, if something we did could attract the crowds like this?'

'Oh, I don't think I'm clever enough for that, and I'm certainly not one for poetry.' Barry leant back on the seat and enjoyed the spring sunshine touching his face.

'What's the difference between a narcissus and a daffodil, do you know, Barry?' It was a genuine question.

'One loves himself and the other doesn't!' Barry laughed at his own joke, and Hannah immediately thought of David.

THE GRANITE CITY

* * *

To David, Aberdeen felt like the coldest place on earth. The wind cut across the North Sea and hit their faces.

They took a taxi to a small housing estate; David was still apprehensive and the thoughts he'd hoped to gather on the journey had completely fled. He was glad Tony had come; he would never have found this place without him.

They knocked on the door of the small council house and waited. David was pleased it was Tony's aunt, Marian McKenzie, who opened the door. She pulled Tony in the house hugging him and kissing him. David was embarrassed and cautiously stepped in behind them and closed the door.

'Look at you. Just look at you.' She tugged at Tony's hair. 'It's good to see you're still alive, young man . . . and David too. Where have you been? You look the worse for wear!'

She led them to a small room and insisted that they sat down while she made them some tea and prepared a meal. There was no sign of Joanne.

David looked around the room and immediately felt enclosed. The pattern of the brown, flocked wallpaper and gaily-coloured Axminster carpet confused him. There was a clutter of ornaments and brasses that made the room look like a Grotto. As he sat, he felt he was in a kind of waiting room, expecting to see the dentist.

'This takes me back years.' Tony wandered around looking at photographs and paintings hanging on the walls. Some were of him as a child; some were of Joanne, and some of his father and his estranged mother.

Marian McKenzie went to the kitchen to prepare some tea and to peel some vegetables to make the boys a meal. She pulled the door behind her, leant back on it, and sighed, 'Now what!'

She was glad Joanne was out shopping, and hoped that she'd stay away long enough so she could gather her thoughts, and see how to handle the situation. The two young men sat in her parlour would have been most welcome at one time and Marian was certainly relieved to know they were safe. She wanted to call Tony's father and David's mother straight away, but guessed that wouldn't be wise, not until she had them in her confidence. Both men looked ill; she'd seen Tony in the hospital, but had expected by now that he would be well, but he was still coughing. David looked much thinner too; more so than she'd remembered him. His dark skin was now pale and insipid looking.

She took a tea-tray into the room and sat pensively with the two young men.

'How's Jo, then Aunty?' Tony started.

'She's okay considering. . . . She's not the same girl though - all the fun's gone out of her. But then I suppose that goes the same for you, Davey. . . . I'm sorry about your father, honey.' She spoke with a soft Aberdonian accent.

David acknowledged her kindness.

'Are you going to stay a day or two?' She quizzed them.

'No Aunty. . . . Just the night, if that's alright with you.'

'Yes . . . yes of course, but one of you will have to sleep on the sofa. I've no more room upstairs.'

A night in this claustrophobic room didn't appeal to David one bit, but neither did spending a night upstairs in a bedroom close to Joanne. 'That'll be me, then. I'll take the settee. I'm kinda getting used to them now.'

Marian paused before she spoke again: 'Joanne won't come back with you, if that's what you want.' She looked at David as she poured the tea.

'No . . . no Aunty. We haven't come to take her back. . . . We just want to see if she's okay, that's all.' Tony said.

Marian was still suspicious of their intentions. She handed them a tin of chocolate biscuits and returned to the kitchen.

David went and sat in the corner by the window to get some light. He picked up a newspaper and flicked through it, reading only the headlines. Tony leant back in the chair and tried to get back to sleep. They were startled when they heard the doorbell ring and a woman's voice. It was Joanne's.

David jumped up as his body responded to the adrenaline.

Joanne came into the room and threw her shopping bags

down on the sofa, delighted to see her brother, then gasped as she realised they weren't alone. 'What's he doing here?'

'Hush, Jo . . . sit down.' Tony whispered.

Joanne was shocked as she glanced across at David and attempted to leave but Tony quietly pushed the door closed.

'Leave her, Tony. . . . Don't frighten her.'

'Don't worry, David, I'm not frightened of you.' she gasped. But Joanne was already lying; she was afraid and felt cornered.

'Then you wouldn't mind answering a few questions, Jo? I'm sorry if this troubles you, but believe you me; David's been hurting as well you know.'

'Please Jo . . .' David said, 'If you want me to leave, then I'll go, but please talk to Tony. . . . Please be honest with us, we have something to ask.'

Joanne's countenance hardened and she bit her lip.

David had the courage to look into her face again, and how much she'd changed. Gone was the lovely young woman that had bewitched him only a few weeks earlier and had tempted him into a final decision of marriage. Her skin was pale and dappled with acne. Her eyes were dull with dark circles beneath them. But it was her hair that had changed the most; it had been cut and was so short that it didn't suit her; in fact, she appeared common and hard, unapproachable and unlovable. And the black leather jacket and short skirt she wore only highlighted her brash appearance.

Joanne's manner with David was as harsh as when he left her at the bungalow but now, with some of her sins to be exposed, she could only look at David with hatred, because he was the one who'd uncovered them. So every blemish on his body, his personality and his slovenly appearance became abhorrent, to compensate for her own flaws. When he tried to speak to her, there were feelings of revulsion for him.

But her look of disgust helped David and gave him courage, as he saw it as a key to freedom; in no way could he propose to this angry young woman, even if he were given reason to do so.

Joanne sat down on a dining chair and folded her arms in

defiance. The two men remained standing.

Everything to David appeared to be surreal. This quaint room in Aberdeen with its china ornaments and Draylon covers wasn't the right setting for what was taking place. He hoped that Marian McKenzie wouldn't return; he hoped she hadn't heard Joanne shouting.

When Tony started to question Joanne, David remained silent.

Joanne knew she was in trouble as the seriousness of her brother was rare. And so he began: 'Have you ever had an affair with David's dad?'

The frankness of his question shocked her; she flushed with colour and held her head low, no longer able to hide behind her hair. 'Man alive . . . ! You're blunt aren't you,' she spat.

'I don't care, Jo. I want some honest answers for both your sakes.'

'Since when has anyone been honest with me?' She lifted her head and looked at David. Yet Joanne knew it was futile to argue with her brother, she'd tried and failed so many times; yes, she was quick with words, but she was no match for him.

'Joanne, this isn't a game. . . . This is real life. We just want the truth. You live in some kind of fairytale world. You can't go on fooling around with people's lives.'

'Oh no. . . . Not like *he* can!'

David lowered his head.

'You nearly killed us both up on those fells, running away like a child that can't get its own way. David's father is dead, and some of the last words he spoke were about you. So answer me, Jo . . . did you have an affair with him?'

The tension was now touching David's soul, his legs became weak and he had an uncontrollable desire to sit down. He fell back with such a crash that the chair was pushed into the wall, knocking a table.

Joanne glared at him. She wondered if he'd fainted, but anger prevented her from helping him.

David composed himself and softly spoke, 'Joanne . . . please. . . . We've come all this way to talk to you. Tony's tired and he's still unwell. I can't bear this arguing anymore. I've had enough. I'm sorry about all that happened, much of it is my fault. I'm sorry if I hurt you. I never intended to. I'm sorry you had to be there when my Dad came back. I only hope my actions saved you from the gun,' he sighed. 'I've been lied to and cheated on so much, and now I just want to know the truth about the two of you. Just tell us and we'll walk away. You obviously despise me now and maybe I can understand that, but I must get on with my life. You're young enough to decide for yourself what to do, but please tell me, Jo, please.'

David's plea touched her heart, but she still felt his reproof. 'You always treat me like I'm a kid - both of you do. But I'm not stupid, I know exactly what I'm doing. . . .' she stuttered. 'Oh my! Your dad said some incredible things, David, didn't he? Perhaps they're true, I don't know. One thing, for sure is. Yes, I did have an affair with him, but I'm not sorry - I won't say I'm sorry!' And she walked from the room, defiant. She wanted to hurt him, again.

To have his fears confirmed, David had to stand. He guessed Joanne would now be crying but there was no way he could bring himself to go and console her.

'Well that's it then, Dave. . . . That's it. I could kill her!'

David knew his costly trip to Aberdeen had revealed the dark secret he hadn't allowed himself to believe. He saw the anger in Tony's eyes but there was no anger with him, he only felt sick and appalled that the young woman he'd considered marrying held this incredible secret, and he'd once thought her so innocent.

'I don't know whether to hope she's lying or not,' he softly spoke.

'She's not lying, Dave. I know this is true. . . . Man, you've had a lucky escape. But I wish it hadn't happened this way.'

Quietly and deliberately, Kathy Keldas put the telephone receiver down, rubbed her hair away from her forehead and dampened eyes.

She was relieved that Marian McKenzie had called, but the

news that her son was in Aberdeen made her shudder; to think he may have proposed a marriage of consolation to Joanne. There was nothing more she could do. She had brooded around the house for three weeks, not mourning the loss of her husband, as many suspected, but mourning the loss of her son.

The fear that one day David would discover the truth about his background had dogged her for twenty-three years. The early years of her marriage had been the easiest to cope with. George had shown her so much love and passion. He had idolised David, treating him, as he had promised, like a real father would. But as soon as the other children came along, things changed. David was pushed into the background, and it was only George's fear of losing Kathy, if he spoke out about David, that kept him silent. Kathy had threatened George that if he ever revealed the truth to David, or to anyone else, she would leave him, and in many of his drunken moments she had feared he would. David, in ignorance, had accepted the rejection of his father, because of the love that was lavished on him by his mother. Kathy loved all her children, but David was special and she had to give him more.

She was devastated when David had shown so much loathing towards her, when she had only ever loved him and done everything for his best interests.

George's death had ended her marriage sooner than she'd anticipated. His Will stated, and much as she suspected, that he'd left the farm and the land to Linzi, Tom and Sarah, leaving David nothing. George had given Kathy the right to live at Keld Head and reap its rewards, as long as she stayed single. There was one consolation, and that was Linzi had returned home for good. The death of her father she had found hard to bear. Her secret visits to the prison had fed her love for him, but now there were only the fields and the buildings to remind her of him.

Linzi was in complete ignorance as to why David had left, and was incensed that he hadn't come back for the funeral. She remembered how much he had chastised her for not attending Uncle Fred's funeral. She thought him a hypocrite. But after her mother told her of the Will, she thought she understood and guessed that David must have known all along about being dis-inherited. Yet she still couldn't understand why her father would have done that to David. But her anger for David soon turned to pity, as she wondered if he was still alive. He'd been so close to death at the hands of her father, he must surely be emotionally scarred. She couldn't bear to think of him in any kind of distress.

Linzi had begged Kathy to help her find him, and couldn't understand her mother's complacency. But Kathy had said she was over-reacting and that David would come home in his own good time. But Linzi wanted to fight for David's rights to Keld Head and thought her mother's actions were unfeeling and unfair.

Then there was relief when Alan had spotted the lights on at the Milton's bungalow and the news that David had been in London with Tony. Kathy was deeply hurt when she heard of Alan's row with him. She'd stayed in all the following morning and sent Alan away on some errands in a hope that she might talk to David alone. She needed to explain to him why she'd lied and done things the way she had. Only they must know their secret. She waited and waited but he didn't call. Kathy couldn't bear the suspense any longer, so had walked down to the bungalow but found it empty. And to hear the news now that David was in Aberdeen, not seeking her or any further explanations, and had gone recklessly chasing after a girl he would be a fool to marry, devastated her.

Alan had made it clear that he couldn't continue to hold down two jobs and the workload had put a strain on their relationship. He had presumed he could step into Kathy's heart, but her coldness toward him had become intolerable. He realised that he could never compete for her affections, as she secretly pined for David. Alan had made the mistake of openly criticising David for his behaviour, but Kathy knew there was little badness in her son. Alan had promised and delivered as much as he could do, but said if David didn't return she should consider selling the cattle, as they were spending excessive amounts of money hiring relief workers.

David slept remarkably well on Aunt Marian's sofa. The heat from the coal fire had warmed him most of the night. He found the cosy little room to be quiet and peaceful, and he no longer felt intimidated by it. He longed for the time when he could sleep in a real bed again. The small bedroom at Keld Head, he didn't desire. The uncomfortable feelings from yesterday had now gone and he felt like the man he was in London: free and contented. The only things he had to consider now were the decisions for his own well being and future; not those of anyone else, not even at the mercy of some girl who'd abused his sense of justice and kindness. One day David would look back and realise he'd been a fool. He did believe Joanne had sincerely loved him; he was in no doubt of that. But her betrayal at the hands of her former lover had revealed a darker side to Joanne, just as the photographs and the writings in her diary had betrayed her. There was no longer any need to sacrifice his future for the one small mistake on his part, for the whole of her sordid past. David felt her sin was greater than his. Tony was right – he'd had a lucky escape, and David should have listened to him sooner. He had suffered at the hands of two women now and wondered if he could ever trust another.

The following morning Marian McKenzie crept into the sitting room to re-light the fire, she looked at the young man sleeping on her sofa but, to a middle-aged woman, he appeared as a boy. She didn't pull back the curtains, she would let him rest. He wouldn't be concerned about her moving about the room. And as she watched David sleeping, she recalled the two grubby little boys playing together, one with bright red hair, one dark, with swarthy skin. Marian had hoped there wouldn't be any trouble over Joanne. She'd heard Joanne yell from the confines of the kitchen but didn't want to interfere. She knew that Joanne had got aspirations over David; but David, who'd witnessed such trauma in his life, could never give Joanne the stable future she needed, and she was as fiery as her red hair suggested.

Joanne used to talk of nothing but David, telling Marian how one day they hoped to marry. She'd said they'd had an agreement since they were children. But she was still too young, only eighteen.

Marian was also concerned that Joanne had spoken too freely of him. Some of the things had shocked her; she'd always considered David to be an honourable young man. When Joanne had returned with the bruising on her arms, Marian worried all the more of her spending a future with David, and tried to talk Joanne out of this infatuation she had. She did wonder if all she'd said was true and if David had really asked her to marry him. Was their relationship as sound as she said it was, or was she just fantasising, as she'd done over many other things in the past.

When Joanne returned after the second shooting at Keld Head and George Keldas's death, she'd changed. Joanne was quiet and, when she did speak of David, she never said anything good about him. Marian had guessed that there had been some kind of rift between them, and when David had turned up with Tony, she'd thought he'd come to take her back. Tony's definite plan to leave the following morning had reassured her, and she was pleased they wouldn't stay for the sake of David's poor mother.

They left without saying goodbye to Joanne. She hadn't risen that morning and, unlike David, had slept badly. Marian had fed them well by giving them a good breakfast. Tony decided to take David to the docklands to see some of the ships in port and as draughty as Aberdeen was, they leant together on the sea wall looking out across the cold North Sea.

Then Tony made a decision: 'I'm not coming back with you, Dave. I'm going to stay here a while. It's for the best. I'm still not well enough to look after myself, and I feel some kind of responsibility towards Jo. She's my sister no matter what she's done. It's not fair to leave Aunt Marian to pick up the pieces and, besides, you need to sort yourself out. You won't want an invalid like me hanging around your neck. I quite like the look of this place; I may get some work here.'

David knew he was right. He did need to sort himself out. He hadn't even considered where he was going or where he would stay.

'So what will you do, Dave?'

'Do you know, I haven't got a clue!'

'I'll give you the key to the bungalow if you like? '

'No . . . no thanks. I can't stay up at Keld Head; not yet anyway. I'll just catch the train back and, maybe, by the time I reach Cumbria I'll have made a decision.'

It was difficult for David to leave Tony at the station. Only a few weeks earlier they had parted on bitter terms, with no loyal feelings between them. Both were bent on their own decisions. They embraced not knowing when they would meet up again.

David sat on the train and the loneliness hit him immediately. He was a man with no identity. The Keldas name that brought so many misgivings was no longer his, and the freedom he'd desired wasn't making him feel as free as he expected.

17

KICK START

David jumped from the train at Windermere station a stronger man. He threw his bag over his shoulder and walked. He didn't feel the need to look over his shoulder, because it didn't matter anymore. He took a bus to Bowness and then headed for the ferry. He knew exactly where he was going.

Bowness was packed with visitors, the early evening sunshine reflected off the lake and onto his face, but he didn't mind. This sunlight hadn't been wasted, as much of it had in London, looking at four grubby walls or sitting on cold steps, seeing nothing but squalor around him. And as spring had trembled nervously to win the battle over winter, David equally trembled as he realised he'd succeeded in facing his fears.

He sat on the wall, waited for the ferry and watched the little boats moored in the harbour, their paintwork of blue, red and white glistening in the spring sunshine as they gently rocked in the calm waters, their rigging and sails, tap - tapping against the masts. Some children were laughing as they fed the ducks and swans that had gathered.

The ferry was heading towards him from across Windermere, the noise from its engine getting louder as it drew closer.

David boarded the ferry and as the old diesel engine chugged on its way, he leant on the rails at the side and looked into the soothing waters below; much more welcoming than the cold North Sea up in Aberdeen. He thought about Tony and wondered what he would be doing, and smiled as he guessed he would be sleeping again.

They were soon across the lake and David jumped off and

headed for the lakeshore, carrying on his back the few possessions he had left in the world. He lingered as he looked through the ruins of the old castle of Nab House, its turrets standing out eerily in the broken sunshine. As he climbed the steep hill, he pulled off his coat; something he hadn't been able to do in weeks, and the warmth of the sun touch the back of his neck.

Uncertain of the correct route, David followed the way-markers to Sawrey and on to Hawkshead, then walked through some fir tree plantations to an open fell with an exposed rocky plateau. He sat down again, in no hurry, and he wanted to drink in the view, as the whole of Windermere stretched out before him. The small boats were now dwarfed like paper toys, and David spotted the ferry once again chugging across the lake.

On the summit of Claife Heights, the small tarns were a good guide to his whereabouts. Then the route took him steadily downhill and continuing westward, he would soon have the little town of Hawkshead in his sights. David started to run as the path continued to descend, and he knew he would soon hit the lane that would lead him to Foxglove Cottage.

David quietly unlatched the door and entered.

Betty Keldas was sleeping in a chair in front of the fire; her glasses had fallen on her chest. A tabby cat sitting on her lap lifted one eye as it heard the intruder.

David carefully laid his bag on the floor and went across to Betty and, as he crouched low beside her chair, he reached over and touched her hand, then gently kissed her forehead.

The old lady opened her eyes and the broad smile that came on her face, told David he was welcome.

She stroked his stubbled cheek with her cold hands. 'Oh Davey . . . Davey. . . . Thank goodness you're safe!' She pulled her glasses back onto her nose and looked carefully into his face. 'You're ill. Let me see to you.'

David laughed, 'No, Aunty, I'm not ill. I'm just tired and maybe I haven't been eating as well as I should, that's all.'

'But we've all been worried about you.'

'I'm sure you have and I'm sorry. I never would have wanted *you* to have worried,' he stressed.

David raised himself and stood pensive before her.

'Let me fix you some food then,' and she held out her hand to him. 'Please help me up.'

David was alarmed to see the deterioration in his aunt and wondered if this was a good idea after all. 'No, Aunty. . . . Let me do it. I don't want to be a burden on you.'

'You, a burden. . . . Never.'

The two kept eye contact for sometime as Betty tried to take in the fact that her nephew, who'd been missing for nearly four weeks, was actually standing in front of her. She took his hand again and playfully shook it as she tried to stand.

'I won't ask where you've been or why you left; that's your business. You must have had good reason - well that's what I told your mother. But please tell me, have you been home? Have you seen her?'

David didn't want to answer the question but went into the kitchen and filled the kettle, then returned and sat on the chair arm beside her. 'Do you think I could stay a bit?'

'Davey. . . . You can stay as long as you like. But, tell me please, does your mother know you're here?' she repeated.

He held his head low, 'I'm sorry. I haven't seen her. She doesn't know where I am, and I can't talk to her; not yet anyway. I don't want to go back. You tell her I'm here, if you like.'

Betty was disturbed. He didn't appear distressed; he was calm, yet definite. 'Then you must make yourself at home. Take your things upstairs. Have the back bedroom. You can have the whole of the top floor to yourself as I can't climb the stairs these days. I sleep down here now. Get a wash and we'll have some tea together. It'll be a treat to have a man around the house again.'

David took his bag upstairs to a bedroom at the back of the cottage. He looked at the old mahogany bed in the corner covered in gaily coloured, hand knitted patchwork squares, he couldn't resist falling on the bed and it creaked under his weight. He threw his arms back in contentment. Then he jumped up again and peered through the panes of glass in the small window; the view was tremendous. He saw clearly the fells he had just walked.

When he went back down the stairs, Betty was in the kitchen cutting some bread. He leant across her and gently took the knife from her hand. 'No Aunty, no. Let me do that.'

Betty followed David around the small kitchen as she gave him instructions. He started to make some sandwiches then hunting through her fridge for some cheese, he noticed that the larder and the cupboards were well stocked. He opened a tin of tomato soup and found some crockery; all the while mindful he didn't knock into Betty and wishing she would leave him alone and sit down.

They finally sat at the dining table together and Betty watched David eating and wondered why he'd got into such a state. He looked thin, his clothes were dirty and worn, his hair was straggly and unkempt, yet his attitude had changed and he was more like his old self.

'What do you intend to do?'

'I'll look after you. . . . I'll get another job and we'll both be just fine.' David was trying to talk and eat at the same time.

'You've got it all worked out then. I'm glad I'm part of your plans.'

'I'm sorry . . . . Did that sound pushy?' He stopped eating and looked at her. 'I shouldn't have put on you like this – but, you see, there was nowhere else I could go.'

'I'm honoured that you felt you could come to me. . . . There's not many that would come to an old woman for help.'

David grinned and for the first time in weeks, realised how good the food tasted. He mended the fire, and stretched his legs out in front of him.

The next time Betty looked at him he was asleep.

She sat and watched him for some time, not daring to move in case she woke him. She realised she had in her midst the precious life of a young man, who had come willingly to find some kind of solace. She wanted to call Kathy immediately, but knew that would be insensitive, and would have to wait until she was alone, however long that would take.

The following morning David woke to the sweet smell of clover as warm air drifted in through his open window. He had slept well in the old bed that he'd often slept in as a child, and each time he turned it creaked under his body weight. He recalled his childhood, waking early and looking forward to spending the day with Uncle Fred at Spickle Howe Farm.

He heard voices downstairs and then, peering through the window, saw a woman leaving. He recognised by her shape that it was Mrs Challenor, a neighbour from the village. A cue for him to get up.

Betty's face glowed as she saw him. He looked well rested, fresher and clean-shaven; his dark hair washed and still wet and shiny, brushed back off his face.

'What can I do for you today?'

'You can have some breakfast first young man. Then you can get some wood in and perhaps some fresh food. I won't have enough to feed a hungry lad like you. I've just told Mrs Challenor that I won't need her help quite as much now . . . I hope I did right?' She looked at him hopefully.

David nodded; it was just what he wanted her to say.

He went into the kitchen and returned with a bowlful of cornflakes and as he sat at the table he told her of his plan for the day. 'I've decided to go to Bowness this morning to get a haircut. Then I can start to look for a job and, when I get back, maybe I could do some washing, please, and some of yours if you like.'

Betty was glad of his enthusiasm. She'd slept badly that night, worrying that she was betraying Kathy in not telephoning her. She didn't want to upset David and could see by his plan for the day that he had not changed his mind. She wondered how he could have abandoned his mother and the farm so easily.

The morning sunshine shone through the tiny windowpanes of Foxglove Cottage, exposing dust and cobwebs that had been neglected. David sat at the table eating toast and drinking coffee, looking out of the window into the garden and keen to get started. 'I'll get off as soon as I can, if that's all right with you?' and looking up at the cobwebs, 'I can do some housework for you when I get back this afternoon.'

'That's good of you, Davey, but how will you get to Bowness?'

'I'll walk or maybe hitch a lift and then get the ferry.'

'You could take the bus and go to Ambleside?' she suggested.

He'd already thought of that, but that meant being closer to Keld Head. 'I'll be fine Aunty. . . . Don't worry about me? I can find my way about here. Now then, what can I bring us back for dinner?' And he rubbed his hands together.

Betty sat at the table with him and started to write a shopping list with such a shaky hand that it was hardly legible. She fiddled in her purse and insisted in giving him money for the fresh meat and vegetables. When David made only a slight attempt to pay, she guessed he was broke.

Betty knew that she would now have a chance to ring Kathy and, as soon he was out of the cottage and she watched him walking down the lane, she immediately picked up the telephone.

'I had a little stray puppy stay with me last night!'

'Did you. . . .' Kathy sounded perplexed.

'Yes, and he's gone out for a walk and he's coming back for his dinner.'

'Are you teasing me?' and Kathy started to worry about Betty's sanity.

'I am love,' she mused. 'It's *your* puppy that I've found.'

Kathy was confused for a moment. 'My puppy . . . my puppy, what puppy? What on earth are you talking about?'

'Not what, but who!'

'DAVID!'

'Yes, David.'

'Oh, Betty. . . . Thank goodness for that. Marian phoned to say he'd left Scotland. I didn't know where he would go next.' She flopped down on a chair by the phone. 'Is he alone?'

'Yes, he is love.' Betty presumed she was referring to Tony.

'Did he say anything about . . . ?' she paused and then continued, 'did he tell you where he's been all these weeks?'

'No dear, and I haven't asked him either, but you needn't worry anymore. You see he wants to stay with me for a while. And I'm afraid to say, he won't be coming home just yet.'

Kathy somehow expected that David wouldn't be coming home just yet, and was comforted to hear that he was back in England, alone and safe.

'You must have had some argument? I'm afraid he doesn't want to speak to you, but he said I could phone you, if I wanted.'

'We did have a huge row, I'm sorry to say. He was shocked at seeing his father again, and then with the shooting, in the heat of the moment, we both said things we'll regret, and let's put it this way, it's all my fault. But tell me, has he talked to you about the farm? I must speak to him about Keld Head.'

'I don't think he'll want to,' Betty said.

'Then will you ask him for me, please. I don't know what else to do with the cattle. We just can't manage without him.'

'I'm sorry, Kathy, but he said he didn't want to come home-he insisted. In fact he's gone to Bowness just now to try and get a job.'

Kathy wanted to run from the house and drive to the lakeshore to meet him and tell him how much she loved him. She wanted to plead with him for forgiveness, but she knew that would be foolish. He was safe at Betty's and he would be loved. She still had faith in him to know she would, one day, see him again.

'I'll have another talk with him when he gets back, but don't worry. . . . Don't call me and whatever you do, don't come to see him or he'll fly again, I just know it!' Then Betty paused, 'there is one more thing though . . . .'

Kathy's heart sunk heavy within her at the tone of Betty's voice.

'He's not the same lad he was. He's thin and looks badly. . . . I'm not sure if he's altogether well. He insists that he'll look after me, but I think it'll be the other way around.'

'Is he agitated again or nervous?'

'No, and that's worrying. He's the opposite - he's calm - too calm, and I haven't seen him like this in years. He's either changed or he's still in shock, but I don't know which.'

With mixed feelings, Kathy put the receiver down. She started to cry, and this time, uncontrollably; was it sheer relief, happiness, sadness or what, she didn't know. She went upstairs to her bedroom, shut the door behind her and fell on the bed. It was sometime before she dared to come out. When she did, her head ached and her eyes were sore. She tried to regain her composure. The children were at home for the Easter holidays, so she quickly washed her face, brushed her hair and went back downstairs.

Tom and Sarah were sat in the parlour watching television. When Sarah saw her mother, she came to her and hugged her around the waist. 'What's the matter, Mummy? Why are you crying?' Sarah didn't want to let her go and clung on to her arm. 'Are you crying because of Daddy?'

Kathy no longer wanted to lie, 'I'm missing Davey, my love, that's all.'

'I miss him too . . . he's gone away forever, like Daddy, hasn't he?'

'No love.'

'Then I'll smack him when he gets back for making you cry.'

The little girl went back to the parlour, sat down beside her brother and whispered in his ear, 'Tom . . . I think Davey must be in prison like Daddy was, and that's why Mummy's crying.'

'Don't be stupid. . . . He's gone because he hates Mum, he hated Dad and he hates us as well!' and with that he picked up a small plastic toy and threw it at the television set.

David's first stop was the barber's shop and being unfamiliar with such places he hesitated as he walked into the small room and asked for a good haircut. The elderly barber was glad of the challenge to attack David's head with his clippers as David sat and watched his dark hair fall to the floor. In the mirror he could see the true lines of his face emerge. He wondered at the man he saw and found it hard to recognise himself. His loss of weight had drawn his face out of recognition, with his short cropped hair and pale skin; his face much thinner, revealed even more, his unusual eyebrows and deep set, blue eyes.

'Well young man,' the barber was triumphant, 'you look a bit more presentable now.'

David fumbled in his pockets for some loose change. 'That's good, because I need to get a job.'

'What line of work are you looking for?' The barber knew who David was.

'Doesn't matter really. . . . Bar work, driving, I'll have a go at anything.'

'Jack of all trades, eh?'

David hesitated, 'well sort of.'

'Get yourself to the hotel across the road. They're looking for a barman. Tell them I sent you and you'll probably get the job.' He wanted to tell David not to mention his real name because with the new haircut, he was unrecognisable as the surly young man everyone had seen in the newspapers.

The next few days were spent cleaning and washing. David cut the grass and weeded the garden; the semi-isolation of Foxglove Cottage suited him with no one to interfere with his life. He bought a post-card from the village Post Office and sent it to Tony, with a cryptic message as to his whereabouts. He made several trips to Bowness, shopping and doing errands for his aunt. Betty had a new lease of life with his presence; she was eating better, her house was cleaner and her mental anguish had subsided.

One evening after David had cooked a makeshift meal, they sat together at the table talking and eating, as had become their custom. 'I spoke to your mother the other day.'

David was non-committal.

'She's glad you're safe and with me . . . but she needs to ask you about the farm.'

KICK START

David was, uncharacteristically, rude to her and stayed silent.

'She wants to know if you're going back, if not she'll have to sell the cattle.'

This suggestion surprised him; he wanted to reply but only out of politeness. 'She doesn't need my advice, she can do what she likes with the farm; it's hers not mine.'

'So you *do* know about your father's Will?'

Of course David didn't know, in fact, it hadn't even entered his head that George Keldas's Will would have been opened in the first place. 'I'm sorry . . . I don't get what you mean.' And the familiar quizzical look returned to his face.

'David. . . . You do know there's a problem with your father's Will. You know he's not left you anything, don't you?'

The words hit him like a sharp sword through his heart. This was the last cutting of any ties: the last insult. No son - no farm - no choice!

At one time, the anger would have made him run, but now he only froze with the realisation of what he'd just been told. He was slow to reply. 'Then I've made the right decision. . . . I'll start work at the hotel on Saturday and earn us a bit of money.'

Betty could see as he pushed his plate of food away, the sadness in his face. He was deeply hurt. He had clearly not known about the contents of the Will. The poor lad, what more could be done for him she wondered? She took hold of his hand. 'You will still stay with me won't you? You won't go away again and leave me?'

David took her tiny, thin hands in his. 'I'll have to stay now, won't I. I think the world of you and I love this cottage - we'll get on just fine, you and me. . . . I chose to come here last week, and although you're no flesh and blood of mine,' (she presumed he meant because she was only his aunt through marriage), 'I've come to realise that blood isn't thicker than water, as they say. I've been shown more love by strangers and friends recently than by my own family.'

The following day was Saturday and David was due to start his new job that evening. He'd bought a pair of black trousers, some brogue shoes and two white shirts. He'd nearly spent all his reserves of money and a trip to the bank confirmed that. He would have to take on as much work as he could get, firstly to pay some maintenance to his aunt, as he couldn't continue to presume on her kindness, and then, for his own self respect.

When he got up that morning Betty was, as usual, up and dressed and hobbling around the kitchen with her two sticks. The back door was wide open and fresh, clean air was bursting in. The birds had been fed and the cat was still hovering for food. As he always did, David came to her, kissed her on the cheek and then went to the cupboard to find a bowl and fill it with cornflakes.

'Come here, Davey . . . there's something I want to show you.'

He could see she was excited as she pulled from her apron pocket a bunch of keys.

'Come with me . . . come with me,' she beckoned him.

He followed her down the garden path, passed the flowerbeds and neatly cut lawn. Concealed in a yard at the back of the cottage was a dilapidated wooden garage, painted with the remnants of flaky, yellow and green paint, and covered in ivy.

'Open the door, Davey.'

She gave him the keys and he unlocked the fragile door.

'Now pull it open . . . be careful . . . be careful, it may be rotten.'

David could see it was rotten and, as he slid the door ajar, she pushed passed him and tried to open it further.

'Let's get some light in here.'

David was wondering, yet smiling at her enthusiasm, and held her fragile arm to steady her.

The garage was full of old junk: paint tins, tools and bits of machinery, metal and wood, but taking up most of the space was a large object in the middle.

'Now pull the cover off?' she asked.

David tugged at the tarpaulin. Dust and cobwebs drifted over him, so he put his hand to his nose to stop himself from sneezing.

'She's yours now, do you want her?'

David saw his Uncle Fred's Volvo Amazon. He hadn't seen the old maroon coloured car in months. He slid his fingers across the rounded bonnet as he admired the coachwork and the large headlamps of the long forgotten car.

'See if you can start her, Davey, please,' and handed him the keys.

'She won't start now!' he laughed. 'Has she been stood in here since Uncle Fred died?'

He unlocked the car doors and jumped inside onto the cold leather seats. He held firmly onto the steering wheel and grinned. Then he slid outside again and found the catch to release the bonnet. He looked at her and rubbed his hand on his mouth, 'you mean I can have this?'

'Well, I've been saving her for you. . . . Freddie always said that if anything happened to him, that you should have her. You do want her don't you?'

He immediately fiddled under the bonnet. 'Of course I want her, she'll do me fine.'

'Can you get her going then?'

'I hope so, but not today. She'll maybe need a new battery, an oil change and spark plugs. . . . The brakes might be seized up,' then he hesitated, stopped and closed the bonnet. 'I can mend her . . . but not just yet, anyway.'

'You will if I pay for it! If you can do the work, I'll tax her and test her and pay the insurance. I can't have you walking and hitchhiking all the way to that ferry every day.'

David left the garage, and tightly held the keys in his hand and restrained himself from throwing them up in the air.

David spent the whole of the next week under the bonnet of the old car and, as he neglected his household duties, Betty wondered if it had been a good idea to give it to him straight away. She missed his company, as he spent most of his time in the garage, then the rest at the hotel. But Betty liked the idea of having a man around the house again, despite him littering her kitchen table with carburettors, air-filters and oily rags as he patiently cleaned them. He so much reminded her of Fred.

David absorbed himself in his new job too. He either walked or hitched a lift to the ferry each afternoon and then caught a taxi home. Most evenings, Betty was still alone. Sometimes, it was the early hours of the morning when she heard him come in and, if he did a split shift, he would stay in Bowness all day.

One morning Betty was sitting at the kitchen table looking out into the garden, David had stayed in bed most of the morning. He'd worked late the night before. He'd slept well but he needed to, as he was working hard, maybe too hard Betty thought. He didn't go anywhere else other than the hotel, then the garage or the cottage, or walking the fells. And, on the few evenings he was home, he sat quietly and watched the television. Despite all its misgivings, the idea of giving him the car had been a blessing, as it kept him occupied, but Betty wondered how long he could keep up this isolation. Living with an old woman wasn't ideal. But this morning David had spent a couple of hours in the garage and as she sat watching from the kitchen window, she heard him try to start the car engine again. It turned over as it usually did, but didn't start, then this time - whoosh! Blue smoke drifted from the garage as the engine spluttered in full flow.

Betty heard the engine start and it had an effect on her she hadn't anticipated. Something ran through her veins like the restoration of life, and not just hers; it was Fred's, and David had done it. Just like when he'd breathed life into Fred on the day that George had shot him. It was David who'd tried to resuscitate him and had kept him alive before the ambulance came. It was David who'd pressed on the open wound and stopped the flow of blood. It was David who'd wrenched the gun from George, risking his own life, as the man laughed and then wept like a child, not regretting that he'd shot Fred, but sorry that he'd missed David. Yes, that old engine ticking over reminded her of a day she'd never dare recapture.

David rushed into the cottage, his face covered in oil and

grime, the whites of his eyes shone with vibrancy through the dirt. He didn't notice that the tears in Betty's eyes were any different to the glaze of moisture her aged eyes always had.

'This calls for a celebration, Aunty.' He went to the sideboard and looked for a bottle of something to celebrate with. Betty wanted to share his glory, but she couldn't.

David didn't discern the tone of seriousness to her voice as she asked him: 'Will you promise to take me to Kendal as soon as you can love?'

'Of course I will . . . I'll take you wherever you want to go - once I know she's safe, that is.'

David quickly got into the routine of the hotel work, despite the unsociable hours. The gift of the car, as old as it was, made his life easier. The physical nature of the work was undemanding, apart from humping of beer kegs up and down the cellar. He enjoyed the companionship too; the other employees found David to be good company and easy going. The other members of staff soon grew to like him despite him refusing any offers of a drink or an evening out. He was a local lad, he fitted in well and caused little friction, except, perhaps, between the waitresses.

Although no one ever spoke of it, it was soon passed around who David really was. They all had read about George Keldas. They wondered why David needed to do bar work and why he now lived near Hawkshead. Some assumed he was living with a woman.

One evening David was working behind the bar, washing a few glasses, when he noticed a young woman walk passed and go to the restaurant; she seemed oblivious to this slim, tidy young barman with short-cropped hair. It was Hannah Robson.

He watched her from the corner of his eye go to the restaurant and sit with a man; the two of them becoming engrossed in each other.

His initial reaction was to freeze. She hadn't spotted him and she certainly hadn't recognised him. He became embarrassed at his lowly status, something he hadn't anticipated.

'Have you got your eye on that girl in the corner, Dave?' the other barman said.

David didn't commit himself.

'Come on, mate, admit it. . . . You've been watching her all evening.'

David didn't know how to reply. 'I just know her that's all.'

'Do you know the old guy she's with then?'

'Yes, I do.'

'You would wonder what a pretty girl like her would see in a guy like him. He's old enough to be her father.'

'I don't think it's anything like that. . . .' David knew to his cost that sometimes young women did like older men but, never-the-less, he defended Hannah, 'you see she works with him.'

'Aye . . . I know she does. Isn't he the vet? They say his wife's left him because of her.'

David picked up a glass and started to rub it dry with a towel. 'How do you mean, I don't understand?'

'Ah ha. . . . There you are; you do fancy her. . . . I knew it!'

David flushed.

'His wife left him recently and he's been seen with that girl, holding hands and walking out with her. My mate who works at the hotel at Rydal fancies her too. She vaccinated his dog. He saw them together on White Moss Common.'

David's instinct was to defend Hannah and Barry, but perhaps some of this was true; a lot could have happened in the few weeks he'd been away, and then living in isolation with Betty. He knew Barry had been unhappy. It was no secret that he and Eleanor led separate lives. But Hannah and Barry: no, that couldn't be true.

He continued to rub the beer glass and the force of his grip broke it clean in two, cutting his hand. 'Ow . . . !' David gasped.

'Steady, Dave. . . . You're cracking up, mate.'

With blood dripping from his hand, David went to the restroom. He put his hand under the cold water in the washbasin. He took a paper towel and held it tightly over the wound. David leant back on the wall, looked at his reflection in the mirror in front of him, and wondered if he liked the man he now was. Why worry about Hannah and Barry; they must do what they want with their lives, as he must do with his. And as he looked hard into his own face, scowling as he did so, he no longer saw the image of George Keldas. His eyes were different than his, also his teeth and his mouth. But the face he saw, he still didn't recognise. And not for the first time, he wondered who the man was who'd given him this life. Did he know or care about a long lost son? The loneliness had returned and he wished that Tony Milton was here; he would know what to do, he would help him. And everything he'd ever known had fled away from him as he clung to the love of an old woman.

David reluctantly returned to the bar; he couldn't risk losing his job, and so, with his hand securely taped in Elastoplast, he continued his work and hoped that Barry and Hannah wouldn't come to him for their drinks.

He watched them for some time as they had coffee and then just as another customer arrived and David served him, they walked passed the bar and only Barry raised his head to say goodnight to the barmen.

Barry Fitzgerald looked back at the dark haired young man and thought he reminded him of someone.

Behind Foxglove Cottage were two small fields, their stone walls reaching high up to the forest. The sheep grazed constantly, filling their bellies ready for the lambs, which would arrive soon. The sturdy little sheep were not afraid of David as he sat on the rocky outcrop above them. The footpath through their territory was well used; these sheep were used to fellwalkers and backpackers.

David sat watching the sheep grazing and looking at the life below him. In the distance, he could see the cars arriving, one after another, to Hawkshead.

This walk got him out of the cottage, out of Mrs Challenor's way. She had come to do Betty's "private" washing. But David knew she would want to fuel the village gossip about him. He also knew Betty would be discreet when Mrs Challenor fished for knowledge about him. So this piece of England that Betty owned, these two fields, were safe territory for David. The very grass he sat on belonged to his aunt. The sheep were there by right too. Betty had let out the field to a local farmer to graze his ewes and the return she got other than the rental, was to see what remained of Fred's land being put to good use and the chance of being able to watch the livestock graze from her window.

Today, as Betty sat in her usual position in the window, she watched David; he had taken to the fells again. He walked the hills a lot, yet despite this, his skin was pale and his body was still thin. He had some appetite, but hadn't put on the weight that he should have by now, during the time he'd stayed with her. The hard work saw to that.

David had also become quieter of late and almost distant, she didn't know why and wondered if something had happened. It was as if something had suddenly changed. She wished he would see his mother and make amends. Bitterness was no way to live a life. She'd tried to suggest it, but he'd rebuffed her and then, in remorse, apologised for his behaviour and kissed her.

The thought struck Betty that he wanted to leave; yet she dare not think it. As changeable and moody as he was, she dreaded him leaving her; to go, just as quickly as he had come.

She prayed for him night and day that he might find some piece of mind. Then she wondered if she was being selfish and should insist that he go home; he perhaps felt obliged to her. Then she thought that he'd come here willingly and, if he should want to leave, he should leave willingly. Betty would not hold him here against his will, and yet she wished she could.

It began to rain, and the fine mist swept across the fell wetting David's face. The sheep made no move, they just continued eating. David pulled up the collar of his jacket and slowly walked back down the hill to the cottage.

'What shall we have for tea, Aunty? I'm starving.' He hung his wet coat on the chair by the fire.

Betty was brave. 'You don't have to eat with me. . . . Why don't you have a run out, get some fish and chips or something - have a drink with your friends.'

David appeared not to hear her and walked to the kitchen and pulled open the fridge door then shouted back. 'My mates are up on that fell side and they don't like fish and chips!'

18

THE VISITOR.

Kathy Keldas ran into the blue-stone hay barn to shelter from the rain; she was breathless. 'For goodness sake, Linzi . . . come inside.... You'll be soaked.'

Linzi joined her mother in the security of the barn, and fell down in the straw and laughed. 'I thought we were going to lose them then, Mum. Why on earth didn't you stop them?'

'Linzi. . . .' Kathy was exasperated, 'those heifers can run a lot faster than I can, anyway, they're bigger than me; they could have knocked me down.'

'We should have used the dog, you know.'

'Oh, Linzi.... Only David or you father could work with that dog. Anyway, we've managed. There's plenty of grass for them now in this paddock.'

The realisation that each small task they did was a challenge for Kathy; things she'd seen David do and had taken for granted. The skill of her son and her dead husband far outshone anything she or Linzi could manage. At least today they had something to laugh about.

They had lost a dairy cow last week; it had to be put down. It had safely calved but, with a weakness in her pelvis, she had slipped and fallen on the wet concrete yard and was unable to stand. Linzi was distraught at the animal's predicament. Alan had tried to help by tying some soft rope around its ankles to support it, but the idea failed. And as a last resort Barry Fitzgerald was called, but there was nothing he could do and suggested the animal be shot. And then Silver had been sick again. She'd developed mastitis in one quarter of her udder.

THE VISITOR

The infection had been missed and had become too severe to be treated. Barry gave her some penicillin, but told them to expect she would lose all productivity on that quarter and would become near useless.

Kathy had wept in frustration because of how much Silver meant to David, and now their best yielding animal would become an expensive burden if they kept her.

She knew if David had been here he would have spotted the infection sooner, and Kathy inwardly cursed him for abandoning her. Linzi and Alan were more open and dared to criticise David's inconsiderate behaviour to her face. Something had to be done, and soon, before the farm fell into ruin. She had to ease the workload for all of them.

They looked out of the barn into the rain as drifts of clouds swept across the sky; some black, some grey, and bringing along with them more water. The fields that were already wet had become sodden and covered the two women in mud.

Wet and dishevelled they made their way back to the farmhouse, walking quickly down the lanes, jumping over the puddles and the small stream that funnelled its way across the path.

'I saw the auctioneer yesterday. He said if we decide soon whether to sell the cattle, he could have an auction arranged for sometime next month.'

'Oh, Mum . . . Dad wouldn't have wanted that.'

'Who knows what your father really wanted, Linzi.' Yet she knew George had got his way in one thing, in leaving David with nothing.

And although Linzi was disappointed, she knew her mother was right. They couldn't farm this place properly between them. Alan had suggested they buy some more sucklers with the money they would make. They already had four heifer calves they could rear on, and they could hopefully make a living at selling a few beef cattle rather than have the hassle of running the dairy herd. They could even buy a few more sheep.

'I know you're right, Mum, but I don't think we should do

anything until we've spoken to David.' As she rubbed her face, rain water ran down her nose.

'If I could talk to him you know I would, but how can I?' Kathy was serious - Oh, how she longed to see him. 'Betty's convinced that he'll leave if we push him. She says he's already unsettled.'

'Then if you can't speak to him . . . I will! There's nothing to stop me is there? I can't see what all the fuss is about anyway. He walks out and leaves you and doesn't contact us at all. He could have been dead for all we knew. . . . And then you go on protecting him all the time and won't say anything bad against him. What's so special about David, anyway?'

'It's not like that, Linzi.'

'No. . . . What is it like then? I don't understand, I'm sorry.'

But Kathy knew she could never understand.

'If you want to see him, you go. . . . You ask him. He may even be pleased to see you, I don't know . . . but be careful mind? Don't go upsetting him. . . . Keep calm. Tell him you've missed him, but whatever you do, keep calm.'

As they approached the farmyard and saw Alan's car parked in its usual place, Linzi took her mother's arm and squeezed it. 'I'll go and see Davey tomorrow.'

They were still talking when they entered the kitchen. Kathy hung onto the door frame as she kicked off her muddy wellingtons. On the kitchen table was a large bouquet of flowers: white carnations, blue iris, yellow chrysanthemums; beautifully arranged and neatly wrapped in cellophane paper, tied with a large blue ribbon. There was no sign of Alan.

Linzi raised one eyebrow at her mother and smirked. 'I'm going for a hot bath. I'll leave you to it!'

Kathy at first hesitated, rubbed her wet hair on a towel and dried her hands and face. She went over to look at the flowers and tried to find a message but there was none; for one fleeting moment, she hoped they might be from David. But before she could lift them from the table, Alan came into the kitchen behind her and the broad and beaming smile on his face told her they were from him. She was disappointed.

THE VISITOR

'Do you like them?' He came closer to embrace her.

She backed away and spoke. 'They're lovely, Alan, but what are they for?'

He pulled her to him. 'Oh . . . things have been a bit tough on us all. I've said things I shouldn't have done . . . and I'm sorry. I'm sure we're all tired and I just want to show you - well, to tell you that I still care.'

'You big softy, Alan.' She gently patted his chest, 'you needn't have done this . . . with all the work you do for us. It's you that deserves presents, not me.'

Kathy gently pulled away from him and, not wanting to snub him, went across to the tap to fill the kettle, knowing she had another problem to face.

She leant against the kitchen sink and folded her arms. 'Alan, I know you still care about me. . . .' she paused - this was going to be hard. 'I'm very fond of you, I always have been; you know that. But please be patient with me. I can't give you anything back just yet. I know you would want it.' She went to unwrap the flowers, not looking at him; the paper rustling as she nervously spoke. 'At one time I did think - well maybe there was something for us . . . and all the time I wanted to divorce George, you knew that. But believe me, it's not been made any easier by his death. I'm a widow and the children have lost their father and, for the sake of decency, I don't think I can commit myself to anything or anyone just yet.'

Alan took hold of her hand and stopped her flower arranging. 'I'm sorry Kathy. I didn't want to seem insensitive. We've been good friends, you and me. I'm sorry I can't do anymore on the farm. I've tried to balance two jobs and it's just impossible. I think that's why I've been moody lately.'

'Alan, you don't need to apologise,' she sighed. 'We moved the heifers this morning like you suggested. What a job we had, we nearly had them in the village!'

'You've done well, Kathy. Aye, you have.'

David slid carefully underneath the old Volvo and pointed his torch on the bodywork. He tapped at the exhaust pipe,

THE VISITOR

checking it for wear and tear. He'd heard a knocking noise and wondered if it had come from a loose fitting. He had promised to take Betty out today; yesterday's rain had gone and the weather was more promising: warm and sunny; Betty called it growing weather.

He shuffled the length of the car on his back on the cold floor, his feet protruding from the side. A transistor radio played, loudly, the Moody Blues, *Nights in White Satin,* and David sung it under his breath, struggling to recall the words.

Someone kicked at his feet and he lay still, not wanting to bang his head. He guessed it was Betty. Then, straining his neck, he looked across at the small feet beside him as they kicked him once again. But whoever it was, was wearing trainers.

'Who is it?'

'Come out of there, Davey, before I drag you out!'

It was a woman's voice, but over the noise of the radio, he couldn't discern whose.

David struggled out from underneath the car and groaned as he wrenched his back in the process. He saw his sister, dressed in old jeans and sweatshirt, her dark hair unkempt and tied loosely in a ponytail.

Linzi grinned and stepped forward. 'Wow, Davey! Look at you, you handsome devil. Where's all that hair gone?'

David brushed the dust from his overalls and leant back on the bonnet of the car to rest his aching back and rubbed his hands on an oily rag. He didn't know what to say to her as he watched her eyeing him, then his car.

She looked again long and hard at his physique and pulled at his overalls to touch him. 'Good grief, you've lost weight. You're skinny.'

'Okay, okay . . . enough of the comments.' He crossed his legs in front of him, still resting his back on the car. 'So, Sister. You've come to see Betty have you?'

'No, you idiot . . . I've come to see you. Don't seem so pleased!' She wandered around the car looking in the windows and went to turn the radio down.

THE VISITOR

'Is this Uncle Fred's old Volvo?'

'It was Fred's old Volvo, now it's mine!' he deliberated.

'Have you done her up a bit then? She looks well.'

'Only the basics, and she's had a good wax and polish.'

'You must look quite a catch going out in this. That's providing you're still single then, eh!'

He smirked at her as she went to sit on an old workbench opposite him and started to fidget with his tools.

'Davey . . . I want to tell you something.'

He lowered his head and waited for her to start nagging at him for leaving.

Linzi was her usual self and got straight to the point. 'I want you to have half my share of the farm, when Dad's Will's sorted out . . . I haven't told Mum, and I can't explain to Tom and Sarah just yet. I don't understand why you've been left out. It's just not fair.'

'Well, thanks for your consideration,' David scowled, 'but I've wanted out for a long time and now I've got the chance.' He made no attempt to move and stood his ground.

She was astonished by his reply and stared at him. 'Oh, for goodness sake. You can't mean that!'

'Oh, but I do mean it. There's nothing to hold me to Keld Head now.'

'So is that why you left us all, just because you *wanted out*!' Linzi was ignoring all the advice that her mother had given her.

David didn't reply.

'Oh, come on David! Don't go all sulky on me. A few months ago, you tore a strip off me for not going to Uncle Fred's funeral. . . . You're a hypocrite, you know! You've left us all in the lurch. I can't believe how you can just walk out on us like that.'

David stayed calm as he spoke. 'Look Linzi, you don't know what it was like to face Dad again, and you won't understand why I left Keld Head and I'm not going to tell you . . . but, I will tell you this, I won't be coming back. I'll stay with Betty for now.'

THE VISITOR

'I'm sorry David, but I could strangle you sometimes. You can be so irritating. Yes, I don't know what really happened, but why leave now? I've told Mum time and time again you're not as perfect as she thinks you are!'

'Oh, thanks. I've never pretended to be perfect.'

'Well, you're just as bad as Dad. . . . He was always walking out on her and now you're doing the same!'

The comparison between himself and George Keldas, hit David hard. He no longer feared George's impropriety, but detested being accused of walking out on his mother. David had hated him for leaving her so often, especially as he now knew the dreadful truth; all the time, making accusations against her, when George was having an affair and playing around with a girl half his age.

David found himself in a daydream as Linzi continued to insult and abuse his name, but he was no longer listening. Then the thought suddenly crossed his mind whether his mother knew or not about the affair with Joanne. He had been so stupid – so slow. All this time he'd only thought about his own selfish pride. How hurt she must have felt if she knew the truth. Was that why she'd been upset by his plan to marry Joanne, and he shuddered at what he may have done.

'David . . . David. . . . Are you listening?'

He was staring into the garden, his eyes now glazed over with moisture.

Linzi jumped down off the bench, and finally reading his mood correctly, went to hug him. And as she threw her arms around his neck, he put his arm across her back and pulled her closer to him and held on to her tightly for some time.

Linzi buried her head in his chest, smelling the oil on his clothes and the warmth of his body. She wanted to cry, but restrained herself and pulled away. She grabbed the oily rag from his hand and playfully pushed it in his face.

'There's one thing I have to ask before I go,' she choked on her words. 'It's the cattle. . . . Mum thinks it's a good idea to sell them and get some sucklers.' Linzi wandered around the car again. 'I don't want to sell them, but if you insist on not coming back, we have no choice.'

'Linzi. . . . It's not my decision to make.' David was sorry about the cattle but he still had self-preservation in mind. 'Just do as you like.'

'Davey. . . ?' she stopped as she was about to leave. 'Please come and see us all soon. . . . Please.'

'I will, I promise. . . . But in my own time. . . . Thanks for coming.'

David continued with his work, going through the motions of the repairs. He tightened and replaced a broken bracket, cursing a bolt that had seized up and corroded and was stuck fast. He kept dropping the bolts then misplacing his spanners, but finally succeeded in tightening the exhaust pipe.

He scrambled from underneath the car again and looked at his watch. 'Oh no!' he threw down his tools and went indoors.

Betty was sat waiting for him. She was neatly dressed and, with the help of Mrs Challenor, her hair was curled, her nose was powered and she had a touch of pink lipstick jaggedly smeared across her lips.

'I'm so sorry I'm late. It took me longer than I thought.'

But Betty knew exactly why he was late: Linzi hadn't left without seeing her, and she was naturally delighted that someone had, at last, come to see David.

She observed his face and, through the dirt and smears of grime, she could see that he looked troubled.

'I'll only be five minutes in the bath and then we'll go to Kendal.'

'Don't rush, Davey, please. . . . Take your time. I want you looking respectable.'

David immediately wondered why.

Betty had been sat waiting for him for some time; so excited about this trip and to see Linzi today was a surprise. Today was wonderful.

David was soon clean-shaven, his short cropped hair, dark and shining and still wet. He decided to wear his newly pressed work trousers and shirt, hoping that he didn't look too much like a waiter. The only problem was that he had no

THE VISITOR

jacket. His only coat was his green Parka that he'd eaten in, slept in, and dossed in, down in London. It was now washed and clean but, never-the-less, inappropriate. The only thing he could do was to wear his old pullover.

'Have you got nothing better than that old thing?'

'What's the matter with it?' He pulled the front of the pullover out from his stomach to look.

'You can't go out in that. Upstairs in my wardrobe you'll find some of Freddie's old jackets. See if one of them fits you.'

Reluctantly, he ran back upstairs and fumbled through the old wardrobe and in amongst the pink and blue Crimplene dresses and old suits he found two jackets. One was a smart navy blazer with brass buttons and the other was a green tweed-shooting jacket.

He groaned, as he tried both of them on and then settled for the blazer.

'There, there . . . look at you now, you look a dandy!'

'Do I want to look a dandy?' David hovered by the door wanting to leave. 'I look more like a pilot.'

'If I'd have known we were going to have this bother. . . .'

'Okay, okay, I'm sorry.' And he fiddled with his collar, hoping she didn't notice he wasn't wearing a tie. 'I'll get the car out.'

Betty hobbled to the front door of the cottage and, resting on her two sticks, took a deep breath. She looked across the fields and saw yesterday's rain evaporating in the sunshine. She tapped the ground with one of her sticks in excitement and a group of sparrows fluttered out from a honeysuckle rambling over the garden hedge.

David pulled the car up to the front door and opened the passenger door. He smiled at her demeanour - this strong willed lady with the courage of a lion. Taking her arm, he gently eased her into the front seat.

Betty was neatly dressed in a light green coat and fawn peaked hat. She rested her two sticks on the floor beside her.

'Which way do you want to go? Straight to Kendal or what?'

'Let's go to Sawrey, then over the ferry so I can see the lake.'

THE VISITOR

* * *

Carefully negotiating the twisty lanes, the Volvo was no longer accustomed to this slow pace. Once at the lakeshore, they didn't have to wait long before the ferry arrived. Betty insisted once they were aboard that she walk out and look over the side, just as David had done a few weeks earlier.

He steadied her by the arm as she leant on the rails, and looked across to Waterhead and could see the Langdale Pikes in full view, but a cool breeze from across the water hit their faces and Betty went back to the safety of the car.

She'd travelled this route many times before, but always with her husband, and to be with David in Fred's old car brought back happy memories. But at ninety-two she didn't know when her final day would come; she had to expect it at anytime. Her heart had jumped a little more of late and she felt fragile, like a small bird nestling in someone's mighty hand. Dizziness at times had overwhelmed her and, if not for David's presence, she doubted she would have had the courage to stay at Foxglove Cottage alone.

'Where exactly do you want to be in Kendal?' David was wondering how on earth this elderly lady would manage the bustle of the town that she was un-accustomed to.

Betty rooted deep into her handbag and pulled out a small card.

David glanced at the inscription as he drove. He noticed the name "Piercy," then abbreviations after it. He saw the number and the street and the word "Solicitors".

He handed it back to her, bewildered.

David parked the car on the tree-lined avenue. Betty held onto his arm and she led him into an old house. The entrance hall was cold; a parlour palm struggled for light as it sat in the corner.

A matronly receptionist welcomed them and ushered them to two hard chairs. 'I'll inform Mr Piercy you're here, Mrs Keldas.' Speaking in an efficient tone. 'You look very well.'

Mr Angus Piercy emerged from his office. He was a tall, thin man, with a cheerful manner. To David he looked business-

THE VISITOR

like in his pinstriped suit. He came across and warmly greeted Betty.

'What a pleasure this is Mrs Keldas,' as he held on to her hand and then stretched out his hand to David. David felt compelled to stand as the man grasped onto him.

'This is my great-nephew, David,' Betty was proud.

'Ah, yes. . . . I do remember you now,' the solicitor said, 'from your uncle's funeral.'

Still embarrassed about his behaviour that day, David had an overwhelming desire to leave, and the corner he now found himself in felt uncomfortable; remorse struck him as he guessed this man would have wondered why he didn't attend his own father's funeral.

'Please sit down, David, and Miss Banks will bring you coffee.'

David was glad to resume his sitting position as Betty was taken into the office.

The matronly receptionist returned with a tray of coffee and biscuits and David struggled with the china, afraid of breaking anything, but happier knowing his aunt was no doubt assuming her own business affairs.

Miss Banks continued to eye David as she returned to her desk. He had certainly cheered what would usually be a dull day. She watched him flick through the newspapers, and could see he was uncomfortable with the large reams of paper of the broadsheets.

David looked about him and felt nervous at the attention. He stared at the bare panelled walls of the office, which were sparsely decorated by some framed certificates and then, fumbled again with newspapers.

It was some time before he heard the door handle of the office twist open. Angus Piercy's voice much louder as they emerged. David quickly stood up.

'Well, good day to you young man, it has been a pleasure to meet you.' He reached out for David's hand again and shook it. 'And good day to you, dear lady.'

David led Betty out into the fresh air, glad of the sunlight.

THE VISITOR

'I'm sorry Aunty, but I'm too warm!' and he pulled off the blazer and carelessly threw it onto the back seat of the car. 'Where now?'

'Now, you take me out to lunch, David . . . and show me that hotel where you work.'

Betty was content that David seemed more at peace today; she hoped she'd given this to him but, as soon as they returned to the cottage, he was outside again, walking up the hill in the late afternoon sunshine. David hadn't changed his clothes, he'd just seen that Betty was comfortable and left her sitting in her fireside chair. She was far too tired to plead with him to stay, and she desperately needed a nap. Betty sighed, 'Oh young man. Don't start wandering like your father. What can I do to help you?'

Betty was right, of course, there was nothing she could do for him; his mind was in turmoil. He needed time to be alone and to think.

He climbed the hill and sat down on a grassy plateau; his favourite spot. He too felt sleepy and in the warmth of the sunshine, took off his shirt, sat back on the grass and shut his eyes; his pale skin soaked up the heat from the sun. He lay with his arms behind his head as a pillow; as dark hairs on his chest and torso were exposed to the sun.

David thought of Keld Head and the busy life he'd had, contrasted with the peace here at Foxglove Cottage. The change had been good for him, he knew that. But it wasn't until Linzi had called today did he realise how much he missed his family. Despite knowing she was only his half-sister, he still had a strong attachment for her. He never-the-less felt angry with his mother, but whether she knew of George's affair with Joanne or not troubled him. He certainly didn't want to cause any more pain and distress by asking her. And, if his mother didn't know the truth, he would have to keep silent. He was certain that Tony would keep the confidence, but would Joanne. She had acted so bitterly toward him, almost hateful. But there was nothing more he could do only to hope, and to live in silence with this knowledge. If his relationship with Joanne had disturbed his mother, he wasn't to blame; he had acted in innocence.

David realised once again that he had broken his promise not to leave. Linzi was right to call him a hypocrite, but maybe not in the sense that she meant. But, despite all this, David could still not come to terms with the idea of going back. He was afraid he would be persuaded to stay. He never wanted to work at Keld Head again; he doubted he could even go near the tower. The image of George Keldas's dead body sickened him, as he remembered his own face and body spattered with the blood of the man he'd believed to be his father.

He wondered who'd cleaned up the mess. Who had scrubbed the walls and floor? Who had milked the cattle that night? It was all a vague blur. He felt uneasy now as Keld Head had a morbidity that he'd never assumed before and it went beyond hatred, as he thought of the place that had the darkest of secrets he could imagine. But this sweet meadow above Hawkshead was warm and light; there was no darkness at Foxglove Cottage. The sun always seemed to shine or the fire would climb so high up the chimney that it would brighten the whole cottage.

David slipped into a deep sleep, dreaming of dark corners, cobwebs and oak beams. He dreamt he was a hostage and someone had tied his hands behind him on a wooden chair. Then another man came along, much like himself and released him, but then started to wrestle with him. But he refused to fight. *I will not do this. . . . I will not do it! I will not be afraid!* Then a tall man in a pinstriped suit came to shake his hand; he congratulated him and said: 'Well done David. . . . You have escaped!'

A rustling noise woke him up, and he opened his eyes and saw a young woman standing over him, watching.

'I'm so sorry about your shirt,' she said.

David looked beside him and saw a small terrier paddling muddy paws across his white shirt and he sat bolt upright.

'It's - it's okay. Please don't worry.' Aware of his semi-

THE VISITOR

nakedness and embarrassed by his pale and bony flesh, David picked up his soiled shirt and slipped it over his chest.

The girl continued to eye him; she saw the jagged scar from an old wound across his mouth, his dark eyebrows and stunning eyes, and she smiled.

'David. . . . It is you, isn't it? I didn't recognise you.'

'Hello, Hannah. I'm er - just getting some sun,' seeing the girl's tanned skin and soft, brown, shoulder length hair.

'I'm sorry about the dog,' she repeated, as the small Lakeland terrier sniffed at David's best shoes. Hannah continued to stand awkwardly before him and then reached down for the dog. 'Jassie . . . Jassie, come here.'

'Are you well, Hannah?' David wanted to keep her attention. 'What are you doing up here?'

'I've come over Claife Heights,' she gestured to the forest, 'I'm just heading for the village for a drink.' Hannah's face glowered and shone. She pulled a small haversack off her shoulders and threw it down on the floor.

'And you David. . . . Are you well?' She was astonished at his appearance, unable to believe this was the same man that had irritated her, then recklessly flirted with her, only a few months earlier.

David began to feel uncomfortable with Hannah standing over him, and tried to get up but struggled with his aching back. He apologised and remained sitting.

'I'm sorry, Hannah. I've been working under my car and I hurt my back. Please . . . Why don't you sit down.'

She untied a pullover wrapped about her waist, folded it, and then sat down on it. 'What an amazing view.'

David looked across at her, happy to be on the same level and, as he glanced at her profile, he had to agree. He pointed at the mountains above them, 'There's the Old Man, then Wetherlam, that's Dow Crag beside it.'

'So, how far have you walked?' she questioned him. He was dressed too smartly for fell walking; his appearance only spoilt by the paw prints of the dog.

'I haven't come far. You see that cottage down there,' David pointed to a group of white cottages, 'I'm staying with my Aunt . . . she lives here. This is her field.' David felt pure elation; he had gone from a nightmare into paradise. The man in the pinstriped suit had told him well done, and it was.

'How's Barry keeping?' David wanted the conversation to continue.

'Oh, yes . . . he's well.' She hesitated a little.

'And are you well, Hannah?'

She laughed at his repetition, 'Yes, yes we're both well, David.' And then speaking more soberly said, 'You know about Barry and Eleanor do you?'

'Yes, yes. How's he coping?'

'He's doing okay really. I guess he's known for some time that things haven't been right between them. I should be in Wales now, but he's asked me to stay on a bit longer. He's been so kind to me - he's treated me like a father and it's the least I can do for him.'

David's eyes widened at this statement and he was reassured. 'So you're leaving for Wales soon?'

'Afraid so. . . .' Hannah pulled at some tufts of grass from beneath her and, as she ripped and tore at them, she subconsciously tossed them into the air. 'There's a practice in Cardiff waiting that specialises in small animals. But I hope I can come back soon.'

David hoped so too.

'You said you needed a drink? Please . . . please come to the cottage. I'll make you some tea, or perhaps a cold drink,' and he raised his eyebrows. 'Do you really need to be in the village?'

'No. . . . No, not particularly. I'd like that, but will your aunt mind?'

'Oh, she won't mind. . . . Besides, she'll be asleep.'

With his back still aching, David struggled to stand. He picked up Hannah's rucksack and threw it across his shoulder.

David left her sitting in the garden and went to get some lemonade. He brought a bowl of cold water for the dog;

anything, to make a good impression. He was pleased all was tidy in the garden; that he'd bothered to cut the grass and repair the garden furniture.

'My aunt will be out in a minute. . . . She'd like to meet you.' He set the tea tray on the grass in front of her.

The old lady came outside into the sunshine and took Hannah's hand and David graciously relinquished his seat for her.

'Aunty, this is Hannah Robson, she works for the vet. You remember Barry Fitzgerald, don't you?'

'Ah, Hannah. I'm pleased to meet you . . . I really am. So you're a friend of Davey's are you?' This was certainly an answer to her prayer.

'Yes, I am a friend - I hope.' Hannah replied.

Betty talked at length to her about the cottage, and about the farm she used to work at Spickle Howe with David's late uncle.

Hannah deduced that she was talking about the old man that had been murdered, and marvelled how much like Kathy Keldas, this old lady managed to keep a sense of dignity about the tragedy that had touched her. She was open and happy, and it had only appeared to be David out of all of them, that had been severely affected by it.

Hannah liked Betty; she could see that David was comfortable and much changed living with her. He was different, not only in his appearance but also in his manner. Yes, Barry was right, she had mis-judged him.

David sat on the garden wall opposite, happy to let his aunt do most of the talking. He looked at his watch. 'Where have you left your car?'

'It's at Bowness. I've come across on the ferry.'

'Oh, dear child. . . . You've come all this way alone!' Betty said.

David laughed, 'my aunt believes in silly stories. There's supposed to be the fabled Crier of Claife, who haunts the woods. He was allegedly sent insane by an "*encounter*" while he rowed his ferry across Windermere. She thinks he's still up there don't you, Aunty?'

THE VISITOR

Betty looked disapprovingly at him, and Hannah said, 'I've had a lovely walk. Please don't worry about me Mrs Keldas. I'll really enjoy the walk back. I'll be fine.'

'I'll hear nothing of it!' Betty tapped her two walking sticks on the ground. 'This mischievous young man of mine will take you back to the ferry,' she insisted. 'David. . . . Please drive Hannah back. . . . It's late and she must be tired.'

'No . . . no really, I'll be fine.'

David jumped off the wall and took her bag. 'It's no good arguing with her, Hannah. I'll take you back. I'll get the car out, or we'll never hear the last of it.'

She put up no further resistance and, for the second time that day, David drove to the ferry.

They talked most of the journey. David told Hannah of his job at the pub, no longer wanting to hide anything. She told him about her job prospects in Wales and how much she would miss the Lakes. This was the longest one-to-one conversation they'd ever had.

He parked the car and they walked down the slipway together; they saw the ferry on the opposite shore, ready to leave.

'Give Barry my regards, won't you,' David said as he stood close beside her, not looking at her but staring out across the lake.

'Why don't you come and see him? I'm sure he'd love to see you.'

David was surprised. 'Do you think so?' He stood bolt upright with his hands pushed deep into his pockets.

'Of course he would. Why don't you come tomorrow night, it's his day off. Maybe we can all go out for a drink or something?'

'Well, if you think he wouldn't mind.' David turned, looked her in the eye and smiled, then picked up her rucksack. He awkwardly slipped it on her shoulders and inadvertently felt the touch of her soft hair on his hand. He felt compelled to lift a lock of hair away from the strap and curl it around her neck.

'Call tomorrow evening then, Davey.'

THE VISITOR

'Tomorrow?' he stressed.

'Yes, tomorrow.'

The ferry approached the slipway and David walked as far as he could with her. And as he watched her playfully wave at him he took in a sharp intake of breath as he realised she had called him Davey.

Betty was talking to a neighbour over the garden wall when David returned. So he dodged inside the cottage and rushed upstairs to his room. He frantically began to sort through his clothes. His laundry basket was crammed full so he pulled out socks and underwear ready to wash. He looked at Fred's old blazer hanging in his wardrobe, pulled it out and muttered as he threw it down on the bed. He thought of his best suede jacket hung in the wardrobe back at Keld Head and knew he had the motivation needed to return. David dropped his shoulders and muttered, 'I'll have to go tomorrow!'

19

KELD HEAD - THE RETURN

The early morning sunshine cast pleasing glances on Keld Head. It had windows like eyes that watched and waited. The slated roof on the farmhouse appeared wet from the glare, despite the tiles being roughened from years of weathering from rain and snow. The porch on the front door was like a large mouth wishing to welcome and to say hello and come inside. It had spat David out but, today, it waited expectantly for his return.

The small Pele tower beside the barn had a flat roof, and it cast a dark shadow on the yard. This was a cold corner. It was never used for animals, only ever used as a store for bags of fertiliser and the like, its value long gone. And no more was Keld Head in fear of Celtic intruders; it had its own civil war, culminating in the death of Fred and George Keldas. Moss had fallen or had been removed by nesting birds from the dark recesses of the tower and it littered the darkened yard. But in contrast there were a few spring flowers growing in crevices on the garden wall, cascading down in lilac and white, glowing in the sunshine and mingling amongst the faded daffodils.

This is where east watched west and grey watched white - a cold war.

David walked out early this morning and noticed the first of the bluebells flowering in the woods, and the wild garlic he crushed under his boots gave off their pungent scent. He wondered if Hannah had seen them yesterday and guessed she would have liked them. He thought she was a spirited girl to walk alone, and he assumed she must be a good walker to come all the way from Nab Point. He smiled when he thought

KELD HEAD – THE RETURN

of his aunt's concern over the fabled Crier of Claife. David had walked that forest night and day and never feared a thing, except his own personality.

He wondered today how it would feel to go back home. It would be easier than he imagined. The day was fine and dry and that helped

The stone signpost bore the name of Grasmere and as David drove on through the busy town packed with visitors, he felt secure with his anonymity. Just a drive up the hill, across the fell road, under the trees and over the bridge to the small hamlet of Keld Head. The old Volvo should have been familiar with this journey.

David tried not to think of whom he might meet or what he might say. He'd been unsettled in the night thinking about this, and decided to just go and get his suede jacket and a few of his belongings. That would surely signal once and for all that he wouldn't be staying. He didn't belong to Keld Head anymore and it seemed to have abandoned him long ago. The only hope he had was that he might meet Linzi first; she'd already been the icebreaker. He felt then that he could leave with no resentment and begin to mend the rift he'd had with his mother.

He swung the car around into the yard, the gate was wide open and all was silent. He didn't look about and resisted the urge to look across to the tower. He walked straight into the kitchen; the door was unlocked. Again, all was silent.

David noticed that the kitchen was as clean and tidy as usual and as he edged quietly around the parlour door, saw the fire was laid ready for lighting, the oak furniture was polished, but the house appeared to be empty.

He called upstairs but still no response. He ran up to his bedroom, jumping two steps at a time as he used to. He pushed open the door and walked in. He felt like an intruder.

His bed was made, his books and papers were all in place, and his clothes folded neat and tidy, much as he'd left them.

Quickly raking through his wardrobe and pulling out jackets, trousers and shirts, David threw them down on the bed. And much like a thief, he rooted through his chest of drawers for pullovers and underwear. He took an armful of clothes and carried them outside and began to fill the backseat of his car.

He'd brought some cardboard boxes with him and, clambering up the stairs, started to pack his personal belongings, and then methodically searched through his bookcase. He unplugged his hi-fi system and boxed up his records. He felt no remorse; he needed to get this job done.

Kathy drove into the yard; she had just taken the children to school and had left Linzi struggling to move an electric fence.

She saw the old Volvo outside the house and hurried across to it. She ran her hands along its bodywork and patted it with gratitude. She muttered, 'He's come. He's come at last!'

On the front seat of the car was a bunch of flowers which she thought must be for her, but in the back, she could see his clothes. Yes, he had come, but with what purpose?

She walked into the kitchen to go upstairs, when David suddenly appeared at the door carrying an armful of books. She looked at him and time froze; images suspended in space, and she wanted to say a name, a man's name, but it wasn't David's. She wavered a moment and as they stared at one another, she fell to the floor like a lump of stone.

David threw down his books and rushed to her, lifting her head and calling her. 'Oh no. . . . Oh no. . . . Mum, please.' He gently patted her cheek, then her hands, as he pulled her close to him. He crouched to the floor with her huddled in his arms as he tightly held on to her.

Linzi came into the kitchen and seeing her mother on the floor, ran across. 'Oh, for goodness sake David, what have you done to her now?'

David stuttered some words. 'Nothing. . . . I've done nothing. She just fainted. I think - I hope.'

Kathy started to come round and as her head thumped so hard, she squinted as she tried to open her eyes.

'Linzi. . . . Hurry. Get her a glass of water. Are you okay, Mum?' David softly spoke. 'Try -try to stand.'

KELD HEAD – THE RETURN

He helped her to her feet and, for the first time in months, Kathy looked closely at her son. 'I'm sorry. . . . I'm so sorry, Davey. I thought you were someone else.'

Linzi looked at her brother, bewildered.

David led his mother to the parlour and sat her on the sofa. Kneeling beside her, he held a glass of water in one hand and supported her shoulder with the other. 'Please drink it. I'm sorry I gave you a shock.'

Kathy continued to stare at David. She had wished and prayed for this moment for so long. There was so much to say to him: the reasons why she'd done things the way she had, desperately wanting to apologise and accept full responsibility for her actions. She gently stroked his cheek; his bold forehead now exposed, and then she rubbed his short cropped hair. 'You just look so different, you gave me a shock.'

She didn't want to tell him how thin he looked. Linzi had warned her, but the scale of it was unexpected. Neither had she seen him with his hair so short in years, not since he was a little boy. His skin looked paler, yet his eyes were clear and blue. He appeared to be calm.

'Linzi. . . . Please leave us alone love, for just a few minutes,' Kathy begged.

Linzi hesitated. She wanted to hear David explain his way out of this one, and to know why they'd argued in the first place. She too had many unanswered questions. But after another purposeful glance from her mother, she left them alone and reluctantly closed the parlour door behind her.

This wasn't what David wanted, he didn't want to speak to his mother, in fact he couldn't.

'I'm just relieved you're safe and well, son. Everything that's happened between us is all my fault,' she looked him in the eyes. 'I don't want you to bear any remorse. I'm sorry, Davey, for the way I've treated you. I never intended things to be like this.'

David couldn't stand to hear anymore of her apology. He didn't want to have to wrestle with more turmoil, and was afraid he might lose the grip on the freedom he had and the prospect of some happiness at last. So he stood up and walked away from her and went across to the fireplace; crouching over the hearth, he took some matches and lit the dry sticks and paper.

Kathy started again, but David interrupted her. He stood and looked, not directly at her, but through the mirror. 'Don't - don't say anymore. . . . I know you're sorry, and so am I. . . . I've just come back for a few things, that's all.'

His cold words hurt.

'I only wanted to explain, Davey.'

'I don't think I can take any explanations just now,' he turned to her again. 'You can't know how hurt I've felt. . . . Almost to the point of feeling betrayed and disowned. I've got to build my life again and I'm slowly doing that. Please be patient with me. But there's just one thing I feel I owe you though - and that's about Joanne.'

Kathy took a gasp of air as she waited for his comment.

'You were probably right to tell me I was a fool to marry Jo, maybe I was, I don't know. I just wanted to do the right thing.'

'And what have you done?'

'Nothing. . . . Absolutely nothing. She doesn't want me anymore,' and he turned his head and finally looked at her. 'And that suits me, I suppose. I just felt I ought to tell you, so you needn't worry anymore on that score.'

David waited and wondered if she would reveal any knowledge of Joanne's relationship with her late husband, but she didn't, so he continued. 'I just had to tell you that's all,' he repeated and shook his head.

'I'm sorry if I seemed over protective,' she softened again. 'I didn't want you to end up in an unhappy marriage, and all for the wrong reasons. For that, I can speak from experience.'

David didn't want to hear anymore and now wanted to go. 'You'll manage won't you? Tell Tom and Sarah I'll come and see them soon.' And he opened the door and left the room.

'David. . . .' she tried to call him back. 'If you ever feel you do want to ask me anything, I'll tell you everything you want to know.'

He stopped at the door, his back still to her and paused, then continued to gather up the last of his belongings.

Linzi, from the viewpoint of her bedroom window, saw her brother leave. She rushed back downstairs where her mother was at the kitchen sink reluctantly preparing lunch. 'Where's he gone now?'

'He's gone back to Betty's. . . . He won't come back now.' Her eyes were full of tears.

'Why didn't you stop him?'

'How could I. . . . He's twenty-four in a few weeks time, he's a grown man, how could I stop him. He must do as he likes.' Kathy was flushed and dabbed the tears away from her cheeks with a paper tissue.

'He can't just leave us, Mum!'

'Oh, yes he can, love. Why should he stay? We never stopped you from leaving and going to college and you didn't have to come back this time.'

'It's different for me though, isn't it?'

'Why. . . . Why should it be any different?'

Linzi was choking on her words. 'Because he's the eldest. . . . He's your son.'

'Yes, he is my son, and that's why, for once in his life, I'm going to let him do what he wants. He's given most of his life to this farm. He's done his bit and now it's up to us.'

Linzi restrained herself from banging her fist on the kitchen table. 'Oh why did Dad have to be so stupid and leave David out of his will? I just can't understand it.'

'Linzi, you should know by now that you'll never understand anything your father did.'

'I think he was jealous of David. You were always fussing around him. . . . No wonder he hated him.'

Kathy didn't want any more of this; Linzi was getting far too close to the truth. 'Stop it, stop it now . . . ! Your father didn't hate David. Don't you see he was punishing me. It was me he hated; it was his way of getting at me.'

Linzi came across to Kathy and huddled close to her, dropping her head against her shoulder. 'I'm so sorry . . . I just don't understand. I miss Dad, and I guess I miss our Davey as much as you do. I just want things to be the same again and I can't bear to see him hurt.'

'He isn't hurting anymore, love. He'll be fine now. He's a strong lad. I can already see a difference in him. He's had a lot to put up with, we all have, but it's over for him now - it's over for us all.'

David didn't want to leave the village straight away; he had another errand to do. He hadn't made a success of this visit, but he'd done what he'd intended, in getting his clothes. The wounds had also been repaired, but they would take a long time to heal, if ever.

His hands were trembling on the steering wheel as he drove carefully through the village street and looked for a place to park. Taking out the bunch of flowers and, un-noticed by anyone, he locked the car; just another face, yet more a part of this little town than most. He walked up the lane to the small churchyard and, shutting the gate, left the majority of the tourists behind; those who were looking for gravestones of a grander nature.

It wasn't difficult to find his objective, as near the wall was a grave with a newly erected headstone, some wilting flowers lay neglected on the turf. David stopped and read:

In Memory of George Samuel Keldas. 1925-1974.
Forty-nine years old.
Loving father and husband

He glared at the inscription for a few moments and repeated the words to himself: *'Loving father. . . . Loving husband.'* She was still telling lies, he thought.

David had had a repetitive vision of a man lying in a pool of blood and he needed to put this vision to rest. The only way he could do this was to be certain that George Keldas was actually dead and could no longer harm him, and today he was given the evidence he needed.

David stared at the grave for some time, assuming the flowers had been left recently by his sister. He wasn't a man for praying, yet he felt if there were a God, he wouldn't be too pleased with his actions. David couldn't ask for forgiveness for himself, because neither could he give it and forgive this wretched man. But standing there alone, he felt some kind of peace, and hoped one day he could be completely exonerated for his actions.

He backed away almost respectfully, and then walked across to a more familiar headstone. It too was sparsely decorated with a simple inscription and a small empty vase lay on the gravel.

In David's hand was the bunch of pink carnations that Kathy had thought were for her. He carefully unwrapped the cellophane wrapper, took the vase and filled it with water from a nearby tap and then, in a meaningful way, tried to arrange the flowers as neatly as he could.

He pondered for a while and spoke softly, 'These are from Betty, with love.' And unobserved, left Fred Keldas's graveside.

David returned to Hawkshead in sombre mood. Betty had an anxious wait for him; he'd told her only that morning of his intention to return to Keld Head to get his belongings, in a hope that she wouldn't warn his mother. He'd begged her not to do so. It wasn't so much as he wanted to surprise his mother, it was more that he doubted his own self-belief, and thought that he might back down at the last minute. He'd also asked her if he could stay at Foxglove Cottage permanently. He could no longer presume on her kindness and hoped she would agree. But of course it was all right, for Betty knew well if he left her now, she would miss him dreadfully. She'd already made up her mind, if he left, she would go too, and move to a retirement home to end her days.

She'd doubted she would live much longer and thought him leaving might even quicken things. She wasn't afraid of death, she'd made her peace with God a long time ago, but now she just wished she could live long enough to see David find some kind of happiness.

Betty didn't intend to tell David this. She didn't want to influence him and make him stay against his will. He had become such a great part of her life, despite having to tolerate loud music playing on the radio and the football matches he constantly watched, and his comings and goings from the hotel late at night.

When David eventually returned with his belongings, he was quiet and pensive, and Betty guessed that things hadn't gone well. She remained quiet as she watched him unpack his things and take them upstairs. When he finally came to sit down, she gave him something.

'This postcard came for you this morning.' And she held up a small colour print of Edinburgh.

He carefully looked at the handwriting and, just as he hoped, it was from Tony. He read it slowly and it simply stated that he was working in Edinburgh and had a job playing sessions music. This brought a wry smile to David's face as he wondered what sort of work it really was, and what pitiful lodgings he would be sharing this time.

Betty also told him of a phone call she'd had that morning. It was from a young woman who sounded much like the girl who had visited yesterday - in that she had some kind of an accent.

Betty complained about her hearing and apologised to David for not getting a proper message. She said the girl rudely hung up when she told her he wasn't at home.

David went to his bedroom, perplexed, and put away his things, hanging some of his clothes in the old wardrobe; Betty and Fred's things were shoved to one side. Next, he set up his stereo system, twisting and unravelling the cables and speaker wires, hoping it still worked. He wished his morning had gone better, and it hadn't left him feeling in the mood he had wanted, so he tried to think about the evening he hoped to spend with Barry and the possibility of seeing Hannah again.

He ran the bath and lay in the soft soapy water and tried to relax; the warmth eased his aching back. Then scrubbing himself meticulously clean, as if he could wash away the past as David wanted to leave a good impression; he'd left too many bad ones with Barry and Hannah. Lying back, he sunk

KELD HEAD – THE RETURN

his head under the soapsuds and washed his hair, flicking water about him. As he lay soaking, he wondered why Hannah had telephoned, thinking she'd called to cancel their evening. Betty had obviously misheard much, as he couldn't imagine Hannah being so rude as to hang up. He worried if Hannah had presumed too much, and that Barry might not want him there. But despite all his quanderings, afraid of a negative response, David wouldn't telephone back; he would go to the surgery in Windermere, no matter what.

Images of Hannah had continually come flooding back to him, and these he hadn't resisted. During the dark days in London he'd thought of her, and on the lonely fells in Hawkshead. He recalled his evening with her on the night of Joanne's wild trek in the snow and wished he'd pursued Hannah then. He remembered being collected from the hospital and her kindness to him. And then the bitter rebuffal, when he'd invited her to visit Tony. When he saw her yesterday she was different; he hoped he was different. But why would Hannah, this attractive and intelligent girl, want any friendship with him anymore? He began to wonder if it was out of pure pity. Maybe Barry had told her to go easy on him, after all he had been a hair's-breadth from death; not once, but twice. But David didn't want anyone's pity.

He recalled her appearance yesterday and how lovely she looked. Her brown hair was beginning to grow much longer, just touching her shoulders, and he recalled how soft it felt when he touched it; the smooth skin on her arms, tanned by the sun and, as he pictured her again standing in front of him, he tried to remember what she was wearing: a pink t-shirt and denim jeans, a silver chain around her neck.

He had felt so numb these past few weeks and whether David could believe it or not, his life was slowly rebuilding. Today he'd made some amends to his mother; she hadn't blamed him for leaving and that vindicated his decision. Yet he was still alone, his self-imposed isolation had been of his own doing, partly brought on by a weak attempt to renew some of his promise. He couldn't alter the fact that he'd left his mother, but he had been freed from his foolish decision to marry Joanne.

But David didn't think that he could continue this lonely existence any longer. Hannah Robson had thrown him a lifeline and he would seize it aggressively and pull himself out of this monastic life he was living.

Grabbing a towel, David raised himself out of the bath with such a surge, that the water and foam splashed all over the floor; he'd made a choice to see Barry and he was going to stick to that, no matter what. He vigorously rubbed himself dry, and was now prepared to go headlong into dressing and shaving and go to Barry's house, even though his thoughts tried to persuade him not to.

David kissed Betty goodbye. She was satisfied with his appearance, as he stood before her dressed in his suede jacket and cream cotton shirt. He hoped his own clothes would mask his skinny body, but his trousers fit him badly and he had to pull the belt tight.

He had hinted to Betty that he might be late home, and David sincerely hoped that he would be. So he sped away; a man on a mission and full of hope.

It had started to rain again and the warm dry air they'd just enjoyed, had turned to a damp and mizzly atmosphere; yet the warmth continued. The meadows lining the road to the ferry were lush and green, as brown and black cattle grazed. David could almost see the grass growing before him as he glanced across. He suddenly felt a tinge of nervousness. He hadn't seen Barry for weeks and the last time he had seen him, he'd rudely walked away.

When David arrived at the practice it was Barry, with a reassuring smile that met him at the door. Barry was pulling awkwardly at a tie around his collar, but dropped it loose to shake David's hand.

Barry held onto David's hand for some time. 'It's good to see you, Davey. Come in, please come in. How are you?' And Barry's usual relaxed and friendly manner did what it always

KELD HEAD – THE RETURN

did for David and immediately put his mind at ease. David followed him into the large and impressive house, to a kitchen where he'd never been before.

'Sit down, please.' Barry patted David on the shoulder again, 'Boy, you look tidier. . . .' and, much like Kathy had, he playfully rubbed David's short cropped hair. 'I'm not quite ready yet, can I get you a coffee or something?'

'No, please, I'm fine,' David replied and sat at the kitchen table. He looked about him as Barry left, and he could see by the general untidiness that Barry was still alone.

David wondered where Hannah was. Perhaps she wouldn't go with them; perhaps she'd intended that all along.

When Barry returned, ready and fully dressed, his dark hair neatly brushed back off his strong forehead, he pulled up a chair and sat beside David at the table. 'So you're living in Hawkshead. How's your aunt?'

'Oh, she's very well, considering.'

'So what age is she now? Ninety-one - ninety-two?

'Yes, ninety-two, nearly ninety-three. . . . She's incredible. I think she'll live 'til she's a hundred!' Bewildered with the small talk, a look of confusion appeared on his face.

'Oh, I'm sorry. We're waiting for Hannah. She's been messing around with a hedgehog all evening. She's only just gone to get ready. You don't mind if she comes with us do you?'

Of course David didn't mind and he enthusiastically shook his head.

'Hannah's a soft touch really. She'd rather look after pets than lumber around with cattle and sheep. She's been a good student for me though, and has been brilliant these last few weeks - looking after me and all. Hannah told you about Eleanor, I gather?'

'Yes . . . yes, I'm sorry.'

'Don't you worry about me. I'll get over it, I'm sure.' Barry paused to control his fractured voice. 'Once we get divorced. Err . . . have you eaten?'

'Yes . . . well no. Not much really.'

'You look like you need a good meal inside you. I'll treat you both.'

'Thank you, yes . . . that would be good.'

When Hannah arrived, the two of them were still making small talk. David was telling Barry of the repairs he'd done to the Volvo.

'Ah, here she is at last!' Barry stood.

Hannah was wearing a pink jersey dress. She had her hair twisted up in a knot and looked sophisticated. David was unsure of how to greet her so he politely rose from his chair and courteously dipped his head; he really wanted to take her hand.

Barry Fitzgerald always succeeded where others failed to bring the best out of David; a side to him that Hannah had rarely seen. She now found David agreeable and could see the good in him, just as Barry had said. And as they sat eating around the table in the restaurant, Hannah started to think of all that had happened to David, as she watched him and Barry chatting. She had pitied him, as David had suspected, but that pity had turned to respect. Yes, she had misunderstood him and she envied his courage and spirit.

Barry looked across and realised that Hannah was being left out of the conversation, although she was happy to watch the two men and just listen. 'Hannah leaves me for Cardiff soon,' and he patted her arm affectionately.

'Yes, I believe so.' David was sorry it was confirmed. 'Will you miss the Lakes, Hannah?'

'I sure will,' she insisted. 'I love it here. If it wasn't for the training, I wouldn't go at all. I just love walking these hills. We have hills in Durham, but not like these. I'm only sorry I haven't been able to walk the high fells. Barry insisted that I never go alone.' Then she joked, 'And he's not fit enough to take me. The other day he took me to see Dora's field and he was so out of shape, I had to pull him up the hill by the hand!'

This frank admittance by Hannah reassured David that their relationship was purely platonic and professional.

KELD HEAD – THE RETURN

'I've never been able to climb Scafell and I would have loved to.'

'Maybe Davey will take you. . . . Will you?'

David was astonished at his suggestion and muttered a reply. 'Yes . . . yes I'd love to. Do you have time before you leave, though?'

'When can we go?' She widened her brown eyes.

David's veins surged with vibrancy; his body trembled with excitement. He had taken his chance and it had paid off. A day out with Hannah was beyond his imagination and yet he was quietly concerned. He still had a bad back from working under his car, and today the pain had begun to shoot down his leg, and his usual elegant stature was reduced to a slight stoop as he walked with a limp.

'You enjoyed that then, Davey?' Barry was now looking at the empty plate.

David stretched back in his chair and contentedly rubbed his hand down his stomach. 'It beats tomato soup and sandwiches any day! That's the extent of my cooking I'm afraid and Betty would survive on the soup if I didn't make the sandwiches.'

David didn't go straight home, but took a stroll along the shores of Windermere, alone. He didn't care that it was still raining, as a hazy moon shone through the clouded night and lit his way. Cool droplets of rain curled down his hair and dripped onto his face. His boots crunched on the shingle on the lakeshore, as he wandered deep in thought, planning in his mind which route to take Hannah up Scafell; excited by her enthusiasm. But down in the recesses of his mind he had a heavy thought, as he knew she was leaving and he wondered if he'd left things too late; he wished it was more than the rain that he could taste on his lips

20

MAN OF CLAY.

When David awoke next morning he could barely move; his back had locked into a position that caused him to bend almost double. He struggled to get out of bed and could hardly stand straight as pain shot down the back of his leg to his knee. He cursed his own stupidity in walking out in the rain, and had assumed that at twenty-three he was indestructible.

David had become like a cat with nine lives. He'd already cashed in two of them by staring down the barrel of a shotgun. For recklessly driving his car down narrow country lanes, he could probably count another two; for being beaten up at a football match, one, and another for sleeping rough in London, where he could have caught pneumonia. He'd also experienced mild hypothermia from spending a night on the fells looking for a desperate woman. That left only two lives intact; he must be more careful and preserve the breath he had left in him. He'd spent far too much, too early, as most of us do

David struggled to wash and change and as he looked at the clock, he realised that it was later than he expected. He had slept through Mrs Challenor doing some washing; Betty hobbling backwards and forwards to receive the milkman, the fish man, the baker's van. He had slept through the phone ringing several times; each time Betty was too slow to answer.

This particular morning with David absent, Mrs Challenor had plied Betty with endless questions of his whereabouts, as he was usually up by now; if not working, he would be gardening or walking, or tinkering about with the car. She thought he must have had one too many beers last night, and complained that the young men of today didn't know when to stop drinking.

Betty too had wondered where David was, and why he was still sleeping. She hadn't heard him come in at all last night and it was only the sight of the car keys thrown on the table that had reassured her he was actually home.

She'd stood at the bottom of the stairs and listened for any movement, but her hearing had failed her. If only she could hear some breathing, some snoring, any noise, just to tell her he was safe. Her weakened legs wouldn't let her climb the stairs; the former dining room was now her bedroom. In frustration, she tapped her walking sticks on the floor, angry at her pitiable state. It was late in the morning when Betty heard the noise from the cistern flush in the upstairs toilet.

David came downstairs and looked rough. Betty thought he probably had a hangover. But, as David held his back and attempted to make himself a cup of coffee she saw the real problem. She reached for her handbag and, tipping the contents out onto the table, found some packets of painkillers and vitamins.

'You'll suffer with your back, Davey. . . . Your father did and your grandfather did - they both had arthritic spines. My Freddie got it badly too.'

David didn't want to disagree with his aunt about the chances of inheriting anything from George Keldas, and continued to sip his coffee and swallow two painkillers.

'It's because I stayed out in the rain for too long last night. It's my own fault.'

'Ah you young ones, you don't know how to look after yourselves.'

'Well it's kill or cure I'm afraid.' And David reached for his jacket and started to leave without eating breakfast.

'Oh, Davey. . . . Not this morning. Please just rest?'

'I can't rest . . . I must walk it off. . . . I need to be fit.' And he left without any explanation.

David limped all the way up the lane and onto the track to Claife Heights, feeling pain with each step. He was angry with himself now; how could he possibly walk Hannah up Scafell? He only had three days to improve.

The grass on the field was slippery from the night's heavy rainfall and as he entered the forest, the lime on the metalled road stuck to his boots. Steam was rising from the trees as the late morning's sunshine evaporated the moisture. The forest appeared to be on fire.

As David continued to walk, the pain in his leg eased as he got into a better stride, and he started to enjoy the fresh air. As it was mid-week, there were few people about, but David still chose his route carefully to keep some isolation, hoping to catch a glimpse of some wild-life. The dark shaded areas of the forest, densely planted with trees, managed to cut out most of the light; all he could hear was birdsong and a faint whistling of the breeze.

He lingered a while in one plantation. He'd walked here earlier in the spring and had spotted a young stag, standing majestically in front of him, its red coat glistening in the sunshine. They had watched each other, motionless, for some time, neither of them daring to move, wondering who was most afraid. He'd hoped he could see it again, and perhaps some young ones grazing with their mother, but today it was too late; they would have been up and breakfasted much earlier than him, and would have gone to ground in the forest, or be nestling in a pocket of bracken on the fell side.

As he walked slowly, he thought he heard a murmuring noise - perhaps the sound of someone talking. He wondered if he was closer to the public-footpath than he'd thought. Perhaps it was the voices of the foresters as they worked in a nearby plantation. He listened again, but there was silence, so he carried on walking.

As he continued, he began to hum to himself and went to sit on a rocky outcrop to take in the view. Again he heard voices and, this time, they were light and cheerful - perhaps a woman's voice or some children playing. He walked on again and continued slowly, watching his footing as he re-entered the forest and, as he trod on wet tree roots, he slipped in the mud and sodden earth and just managed to keep standing.

The voices remained with him; neither louder nor softer, and he realised they were coming from behind him. He stopped to listen but the voices stopped again. He wondered if he was hearing things, and that maybe he had drunk too much last night after all, or was it just a ringing in his ears. David, amused by it, lightly tapped his head and continued. All was silent again.

He crossed another metalled road and re-joined the forest, when he heard what sounded like a child's laughter. Again he waited and listened and it stopped. He was perplexed and was beginning to feel uncomfortable, when he heard another voice, and this time it was calling his name. It reminded him of the night at Keld Head when he'd re-traced his footsteps in the snow, worrying who was behind him, afraid he was beginning to act like his father. But this time he had nothing to fear. It was just coincidence that it sounded like his name.

Then he heard it clearly, not just the name David, but David Keldas. Someone was really behind him; a woman or a child was calling his name and telling him to stop. Maybe it was Hannah he thought, and waited for her to catch up. When no one arrived he retraced his steps, and then off into the distance and into the trees, he caught sight of a red garment as someone ran away from him.

David heard the laughter again and, angered by the teasing, pursued. But he could hardly run; his leg and his back ached too much. He certainly wasn't afraid of Betty's fabled ferryman as he walked on, avoiding the footpath and followed the stalker deep into the forest.

In the density of the trees, he lost the figure and lost his bearings. He stopped and listened again and heard a whispering and laughing and instinctively headed for the noise. As uncomfortable as it was, he started to run, his leg painfully jarring as he stumbled again on some branches and tree roots and, as he jumped over the dead bracken and broken branches, he scratched his face and tore his jacket on some sharp stalks. He could make no advance on the stalker and yet continued on, not wanting to lose ground, gasping and panting with each breath.

Then he heard it again: 'Run, David . . . run!'

He heard it time and time again; it wasn't his imagination.

Pursuing faster, David slipped, struggled, and slid about in the mire, splashing through boggy patches black with peat that saturated his trousers. Out into the sunlight and then back into the shade. He was making headway now and the laughing stopped.

He saw the shape of a small slim frame; someone wearing a red knitted hat and dark clothes. It looked like a boy.

'Stop. . . . What do you want?' David shouted. But they ignored him and continued to run from him. And now he could only hear their breathless gasps.

With a strength David thought he didn't own, he ran on faster and as he approached the stalker, he lunged out and grabbed their jacket, but they slipped from his grasp. And as the pain in David's leg gnawed at him, he again shouted in despair, then stopped.

'Please wait? Who are you? What do you want?' But he was ignored.

David chased again, and this time he managed to catch hold of the person's jacket and then, lunging his body onto the legs, grabbed hold, and both of them went crashing into the mud on the forest floor.

David held on tightly as the stalker tried to wriggle free, kicking him and muddying him. And as they wrestled together, both twisting and turning, David saw the face of a girl, afraid, and struggling to release herself from his grasp. She ran free and again David pursued. She grabbed a broken branch and hit him on the shoulder, but he knocked it from her. Then, finally, his manly strength once again knocked her to the ground.

As she struggled to free herself, David caught her shoulders, turned her body over, and knelt beside her. 'What are you doing? What do you want?' He shouted desperately as he looked into her muddied face, and could see clearly that it was

Joanne. David held his head high and dared to look in her eyes.

'Don't hurt me, Davey, please. Don't hurt me!' She was gasping and laughing at the same time.

David didn't release his grip but held her tightly by the shoulders, thinking her back must be as saturated and filthy as he was. 'What do you want, Jo? You're crazy!' And he pressed her shoulders further into the ground.

She shook her head and tried to wriggle free, but this time his grip was too strong. 'Do you want to kiss me again? Do you?' she struggled for breath.

David didn't want to kiss her; he wanted to slap her face, and it took every ounce of restraint not to.

'What do you want?' He shouted again, still holding tightly onto her. 'Why are you following me? Why are you doing this to me? What have I done?'

'No, you never think you've done anything wrong, do you, Davey. . . . You think you can mess around with my feelings!'

'Joanne. I've never messed around with you!' He gave her a look of deep reproach. 'I only kissed you once – maybe twice, that's all!'

'Oh yes, it doesn't seem much to you does it,' she spat. 'It didn't mean much to your father either!'

'I don't want to know about him!'

'No, I don't suppose you do,' she stopped struggling. 'But you're going to. That was just how it started with him, just a kiss - just like you . . . then one more . . . then one more!'

'Stop it, Jo. Just stop it!' He shook her by the shoulders.

'No, I won't stop it. . . . That's it . . . close your ears. I never will stop it, I never will. He thought he could come to me at his beck and call. I was only a kid, Davey . . . I was only fifteen. I couldn't handle him. I didn't know what to do. I was afraid! He was manipulating me.'

David was stunned to silence.

'Sometimes when you were out looking for him, and you thought he was on the fells, he was with me! Can you believe it? What a joke! Oh yes, he thought it was so much fun. He laughed at you all. But I couldn't cope anymore. I knew it was wrong - him and his secrets, but I couldn't stop him. So I started tormenting him, just like I tormented you. I threatened to tell your mother, but I didn't want to hurt her. In that, I was loyal. So I told him you were trying to take over the farm, and that he should get back before you ruined things, but he still kept coming back, so I just carried on teasing him; following him day and night as often as I could. I harassed him so much; made him nervous and suspicious of everyone. Yes, it was me, Davey. I repaid him for all his abuse. Oh yes, and then you came along - just the same - just like him. But you, I'd longed for . . . ! I hoped you would save me, but you were just the same - just a kiss, that's all, and then it stopped. That was just as bad. Just one kiss huh! Is that what you thought?'

The laughing stopped and Joanne began to sob pitifully. David loosened his grip and she propped herself up.

'Oh, but I loved you, yet you didn't care, did you, just like him? I thought you were kinder, but you weren't - you were just the same, so I started to follow you. I drove you crazy, didn't I?'

'Then you'll follow me no more!' David didn't want to hear any more and he started to pull himself away, but she grabbed him by the collar.

'That's right. . . . Leave me here in this filth! That just suits you doesn't it?'

But David no longer cared. He pushed her away, struggled to his feet and walked away. He realised how wet and cold he was. His leg was aching more than ever and he felt numb with pain.

David slowly walked down the hill and through the trees, away from her foolishness. He no longer cared, he wanted another woman and the chances of her loving him were a mere glimmer and he didn't want to do anything that would put out that spark; thinking of Hannah - nothing but Hannah; her soft hair, her gentle manner, her large brown eyes. He wanted to say her name in reassurance, to protect himself from his own evil thoughts. *Oh my, how this hurts, how this hurts!* He staggered on like a man lost. His eyes wide open, yet walking blindly. He must get home and wash himself free of this disgust.

A blow hit him so hard in the back that he fell to the ground, gasping for breath, and his lungs stupefied in a spasm. David fell onto his knees, grasping his chest and, as he turned, he saw Joanne standing over him, holding a stump of wood in her hand.

Every ounce of strength left in his body surged as he threw himself at her again, knocking her to the ground. His whole body weight bearing down on her as she screamed. 'Oh, yes, that's it. That's it, Davey. . . . Why not finish me off? You can't take any more can you? You're weak, you are, just like your father, and look how he ended up'

'He was a fool Joanne, but he wasn't weak. . . . You killed him!'

'Aye, but he killed me first.'

As eye met eye, and David reflected on what she had just said, his eyelids lowered. Then she continued, 'I saw him point that gun at me, Davey. He wanted me out of the way. But you wouldn't harm me would you? You're different in that!' He was so close to her she could smell him. 'Huh, but then maybe he was telling the truth for once. Maybe you're not even his son. What a shock for you, eh?' And Joanne's breathing laboured as David put his hands around her throat and tightened his grip.

'Stop it . . . stop it. You're hurting me!' She clasped her hands around his wrists, but he was too strong for her.

David couldn't resist. He desperately wanted her to stop talking - he must silence her, but she wouldn't stop.

'That would be some secret, Davey. . . . Some secret, if I let it out!' her voice was fading.

'God have mercy on us, Jo!' And he squeezed her neck tighter.

David's eighth life passed before him, and he'd survived. His only hope rested in the hands of this girl. He wanted to stop her slander and silence her forever, so he squeezed his hands tighter around her throat and saw the very life start to drain out of her.

Joanne stopped talking, her eyes reddened and she looked mercifully at him; her face turning blue. She squeezed her hands on his; desperately trying to pull them off her neck. She reached up and touched his face and managed to claw her fingernails into the soft tissue of his cheek and scratch at his eyes. It was the last pain David could endure.

Joanne struggled free as David fell over on the wet earth. She stumbled away from him, gasping, sobbing and crying out loud.

David crawled on hands and knees to find a dry piece of ground, his breathing was heavy and laboured and his jaw quivered with shock, as he propped himself up against a tree to support his back. He had so much to take in, yet his head was wet and cold; he couldn't think straight. Once again Joanne Milton had got the better of him. Was it truth or lies she'd told; he no longer cared. She must do as she likes; say what she wants, he didn't mind. All he knew was that he must see Hannah again and take her to the mountains. He would walk the valleys and hills with her and hope she would love him the more for it.

David struggled to his feet and as his knees trembled under his bodyweight, the pain in his back, intense. He realised he was totally lost.

He took off his wet coat and rubbed some of the excess moisture from his trousers, then wiping his face with a handkerchief, he saw it was smeared with mud and streaks of blood.

Betty pulled a few dead leaves away from the red geraniums on her kitchen windowsill, and their fragrance delighted what few senses she had left. She watered them and placed them back on the windowsill, then she saw David coming into the garden with his coat folded up in a bundle and held under his arm. He looked wet and dirty and, with the dim eyesight she had, she saw blood on his face.

He bent over awkwardly by the door and tried to kick off his boots; throwing his coat down on the floor in the porch. David didn't look at Betty, and acted as if she was invisible and went straight over to the kitchen sink, ran the hot tap and washed his hands and face, recklessly splashing water everywhere. Barely clean, he dried himself on a towel, soiling it with blood and grime.

'Do - do you think I could have some more painkillers, Aunty?' still not looking at her.

Betty put down the small watering can and went to look at him closely. 'Whatever's the matter? Have you fallen?' Then she hobbled away to find her handbag and gave him the carton of pills. His hands were shaking as he fumbled to open the seal on the container and poured several pills into his hand.

'Don't take too many!' Betty reached across to take the carton from his hand. 'Oh my goodness! What have you done? You're hurt?' She came up close to his face and peered into his eyes.

'I'm okay . . . I'm going to have a bath.'

David put his head down in shame and moved away, leaving Betty alone with her thoughts. Something was seriously wrong, and she had a feeling he wasn't going to tell her what it was.

Poor Betty; unaccustomed and frustrated with the lives of young people, put the kettle on to make him a hot drink, but David never returned to receive it.

She heard the bath water running, then she heard it emptying, and then there was silence. She shouted upstairs: 'Davey . . . Davey. I've made you a drink! You have to be at work soon.' But he didn't reply.

Betty knew it was futile to coax him downstairs. David knew that he was well out of her reach.

It was late in the evening before she heard him stir, and as he crept down the stairs wearing a clean t-shirt and jeans, he looked solemn as he stood at the door. His skin was grey and his eyes were reddened.

MAN OF CLAY

'I'm sorry. I'm so sorry. I've brought nothing but trouble for you, haven't I?' And he stood shivering in front of her.

'You're hurt, Davey. . . . Let me help you. Come and sit down by the fire. You're no trouble.'

David sat down and held his aching back. Betty bustled into her makeshift bedroom and brought out a pink eiderdown and lovingly covered him with it.

He wanted to laugh at it, but couldn't.

'Let me call a doctor . . . or your mother?'

'No, please . . .' speaking in low tones. 'It's just my back again, that's all. I'm sorry. I'm sorry.'

'Did you fall?' she asked him for the second time.

'Yes - yes I fell. I slipped on some rocks on the hillside.' He hated to lie to her, but he couldn't tell her the truth; he didn't know the truth. Joanne had confused him with her ramblings, that he no longer understood anything. So he wrongly believed what he said didn't matter, either.

'Do you want to me to telephone the hotel?'

'No - no please it'll be okay,' he insisted.

Betty knew it wouldn't be okay. He should have been at work two hours ago. He had let the hotel down and that wasn't like him.

She went into the kitchen and started to cut a piece of ham off the bone, nearly cutting her fingers. She buttered some bread and opened yet another tin of tomato soup. She spilt half of the contents of the teapot on the kitchen table; her hands shaking, not just with age, but with anxiety.

Betty placed the meagre meal on a tray and set it down on his lap. He was laid back in the armchair, his head was on one side and his eyes were closed.

'Please eat it, love. . . . It'll do you good.'

Although David knew the meal had been lovingly prepared, he looked at it with contempt and wanted to push it away. He hadn't eaten all day, yet he felt no hunger, only sickness.

Betty didn't see much more of him for the next few days. He stayed away from work; he stayed in bed most of the time, coming down only to eat a few slices of toast or for more painkillers. Then one evening, David came downstairs fully dressed. He was clean-shaven, rested and looked better. Betty finally managed to make him smile as she warmly stroked his face. The grazes on his cheek and his forehead were beginning to heal, but leaving dark lines where the skin had scabbed over.

He made no further attempts to go to work, but took his muddy walking boots and cleaned them over the fireplace.

The following morning David was up early and dressed before Betty was even awake. She heard the engine of the Volvo start up. He had left her a note on the table:

Gone to Scafell with Hannah Robson. Don't wait up for me.
David.

Betty was fast running out of patience with him and slapped his note down on the table. 'Oh you silly boy! You silly, silly boy!'

David arrived at the surgery and swung the car around in the driveway, flicking gravel and stones across the yard. He was early, so he didn't knock the door but waited in the car. Hannah soon appeared and just to see her face was a boost for him. He was relieved she hadn't changed her mind.

Hannah had been ready and waiting for some time. She was excited about her day and hoped that David hadn't changed *his* mind.

She had made sandwiches, bought fruit and chocolate, and done a flask of coffee and some juice, just as promised. Hannah was well prepared and David was pleased she'd been sensible in what she'd chosen to wear.

He edged out of the car to help and hoped she didn't notice his bad back. But she did see it. She saw it straight away. Hannah also noticed he appeared nervous, and could see scratches on his face and he looked vague and distant.

David barely greeted her as he put her things in the boot of the car. He packed away the foodstuffs into one rucksack, intending to carry most of the weight himself.

They sped off to Keswick, quickly through Dunmail Raise; he was driving far too fast. When he spoke to her, he spoke erratically, and his sentences were disjointed; almost rude.

Hannah was disappointed in him. She had looked forward to this day; butterflies were fluttering around in her stomach at the thought of seeing him again. Then there was the excitement of the walk; to see new places and to climb the highest mountain in England. And it was David's presence that excited her most. But, today, he appeared to be his old self: the moody young man that she'd first met and, if he remained the same, she doubted she could enjoy her day at all. But Hannah was now committed.

They parked on a small lane with a few other cars, and lifting her things from the boot of the car, David spoke softly, 'Are you ready for this, then?'

Unbeknown to Hannah, David also felt nervous. All he'd hoped for was to be here with her. Doubts of her intentions flooded relentlessly in his head and he felt unworthy to take Hannah anywhere, and wrongly thought that she'd agreed to come, only because it was a chance to walk the high fells. He had been fooling himself in thinking it was him she wanted.

As he lifted the larger of the two rucksacks onto his shoulder, Hannah noticed him wince; there was definitely something wrong. She then remembered how he'd struggled to stand up when she had met him in Betty's field.

'David, are you sure you're alright to carry that?'

He was embarrassed at her questioning and didn't reply.

He set off at pace through the small farmyard and on to Stockley Bridge. Hannah striding out to keep just one pace behind him. She watched his elegant stride, as he walked tall and fast in front of her, yet there was still a slight limp that she hadn't noticed before.

They walked up the gradients to Sty Head Ghyll, and despite his limp, David was certainly fitter than Hannah. She stopped several times to catch her breath and he politely waited for her and then as soon as she was rested, he would ask if she were okay, then start up again, yet he continued to limp.

When Hannah stopped to take another rest, she shouted to him, 'David. You're limping. Are you sure you're okay?' She was insistent this time.

David wasn't okay. His back was already aching and he could feel a burning sensation down the back of his leg. 'I'll be all right. I've had a bad back that's all, but I'm used to it now,' he snapped back at her.

Hannah was irritated at his manner and her eyes widened as she too lost patience with him. 'We're not going to play these silly games again are we!'

Her words struck him hard. She was right to give him the discipline; he knew he was being a fool. Taking a step back onto the soft grass, David sat and waited for her. He lay back on the grass to ease his back and Hannah came and sat beside him.

'I'm sorry, Hannah. All I wanted was to take you on this walk.' He couldn't look at her face, so just looked up at the blue sky. 'My Aunt Betty thinks I've got sciatica. She's been plying me with painkillers for three days now, but I'm not feeling much better.'

'Why didn't you tell me? We could have gone another day.'

'But when, Hannah? When? You're leaving soon!' He propped himself up on his elbows, took the flask from his bag and poured some coffee, then he looked at her warm face and it compelled him to smile.

'How much further is it?' she spoke softly.

'A long way yet. We have to get to Sty Head Tarn, then a steady climb up The Corridor, and then it gets rocky.'

She touched his arm with her hand. 'Can you really go on?'

David knew he must be strong, but her kindness weakened him, much like Tony's had during their stay in Blackpool when he had wept in his friend's arms. He wanted to touch the girl's face and stroke her hair, yet if she only knew that a few days earlier he had tried to kill another with his bare hands. But now he was here with Hannah sitting beside him, so lovely, gentle and trusting. She mustn't know the thoughts that were swimming around inside his head.

Hannah could see he was troubled. She knelt upright and fumbled inside the rucksack for some chocolate and handed it to him, then looked determined into his eyes. 'We don't have to climb Scafell today. Let's just enjoy the hills and each other's company. I promise you, I'll come back in summer and you can take me then! Anyway, I'm already tired. You may have a bad back, but there's nothing wrong with your lungs. You've tired me out. Let's rest awhile and see how we feel?'

Totally defeated, David agreed and chose a detour. And so they diverted onto the beautiful mountain pass, along a stream of water, cascading and foaming, blue and white in the sun, bordered by rocks that glistened white.

David knew she was wiser than he was. He was a fool to risk her life and his own, just to save his flagging ego. The mountains could be dangerous places if the weather changed and already darkened clouds were appearing on the horizon. David felt easier as he realised Hannah was just concerned for his injury. The more he relaxed, the more he talked, pointing out to her the surrounding fells, telling her their names.

'You must know a lot about these hills, Davey. . . . You should bring people up here - become a guide or something.'

'Ah, no, I don't like walking with crowds,' he smiled, 'two or three's enough for me.'

'You should let Barry look at your back. He's always illegally treating himself to the drugs at the surgery.'

'I bet he is. He wanted you to stitch up my busted lip, remember?'

And the memory of that reminded Hannah of how much she had changed in her opinion of him, because now, looking at his face and attracted by his humility, she knew she would do anything to help him.

They sat down beside a tarn and a cool breeze caused her to move closer to him. She took a bottle of juice from his hand, and drank, then pulling open an orange and breaking the segments gently, they shared them like children.

'What about your family name? It sounds very old. . . . What does Keldas mean? I've never heard it before.'

David was embarrassed at this question and was reluctant to answer. 'A Keld is a spring or a well. Like the farm - Keld Head. It was built near a spring, you see. Our family name was Kellet really, but my great-grandfather was an eccentric and he changed our name to the old Nordic meaning of Keldas.'

'Has your family lived here for generations, then?'

He paused and was unsure how to continue. *What family was this!* His mother was from Lancaster and that was all he knew; there was no ancestry to talk of. And as he bowed his head a little, Hannah realised she'd been insensitive. 'I'm sorry. I didn't mean to pry. It must hurt you to talk about your father.'

David knew he couldn't lie any more. He wanted to be honest with her and clear his name; he'd once been proud of his family, but no longer. He guessed Hannah had been wary of him in the past, and was uncomfortable with his moods. He didn't want her to think it was anything to do with him being like George Keldas. He believed he was no mindless and abusive womaniser. He was as honest and as faithful as they come.

'Hannah. There's something I must tell you, and I don't quite know how to say it.' There was sadness in his eyes. 'I want to tell you before anyone else does. You see George Keldas wasn't my real father. I don't know who my real father is!'

Hannah felt like she had electricity running through her veins. 'Please don't, Davey. . . . You don't have to tell me this,' and she looked away from him, but he held her shoulders and turned her to towards him, lifting her a little. Then realising he was squeezing her shoulders as hard as he'd squeezed Joanne's neck, his fingers trembled and he pulled his hands away.

'Yes, I do. I do!' he emphasised. 'You're my friend, I hope, and I wanted you to know the truth. I didn't want you to be afraid of me. I can't expect you to understand what I've been through. . . . I guess I've had some kind of trauma. Things have been hard, but I'm getting better. I just wanted to tell you.'

Hannah pulled away and hugged her knees into her chest, then folded her arms around them, and repeated herself, 'You didn't have to tell me this, Davey . . . ' she hesitated, 'because I already knew!'

David's mouth dropped open. 'I'm sorry, I don't understand. How did you know?'

Hannah could see she'd had gone deeper into this man's heart than she'd intended. She would never forget the look in his eyes. 'Because Barry told me. . . .'

'And how for pity's sake did Barry know?' He threw his head back.

Hannah didn't want to say anymore as she watched him lie back on the grass and rest his head on the soft turf.

David should have felt a great relief but he didn't, he felt ill at ease and confused. Then he quickly sat up again and said, 'How did Barry know? Who's been talking about me?' and this time he was angry and insistent.

'Oh Davey . . . Davey. . . . You are so slow at times!' She looked longingly at his face and his blackened eyes pierced her. 'Nobody needed to tell him,' she stressed. 'No one . . . no one!'

David looked at her and tried to grasp the meaning of what she'd just said, but couldn't.

'Oh for goodness sake, David. . . . You're Barry's son!'

David was motionless. He felt like he'd been given a golden nugget, a diamond, and a prize of highest value. This cannot be true. It couldn't be as simple as this.

'What – what do you mean, Hannah? I don't know what to say. How do you know this? It's impossible!'

She came up closer to him and wished she hadn't told him, but how could she have prevented it. 'Hush now. . . . Don't speak anymore. You must have time to take this in. I'm sorry Davey, I'm sorry. I shouldn't have told you. Please don't think Barry's been gossiping about you. . . . I've only known myself a few weeks. He wanted me to know how much he cares for you. Yes and I care for you, too.' she put her hand on his arm and squeezed it. 'On the day that Eleanor left him, I came home from a shopping trip in Kendal, and he was sitting in the office looking at some old newspaper cuttings he had about you; those taken with him, when you were a boy; those of George Keldas and the shootings at Keld Head. He started to cry and I felt so embarrassed. I didn't know what to do. I couldn't stop him. But Barry said he wanted to treat me like a daughter and that I should know about him and Eleanor. He told me he'd had a relationship with your mother when they were younger. He told me you were his son and that you didn't know. He told me everything, Davey - everything, and I promised I'd never tell a soul. Oh, don't you see, you're so like him; those eyes of yours. The day I saw you at Hawkshead and you'd had your haircut, I couldn't believe the likeness. You even act like him; you're sensitive, just like him, and I know why you found it hard to cope with the situation at Keld Head: you shouldn't have been there.' She paused and then said, 'come on, let's walk, I'm getting cold.'

'No, wait, Hannah - please. I can't take this in. I feel embarrassed - naked.'

'Don't be, please. . . .We must walk, Davey. You need time to take it in.'

David struggled to his feet. And as he held out his hand to help her to stand, he refused to let go.

Hannah felt his body trembling through hers, as they walked side by side, hand in hand, then she squeezed his hand in response. She talked non- stop about the beautiful scenery; anything to distract him from asking more questions.

David would never recall any of the steps he took that day, despite the fact that his back ached like nothing on earth.

At first he felt ashamed of his mother and Barry, then delight, but then there was repulsion. Then he felt risen by his new status, then he felt low, as he considered his conception and became as small and insignificant as the embryo he'd been. He thought he'd been moulded like clay in someone's hand.

Hannah never intended to tell David the truth. Barry had assured her that he was in ignorance. And she worried if she'd done the right thing. Yet with the respect she had for David, she could no longer see him suffer.

The white rocks in the ghyll glistened in the sunshine. Tufts of lilac coloured heather and bright green strands of fern sprouted in the crevices of the rocks. White and grey, fluffy clouds dappled the sky. The noise of the water was refreshing as it splashed down the valley and made its way to Stockley Bridge and Derwent Water. A cool breeze blew on their backs. Hannah and David were bonded by a secret and it was the emotion of the moment that made David believe he now loved her. He hoped he could see her every day until she left. He was happy, it was she who'd revealed this truth to him, and no other. He found himself inwardly saying Barry's surname, repeatedly: Fitzgerald - Fitzgerald. But he knew it was a name he could never bear.

David fell into the car; the relief was intense.

He didn't need persuading to stop for a cold drink on the way home as their conversation flowed light and easy. Hannah promised to meet him the following night if he wasn't working, and a pang of anxiety touched him as he wondered if he still had a job.

As they sat outside a bar in the last of the afternoon's sunshine, David told her all about his time in London. He told her of Banjo and the boy, Twist, and how they'd helped Tony get better.

Hannah told David how much Barry had worried about him while he was missing, and had spent an agonising three weeks, until they heard he was safe.

David put his arm around Hannah, and she leant back on his shoulder. He felt her soft brown hair touch his face. 'Hannah. . . .' he softly spoke.

She looked at him and knew exactly what he wanted. She reached across to kiss him but she didn't notice him hesitate.

The day drew cooler and a strong breeze was beginning to emerge as David drove her home. 'It looks like we've had the best part of the day,' she said. 'Oh, Davey, I nearly forgot,' she sounded excited. 'There was a piece in the local newspaper about a girl that had been assaulted on Claife Heights. . . . Can you believe it . . . ! Your aunty told me it wasn't safe to be up there alone. Just think, it could have been me!'

David's heart fell heavy; the weight was back and dragging him into the mire and, as he stared out into the distance, he gripped the steering wheel with his hands and muttered, 'It could never have been you, Hannah - never.'

21

A CAPTIVE AUDIENCE.

Betty sat in the parlour window watching the road. She nibbled at some small squares of pork pie placed on a pretty floral china plate. She'd saved some for David, hoping he wouldn't be as late home as his note suggested.

She had tried to stop herself from worrying about him too much. There was no point; the Keldas men always did as they pleased. At least the weather had stayed fine and the mountain-tops were free of mist, with just a few clouds lingering. But as the late afternoon brought more cloud and the day deteriorated, Betty saw specks of rain appear on the window, and she hoped David had finished his walk.

Betty had missed him dreadfully today. Perhaps because she knew he was with Hannah. She should have been delighted that he'd found a friend, and the girl was likeable; but Betty hoped this Hannah could cope with David's problems. She also wondered how sincere Hannah's friendship was and Betty dreaded she might disappoint him.

David had certainly been happy the day they'd sat together in the garden, and Betty wondered if Hannah could lift him out of the desperate state he had sunk into. Nevertheless, she still felt a kind of loneliness. Having David live with her these last few weeks had been better than any medicine the doctor could prescribe. She thought that perhaps now her useful life was over. She had cared for her husband for over sixty years and, regrettably, not had any children; David was the closest thing to a son she had. But Betty feared, much like Kathy a few weeks earlier, that she was losing him. The one consolation she had was to have been a refuge for him when he most needed it.

A CAPTIVE AUDIENCE

At a time of life when some would feel useless, Betty felt that she had struck gold. She'd found one, final and ecstatic, rush of life surge through her veins.

Betty saw a white car coming slowly down the lane and pull up outside the cottage. Her heart jumped when she saw a policeman open the garden gate and knock on her door; it must be David; something had to be wrong. Betty was so afraid that a great weakness came over her and she was unable to stand, so she feebly called out and asked the man to enter.

'I'm sorry to disturb you, Ma'am,' and as the policeman opened the cottage door and saw the old lady, he bowed his head in respect. 'Don't be alarmed.'

'Please, officer . . . please sit down.'

'No that's okay, Mrs?' he hesitated. 'I'm sorry I don't know your name?'

'Mrs Keldas . . . Betty Keldas.'

'Ah . . . right. Mrs Keldas. We're just making house to house enquiries . . . perhaps you can help us?'

Betty was relieved by his reassurance.

'A young woman attacked up in the forest on Wednesday morning,' he said. 'Have you seen anyone acting suspiciously or heard anything?'

'No . . . . Certainly not.' Betty told him. 'Many people come this way, because of the footpath.'

'Do you live here alone Mrs Keldas?'

'No . . . . My nephew lives with me . . . he's a good lad, there's not many that would take care of an old woman like me. Oh, look . . . here he is now.' Betty saw David's car pull into the driveway and as he walked through the garden his lameness was obvious.

The policeman waited for him to enter, and having time to examine David's face wasn't sure if he knew him or not.

David threw his keys on the table, put down his rucksack and spoke abruptly. 'What can we do for you officer?' David could see a look of distress on Betty's face and continued to speak authoritatively. 'Is everything all right?'

'So you must be Mrs Keldas's nephew?'

'She's my great-aunt actually. . . .' David tried to be clever and continued to look scornfully at the policeman.

'And what's your name then, son?'

'David . . . David Keldas.'

The policeman came forward to formally shake his hand. 'Ah, I thought I recognised you. You're from Keld Head, aren't you?'

David nodded in response, as he in return recognised the policeman as one of many that had called at the farm over the last few months.

The policeman asked David the same question he'd asked Betty, but this time he worded it differently. 'Were you in the area, or did you see anything suspicious on Wednesday morning?'

David was in a trap and cautiously replied. 'Why do you ask?'

The peculiar look on David's face and his manner irritated the policeman. 'Just answer the question, please?'

Betty had been watching for David's reaction and quickly interrupted. 'He's been sick. . . . He's been in bed all week.'

'Is that right? So you haven't seen anyone acting suspiciously?'

In sheer disbelief at how his aunt had replied David repeated. 'No . . . no *why*?'

'And where do you work?'

'I'm off sick at the moment. . . . I'm a barman.'

'A young woman was attacked up in these woods and I wondered if you knew anything about it?'

David denied all knowledge.

'Well, that will be all for now, Sir . . . but if you do hear of anything, please call us won't you. We want these hills to be a safe place for people to enjoy.'

The policeman returned to his car and met his colleague on the lane. 'Do you remember the lad from Keld Head? George Keldas's son. Well, he's in there. He's got scratches on his hands and face, and has a bad leg. . . . I don't trust him at all. The old woman covered for him.'

A CAPTIVE AUDIENCE

* * *

Betty saw David wipe his brow as the policeman left. He grabbed his bag to go upstairs and change. 'Don't you dare go anywhere young man. . . .' Much strengthened, she rose to her feet. 'You come right here and sit down now!'

Fearing her wrath more than the policeman's, David knew he was in trouble. Yes, his elderly aunt had covered for him and, although she was very old, she certainly wasn't stupid.

'Now you tell me about your day?' as she resumed her place at the table and David was compelled to join her.

As he sat before her, he put his hands nervously behind his head and then brushed his fingers through his dark hair, making the short black strands stand on end.

'I've had a brilliant day with Hannah. . . . We didn't make Scafell, my back was too bad. I've taken her home and that's all. . . .' He raised his eyebrows arrogantly.

But that certainly wasn't all; he had no desire to confuse his aunt and tell her that he'd learned Barry Fitzgerald was his real father.

'And that's it, is it?' she replied. 'So what about Wednesday, David?' her look was determined. 'I want you to tell me about Wednesday? What really happened up in that forest?'

David glared back at her unable to answer. He couldn't lie - not to her. He just sighed and shook his head.

But Betty was a match for him and cruelly waited, knowing he would feel compelled to fill the silence.

He sat forward in his chair and came closer to her. 'Aunty. . . I can't tell you what happened but, please, trust me.'

She saw David's skin glowing with colour from the sun and the exertion of the day, and it belied the fear of his sin being discovered, as he appeared less strained than he had been in weeks.

'I may be in serious trouble. . . . You see, I met a friend in the forest. . . . Someone who has a grudge against me and, shall we say, things got out of control. . . . Thankfully, I've harmed no one, though, you must believe me.' David was relieved that Joanne's strength had prevented him. 'I've probably been hurt more than anyone has.... If I have to suffer for being human, then so be it, but please believe me, none of this - none of it, is my fault.'

'David.... You're not making any sense?' Betty softened.

'You must trust me, then. I can't tell you what happened ... but I'm so sorry if I've worried you.'

'If you insist you can't tell me, I can't make you, but when will all this end?'

'I don't know ... I just don't know ... I wish I did. I feel I'm being punished for something - for someone. I don't know what.... There's a bitter after-taste in my mouth from the things my father did.... But I've had a great day with Hannah, and I think a lot of her and I hope she feels the same way about me. I want to rebuild my life. I thought after today things would be better, but I'm not sure anymore.'

'Davey ... if you can't speak to me about what's happened, please speak to someone.... Your mother ... this Hannah.'

'There's no one else I can talk to about the trouble I might be in.' David knew there was someone, and that was Tony Milton, but he was hundreds of miles away in Edinburgh, yet how could he tell him he'd tried to strangle his sister. He also knew if he were found out, he might lose Hannah and, for the chance to keep her, he would do anything - anything. But why should he bother to preserve George Keldas's name and keep silent about his abuse. He had done nothing for him only abuse him too. But it wasn't just his name, he had his mother and his sisters and his brother, and then there was Betty; there was Keld Head and everything he'd ever known. He cursed the man; he despised him, and began to pity Joanne the more. If what she'd said was true, she wasn't totally to blame, and perhaps her way of handling things was a just punishment for a wicked man. But to punish him as she'd done; how could she. She had driven him to violence, and must despise him now.

David knew he must fight. He mustn't let go. Hope was in his grasp and it was so real and close, that he could touch its warmth.

A CAPTIVE AUDIENCE

He wished now he'd stayed longer with Hannah, but her revelation about Barry had made it awkward for them both. David felt he couldn't see Barry; he would have to be mentally prepared, and Hannah would have let him know she'd told David the truth. Barry was still a friend and David knew, eventually, their relationship could change.

He recalled Barry's kindness to him, how they had often worked together, laughing and cursing at the cattle, struggling with their various ailments. How Barry knew all the time that David was his own flesh and blood. He remembered sitting with him on the straw bale in the loosebox; the intimacy they had as he'd unburdened his mind about George Keldas's trial. What must he have thought? Did he say anything that would have hurt him? Had Barry enjoyed their meal together, and David wondered how he'd felt, sitting with his son and the girl he wished was his daughter. Yet David never once considered why Barry hadn't told him the truth.

He'd had some wild ideas at one point that Alan Marsh could have been his father, but had never considered Barry Fitzgerald. He knew they'd all been friends as young people, and knew that his mother did have some kind of a relationship with Alan, but he had cringed at the thought.

Then the question arose of why his mother actually married George, and why did they decide never to tell him the truth. Was it just as George had said, and he had kept his promise not to tell? But now David's new heritage had at last given him a sense of respect and a full identity. But this latest incident with Joanne, if the police discovered the truth, gave him further reasons to worry. How could he possibly hurt Barry; he would wish he'd never fathered him at all. Even though the reproach would be silent, it would hurt.

David spent the following morning tidying the garden. Despite the fact that his leg and back were still aching, he cut the grass and washed the car. As late morning approached, he knelt on the lawn to clean the mower. He'd carelessly smeared grass and oil over his t-shirt and jeans. He was still unshaven and looked grubby; he smelt of newly cut grass.

David had been humming to himself and whistling, when he heard a car pull up on the lane and stop outside the cottage. He looked up and saw the same policeman that had called yesterday. The man approached and stood tall above David as he continued to kneel on the grass.

'Good morning, David,' the policeman had a partner standing with him.

David didn't rise and, kneeling on the damp grass, felt totally defeated. He'd hoped they wouldn't return, but to come today at this time, just when he was about to wash and change and meet Hannah.

'So then, young man. . . .' the policeman began.

David struggled to his feet holding his aching back.

'Some of your neighbours tell me that you're partial to walking up in these woods. In fact, some have gone as far to say that you probably walk these woods every day. Is that so?'

'I walk up the Heights a lot . . . yes.'

'So could I ask you again, if you were up in these woods on Wednesday, May the 3rd?' The look was serious.

'I possibly was. . . . I can't remember.'

'Then why did your Aunt tell us you were at home and sick in bed?'

'I have been sick. . . . I have a bad back. My aunt's an old lady, she must have been mistaken by the date.'

'Then if you were sick, why didn't you call work to tell them. They'd no idea where you were.'

David was pained to know that the police had been checking up on him.

'I think it might be an idea, son, if we talk about this a bit more!' The policeman looked at the cottage door wide open and, guessing that Betty was inside, continued. 'We either do it here or - you know the rest!'

There was no escape for David; he was in deep trouble and not wanting to cause his aunt any more worry, relented. 'I'll come with you . . . but please let me tell her where I'm going.'

David went indoors and kissed his aunt goodbye. Betty had

seen him talking to the policemen and she knew why they'd returned.

'Please don't worry, Aunty. . . . It'll be all right. I'll sort it.'

But Betty was worried; she was desperately anxious for him, and felt he was walking out on her life for good. She'd guessed this time would come, but not in this way and not with these men. She watched them drive away and immediately went to the telephone and did something she should have done days earlier, and called David's mother.

'Right David. . . . Just answer our questions and you'll be home before you know it.'

The cold room smelt of disinfectant and was lit only by an artificial light. David was sitting on a hard chair, his hands clenched together and resting on the table in front of him. His eyes were piercing the table; he was a faded mirror image of George Keldas.

'On the 3rd of May, a young woman was assaulted on Claife Heights, and was left injured and soaked to the skin. If not for a couple of passers-by, she could have died of exposure. Now lad, I'll ask you again. Were you up in the forest on Wednesday morning?'

'Yes . . . I was.' David quietly replied.

'And did you meet anyone?'

'I was alone.'

'And did you meet anyone one!' the policeman repeated.

'I saw a few people, yes.'

'Did you talk to anyone?'

'I may have done.'

The detective banged his fist down on the table. 'Answer me properly, lad!'

David was shocked at this outburst and ashamed. He felt disgusted at his own attitude and appearance. These two men were smartly dressed: one in a uniform, the other in a suit, and yet he was in old, dirty clothes and he could smell the grass cuttings and body odour on himself. He looked wretched.

'You have some scratches on your hands and face,' the

policeman continued. 'Where did you get these?'

'I caught myself on some branches.'

'Stand up – take off your shirt?'

David felt humiliated by this question and reluctantly rose to his feet and complied. And as he stood before the two men, cold and semi-naked, he wanted to cross his arms over his body to cover himself, despite knowing his chest was clear of marks.

'Move closer.…Turn around?'

David obeyed and one of the men came up close to examine his back.

'How did you get this bruising?'

'I fell against a tree.'

'Put your shirt back on and sit down.' The policeman resumed. 'Do you know a young woman called Joanne Milton?'

There was a long pause before David could continue.

'Yes, of course I do.'

'In December last year, you were involved in an incident, where Joanne and her brother were admitted to hospital suffering from hypothermia. The nurses told us Joanne had bruising on her arms and back and you were with her that night. On Wednesday, that same young woman was assaulted on Claife Heights. She was admitted to the same hospital with bruising on her neck! Now, David, can you tell us about this, please?'

'Joanne's a strange girl. . . . She does things to herself.' David foolishly continued remembering Linzi's former explanation. 'Anyway, she shouldn't walk the fells alone. It's not safe.'

'You're irritating me now, David! Did you assault Joanne Milton on Wednesday the 3rd of May?'

David paused, he'd remained firm, he hadn't lied so far and he didn't want to lie, but what could he say. Whatever he said would condemn him. He was trapped and completely lost. He didn't know what time it was; surely, he should be with Hannah by now. What would she think of him if she knew he was here? If she knew he'd been minutes away from murder.

A CAPTIVE AUDIENCE

Yet he could not let her go, this still wasn't his fault, his only hope would be lost if he told the truth.

'I did not.' he lied.

The detective slapped his hand down again on the table. 'Get him out of my sight!'

David was pulled up out of chair by the arm and led to a small room with just a bed and a hard chair. 'You're not going home yet. So don't think we've finished with you. I can hold you as long as I like.'

As the door banged shut behind him, David went across to the bed, sat on the mattress and put his head into his hands. He wondered how low he'd sunk and felt humiliated to be treated like a criminal. This was all Joanne's fault. She had thrown a wild card, and she may have succeeded in getting her revenge. Was he also to be punished for the sins of George Keldas?

He didn't know what Joanne had told the police. Had she spoke the truth? Did they really know it was him that had assaulted her? And now he too had lied, he was worth nothing. He had sunk as low as all the others: his mother, George Keldas and Joanne. He had despised them for their deception and now he despised himself.

David fell back on the bed, resting his arms under his head as a pillow and stared at the ceiling. He lay quietly for what must have been hours. He was alone with his destructive thoughts with no concept of the time. Hannah lost; the farm lost; probably his job; he was disowned by all; even his real father would surely hate him now.

David heard a woman's voice outside as the door unlocked and it immediately comforted him. He sat up on the bed and waited, expectantly. His mother came into the room, with a tall man wearing a pinstriped suit.

David got up, his head bent low, and moved slowly across the room and hugged her; she pulled his head close to her bosom.

'Davey - Davey. What are we to do with you?'

She lifted his head and looked him in his eyes. 'Come on,

son, we must talk.'

David looked up at the tall man and recognised Angus Piercy, Betty's solicitor.

He took David's hand and shook it. But David was ashamed to stand before this immaculately dressed, elderly man.

'David . . . please sit down. . . . We've come to help you.'

'Just tell us what happened. I know you couldn't have possibly hurt that girl.' Kathy said. 'You can trust us . . . please tell us.'

'It's true....I've been charged with assault. It would be better if we were alone, Mum.' David spoke in soft and broken tones.

'I think it's time we did some straight talking, David, and Mr Piercy should stay.... He can help you.'

'Then if that's what you want,' and David began.

David took hold of his mother's hand. 'If I tell you truth, it'll hurt you so much, but I don't think I can keep it inside any longer. I'm sorry it has to be this way . . . I'm so sorry.'

His face was pale and his eyes looked grave. Kathy wondered what he'd done that could upset her so much and she looked questionably at Angus Piercy.

'I did hurt Joanne. . . . I tried to kill her. . . . I wanted to kill her. I could have done it with my bare hands!'

Kathy rose from the chair, but David gently held her arm and sat her down again. 'No, you have to listen. . . . You must know why I did it. You must trust me.'

David told them everything. Of Joanne's affair with George Keldas. How she said he'd abused her and then how she'd stalked him in retribution. How David had unwittingly kissed Joanne, and how she'd followed him and pestered him ever since. He told them about the night on the fells, when Joanne refused to come home if he didn't give her a promise of marriage. Then there were the endless letters she'd sent him when he was still at Keld Head. The phone calls and her diary, explicitly describing the relationship with George Keldas and the love and fantasies about himself. And finally, how they had met on Claife Heights, when she had taunted him. How she'd struck him on the back with a heavy branch of wood; a blow so strong that David thought it could have killed him if it was any higher, or on his head, which he was certain it was intended to be. That she'd blackmailed him, saying she knew George wasn't his real father, and threatened to expose it to everyone. And that he now knew the identity of his real father.

David looked into his mother's eyes and witnessed the reaction he had waited long months to see.

'This is all my fault, Davey. I'm so sorry. . . . It's not your fault. You shouldn't have to go through this hell.' She shook her head; her heart now heavy.

Angus Piercy interrupted. 'David. . . . Do the police know any of this?'

David looked at the kindly man, and strengthened by his mother's apology said, 'No, I don't think so . . . but I don't know what Joanne's told them.'

'Have you admitted anything?'

'No, I lied.'

The solicitor shook his head. 'Do they have any evidence against you - anything that could prove you were with her?'

'But I'm guilty. . . . I did hurt her.'

'Then it must be self-defence - you were provoked. If they have no evidence, they cannot keep you here long. Leave this to me. You must come too, Mrs Keldas, please.'

David paced the floor of the small room and wondered if he had any hope left. He remembered the clock in the interview room and knew he should have been with Hannah by now. He cursed and gently banged his head against the cold wall.

It was some time later in the evening when the door was opened again and one of the policemen called him. 'Right, Keldas. . . . Out!'

David slipped from the bed expecting another interrogation.

'You're let off this time. . . . But don't go anywhere near that girl again. You're both lying and we know it. She insists she doesn't know her attacker and she says it certainly wasn't you. But we know it's you all right . . . she's dropped all charges. I don't believe either of you, and you've both wasted our time.'

A CAPTIVE AUDIENCE

David found it hard to believe he was actually free and was stunned as he wandered into the dark hallway of the police station. Kathy was sitting alone on a small bench.

'Come on, son. . . . Let's get you home.' She led David out into the cool night air, holding firmly on to his arm as if to guide him.

He took a deep breath to fill his lungs and remove the stagnant air of the police cell from his body. Then the beaming headlights of a car shone across the car park and David saw a Mercedes waiting, with its engine running.

Barry Fitzgerald came over and put his arm across his son's back and guided him to the rear seat. As they drove away, David could hear his mother's voice quietly talking to Barry, as she sat beside him in the front seat. David fell asleep. He didn't know where he was going; he didn't really care.

The large bed was snug and warm; David slipped under the covers. A hot bath had rested his muscles and the chicken broth his mother had made, reminded him of life back at Keld Head; the glass of brandy Barry had given him, stood empty at his side. The cotton sheets felt soft and comforting to his body. David had said very little as he entered his father's house.

As daybreak crept into the bedroom, David lay awake, not knowing if he had slept. And as he listened to the dawn chorus, he looked around at the opulence he found himself in. His soiled clothes still lay in a neatly folded pile on the chair beside him. He heard a few cars driving by and the clinking sound of milk bottles as a milkman delivered.

He began to contemplate, that, if not for his mother, he would probably still be in the prison cell. He attempted to sleep again but the more he tried the more sleep fled from him. He wondered where Hannah was; was he close to her room? Yet, he had no desire to look for her.

Through half-closed eyelids, David looked at the plush carpets, the soft furnishings of turquoise jacquard and lace. He wondered what life would have been like if this had been his home, and he'd been reared by his real father. And, as he mused over his surroundings, a shivering feeling stole through his body as if he had been woven in the womb and re-born, like he had come into the world with just the skin on his body, and through a hard labour.

David heard the bedroom door open as it brushed on the fibres of the deep shag pile carpet. He sat up in bed, stretched and brushed his hair straight with his fingers.

'I'm sorry it's early, Davey, but I couldn't sleep.' Barry lifted David's folded-up clothes off the chair and put them on the floor. He sat beside him on the bedside chair and handed him a mug of tea.

'Don't worry. . . . Neither could I.' David yawned. 'What time is it?'

'It's five-thirty and I have to be in Kentmere by seven. I wanted to speak to you before I left. . . . This is a funny kind of meeting place isn't it? I never dreamt one day you'd be sleeping under my own roof.' Barry looked closely at David expecting to find a clue to his feelings, but found none.

David leant back on the softly padded headboard and sipped his tea. 'Thank you for looking after me.'

'It's something I should have done years ago.'

David smiled and Barry knew he could continue.

'I just wanted to tell you I'm sorry - if you can accept my apology. But I wanted to tell you not to hate us, especially not your mother. I'm just as guilty.'

'Please . . . please don't. You don't have to do this.'

'No, you're wrong. I do have to do this. I couldn't bear for you to think badly of your mother and me. Please don't speak now, and just hear me out. I must explain.'

David looked at Barry and for the first time in his life, saw the face of a father he respected, and tried to see himself in the man's eyes. Although David's own eyes were heavy through lack of sleep, they widened as he saw a mirror of his own reflection and wondered why he'd never noticed it before.

'Your mother and I were young. . . . I was still at university and she was already engaged to George. We made a big mistake, Davey, and although we dearly loved one another, it was too late. She told George she was pregnant by me, and that she must break off their engagement, but he pleaded with her. He promised her he would look after you as if you were his own and never tell a soul. It broke my heart to see her marry him. I felt helpless. I had years of studying in front of me and at the time couldn't have given you the life you deserved. I finished my training and married Eleanor and I stayed here so I could be near to you. I tried to help you with the farm bills, not to make them so high. . . . Eleanor never wanted any children, but that didn't matter because I had you. I could satisfy myself by coming to the farm now and again - that made me happy. Before George was taken to prison, even before he tried to shoot you, I could see you were unhappy. I argued with your mother that we should tell you - in fact, I begged her, but she thought, and perhaps wrongly, it would hurt you more if you knew the truth. We made a bad decision, Davey, and I've found it hard to live with, and I guess so have you.'

David listened to every word he said, trying to put the jigsaw pieces of his life together. Although Barry's explanation wasn't complete, it was sufficient to satisfy him; he guessed one day he could learn more.

'I hope someday you can forgive me, I can't stand it, that you might think badly of me,' he repeated.

David didn't realise, but Barry's desire for love reflected his own. They had both been denied it and as David listened, he knew why he'd always felt comfortable with this man.

'Your mother thinks we should still keep things quiet, but that's up to you, now.'

'I don't want anything to change. I've had a rough time, but I feel safe now. I don't even feel I deserve this attention.'

Barry stood up and collected the empty beakers. 'Then stay with me a day or so. Hannah leaves on Tuesday and I think you'll want to be with her as much as I do. Oh, by the way, we've told her everything. She's in surgery this morning, but I've given her the rest of the day off. Get some rest and make yourself at home, because that's how I want you to think of this place if you can.' Hope was within grasp.

After Barry left him, David felt peace return. He belonged to someone, he was loved again and everything he had ever wanted was in his hands and ready for the taking. But this luxury could never be his home; he'd thought Foxglove Cottage to be a haven and Betty was the only one who'd loved him when he needed it. David didn't know if he should stay long with Barry; he loved Betty too much.

He slipped back down under the sheets and, finally, slept.

Hannah had taken full control of Barry's kitchen. She had tidied the cupboards, re-stocked the fridge and cleaned the cooker and worktops; all that Eleanor had neglected.

She started to prepare some bacon, carefully removing the rinds with scissors. She washed some mushrooms and tomatoes, put coffee in the percolator and poured two large glasses of orange juice. The sun poured down into the kitchen and onto her face. Hannah felt a kind of euphoria today and she knew why.

As she worked, she became aware someone was watching her. She turned and saw David standing behind her, wearing Barry's navy blue bathrobe. He looked scrubbed and clean, his face a little puffy from sleep.

'Good morning, or should I say good afternoon, David.'

He stayed motionless at the door, unsure of what to do. He hesitated, and then padded bare foot across the cold lino towards her.

'I have strict instructions to get you some breakfast.' Hannah's face said everything.

All he could say, was, 'thank you.'

David sat at the table and watched her working as she started to fry the eggs and grill the bacon. She chatted to him nervously about her morning's work; how she had removed some rotting teeth from a poodle, and helped give an elderly Labrador a hysterectomy.

David had the appetite to eat everything Hannah gave him, as she sat opposite him across the table. When he finished, he reached across the table to take hold of her hand. 'I'm going to miss you, Hannah.'

'I don't want to go, Davey. I don't want to leave you and Barry.'

'I'm flattered you feel that way. I can understand it about Barry, but I'm not worth it. . . .' and he shook his head. 'I must persuade you to go, as much as I want you stay. . . . Don't hang around for a loser like me. You can't let all those years of work go to waste.'

'But there's so much here for me. Barry said he would have given up everything he could for you, but your mother wouldn't let him.'

'Maybe she was right.' David squeezed her hand. 'I can give you nothing. What have I got? An old car and that's it! I've no money and probably no job . . . oh, yes my genetic makeup may be accounted for now,' he wryly smiled, 'but look at the upbringing I've had. Surely, George's influence will have more say on my character than Barry's ever will. I'm at rock bottom, Hannah.'

'None of that matters. It's you - it's you that matters, can't you see it,' then she laughed. 'I think I hated you once, you know, but that didn't last long. When I saw you with Linzi at the bus-station, I thought you were lovers, I was so jealous. When I thought you had something going with Joanne Milton, I found myself hating her. Any way, you do have something: this house is rightly yours and this wealth.' Hannah gestured. 'Barry will look after you now.'

'That doesn't matter to me. . . . I'd rather live at Foxglove Cottage and sleep in my aunt's rickety old bed. This luxury isn't for me.'

Hannah knew David was right and was pleased he was no gold digger. His honesty endeared him more to her.

'On the day of Uncle Fred's funeral I vowed I'd never leave Keld Head or marry any one. And I think that decision influenced my behaviour - I was rude to you, I know. And I've done nothing these last six months to make up for it. I only flirted with you to satisfy my own desire.'

'Oh . . . thanks, Davey! And is that what this is all about?' Hannah held her gaze at him - she had to be sure.

'No, it isn't . . . I'm sorry. I'm useless with words. I want more than flirting, Hannah. But remember I would have been in prison, if I hadn't have lied. I could have killed Joanne you know!'

'Oh, for goodness sake, David! Stop it. I could have *killed* her too, when I found out what she'd done to you.' Hannah gathered up the empty dishes and took them to the kitchen sink and, turning her back on David, began to run the hot water. It didn't matter what he said; Hannah's feelings for David had taken over and her heart was careering out of control. There was nothing more he could say that would change her opinion of him. She knew she was being irrational. She lowered her head and wanted to cry. She stood for a few moments unable to speak and wondered how he would respond.

Then she felt David slide his arms around her waist and envelop her. He leant on her back and began to kiss the nape of her neck and her hair, whispering and breathing softly in her ear. 'I'm sorry, Hannah, I've made you cry . . . I only want to do what's best for you.'

She reached back and their hands entwined; fingers were bound together as an unbreakable chain.

22

WITH GOLD

Kathy once again tried to take charge of her son and, for now, he let her. She understood that their relationship would have to take on another aspect; if David put his foot down she would have to relent and, besides, there was now another woman in his life who would have a greater influence.

Kathy liked Hannah. She was a pretty girl, sensible too, and would be good for David. But it was Hannah's bond with Barry that recommended her the most, and if Barry didn't think so much of her, Kathy doubted she would.

Hannah had also made David happy again. He laughed and teased as he used to. Some of his wit he'd learned from spending long days with Tony Milton.

Kathy had been devastated about the behaviour of her dead husband; she never believed him to be the adulterer as he'd rightly accused her. She was still uncertain if they'd been told the truth and perhaps Joanne Milton was fantasising again. But it meant her relationship with Barry could take on a new meaning, as David was no longer ignorant of the past. Yet, even in this, she would have to be cautious and not cause any gossip. She would continue to keep David's genealogy a secret.

David still refused to talk about Keld Head and showed little interest in the farm. It disturbed Kathy to think how much work he'd left her with, but she treated it as a just punishment for her error. And as much as she wanted him back, it had to come from him, but it didn't.

On the first occasion when they were alone at Barry's house, she confronted him about Keld Head.

'David, you must think about your future. What are you

going to do? Will you come back to Keld Head?'

He looked at her, bewildered. 'No, I'll go back to look after Betty and try and get another job. . . . I can't leave her now.'

Kathy was ashamed she hadn't considered it; she was still thinking of herself. 'Then you're more righteous than I am, son. Don't worry about money; look after Betty and we'll help you out. She isn't short of a penny or two. If you go back to her, she'll do anything to see that you stay. If Betty can see out her days with you, she'll be happy.'

David had already thought this out.

On Hannah's last few days, they were inseparable. They had walked together, laughed and played like children, tormenting Barry with late nights and loud music. He said he would be glad of some peace, but that was a lie.

The morning Hannah was due to leave was a scorcher; deep blue sky was speckled with white fluffy clouds, which floated across the horizon on gentle breezes. The fells stood out gloriously, enticing her to stay; but she was committed to go.

The emotional rescue of David had taken its toll on Hannah's feelings. But the few days' rest with him and his happy and cheerful manner bonded them closer.

She learned how alike Barry and David were, not only in appearance but also in disposition. In fact, Hannah was glad David was returning to Betty's cottage before their connection was discovered. Their obvious similarities may have given away their true relationship to anyone who saw the two men together. But Hannah had more than one concern about David, as he never mentioned Joanne Milton to her and, in some ways, she wished he had; she hoped David had nothing more to tell, but his silence on the matter did nothing to reassure her.

David packed away his few belongings in a holdall and put them in Barry's spare car. Hannah insisted she be the one to take David home to Foxglove Cottage. Home, was the expression David had used when he left Barry. He didn't mean to infer any disrespect for the kindness he'd received, and neither did he want to snub Barry's offer of a roof over his head; he knew he may need it one day.

When Betty saw Hannah again, she peered into her lovely brown eyes. She remembered the young woman now; her features had become lost in her memory. But Betty hadn't forgotten how easy David was with Hannah, and she understood why he liked her.

Betty had only been given a partial explanation of why David was in trouble with the police, and had only been told he'd had a row with Joanne and she had attacked him; Betty had surmised that Joanne and David must have been lovers at some time. She was pleased this was no longer the case: she didn't care for Joanne Milton.

'Sit down, Hannah. Talk to my aunt and I'll make some tea before you go.' David ushered her into Betty's parlour.

Hannah looked around the room at the furnishings, old and dated, yet becoming for Foxglove Cottage. This was the first time she'd been inside the house and could see why David loved it here. It had a smell about it which she found reassuring, a little fusty and old, but welcoming. The sun had cast a pleasing glow to the parlour as Hannah looked out of the window; a velvety purple clematis tumbled in the breeze above the lintel.

She went across to the mantelpiece and picked up a photograph. 'I've seen this one before.'

'Yes, David was about thirteen then,' Betty said. 'He won that prize for the best calf in show. That's Mr Fitzgerald with him. You can take it if you like.'

'Oh, no, I couldn't possibly . . . it's yours.' Hannah put the photograph back in its place and sat down.

'No, take it please. I have a tin full of them in my dresser. I have that one three times over. I'll maybe show you them all one day.'

'If Aunt Betty wants you to have it, Hannah, take it, or we'll not hear the last of it.' David said.

'So, Davey, I hope you haven't got used to the finery up at

that big house in Windermere; you'll come down to earth here. It was good of Mr Fitzgerald to help you. He's been a good friend to your family.'

David eyed Hannah, but she was still looking at the old photograph; this was David's problem and time for him to change the subject.

Hannah left him at Foxglove Cottage, with eyes full of tears. She cried all the way to the ferry. The photograph of David and Barry was on the seat beside her and each time she looked at it, more tears came. David had hugged her and kissed her, and had helped her to leave, yet she couldn't speak; he had found it hard too. He promised to write and call when he could and she wondered how often that would be.

Alan Marsh swept the floor of the dairy and glanced around the door as he thought he heard the Mercedes leaving. He had been fumbling around looking for more work to do; he should have been in Barrow-in-Furness by now. He'd been called in to help Barry with a heifer that was lame and needed an injection of penicillin.

Alan had noted that Kathy spent a lot of time in Windermere visiting David. He was pleased David hadn't got into any serious trouble, but what the trouble was, he didn't know. He didn't understand why Barry had put David up, thinking rightly that David had some attachment to Hannah.

He could visualise David going out of control with his abrupt manner, his self-centred attitude, and now this trouble with the police. It irritated Alan not to know why the police had held David for so long. He thought perhaps it was for a serious motoring offence, like drinking and driving. Alan had even spent some evenings at the hotel where David worked, hoping that someone would gossip. But all he heard was that David had been sacked for not turning into work after the police had called. Alan felt David was turning into a waster and had no time for him anymore.

Then Kathy had invited Barry in for coffee. Alan was hurt

that he hadn't been confided in. He also knew that Barry's wife had left him, and that he and Kathy did a have a brief fling when they were teenagers and he feared Barry might get back into Kathy's life.

As much as Alan had wanted Kathy; he had once hoped he could have married her. But now he knew he couldn't deal with David's prominence in her life. Tom and Sarah, well, they were just kids, and he did have a good relationship with the boy; poor thing, he'd now been deserted by his father and his brother. Alan guessed that Linzi's moods would drive him crazy, and he wondered if his relationship with Kathy would have to remain as it always had been: just good friends.

As Barry left, Alan went indoors in an excuse to tell Kathy he had to leave for Barrow. She appeared calm and happy. Her hair was neatly styled in a knot and twisted up on her head and her lips were glossy with lipstick. The work clothes had gone and she was wearing a pretty summer dress and this week, since the incident with David, she had left the house every day neatly dressed, and Alan guessed that this wasn't just to please her son.

'You look radiant today,' he looked longingly at her.

Kathy realised he would feel abandoned and immediately attempted to make some coffee to compensate him.

'No. . . . No coffee. I didn't want to leave without seeing you.'

'Well, thanks again for helping. I don't think we could have managed it ourselves.'

'No, I don't suppose you would. It's a pity you have to manage on your own at all.'

Kathy didn't want any old wounds re-opened. She knew exactly what Alan thought of David and hesitated before she spoke. 'When will you come again?'

'I may pop back tonight,' he said hopefully.

'Ah . . . I won't be in.'

'That's okay, don't worry.'

'Well, it's Barry. He's feeling down at the moment and I promised I'd call. Hannah's gone today, you know.'

'Yes, but isn't David still with him?' Alan hinted.

'No. . . . No, he's back at Betty's today.'

Alan's mind mused over the situation. 'Well, I'm off then.' And realising he was no longer required, headed for the door.

'Alan,' she called him back. 'Don't go yet. There's something I want to tell you. It's hard for me to say this.'

'I don't think you need to say anything, Kathy. . . . It's you and Barry isn't it?' And he held on to the door handle.

'Oh Alan.' She couldn't stop herself from moving in close to him. 'You've been a good friend. You've stuck with me through a lot, and I've always been open with you about my feelings. I hope I've never led you on, have I?'

'No, Kathy, you haven't. I've led myself along,' he sighed.

'I don't know what will happen between Barry and me - if we can catch up after all these years. Will you be hurt if we can make it work?'

Alan pushed his shoulders back and took her hands. 'Don't even think it, Kathy. Why should I deny you any happiness?'

'Alan, you are a wonderful, wonderful man. And I love you dearly.' She kissed him on the forehead and he moved away.

David continued his existence at Foxglove Cottage living in a kind of euphoria because everyone that mattered loved him again. And the effect this had on his well-being was apparent. And as spring turned into summer, David's skin tanned and his blue eyes shone, and he kept his hair short. He found some lunchtime work at a bar in Hawkshead, which meant he didn't have to worry about being away from Betty for too long. It gave him the escape he needed from caring for her, and enough money to pay some of the household bills and put petrol in his car.

He rarely left Hawkshead for days at a time, except for the occasional invitation to Barry's house. Barry also called at the cottage regularly, as it gave him some insight into Hannah's life, as she wrote long letters to David.

Betty had welcomed Barry, and found something pleasing about him. He reminded her of David. Perhaps that was why she liked him. But she couldn't understand why they met so often; he was too old to be David's friend.

Kathy was never away from the cottage, bringing casseroles, cakes and puddings and any home cooked food she had time to prepare. Betty felt this was unnecessary, as she and David were happy living on sandwiches and soup.

David continued to do more work around the cottage. He painted the outside of the house, spending long days up a ladder, stripped to the waist, whitewashing the walls and painting the window frames. He repaired some of the guttering, pointed some of the outside wall that had crumbled, with mortar. He put some plants in the garden: marigolds and petunias; he chose Betty's favourites. And then when he was tired, they would sit together in the garden under the hot sun, Betty beside him, wearing a large straw hat to shade her from the heat. She slept long and contented now.

Mrs Challenor had to be called in to help her bathe. Kathy washed and set her hair, and it was David's job to clean the house and do the washing and ironing. He even found time to paint the kitchen.

Betty's jumping heart told her this would be her last summer; so she spent the time completely indulged in her nephew. She felt that she'd reached a happiness she had never known. But she had moments of confusion and sometimes didn't know if she was talking to David or her Freddie; she wondered why Fred should have to work at the pub in the village at lunchtime. David agreed that for one day a week he should have a day off, away from Betty, and even on those days he could never return to Keld Head, so he just walked.

Betty was fragile as she entered her ninety-third year and David his twenty-fourth. It was apparent that there were some things he could no longer do for her. But her desire to stay in the cottage with him and see out the rest of her days meant they had to bring in outside help. And in the long evenings when she slept, David could only sit and watch, frustrated at his inability.

In those quiet evenings he wrote his letters to Hannah. She'd insisted he tell her everything about the building repairs and the painting of the cottage; almost every cup of coffee he had. One morning David collected the mail from the hallway floor and, as he always did, read the handwriting on each envelope first. There was nothing from Hannah, but there was a letter with an Aberdeen postmark. He knew it was from Joanne.

His immediate response was to throw the letter on the fire, but he held it for some time in his hand, staring at the writing, expecting more abuse or emotional blackmail. He tapped the letter on his hand and then, in a desire to prove himself undaunted, went to his bedroom, flopped down on the bed and ripped the envelope open.

25 Claire Terrace.
Aberdeen

Dear David

Tony has insisted that I write to you, he has been playing "Big Brother" again. It's a few weeks since I met you in the forest and I'm sorry to hear that you have a bad back. I hope it's better, and I hope I didn't aggravate it too much.

Tony is back with us again for a little while. He's well, and surprise, surprise is earning good money as a session's guitarist. We were relieved that you didn't have any more trouble with the police. Tony insisted that I apologise to you, but I cannot do that.

I just wanted to tell you that I never intended you to get into trouble. After you left me, I sat by a tree and tried to breathe properly again - you did hurt me, Davey. I tried to clean myself up a bit and dry myself. I think I was crying, when a couple walking their dog passed by. They were worried about me. They walked me back to their car and took me to the hospital and they must have called the police. It was the police who forced me into making the charges.

I was sent back to Aberdeen, to stay with Aunty Marian again. When Tony arrived and we had another row and he insisted that I dropped all charges. The police asked me if it was you that had hurt me, but I lied and said I didn't know my attacker. But I was still angry with you Davey.

By the way, I hear you are going out with Hannah Robson. I hope she can make you happy.

I don't know if I can ever say sorry for what I did. You'll never know what it feels like to be pushed around and hated by all. Everyone loves you, Davey. My Mum left, Dad's never at home, Tony's always teasing me. Then there was George, then you. I never loved him, Davey, I hated him. I only ever loved you. I only wanted to be loved like you are, but I guess I don't deserve that now.

Incidentally, Dad is selling the bungalow. He says it's of no use to us anymore.

Tony said I had to tell you he's coming down to see you soon. Please try not to hate me Davey, will you. I will always love you.

Joanne

David placed the letter down on his chest and wondered at its sincerity. He knew Tony would never have asked her to write; that was another lie she'd told.

If Tony had been the instigator of his freedom, he inwardly thanked him. But he would find it hard not to hate Joanne. She had done him so much harm, but he did pity her, she was only eighteen and just a kid. He feared she would never trust anyone again because of George's badness and his own loose conduct.

He tore the letter into small pieces; he wouldn't tell Hannah she'd written.

Linzi buttered the bread, spreading it thinly in an attempt to make it go further, and then piled the slices on the plate. Her mother was beside her at the kitchen table, filling the slices with egg mayonnaise, some with grated cheese or a layer of ham and tomato. She cut them in half and arranged them on a large blue plate. There were pork pies, cut into quarters, and a few bowls of crisps and green salad garnishes.

'I hope we've done enough.' Linzi brushed her hair from her eyes trying not to coat herself with butter.

'Well, they're not coming for the food. A cup of tea and a sandwich is all I can offer. If it helps sell the cattle, it'll be worth it.'

'I still feel uneasy about it. . . . What time do you think they'll start to arrive?'

'Well, knowing these farmers, they'll want a good look at the cattle first. The catalogue was well written, but your Dad always liked to weigh an animal up long and hard before he spent any money.'

'I hope we're not doing wrong by him.'

'Look, Linzi . . . this is your farm now. If you want to get up at six each morning to milk these dairy cows, we'll keep them; but you can't can you? None of us can. Besides, we can't afford to keep paying the relief milkers. . . . No, love, I'm certain we're doing what's best. With all the upheaval in Europe as well; your Dad said it would spoil farming.' But Kathy knew that Linzi's concern ran deeper than the money.

'It'll be sad to see them go, all the same.' Linzi continued to moan. 'All the hard work that went into breeding them and our Davey's not interested anymore.'

'Oh, he's probably switched off, Linzi. You know what he's like. It'll bring back too many bad memories to think of Keld Head. . . . Anyway, he'll be pining for Hannah, and Betty will be driving him crazy.' Kathy smiled as she thought of David trying to satisfy Betty's finicky ways, making breakfast and getting into trouble for putting too much butter and marmalade on her toast and putting too much milk in her tea.

'I still feel angry with him though. He could have at least come to help us today.' Linzi slapped the last piece of ham on the sandwich and placed it with the others.

'If he'd have wanted to come, he would have.'

'Then he must really hate this place.'

Linzi still didn't understand why David had left, and assumed he was afraid. She too found it hard working among the buildings that her father had once worked, not because of fear, but because of the memories. But Linzi never saw her father with a shotgun in his hand. She wasn't there to witness his death or to hear the great noise as the gun went off, or see his dead body. Linzi often sat alone in the tower, crying; she knew her father took his last breath there, and she would sit and wonder how she could give it him back. She once asked her mother if David ever mentioned his final words. But Kathy had lied, saying David was more interested in protecting Joanne than listen to anything that George had said. So Linzi had to be content with the last words her father had spoken to her at the prison, and then it all made sense: *"Davey's laughing at me, isn't he? It's as well he doesn't come or I'll finish the job off proper. Take his money now, because he'll soon have none!"* Linzi knew David had been punished by her father's death; he had no money, and her father had got his wish: his death was the only way he could have succeeded.

Farmers were talking, grouped together in corners of the yard, some swearing, and some laughing. A few of them were dressed smartly in tweed and green jackets, and others looked like they'd just fallen into a midden. Blue smoke was drifting in the air from cigarettes and pipes. A small queue formed to inspect the cattle, which were eating the clean straw, unaware that they were about to leave their home. Kathy watched the farmers wandering about the farm buildings; many had never set foot in Keld Head because of her dead husband's suspicious nature. Some had only come to see what sort of a job the Keldas women had made of the place and to see for themselves, if the rumours were true, that David Keldas had abandoned his family.

Before the bidding was due to start Kathy came indoors to make more tea and fill the urns with hot water. She had set up a makeshift dining area under the hay barn and had put out a trestle table, spread with the pies and sandwiches.

She stopped and looked out of the kitchen window as she waited for the kettles to boil. Linzi was right: George would have hated this; strangers on his farm, with cars parked in the yard and lining the lane. She also had worried if they were making a mistake, but it was too late to change their minds; soon the bidding would start and Kathy knew that by three o'clock that afternoon, most of George's cattle would be scattered the length of the county.

Kathy had promised the children a celebration meal that evening. She'd put a large piece of sirloin in the Aga, and later she would make some Yorkshire Puddings and a trifle, she'd even bought a bottle of Champagne.

As she stood watching, waiting for the kettles to boil, more people arrived. She looked out and saw a small group of young men over by the tower, laughing. She saw Darren Watson, David's friend from college, and she guessed he'd come to see Linzi; there was definitely something going on between them. She watched them thumbing through their catalogues and arguing the details; John Cardwell the auctioneer was with them.

A kettle started to boil so she went across to fill some flasks with hot water and then returned to her vantage-point at the kitchen window. The laughing continued and Kathy lifted her hand to her mouth as she spotted David with Darren Watson, he was pointing at the catalogue. Somebody else approached and shook David's hand, another came and patted his head.

'Oh, thank you, God. . . . Thank you, he's come,' she whispered.

David took off his jacket, rolled up his shirtsleeves and sat back on the dining chair. Moss jumped up at him and licked his hands and face, sniffing at his body.

'Would you like to stay for tea Mr Cardwell?'

'No thank you Mrs Keldas. I think you all need a bit of peace and quiet now. No need to worry about milking anymore eh, Davey?'

David didn't reply, but just politely smiled and continued to play with the dog. He couldn't speak, as he too was choked inside to see some of their best dairy cows bundled into the back of a wagon, never to be seen again.

WITH GOLD

Linzi and Alan came in laughing at some joke a farmer had told them. She went to David and flung her arms around his neck and smothered him.

'Okay, that's enough!' loving the distraction and the attention.

As evening approached, Kathy laid the table and set it for seven: she and Linzi, Tom and Sarah, Alan, David, and Barry. She was relieved at the success of the day: enough money to buy the new beef cattle and some to spare. Her friends about her; her children, her son and her lover. There was an empty chair at the head of the table opposite her.

She didn't believe in spirits, but a wave of sadness overwhelmed her to see George's empty chair, as if his absence had struck her for the first time. She looked across at his photograph on the wall, saw his handsome face and felt his gaze. But Kathy was no longer afraid of George or his reproach, he had deeply insulted her loyalty and his jealousy had probably caused his own ruin. She could only thank him for a few important things: their beautiful children: two daughters, and a strong son in Tom, a home and the livelihood she had.

She watched Alan talking to Barry, complaining about the price of animal health products, and she was happy she'd been able to keep his friendship. She looked at David and Linzi, who were now arguing because David refused to take her to see Darren Watson that evening. The two youngest were chasing their food around their plates with their knife and forks, eating only the beef and the Yorkshire Puddings. Sarah tried to steal one of Tom's puddings, so he jumped up from his seat and, taking his dinner plate with him, went to sit in the empty chair at the head of the table.

'Tom. You get out of there! Get back in your own chair. If anyone should sit there now, it should be Davey.'

David glanced across at the boy and then looked at his sister. 'Leave him be, Linzi,' he softly spoke.

It was late in the evening when David left Keld Head. He'd had a wonderful day being with his family, but he had missed Hannah. He intended to write to her tomorrow and tell her the details; she would be pleased he'd gone. David had even taken a little pride in himself today, as he realised that it was some of the breeding he'd introduced that had helped them get a good price for the cattle. He also felt the way was open to return when he could, but only to see the children. Tom would barely speak to him and David knew it would take time for him to be forgiven. Sarah: she was more open and had accepted him straight away; she really believed that David must have been in prison like her father.

David was still uncertain where his future lay, it certainly wouldn't be at Keld Head; that, he'd resolved some time ago. The only thing he was sure about was that he had to take care of Betty. As for Hannah, he would have to be patient. He would never stand in the way of her studies; she had another year to go at least, and that would give him time to get his life restored and maybe save a bit of money.

He sped along the dark and twisting lanes back to Hawkshead, flinging the old car around each bend, he was tired and content, but anxious he'd left Betty for so long. He had managed to persuade Mrs Challenor to sit with her for some of the day, but David guessed by now she would have gone and Betty would be starting to fret. He hoped she would be in bed and anticipated glancing around her bedroom door just to say goodnight. As he approached the cottage, he saw most of the downstairs lights were still on.

Betty was sitting in her chair watching television, wearing her pink nightdress and dressing gown ready for bed. 'Oh, Freddie, you're late tonight. Where've you been?' she whispered.

David went across, crouched by her side and kissed her on the forehead. 'I'm not Freddie, Aunty. . . . It's me, David!'

'Let me look at you, Davey. Oh, I'm sorry love. I'm getting confused again aren't I?'

'Would you like me to make you some supper, Aunty?'

'Just tea, not too much milk. That would be lovely, Freddie.'

David stood up and went to the kitchen and, momentarily,

shut his eyes. He had learnt there was no point in explaining again.

He set a mug of tea on the table beside her and told her about the sale.

'Tell me again, why your father's selling the cattle, Davey?' she said.

'Ahhh...' he shook his head. 'We'll talk about it in the morning. Are you going to bed now, Aunty? Do you want me to help you?'

'No, love. . . . You get off. I'll have my tea first then I won't spill it.'

He kissed her cheek and went upstairs, carrying his mug of tea in his hand.

David was soon asleep but, by two o'clock in the morning, was awake and turning restlessly in bed and couldn't settle. He'd eaten far too much that his body had become unaccustomed to. David got up and fumbled in the bathroom cabinet looking for some Rennies and then wandered back to his bedroom, but as he glanced downstairs, there was a glow of light coming from under the stairway door.

He crept downstairs and pushed open the door and could see Betty sitting exactly where he'd left her. The mug of tea beside her was untouched.

'Aunty . . . Betty, are you okay? What are you doing?' He leant over her and touched her hand to rouse her, but all he could feel were cold, lifeless and rigid bones. He didn't need to examine her further; his hands were shaking as he put out the light and then, kneeling beside her, flopped his head down into her lap.

In the stillness of the night and in the darkness of the room, lit only by the orange embers of a dying fire, David wept, his shoulders heaving with the weight of his loss.

He stayed with her until daybreak, not wanting to leave her alone. David carried Betty's small and fragile body back to her room and laid it out gently on the bed. He pulled the bedclothes up to her neck and covered her in the pink eiderdown, as if she was sleeping. He waited until a reasonable hour before he called the doctor and the undertaker.

David didn't know that Betty had died only minutes after he had gone to bed. She'd been unwell all evening and had felt sharp, crushing pains in her chest. She thought she was waiting for Fred to come home; she wanted to stay alive so she could see him one more time.

Betty had looked into his face and seen his warm eyes and the love he had for her, and was glad he was happy. She thought he must have been looking for George on the fells.

David Keldas hated funerals, especially when it rained but, today, it was warm and sunny.

Kathy sat beside him on the front row of the chapel, with Hannah at his other side. Sitting so close together, David felt warm and clammy, his body sweating from the exertion of carrying Betty's coffin on his shoulders, bearing the weight with three others.

Hannah was glad the sun shone for Betty. This lady deserved a good day.

She felt David's body trembling, so she rested her hand on his arm. They stood for the hymn and then listened as the clergyman delivered his sermon. He appeared to direct all he said to David. Hannah didn't know how much the eye contact was unsettling him.

The clergyman spoke about the courage of the young and their willingness to take care of the elderly. He mentioned a few light-hearted comments about Betty's feisty character, people laughed in low tones, not certain if they should.

David wished the clergyman would look at someone else; he didn't want to be the focus of attention and was glad that most of the congregation could only see the back of his head; he was unaware of who was behind him.

After a prayer at the graveside, David threw a handful of soil on the coffin. It wasn't until most of the mourners had left, that he had the courage to look around. Hannah was standing by his side, still holding on to his arm.

Hannah saw David smile and loosen his tie, letting it hang

untidily around his neck. He winked at her, happy that the serious part of the day was now over. Hannah realised she needed reassurance, rather than him.

David didn't particularly want to stay with the other mourners who'd been invited back to Keld Head, but this was Betty's day, and he must show his respect for her. He couldn't let her down and go on a drinking binge, as he'd done on the cold wet November day of Uncle Fred's funeral.

'Aren't you going to speak then, Dave? I nearly didn't recognise you with that haircut?'

David turned to see Tony Milton. He wanted to throw his arms around him but was restricted by Hannah's arm. But he couldn't stop himself from moving his body in closer. 'Never mind my hair . . . where's yours?'

Tony eyed Hannah who was holding even more firmly to David. Then taking her hand in his, he kissed it. She was taken aback by his forwardness.

'Are you coming back to Keld Head for a bite to eat?' David asked.

'Aye, if you'll have me. . . . If you've still got time for an old friend.'

David walked towards his car and Tony stopped. 'Er, if these are your wheels, I think I'll walk, thanks. I need to take in some of this air. I guess I've missed this place. Besides, I've got my image to think of.'

Out of the corner of his eye David was aware of a tall man approaching and wasn't surprised to see Angus Piercy. He warmly shook his hand.

'Thank you for coming, Mr Piercy. Will you come back to the farm for a drink?'

'I'd like that, yes please. But is there somewhere we could speak privately, first?'

David hadn't noticed the brown envelope he'd waved in his hand, but Hannah had. She knew this was the solicitor that had helped David get out of police custody, but she knew no more.

'Please come to Keld Head. I can see you there,' David was

reticent. And as he and Hannah drove slowly back through the narrow village street, up the hill and on to the moor road, for the first time in weeks there was an uneasy silence between them.

David took Angus Piercy across the yard into a small office that once was a tack room. It still had some shabby saddles and bridles and other leather items hanging on the walls. There was an empty glass cabinet that used to house George Keldas's rifles.

David offered the solicitor the only chair; he felt uneasy standing in this small room with such a tall man.

'I won't sit down thank you, David.' Angus Piercy sensed David's anxiety. 'I would be happy if you did though. Relax will you.' But David continued to stand and put his hands in his trouser pockets and rested his loins against the desk.

Angus Piercy pulled the envelope from his jacket pocket and David shuddered.

'Now, David . . .' the solicitor put his glasses on. 'I have something important to read and it concerns your future,' he looked at David down his nose. 'You will be sorry I'm sure, at the loss of your great-aunt, but in the event of her death I've been instructed to act on her behalf to be the Executor of her Will. And I am happy to read to you her last Will and Testament. If you would like to hear it.'

David legs trembled and in the heat of the small office, felt perspiration trickle down his spine and probably stain the deep blue shirt he was wearing. He brushed some sweat from his forehead with his hands. 'Er, yes. . . . Please - please do.'

This is the Last Will and Testament of Elizabeth Mary Keldas, of Foxglove Cottage, Hawkshead, Cumbria, made on the first day of May, Nineteen hundred and seventy-four.

I hereby revoke all former wills and codicils and other testamentary provisions made by me and declare this to be my Last Will and Testament.

I appoint on the day of my death, my solicitor, Angus Robin Piercy, of Preston House, Kendal, Cumbria, to act as my Executor.

WITH GOLD

I devise and bequeath that my great nephew, David Robert Keldas, of Foxglove Cottage, Hawkshead, all my estate: financial, real and personal.

I witness hereof, and I have set my hand this day and year first written.

Elizabeth Mary Keldas.

'Do you want me to continue, David?'

He just nodded.

'This is a very simple will, because you are the sole benefactor. Betty has left you all her property - that being Foxglove Cottage and the land at Rye Hills. You will inherit all her estate, personal goods and capital, would you like to know how much that may be?'

'I'm sorry. . . . But I can't grasp what you're saying.' David shook his head as if to waken his brain to activity.

'Well, basically, you've been left everything she had. All her property, money and shares, which, when calculated, will be a considerable amount.'

David walked across the office and looked into the empty glass cabinet at his reflection. 'This can't be true.'

'Do you want to see it for yourself?'

David spun around and took the paper from him but could barely read its contents. He only saw his name and he repeated it aloud: 'Keldas . . . Keldas . . . Keldas.' He dropped his hands and still grasping the papers, said, 'She can't do this . . . I can't take this. I'm not her relative and you know that!'

Angus Piercy pulled the chair out from under the desk. 'Sit down David and listen,' and this time he obeyed.

'This is a legal document and it cannot without any great contest be changed. It may be so that you're not Keldas by birth, and perhaps your aunt didn't know that, but that's the name on your birth certificate and, I assume, that's the way it's going to stay. And although you're not related to her by blood, neither was she Keldas by blood, she only became so by her marriage to Fred. This was still her dying wish that you inherit everything. The money she had was left from the sale of

WITH GOLD

Spickle Howe Farm after she bought Foxglove Cottage. But let me tell you the circumstances of her writing this.'

The chair that David was sitting on felt like it was moving.

'Her original estate was to be split between you and your brother and sisters. But when you went to stay with her and look after her, as nobody else had . . . '

'I only went out of sheer need. I couldn't come back to Keld Head; this place sickens me. . . . It was pure selfishness that I went to her. I was afraid.'

'Listen, David. When you brought her to my office a few weeks ago, she told me that George hadn't left you anything in his Will. Of course, I already knew, as I'd been his solicitor too. It was a travesty what he did to you and, at the time, I tried to reason with him to reconsider, but there was no reasoning with George was there. Back then I didn't understand why he could do this to you, but I have to do as my clients instruct and this was the same with Betty. When you told me you knew George wasn't your father, it all made sense. I'm glad Betty never knew the truth; she wanted to make up what she thought you deserved. She told me you'd brought her so much happiness, especially of late. She could have changed her mind when you had your brush with the law, but she didn't. No, David, even if she knew the truth about you, I'm convinced she wouldn't change her mind. Remember, Fred Keldas gave his life to protect you and now Betty wants to give you his estate!'

'Well, what can I do?' The shock was still apparent.

'Nothing lad, nothing. Just enjoy your life and the hope she's given you.' With that he shook David's hand and left.

Well done, young man - Well done. The man in the pinstriped suit had said.

Hannah mingled with the other guests around the farmhouse. Kathy had put on a good spread of food, yet Hannah ate very little. People were talking, drinking tea or a glass of sherry, but Hannah felt isolated. Most of these people were strangers. Some were from Hawkshead, some were David's relatives, and some were Betty's old friends. She wished David would come back; he'd been too long with the solicitor.

Hannah cursed the man for coming today; David wasn't outwardly grieving, he was being strong and she wanted him to stay that way. But she guessed he was in trouble again and his mood would soon change. She watched Tony Milton flirting with Linzi and felt it inappropriate for a funeral. She had no desire to join them. The boy, Tom, was sitting alone and he appeared to be sulking. He ignored Hannah and she assumed he was jealous of her relationship with David. She could have played with Sarah, but she was too tired after the journey up from Cardiff that morning. She wished Barry was here, but he had to leave early for a business meeting. So Hannah resorted to washing some dishes and continued to look out of the window into the farmyard for David. She saw the tall man leave the office. The door was wide open, but David didn't come out. If he was in any more trouble, Hannah doubted she could cope. Despite the circumstances, she'd looked forward to seeing him today and his composure had lifted her, but now her mood was low; the funeral had reminded Hannah of her mother.

Deep in thought, she put down the tea towel and continued to watch the office door. There was still no sign of David, so Hannah decided to find him and confront him with her feelings. She slipped from the kitchen unnoticed and marched across the farmyard and as she approached the office door David emerged.

He spotted Hannah and, to tease her, took the grin he had off his face, bowed his head low and looked solemn.

Hannah saw David's countenance and muttered, 'Oh, not the moods again, please, please, not today. What is it now, DAVID!'

David continued his sham and looked woefully at her. 'I've got something to tell you.'

With that, the spirit within her rose and she snapped. 'What more can you tell me, David? What else have you done?' Hannah's face flushed with emotion and she ran from him across the yard and towards the tower.

He followed and shouted, 'Don't go in there, PLEASE . . . !' And he grabbed her arm, but she resisted him and went into the tower.

Hannah stood in the gloom of the four stone walls and wondered why he hadn't followed her. It was a few moments before he came inside.

David looked at Hannah and she was standing where Joanne had stood months earlier. Her face was blurred as he saw the image of Joanne. He heard voices in his head saying: "*Meet me in Keswick, at the Moot Hall. Catch the bus and I'll bring you home.*" Then he heard: "*You're a bastard, Davey. There, I've said it. You're no son of mine. . . .*' David felt a crushing pain in his chest and his throat constricted.

She watched him sway and his hand rested on the wall, then Hannah thought she saw him grasping the stone with his fingers. She noticed beads of perspiration over his forehead. Then he spoke, but his voice was shrill, as if it was constrained. 'Hannah please listen to me. . . .' he was desperate and grabbed her arm.

'I can't, David. . . . You've hurt my arm. You're always hurting me, and I can't take anymore. . . . I've tried hard, but I can't help it.' And she pulled away from him.

Standing in the place he least wanted to be on this earth, David knew if he left, she would leave too. Then he saw her clearly, and it was Hannah, lovely Hannah and a single teardrop rolled down her cheek. He took a step forward and caught her hand.

'Are you going to walk out on me, Hannah? Are you going to leave me before you know what's in this letter? Are you going to judge me again?' and he waved the envelope before her. 'This - This will affect my future - your future, I hope!'

'Do we have a future, David?'

'Listen to me, but, first, let me take you out of this hell hole!' He led her by the hand, took her into the office and shutting the door behind him, fell back on the timber as if to keep all the evil out.

WITH GOLD

'Read it, please . . . read it,' and he pushed the envelope into her hand.

Through a haze of tears Hannah read the document and knew once again she had wrongly judged him. 'I'm sorry, Davey . . . I'm so sorry. . . . This is amazing news!' her face brightened as she brushed her wet cheeks with her hand. She fell into his arms and wept at her own foolishness and his kindness. And in the seclusion of the small room, he wrapped his arms around her. 'Hey, hey, hey . . . come on. Please don't cry.'

'I'm so sorry, Davey, I'm sorry, I didn't mean to hurt you and go in the tower. . . . I didn't know where I was!'

'Forget the tower, Hannah, and listen to me?' He took a clean and folded handkerchief from his pocket and dabbed her eyes.

'Don't you see, Betty's given me a chance? I lost so much: a father, a home, a livelihood, but I've gained. I've now got a beautiful home in Hawkshead. I've got a wonderful father and enough money that I needn't worry anymore. I've got my family back and, though I've lost Betty, she's given me a future. And I've got you, I hope. Do I Hannah?'

She bent her head onto his chest and couldn't speak. Then looking up she saw the cool gaze of his unfathomable eyes, which irresistibly held her attention and forced her to look at him, as they always did.

He lifted her chin. 'I want to ask you to marry me, Hannah, but I know you can't commit yourself - not yet anyway. But will you think about it next year when you leave college?'

He hadn't said he loved her, he just talked of marriage and Hannah knew from his relationship with Joanne that the two were completely different in his eyes. But she loved him intensely, yet daren't say it. The words were bursting on her lips but instead she said: 'You have something, David, you know that? I don't know what it is. . . . People like you, and that makes me feel secure. You have tenacity and strength; a kind of northern spirit.'

He stepped forward and his kiss was spontaneous, the

passion, strong, but the motive was uncertain.

Then Hannah smiled again, in fact she wanted to laugh; the man she'd once hated had just said he wanted to marry her. She looked at his face; how smart he looked today, how slim and elegant he was. Barry had told her not to prejudge him and she hadn't listened. Then she quietly replied, 'I think I would love that more than anything, Davey - to be here in the Lakes with you, in Foxglove Cottage.'

David mingled politely among the other guests, keeping one eye all the time on Hannah. He'd decided to tell his mother later about his legacy, but maybe not tell her about his half hearted proposal; he guessed she might not be pleased.

Tony Milton came over. 'Look I'm off now, mate.' he slapped David on the shoulders again. 'I need to see a man about a dog!'

'If you'll just give me a minute, I'll walk down the lane with you. '

David pleaded with Linzi to sit with Hannah, then he jogged down the hill to catch Tony up.

He heard Tony singing out loud and laughing as he approached. 'So, Dave. . . . You've got yourself a regular bird then have you?'

'Aye, something like that. And how's things with you?'

'Hunky dory, I think. . . .I've got enough work coming in to pay the bills.'

'You're not living in some doss-house again are you?'

'No, I'm not. . . . I'll stay up north for awhile. I've got a decent flat in Edinburgh. Oh, and yes, I'm still seeing Kelly, my little blonde nurse. Do you remember her?'

'Yes, the one that hated me!'

'Yes, that's the one. . . . She still hates you by the way!' Tony stopped in his tracks, thrust his hands in his trouser pockets, and then, with the toe of his shoe, played with some gravel on the lane. 'You were in big trouble you know, mate. Kelly said the police were around the hospital asking awkward questions. I told her some things about you and Joanne, and what she was really like and I guess she must have defended you.'

David bit his lip. 'I suppose you both got me out of trouble then?'

'I guess I owed you one, didn't I. So, what now, Dave? What are you gonna do?'

'Stay in Hawkshead, I hope. . . . I've seen a job for a National Park Warden. I'll go after that, earn a bit of brass and then see what Hannah's doing this time next year.'

'So that's it then mate, sorted?'

'Well almost.'

They continued walking down the hill, two tidy young men dressed in smart suits; both happy, both changed, building new lives and silently reflecting on their past.

David put his hand in his pocket. 'I've got something for you, but you'll have to catch it . . . !'

They stopped and David threw the glass snow scene globe up into the sky. And as the snow swirled and swirled around the tower as it slowly spun, the two men, in contest, raised their arms and jumped high in the air to catch it.

THE END